Heaven's Shadow
Book 1: Heaven's Shadow
Book 2: Heaven's War
Book 3: Heaven's Fall

HEAVEN'S
FALL

Ace Books by David S. Goyer and Michael Cassutt

HEAVEN'S SHADOW
HEAVEN'S WAR
HEAVEN'S FALL

HEAVEN'S FALL

David S. Goyer &
Michael Cassutt

ACE BOOKS, NEW YORK

THE BERKLEY PUBLISHING GROUP
Published by the Penguin Group
Penguin Group (USA) Inc.
375 Hudson Street, New York, New York 10014, USA

USA I Canada I UK I Ireland I Australia I New Zealand I India I South Africa I China

Penguin Books Ltd., Registered Offices: 80 Strand, London WC2R 0RL, England
For more information about the Penguin Group, visit penguin.com.

This book is an original publication of The Berkley Publishing Group.

Ace Books are published by The Berkley Publishing Group.
ACE and the "A" design are trademarks of Penguin Group (USA) Inc.

Library of Congress Cataloging-in-Publication Data

Goyer, David S.
Heaven's fall / David S. Goyer & Michael Cassutt. — First edition.
pages cm
ISBN 978-0-441-02093-5 (Hardcover)
1. Human-alien encounters—Fiction.   2. Space flight—Fiction.   I. Cassutt, Michael.   II. Title.
PS3607.O925H425   2013
813'.6—dc23
2013006738

FIRST EDITION: August 2013

PRINTED IN THE UNITED STATES OF AMERICA

10 9 8 7 6 5 4 3 2 1

Cover art by James Paick.
Cover design by Lesley Worrell.
Interior text design by Tiffany Estreicher.
Interior illustration by Steve Karp.

To Ginjer Buchanan

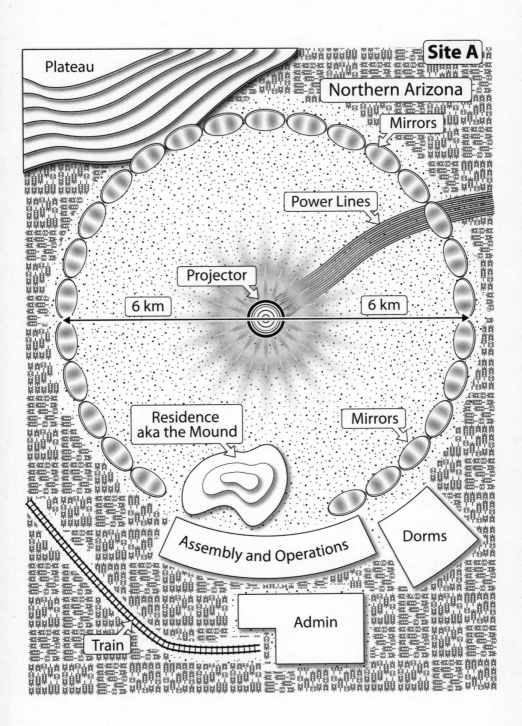

Site A

Plateau

Northern Arizona

Mirrors

Power Lines

Projector

6 km   6 km

Residence
aka the Mound

Mirrors

Assembly and Operations

Dorms

Train

Admin

Dramatis Personae

The Crew of *Adventure*

RACHEL STEWART-RADHAKRISHNAN, commander

PAV RADHAKRISHNAN-STEWART, pilot

ZDS ("ZEDS"), a Sentry

YAHVI STEWART-RADHAKRISHNAN, passenger

XAVIER TOUTANT, passenger

SANJAY BHAT, flight engineer

In Bangalore

TEA NOWINSKI RADHAKRISHNAN, former astronaut

TAJ RADHAKRISHNAN, former vyomanaut

WING COMMANDER KAUSHAL, commander, Yelahanka Air Base

MRS. MELANI REMILLA, director, Bangalore ISRO

SURESH KATEEL, Indian politician

COLIN EDGELY, leader of the Kettering Group

CHIEF WARRANT OFFICER SINGH, leader of the security team

WARRANT OFFICER PANDYA, security team

AIRCRAFTSMAN ROI, security team

EDGAR CHANG, media representative

KALYAN BHAT, bereaved relative

ARUNJEE LIN, media representative

URVASHI MURALY, media representative

SURINA, nursing assistant

ISHAT, crematorium worker

On Keanu

HARLEY DRAKE, former astronaut

SASHA BLAINE, former astronomer

JAIDEV MAHABALA, engineer

VARIOUS YAVAKI
  NICK BARTON-MENON
  ROOK
  ELLEN WALKER-SHANTI
  DULARI SMITH

MAREN HOUTMAN, art sector

JORDANA SWALE, agro sector

ZHAO BUOMING, former spy

MAKALI PILLAY, exobiologist

DALE SCOTT

At Site A

REIVER AGGREGATE CARBON-143/A72, combat and assembly
formation

WHIT MURRAY, junior engineer

TRANSFORMATIONAL HUMAN EVOLUTIONARIES
    COUNSELOR KATE
    COUNSELOR MARGOT
    COUNSELOR HANS
    COUNSELOR NIGEL
    COUNSELOR CORY
    COUNSELOR IVETTA

RANDALL DEHM, engineer

JAMES DE LA VEGA, program manager

Pilots

STEVE LIU and **JO ZHANG**

BENVIDES and **QUENTIN**

Prologue

THURSDAY, APRIL 12, 2040

SEC DEF TO CONGRESS: QUOTAS NOT MET, BIG CHANGES LOOM!

CHINA THREATENS SANCTIONS; PRESIDENT GERRY LAUGHS

STOCKS UP ON SEC DEF THREAT

SUMMER '40-CAST: IT'S A DRY HEAT!

YANKS' ROBO-ARM TOSSES 4TH STRAIGHT PERFECT GAME!

LILY MEDINA WEDS HER FOURTH—THIS YEAR!

HEADLINES, *NATIONAL TIMES*,
7 P.M., THURSDAY, APRIL 12, 2040

WHIT

Whit Murray thought: *Something is happening.*

He had no information, no warning. There was no visual cue. Yet he felt a cold tickle at the base of his neck.

It was eight in the evening, the sky still light even though the sun had set. Whit had just left the North Nellis metro stop and was hurrying toward the dorm. He was tired, he was hungry (he'd worked past closing time at the Installation cafeteria), and he was eager to score one of the top bunks.

Then he realized he was alone on the sidewalk.

On the tall side—at least compared to most of his contemporaries— Whit tended to slump when worn down. He was large, but not fit, certainly not coordinated in any sense of the word. His gait, especially tonight, was more of a shamble.

He also had one of those faces that teenaged humans constantly misread. It had to do with his eyes, which were frequently open wider than strictly necessary, giving him an expression of superiority or disdain, none of it what he felt, but enough to encourage the odd elbow from a fellow traveler on a bus and even a couple of actual beatdowns inside the Installation itself.

Posture, visage, aloneness, it all added up to robbery victim, or target for the Aggregates.

For some reason—possibly gestures and nonverbal cues from his co-workers all day—Whit realized that he wasn't going to be robbed.

He was going to be ambushed by an Aggregate, and likely taken somewhere he didn't want to go.

It had happened to others. It had happened to his father and mother.

As he continued on his way, though more slowly, glancing left and right, seeing no one—no human beings—Whit wondered why the Aggregates never sent warnings, or even benign messages.

Maybe they found some value in shock and surprise. Of course, Whit wasn't going to be surprised. The Aggregates had been dealing with humans since before Whit was born, yet they continued to underestimate the informal, off-the-grid ways in which information flowed from one person to the next.

No matter. Whit was on alert, and ready for the encounter.

All he could do was wonder: Where were they sending him? And why? He was a junior containment specialist spending more time on education than hardware development. What good would he be anywhere else?

Well, there was manual labor. Maybe his size had caused the Aggregates to reclassify him.

Off to his left he could see the glittering towers of downtown Las Vegas. Whit did not gamble; he knew no one who patronized the casinos, though clearly there must be hundreds of thousands who did. The money eventually went to the Aggregates. *All* money went to the Aggregates. He remembered his father complaining that it was bad enough aliens had taken over the United States and now controlled the government . . . but they also let the roads turn to potholes and allowed buildings to collapse. "No matter how powerful they are," Andy Murray used to say, "when people see everything going to shit, they're going to rise up."

Of course, expressing sentiments like that had led to Andy's disappearance . . . and so far, he'd been wrong. There was no sign that citizens of what was now called "Free Nation U.S." or any humans under the Aggregates were going to throw off alien oppression. There were too many, they were too powerful, too all-knowing, too ruthless.

And they had too many humans on their side.

The first sign of an Aggregate "ambush" was always the team from Transformational Human Evolution (or THE): three (never fewer) of the handsomest humans anyone ever saw, at least one of them female. They stepped out of the shadows as if they had somehow materialized.

The woman in Whit's trio was a redhead in a dark blue business suit with a nice skirt. She had eyes so green Whit could tell, even in the darkness.

"Whitson Murray?" she said. She had some kind of accent, too, vaguely Eastern European, what always sounded like Russian to Whit. (THE liked to have its action teams working in countries other than the ones they were born in.)

"Confirmed," he said. Who else would he be? Obviously they could read his data. (And probably just as obviously, they only wanted to note the delta between his data and his response.)

"I'm Counselor Kate; this is Counselor Margot"—another woman, middle-aged, pleasant, and sort of motherly, with a hint of Italian in her voice—"and Counselor Hans." A man not much older than Whit, but taller, clearly stronger. "We represent Nevada Aggregate Twelve-Ten, and we bring you the joy of a new mission."

All three members of the team turned, like dealers in a hardware showroom, revealing half a dozen units of Nevada Aggregate Twelve-Ten.

Whit hadn't seen them arrive—more fuel for the teleportation argument.

He always wondered—did the Aggregates ever go anywhere in groups smaller than a dozen?

The individual units of this Aggregate formation looked and probably were identical, as if assembled in the same factory. But they were capable of independent action, and the one on the far left stepped forward and spoke to Whit.

"Junior Specialist Whitson Murray," it said. When the Aggregates first revealed themselves, fifteen years ago, everyone expected them to sound like machines—about as articulate as Siri III on the iPhones everyone carried then. But they turned out to have sweet, almost childlike voices. Whit knew that if he closed his eyes, he might think he was being addressed by an eight-year-old.

A dangerous and articulate eight-year-old. The rule was, lower your head a bit and don't look threatening. So he did as the sweet-voiced member of the formation continued: "Your development records demonstrate great mathematical and engineering skill."

The proper response was "Thank you," and you can bet he offered it, even as he thought, *Duh, why else would I be working at the Installation?*

"Your work in Department Ninety-One is terminated effective tonight."

Which was not great news: When you were out of work, you were out of the dorm. When you were out of the dorm, well . . . Counselor Margot had mentioned a "new assignment." Whit held the humble posture.

"You are being transferred to Department Two Hundred Ninety-Two effective eight A.M. tomorrow."

"Thank you," he said. "I look forward to new and challenging work." Whatever it was.

"Your future is bright, Mr. Murray."

And with that, the speaking unit stepped back in line, and the whole crew marched forward into the Nevada evening, in the general direction of the metro stop . . . Hell, he thought, maybe they were headed to the Atlantis for a round of roulette and a few drinks.

Whit would never know. He was left with his friends from THE.

He shifted his backpack. "Do I have to relocate?"

"Not far," Counselor Margot said. "Department Two Hundred Ninety-Two is located in northern Arizona. You will also hear it called 'Site A.'"

That was a relief. Because if THE had told him, *Your new job is in Cairo*, he'd have to get to Cairo tomorrow. Which would leave no time for packing: He would simply have to turn, get to McCarran, and get the first plane to Egypt, leaving behind whatever clothes and possessions he had in his locker.

There would be some allowance for the time change—but he would have to be there by close of business.

"How is this different from my current work?" Which was designing and testing subsystems for power beams.

"Our world is about to be invaded," Counselor Kate said. Whit was getting the idea that her role in the team was to be dramatic.

His reaction must have shown skepticism. (In addition to having a face that encouraged people to get pissed off at him, his face hid nothing.) Counselor Hans hauled out his pad and displayed it to Whit.

It showed a surveillance camera image of a bullet-shaped vehicle, half-shadowed, obviously in space. "This vehicle took off from Keanu three days ago. It will land somewhere on Earth tomorrow, we believe."

"What kind of invading force is that?" Whit said, never unable to keep from saying what he thought. "One ship against a planet?"

"One ship can unleash any number of devastating chemical, biological, or cyber weapons," Counselor Hans said, sounding a lot like the kind of person who would coldly unleash any one of them. "And we cannot assume this will be the only one, merely the first of a possible wave."

"I'm as concerned as I am intrigued," Whit said, truthfully. "But what—?"

"We're preparing to strike back, if necessary. A team has been in place for a year . . . but now it needs to be expanded with young, fresh minds like yours."

"I don't know anything about spacecraft or orbital mechanics," he said. He didn't even know enough about spaceflight to understand the possible jobs.

"The nouns change," Counselor Kate said, smiling, "but the verbs remain the same."

Before Whit could ask what the hell that meant, Counselor Hans said, "If you can understand fluid dynamics, you can do orbital mechanics."

Okay, so he would be doing orbital mechanics now. Forget the two years he'd just spent on electromagnetic fields and plasmas, something he'd been studying since age fourteen. You didn't say no. You wouldn't die—not immediately. You'd just lose the Aggregates' trust while winding up on THE's shitlist, meaning you would be "offered" a position in the agro or enviro sectors, likely on some grim cropland or drowning seacoast, where lives tended to be shorter than in the cities of this great land.

That's what happened to Andy Murray—and he lived two whole years after declining a transfer.

"No" never occurred to Whit.

Besides, he was intrigued. He had heard about the return of the rogue Near-Earth Object Keanu, of course. Even THE and the Aggregates couldn't stifle that information. Like everyone, he knew the story of the savage takeover of the NEO by terrorists, the extermination of intelligent nonhuman life forms, and the NEO's attempt to flee the solar system.

When Whit was thirteen, there had even been a TV series called *Planet X* that told an exciting story about humans landing on a Near-Earth Object and behaving stupidly—and discovering, among other things, that there were zombies on the NEO.

Or something like zombies. Dead humans brought back to life. For a while.

Everything went to shit and the humans—alive and formerly alive—wound up taking over and sailing the NEO out into the universe to fuck more people up.

It was supposed to be science fiction, but everyone said it had a lot to do with whatever had happened on Keanu before Whit was born.

Either way, these people sounded bad.

"It's a scouting mission," Counselor Hans said, "prelude to a full-scale invasion."

"From space?"

"They're going into orbit," Counselor Margot said. "Not far away."

"I'm in." Whit wasn't convinced, but he had no options.

It took maybe three seconds for Counselor Hans to squirt Whit's new employment info data to his pad. "Good luck," he said. "Earth needs you." He sounded as though he actually believed it.

"You should get Transformed," Counselor Margot said. *Of course,* Whit thought. *There's always the recruitment pitch.*

"I'm thinking about it," Whit said, as he put some distance between himself and the trio from THE. If he didn't hurry, he was going to be too late to grab any food from the dorm's cafeteria, and that would truly suck.

He would actually consider getting Transformed under one condition, which he could never utter aloud:

Bring back my father, you bastards.

Meanwhile, he had to be on their side.

Day One

FRIDAY, APRIL 13, 2040

QUESTION: In all your time away from life on Earth, what did you miss most?

RACHEL: (long pause) Pizza.

INTERVIEW AT YELAHANKA,
APRIL 14, 2040

RACHEL

"It's so big!"

Rachel Stewart's first view of Earth, as she returned from two decades of exile, was a shock:

Earth looked exactly as she'd pictured it.

When she and her crew launched from Keanu, their Near-Earth Object habitat for twenty years (and currently making its own approach and preparing to go into an orbit beyond the Moon), their former home world looked like a fat whitish-bluish hemisphere. Rachel had learned long ago that the Moon was the size of a dime held at arm's length. In her case, on launch day, Earth from five hundred thousand kilometers was about the size of a quarter.

Keanu and their transfer vehicle, *Adventure*, were approaching the planet from its southern pole, so what they saw, in the relatively few times cameras or windows were pointed earthward, was the Antarctic surrounded by ocean.

To Rachel's surprise, having grown up with the threat of melting ice caps, Antarctica was still white and snow-covered. How deeply, she had no way of knowing.

But it was reassuring. Especially as *Adventure*'s speed increased as the vehicle flew closer—so much closer that Rachel revised "flew" to "fell," since that's what they seemed to be doing.

The only response to Rachel's comment came from Zeds, the Sentry pilot, in his Hindi-tinged English. "I thought human childhood habitats looked small when revisited." *That's what happens when you raise aliens as if they were human*, Rachel thought. *They grow up just as argumentative as their two-armed cousins.* The sarcasm was apparent even through Zeds's environment suit. (It was odd for Rachel to know that *Adventure* had originally been built by and for Sentries—but the Sentry pilot was the one forced to wear a suit.)

"Shut up and land this thing," Pav said. That was her husband, Pav Radhakrishnan. Now thirty-six by Earth's calendar, he had grown stolid and confident while still, in stressful moments, capable of acting like a hotheaded teen male.

"Daddy!" That was their daughter, Yahvi, fourteen, speaking from her couch slightly behind Rachel's left shoulder—sparing Rachel the wifely duty of correcting her husband, a job she never liked and wasn't good at.

There were actually six in *Adventure*'s cockpit: Rachel and Pav and Yahvi, Zeds the pilot, plus Xavier Toutant and Sanjay Bhat. The latter two, like Rachel and Pav, were members of the original HBs—the "Houston-Bangalores" who had been scooped off planet Earth twenty years back and transported to Keanu. Xavier came from Houston; he had been the HBs' scrounger and jack-of-every-trade for two decades.

Never shy, he grunted and said, "Let's just do it the way we practiced."

Sanjay, on the other hand, was one of the quieter members of the Bangalore crew. . . . Rachel hadn't even known his name until at least a year after their arrival on Keanu. Granted, there were more than 180 people to meet and get to know in those days, after humans expelled the Reivers from Keanu . . . but in the confines of the human habitat, it wasn't as though Sanjay could easily escape attention.

But he had.

Nevertheless, he had proven himself to be one of the masters of the proteus, Keanu's 3-D printing and fabrication system . . . the nearly magic Architect technology that allowed humans to (a) get rid of the Reivers, (b) make supplies and equipment, and, ultimately, (c) turn themselves into the galaxy's smallest spacefaring civilization. If anyone could take credit for the design, construction, and operation of *Adventure*, it was Sanjay.

"Entry interface," Sanjay said.

Adventure began bumping at just that moment, much like an airplane hitting turbulence. As her mother, Megan, had reached for her hand during flights across the Rockies and into Houston on horrible stormy afternoons, Rachel reached for her daughter's.

She had faith in *Adventure* . . . as much faith as anyone could place in a machine that was several thousand years old and built by a race of sentient aquatics on a world far, far away.

It was, when she looked back, a crazy challenge—outfitting an ancient spaceship preserved in vacuum for centuries. How do you do that?

Well, first you turn the work over to two dozen former Indian Space Research Organization (ISRO) spaceflight engineers. Given the proteus tools available to use in the Keanu system, the largest challenge was . . . theological. That is, technical challenges turned out to have possible solutions, all of them workable, in theory.

What kind of propulsion system should the Sentry vessel have? Thermal protection? Environmental?

Should it spin or tumble to provide artificial gravity?

The development took six years, once Rachel and the others realized they were truly headed back toward Earth and would inevitably have to land there. Some of them, anyway. (And as the anointed ruler of the HBs, a job she kept trying to shed, Rachel knew it would have to be her.)

First, the HBs had tried to create an indigenous lander. After all, they were already using proteus printing to fabricate engines, control systems, environmental systems, seats, and everything else . . . why not the actual shell or, as Sanjay and former astronaut Harley Drake kept telling her, "The bus, Rachel. It's called a *bus*."

Their first "bus" was a stubby, short-winged thing like one NASA had tried to build around the year 1995. It was called the X-38, Rachel thought—she remembered her father, Zachary, talking about it. It never flew as more than a prototype, but it was the model they used.

And during its first launch from the surface of Keanu—*launch* being an extreme word for a process that essentially involved squirting some reaction mass downward, causing the X-38 to float off the surface—the vehicle failed. Some defect in their design or manufacture caused the X-38 to break up when its main engine fired to put it in a big looping test orbit.

Two HBs died, including Shane Weldon, one of the original space professionals from NASA who'd run Zack's mission to Keanu.

So, with time running out, and no wish to come up with a new design and risk another failure, Rachel and Sanjay and company turned to the Sentry ship that had been parked on the surface of Keanu.

The Sentry ship was a needle-nosed, stubby-winged thing that looked like a tapered artillery round. Over the centuries it had been stripped and looted like a pharaoh's tomb; when humans first discovered it, it was literally just a shell.

But what a shell! Sanjay and his team were amazed at the structural integrity of the Sentry ship the first time they pumped air into it. "The leak rate is better than *Brahma!*" *Brahma* had been the Coalition craft commanded by Pav's father, the one that landed on Keanu back in 2019 a few hours after Zach Stewart's *Venture* spacecraft.

Once the HB team proved that the Sentry ship would hold air, it was time to equip it with propulsion systems and fuel tanks (all of it, every molecule, arranged and/or manufactured in the human habitat) and items like storage lockers for food and cargo, and seats (human-sized, except for one) and controls and . . . well, a shitload of equipment. Since the cockpit was designed for Sentries, who were generally a half meter taller than humans, five of the seats wound up having to be suspended in the middle of the volume, "like flies in a spiderweb," in Sasha Blaine's unhelpful words.

One other major task was coating the exterior of the Sentry ship with a thermal protection system. Sanjay's rudimentary analysis showed that the "metal" of the Sentry shell was unknown. Obviously, as Harley said, "given that it's lasted ten thousand years, it must be pretty fucking robust." But they had no way of knowing how it would withstand the thousand-degree temperatures of reentry into Earth's atmosphere.

So they elected to coat the entire exterior in the same material used for the X-38 . . . a light silica-based compound that had been evolved from the space shuttle by *Brahma*'s engineers. The extra layering spoiled the

Sentry ship's clean, classic lines . . . but everyone felt safer knowing that they had protection during reentry.

This work took years. In fact, when *Adventure* finally launched four days ago, Rachel was still not sure they had done everything possible, run every test.

They had, however, taken time to do one old-fashioned thing: They had given the Sentry ship a name, *Adventure*, partly to honor the original *Venture* that brought Rachel's father's crew to Keanu . . . but mostly to remind them of their new mission.

But they had simply run out of time. Keanu was approaching Earth, where it would be a fat target for Reiver weapons. Jaidev, Harley, and all the HB leadership had agreed: *Adventure* had to reach Earth at the first opportunity.

Now here they were, passing the Antarctic, dropping lower and lower, over the empty expanse of the Indian Ocean. To their right, roughly northeast, they could see a huge cloud formation. "Cyclone," Pav said. "Bad news for Indonesia."

"Is it still called Indonesia?" Xavier said.

A new voice sounded inside the cockpit. "*Adventure*, this is Bangalore Control—" Rachel sat up at those words, since she remembered hearing them from *Brahma* mission director Vikram Nayar back during that horrible week of the *Venture/Brahma* landings, the deaths, the mess that led to her arrival on Keanu.

Rachel and the HBs had been in touch with Earth for thirty months, of course. Carefully. The HBs suspected that the Reivers had reached their home world as many as nineteen years in the past, once they'd been expelled from Keanu. But they had no information about the success of their invasion, the extent of the infection. Well, there had been stray, strange transmissions warning Keanu and the HBs to . . . stay away.

As if they would. As if they *could*.

There had also been odd, plaintive transmissions from India and the United States, people asking for information on loved ones lost twenty years ago. Sasha Blaine began to build a database, but it was already heartbreaking: They knew that a handful of names were not among the HBs, meaning they had gone missing—or died—on Earth in 2019.

"Bangalore, *Adventure*. At forty-five thousand meters, descending.

Are you tracking?" Pav was handling the communications, for obvious reasons. He was human; he was from India; and he had been Keanu's only voice link with Earth so far.

"We are tracking you," Bangalore said.

Pav glanced over his shoulder at Rachel. "So they can still do that much."

Their imaging systems and signal intercepts had led the HBs to believe that humans had given up spaceflight. They had detected no air-to-ground transmissions (an obsolete phrase, but still the best they could do) from lunar bases or Mars orbiters. They weren't even sure there were still space stations.

What popular or historical material they had managed to screen confirmed this: The last two space missions in the history of human spaceflight had been to Keanu in 2019.

Popular history and entertainment mentioned "visitors" and "bene-factors" known as the Aggregates, but with few useful details. Earth had changed in twenty years, obviously. The global environment had continued to evolve; Arctic ice was largely gone and sea levels had risen.

There had been the usual wars, all of them regional. Some nation-states and associations seemed to have disappeared; there was no mention of a United Nations, for example. They saw references, however, to the Free Nations and the Western Alliance. (Overall, they didn't see nearly as much broadcast material as expected, though surely their position—far out of the solar system plane—their sheer distance, and their lack of a receiving network had a lot to do with it. There was also the reality that most of Earth's communications were now short-range or through fiber-optic nets, not spewed into the galaxy at large.)

What was most intriguing was the rise of a religious-scientific movement called Transformational Human Evolution. The HBs had not been able to find out just what it was, only that a lot of people—in the tens of millions, possibly hundreds of millions—were members.

If you look at it one way, Rachel thought, *we're arriving as emissaries . . . another way, as scouts.*

Another way—as irresponsible parents. She and Pav had spent hours debating the wisdom of bringing their daughter on such a dangerous voyage. It wasn't just to give her the kind of educational sightseeing trip

Rachel's parents had given her, though it seemed appropriate that Yahvi should visit her ancestral world.

The reason was this: While *Adventure* was capable of being refueled and could conceivably have launched in a high, looping Earth orbit that might have eventually taken the crew back to Keanu . . . Rachel and Pav fully expected this to be a one-way trip.

When they left Keanu, the six of them were saying good-bye to friends and their home.

And, given those circumstances, Pav and Rachel were simply unwilling to leave Yahvi behind.

As they dropped lower, the initial buffeting lessened and they found themselves in the rosy glow of plasma. "We're leaving a bright streak across the Indian Ocean dawn," Sanjay said.

"How is the temp?" Pav asked. Why, Rachel didn't know. If it was too high, they were in deadly trouble. It wasn't as though they could do anything about it.

"Shields are holding," Zeds said, which almost made Rachel laugh, since it sounded like a line from a movie she remembered watching with her parents.

"How unlikely is this?" Xavier said. "A ship designed to return from Keanu to the Sentry world ten thousand years ago and God knows how many light-years from here . . . and now it's landing on Earth!"

Rachel could see Pav shrug. Zeds just grunted, a peculiarly human reaction.

Things began to happen very quickly now. A guidance system was doing the actual piloting: Zeds and Pav were simply monitoring—or, in Pav's case, worrying aloud.

They were low enough now, over the Laccadive Sea, that Bangalore had had to alert air traffic to their passage—but still high enough that they could see, off to the right, the northwestern coast of Sri Lanka.

But just like that they were over India proper, heading directly north up the tip of the subcontinent. "Was that Madurai?" Yahvi said. Rachel had asked her to keep quiet at this time, but at fourteen it was hard to remember parental orders—Rachel knew from experience. And besides, she was proud of the fact that her daughter had tried to learn terrestrial geography.

"Not yet," Pav said. He had actually flown over Madurai as a boy.

"Coming up on the big swoop," Zeds said. "Ready to rock it."

The "big swoop" was a vital maneuver. . . . *Adventure* was currently flying nose forward like a reentering space shuttle. Unlike that vehicle, however, it could not lower landing gear from its belly and glide to a stop on a runway.

Adventure would have to fire its main engines, which had so far been used rather sparingly, first to lift the vehicle off the surface of Keanu four days back, then to change its trajectory, essentially slowing it down, putting it on a shallow "flight" toward Earth.

The stress on the vehicle would be immense. But, having shed much of its original thirty-eight-thousand-kilometers-an-hour speed diving into the atmosphere—turning velocity into heat—*Adventure* now began to ascend, gaining a bit of altitude (and reaching thinner air), going nose up, up, up, and up until the vehicle was standing on its tail . . . and the crew left feeling as if they were weightless and motionless.

They weren't, of course. They were still flying toward Bangalore at a good clip.

Stress on the vehicle aside, there was also stress on the six of them— the only real g-forces they experienced during the flight. They now felt as though they were being pushed deeper into their couches, possibly with the addition of a fifty-kilogram weight on their chests.

But that lasted only for a minute or two. Zeds was especially silent and obviously struggling. Rachel had learned that the gravity of the original Sentry world was half that of Earth, and the Sentry habitat was stabilized close to that. (Sentries always seemed unhappy when they entered the human habitat; it was due to being twice as heavy as they liked.) Zeds wore a protective suit that offered support, but he still had to be feeling flung about.

Rachel and the other humans were in street clothes. They weren't expecting multiple g-forces, or not for more than a few seconds, so suits weren't needed.

Xavier did utter "Shit" a couple of times. And there was at least one audible whimper in the cockpit. *That was me,* Rachel realized.

"Good job," Pav said, surely intending that for *Adventure* herself.

As things smoothed out, Rachel began to feel relief—she had not realized just how worried she had been about the big swoop.

Now she and the others felt as though they were falling backward, as *Adventure* rode its rocket down and to the north. A rearward-facing camera showed a large city passing beneath them . . . Bangalore. But they were going too fast and their field of view was too narrow to identify any landmarks, just the mass of the big city itself.

When the HB Council decided that landing in India was preferable to Houston or Florida in the United States (there were more of the mysterious THE folks in America than anywhere else), Bangalore became the choice.

The actual target was an Indian air base north of the city called Yelahanka, which had been chosen primarily because it was the closest controlled airport to the former Bangalore Control Center. The mission control building and surrounding territory had been destroyed by a Keanu vesicle in August 2019, but a larger space research campus survived.

"Two thousand meters," Pav said. "Descent speed is good."

"Feels a little sluggish to me," Zeds said.

The moment he uttered those words, *Adventure* shuddered and a red light flashed on the control panel. (The designers had kept the earthly conventions wherever possible.)

Before Rachel could react—or even feel fear—Yahvi's hand landed on her shoulder.

"Relax," Zeds said. "We're still good."

"But losing some altitude," Pav said. For a moment, they exchanged terse, operational chat, like all pilots Rachel had ever heard on every airplane flight she'd ever taken.

"I saw a flash from one of the screens," Pav said.

Then Zeds added, "I think we lost part of the tail."

Hearing that, Rachel almost choked. The tail was actually a set of four fins, each providing aerodynamic control and landing support. Losing one or part of one might not be fatal, but it was certainly not *good* news.

"We're holding steady," Zeds said after a long ten seconds. "Still under control."

"A heads-up would have been nice," Pav said.

Rachel wished again they could have kept constant contact with Keanu, a hopeless task given the NEO's distance from Earth and the lack of relay satellites.

The ultimate mission? Historically humans thought about visiting other worlds in order to explore. But no matter how much it had changed in two decades, Earth was their home . . . so exploration wasn't the goal.

Another classical reason was to find some vital element or mineral, and God knows the Keanu HBs could have used food, clothing, and any of a hundred thousand items from Earth, from books to shovels to electronics. They had been able to fabricate many items, but they were only as good as their memories—or ability to reinvent certain items. (It would have been great, Rachel believed, to have been able to buy an RL-10 rocket off the shelf, rather than try to fabricate something like it.)

Another motive for great human voyages, of course, was war.

So, really, the flight of *Adventure* was a bit of all three. Which made it sound as though there were a real plan. But for the first ten years of her life on Keanu, Rachel and her colleagues had concentrated on surviving in their original habitat, all the while trying to learn how to control the NEO.

That job had previously belonged to a race called the Architects, the original builders of the NEO who had launched it on its ten-thousand-year mission.

But the only Architects the humans had met had been Revenants . . . formerly alive beings revived to communicate with humans, to tell them, in Rachel's view, just enough to make their lives difficult.

Eventually, using clues from the last Architect, the HBs had learned how to "fly" Keanu, turning it back toward the solar system for this curious mission.

Missing tail fin or not, *Adventure* was still flying, still descending at a survivable rate. Pav reached to his left and patted Zeds on the shoulder, or one of the pair on the Sentry's right side. "Looking good!"

Rachel allowed herself to feel hope—right up to the time *Adventure* crashed.

It wasn't a serious crash, an auger-in at great velocity. No one would have survived that.

But it was a hard thump down, the silvery shell smashing tail-first into a grassy apron north of the main Yelahanka runway.

Pav's last words were, "Too fast!" Rachel had sat through a number of simulations, though nowhere near the number Pav and Zeds had performed. She could read the changing numbers—altitude and speed—and saw that the altitude number was getting low while the speed remained too high. (When, in rehearsals, she pointed this out from her backseat spot in the cockpit, Pav would often remind her that it was her *father* who was the astronaut, not Rachel. Of course, she could and did say the same to Pav.)

She wondered what "too fast" meant. As in too fast for comfort? Or too fast for survival—

In those twenty seconds, Rachel watched the view screen with horrid fascination, the tarmac rushing toward them not much faster than it had in their sims, Yahvi saying, "Mommy . . . !" Even Xavier couldn't go silently into that not-so-good night, moaning, "No, no, no!"

She was thinking, *I'm going to die here, stupidly and so will my daughter. Why did I put her at risk?*

"Are we on the runway?" Pav asked.

Rachel wanted to scream, *Who cares?* But Zeds answered, calmly, "No, but I think it's going to be okay—"

They crunched with a sound like a Dumpster falling two stories onto concrete. The impact was greater than the worst airline landing Rachel had ever experienced. The couches cushioned the impact, but a large piece of the control panel broke off and fell, barely missing her and Yahvi.

Adventure rocked, shuddered, seemed to sink into the grass . . . then finally settled, at a bit of a list. They were on their backs, pinned like insects, looking up, feeling full Earth gravity after several seconds of multiple Earth gravity. Rachel felt sick to her stomach.

"Bangalore, *Adventure*," Pav radioed. "No matter what it looked like out there, we're down and safe." Then he glanced over his shoulder to give Rachel and Yahvi a smile.

At that moment, Xavier said, "Oh, Jesus Christ!"

Seeing what Yahvi, Zeds, and Rachel could not, Pav's expression changed. He touched his headset. "Correction, Bangalore, we're going to need emergency medical assistance!"

Now they all looked toward the rear or bottom of the cockpit, where they saw Xavier, his restraints unhooked, trying to get to Sanjay's couch a meter away. It likely didn't matter; Xavier wouldn't be able to do much.

The broken panel section had hit their genius designer and engineer right in the head.

Rachel was thinking, *First* Venture, *then* Brahma, *now this.*

The Stewart and Radhakrishnan families should never be allowed to land another spacecraft.

I come from a small town, very few people, where the number doesn't change much over the years. For example, whenever a gal gets pregnant, some guy leaves town.

DALE SCOTT'S FAVORITE JOKE,
TRANSLATED FROM THE ORIGINAL BABYLONIAN

DALE

"How'd you get it moving, Harls?"

Dale Scott may have spoken a bit louder than necessary, and his words were nothing like a greeting, all of which explained why a bald, middle-aged man wearing a silly flowered shirt and baggy shorts (which exposed shiny new flesh-colored legs) started as if he'd been shot. Then he turned with a look of genuine surprise.

To be fair to Harley Drake, it had been some time since he had seen Dale—and their last conversation had been angry.

Making matters worse, Dale had totally ambushed him. It was still very early morning, Keanu human habitat time. The glowworms on the ceiling above were just beginning to grow brighter, heralding a new day of earnest productivity and blind, robotic denial—at least as Dale thought of it.

But Harley Drake, Dale's long-ago astronaut colleague and Keanu nemesis, was more aware of the lingering mysteries and unanswered questions concerning their space home of two decades.

As far as Dale knew, every morning since that first month, Harley had visited this part of the habitat, the area known as the Beehive, a magical collection of honeycomb-like cells ranging in size from squirrel to elephant. For several months back in 2019, dozens of living creatures had emerged from the Beehive—reborn on the Near-Earth Object after their DNA or computer code or 3-D map or "soul" had been retrieved by Keanu's systems, then imprinted on a suitable collection of nanotech goo, to be combined, transformed, and rearranged into a living creature indistinguishable—at least by any measure the Houston-Bangalores possessed—from its dead original.

People emerged from the Beehive, too. Not many, and not for long. Shortly after the arrival of 187 involuntary human immigrants to Keanu, the Beehive stopped reviving humans, stopped creating Revenants. The reason was unknown, maybe unknowable, but Dale suspected that everyone was relieved. Over the years, all of the HBs began to believe that the Revenants would never come again.

Harley Drake was the only real exception. Dale suspected that the former mayor of the HBs came to the Beehive every morning, ritualistically, to see if any additional Revenants had come back . . . or to make sure that they hadn't.

Today, however, he found Dale Scott.

"Fuck you, Dale."

"Nice talk."

"You scared the shit out of me."

"Not my intention."

"Yet, it happened. You chose to lurk there instead of walking up to the Temple during working hours."

"True," he said, "but the Temple is so crowded with—"

"People who hate you?"

"As cruel as it is true."

Only now did Harley meet Dale's eyes. Until this moment Harley had been looking past him, at the stale-smelling maw of the Beehive. But it wasn't rudeness or extreme caution that kept Harley from engaging; it was history. Harley had been a well-regarded test pilot and NASA astronaut up to two years before the whole Keanu debacle.

But during a trip to the Cape he had been injured in a car crash that took the life of Megan Doyle Stewart—wife of astronaut Zachary Stewart (and later a Revenant). He had lost the use of his legs, a condition that persisted for years on Keanu.

Harley was an adaptable man and he made the best of his situation, but even after Keanu technology managed to make him mobile again, those special habits died hard. He was no longer used to seeing eye-to-eye—in every sense of the phrase.

"Exile hasn't been good to you, Dale. You look like the Unabomber, and the blue bag is a bad fashion choice. Maybe you ought to come back to the habitat."

Dale had believed he was long past the time when Harley Drake could insult him. He felt that he had thrived in exile. But Harley's words forced him to touch his face, recognize that he wore a patchy beard. His hair was long, too, what there was of it: bald on top, his fringe reached to his neck.

Even his face had changed: His nose was bent, thanks to an accident a decade ago. And there were markings . . . tattoos of a sort . . . on one cheek and both arms and lots of other places Harley Drake could not see.

And Dale's clothing? The faded sky-blue jumpsuit modeled after the uniform he and Harley had worn in their NASA careers was looking shabby. "You know how it gets," he said. "Live alone—"

"I have no idea. What is it you want? Food? A bath? Better clothing?" Here Harley almost spat the word: "Forgiveness?"

"And what the hell did you ask? Get what moving?"

"Keanu."

"We turned it around years ago. You were there."

"Turning it around and guiding it into Earth orbit are two entirely different challenges." He smiled. Harley said nothing. *Fine,* Dale thought. "I came here to help you out and maybe offer a trade."

"Don't take this the wrong way—or maybe you can take this the right way—but I don't think you have anything to offer."

"There's trouble with Rachel Stewart."

Now he had his attention! "What the hell are you talking about?"

"I know that she and Pav and four others landed on Earth yesterday, in India. I also know that you are in touch with them, but not as much as you'd like to be—or should be."

"Fine, and no big secret, by the way. So what?"

Before Dale could answer—he hesitated because he was still not sure exactly what he wanted to reveal—both men heard Harley's name called.

Looking concerned, Sasha Blaine arrived, a whirling vision in scarves and long red hair. She was in her early fifties—a dozen years younger than Drake—taller than most men and, with a bit of added weight, larger, too. Dale knew that she was fiercely intelligent—emphasis on *fierce*—a Yale mathematician who had the bad luck to be working in Houston mission control at the time of the *Destiny-7* fiasco, and the Big Scoop that followed.

She had never liked Dale. "Get away from him, you son of a bitch."

"We're just talking, Sash," Harley said. It didn't seem to satisfy Sasha; she stood there with arms folded, as if daring Dale to launch a personal assault. "Dale was just about to tell me how he knows the details of Rachel's mission."

This information didn't lessen Sasha's annoyance to any detectable degree. She simply said, "Bullshit. He's been living in caves for years."

"I've been spending most of my time in the Factory," Dale said. "The rest of you should visit. You might learn something."

"Like what?" She was still ready to spring at Dale.

"Like the fact that your big secret surprise landing was not only expected all over Earth, the vehicle was attacked. And whatever you've got planned next, it's not going to work."

Now Sasha turned to Harley, who said, "I think it's worth a listen."

"Then," she said, "he can come back to the Temple. For however long it takes to hear him out . . ." And she turned to Dale: "Then you go back to the hole you crawled out of."

The day *Adventure* returned to Earth, Dale Scott returned to the Beehive, his first visit to the human habitat in three years.

As Harley and Sasha's greeting showed, he hadn't asked permission. While his former hab-mates had their mayor and council, they never had sufficient reason to establish a police force, much less an immigration service. There weren't enough of them. They were also pretty well behaved.

In fact, with the exception of Zhao Buoming, a former Chinese intelligence agent and murderer (he killed a man on the Houston-Bangalores' first day aboard Keanu), now solid citizen, Dale Scott was the community's most notable bogeyman. His crimes fell into categories like "vagrancy" and "petty theft" (which implied private property, a fairly dubious concept given the way the HBs operated), or "failure to contribute communal labor." Guilty of that charge!

It really came down to, "Scott, you have a bad attitude." Well, shit yes. It had ruined a marriage and an astronaut career and had made his life on Keanu miserable.

It wasn't as though he hadn't tried to change. During the weeks that followed his arrival, his overland explore with Zack Stewart and Makali Pillay and Wade Williams and Valya Makarova—a space trek that may have saved Keanu from the Reivers!—Dale had consciously and openly tried to listen to others, to do what job-jar tasks needed doing, to share, to smile.

To no avail. True, Zack Stewart, Wade Williams, and Dale's lover, Valya, had been killed in the big trek. Also true, while the Reivers on Keanu had been exterminated, untold numbers had escaped, not only stealing the only obvious means of transport off Keanu but surely heading for Earth.

For some reason Makali, the Aussie-born exobiologist who was just as much a part of the overland trek to the Sentry habitat as Dale, escaped all blame for what went wrong.

After a year of sanctions that resembled the silence that offenders received at military schools, Dale finally confronted Harley Drake. "What did I do wrong?"

"You lost Zack Stewart. Williams died. Your girlfriend, too."

"You know the conditions were insanely difficult. Makali and I were lucky to survive!"

"I know. And you're a pilot, so that's your story and you're sticking to it."

"Come on, Harls! Are people saying I killed the others? Wouldn't that be kind of suicidal?"

"People are saying," Harley said, "that you might not have tried very *hard* to save them."

"I didn't want to save Zack Stewart?"

"You mean the guy who kicked you off ISS and ruined your life?"

Dale closed his eyes. This conversation had taken place near the interior wall of the human habitat . . . the one opposite the Beehive. Looking back toward the Temple, three kilometers distant, Dale had been able to see evidence of progress and industry . . . fields under cultivation, small structures built, people moving with purpose.

They had all done well in the first year . . . avoiding starvation and plagues and the sort of conflicts that frequently—automatically?—afflicted small human groups in isolation.

Dale had tried to be part of it. He had wanted to work with the Bangalore magicians Jaidev and Daksha, the geniuses who devised the "poison pill" that killed the Reivers, who then turned their considerable skills to learning and operating Keanu's proteus printing and fabrication system, turning out everything from T-shirts to coffee cups, from penicillin to sweet corn. He possessed a degree in engineering, didn't he?

So, it turned out, did most of the HBs. It wasn't really a surprise, given that the Bangalore Object scooped up staffers from ISRO mission control.

"There's a huge delta between thinking a guy did you wrong, and killing him."

"Letting him die," Harley had said. "But I take your point."

Accompanied by Camilla, the child Revenant, Zack Stewart had died a hero's death, carrying a thermonuclear trigger into the deadly core of Keanu in order to reboot its power system. Dale had been so impressed that for several moments, perhaps hours afterward, he had forgotten what a smug, arrogant, entitled prick Stewart was. "I can't believe that's the reason no one is talking to me."

"Some people are talking to you, Dale. I am." Which was true, but irrelevant. Dale Scott and Harley Drake had too much history to overcome. They would always talk, even if it meant arguing.

"You're not enough, Harls."

Harley Drake shook his head, then said, "Okay, it's more than that."

"So you acknowledge that I do have a problem."

"You are no one's idea of a team player. You are all too willing to let other people work so you don't have to. You will screw any woman who gives you a moment's opportunity.

"And, worst of all, I think, you can't be throwing around terms like *haji* and *camel jockey* and expect people of Hindu extraction to like and trust you. I don't even know what the fuck you were thinking—I mean, *camel jockey*?"

Dale opened his mouth to protest that he hadn't used such terms, or wouldn't if he thought about it, but the *camel jockey* confirmed it. The automatic use of derogatory terms just came easily to him by nature—nature reinforced by two unpleasant tours of duty in Iraq thirty-five years earlier.

"Can I apologize?"

"I'd recommend it," Harley said. "I wouldn't put much hope in a reprieve."

"So this is some kind of life sentence."

"It's a small group with a long memory. All you can do is give it time."

Giving things time was never one of Dale Scott's talents. If the HBs were going to isolate him, he would simply withdraw.

And he had . . . ultimately to his great benefit.

Thinking of long-dead Zack Stewart, Dale felt a bit smug and entitled himself as he accompanied Harley and Sasha deeper into the human habitat. As he met the eyes of original HBs and the first generation—*yavaki* was what they called each other: "young ones"—Dale sensed their defensive pride in their tidy fields and residences, in the cute little walkways and gardens.

Yes, it was nice, but it was also suffocating.

He never understood everyone's doglike attachment to the human habitat. Yes, it was where they all arrived—and the place that the Architect/Keanu had modified for them. But Keanu was around a hundred kilometers in diameter, and mostly hollow. It could have held twenty equally useful habitats.

Harley had tried to find as many as he could. It had not been easy; up to the week after his arrival on the NEO, to the moment of core reignition, Keanu had possessed a series of subway car–like pods that zipped through the same web of tunnels that allowed nano-goo to flow.

The cars still existed, and still looked as though they were functional, but the control system had ceased to operate. It was as if Zack

Stewart's brave, self-sacrificing reboot had brought Keanu back online in safe mode . . . basic systems like propulsion and life support working, but none of the extras.

So Dale had been limited to the habitats he could reach on foot, which turned out to be four: the Sentry space, which was aquatic and filled with what he considered giant lily pads. And Sentries. Dale had not enjoyed his first visit to the Sentry habitat, when he was in flight and Sentries were the enemy. And while hostilities had ceased by the time of his second visit, it was an oppressive place: wet, damp, smelly.

Adjacent to the Sentries was a dead habitat, one that he and Zack Stewart and crew had crossed in their inner space trek. Poking around in that ruined landscape was fascinating and also bittersweet, because it reminded Dale of his dreams of exploring the Moon—dreams that had largely been killed by Stewart.

Dale had also ventured into the realm of the Skyphoi—that was the way he thought of it—the air-based creatures who communicated by changing colors and seemed blissfully unaware of such mundane matters as buildings or vehicles or, as Dale had proved, visitors.

The Skyphoi habitat was cylindrical in cross section, like the others Dale knew, but was filled with a thick atmosphere and clouds of living things, like airborne algae, and lacked a proper floor. Entering it, Dale had had to descend to the lower hemisphere, an incredibly disconcerting voyage that reminded him of a hike he had taken to the bottom of the Grand Canyon . . . without the charming scenery or the Colorado River.

No alien entity had landscaped the lower half of the Skyphoi cylinder, either, so it was filled with boulders and fissures (even in Keanu's relatively benign internal climates, weathering still left its mark, especially over a few thousand years) and tons of debris, garbage, and what surely had to be Skyphoi guano.

The smell alone had been enough to cause the intrepid explorer to turn back. Then there was the suffocating, potentially toxic Skyphoi atmosphere.

No, Dale had probably spent more time in the Skyphoi habitat than any human, but the competition was non-existent.

And the Skyphoi remained a mystery, the darkest of the three bad habitats.

Dale didn't really want to criticize his fellow HBs for their lack of curiosity, but he was pretty sure that he was the only one who had seen them all, who would know much of anything about them, firsthand. At least on purpose.

Not that he was an explorer at heart. His wanderings had been forced. So now he lurked, he skulked. He had—no doubt about it—spent far too much time alone.

But now, today, this moment, he was back among . . . people.

And their unique environment.

They're here! The outbound Keanu vessel we've been expecting entered Earth's atmosphere early this morning, Perth time, and appears to have landed in southern India . . . likely Bangalore.

We, which is to say Colin, were actually able to track them on approach—a bright streak across the sky, like a meteoroid.

We were unable to intercept any useful telemetry (they may not have been transmitting it or, if so, only in a direct beam to Keanu) or voice, only bursts of what was clearly communication, but likely scrambled.

Of course, this means other parties were surely able to track them, too. And there are indications that someone—guess who?—took a shot at them during final approach.

But none of our eyes and ears in Bangalore reported any crash. And the total blackout of Keanu-related news—and the sudden disappearance of General Radhakrishnan and Director Remilla of ISRO—suggests that the Keanu folks made it, and are safe.

Of course, none of us are truly safe.

But this may be the first step.

ENCRYPTED MESSAGE TO THE KETTERING GROUP,
APRIL 13, 2040

TAJ

Taj Radhakrishnan ran out of Yelahanka's operations center, intending to leave his wife behind. "No, you don't," she shouted, "not without me!" And she followed him.

Taj was too concerned with what had just happened north of the Yelahanka runway to really care about his wife's actions. She was not a member of the official welcoming committee and should not have been in the air base operations center at all.

But Taj and the other committee members had allowed it, given that Mrs. Radhakrishnan, the former Tea Nowinski, was a space professional and a NASA astronaut—in fact, the commander of the first piloted lunar landing mission of the twenty-first century back in 2016. She may not have worked in the field for twenty years, but, then, neither had Taj.

Perhaps it was that layoff that contributed to his wife's loss of operational discipline—the urge that allowed her to race for Taj's Jeep as it and several similar vehicles started heading for the landing site.

"I want to see them!" she said.

"Get in." She had a right, after all. Taj had wanted Tea with him from the beginning but had run into a bureaucratic barrier: If the welcoming committee had no room for a long list of local politicians, ISRO certainly didn't want Taj making room for Tea Nowinski Radhakrishnan, even if she was stepmother to one of the *Adventure* crew . . . and former quasi-stepmom to a second.

The driver gunned the Jeep with purpose, violently flinging Taj, Tea, and the fourth party, Wing Commander Kaushal, side to side. "Careful!" Kaushal snapped. He was a round little man—short and so fat that Taj wondered how he passed the annual fitness exams. But then, Kaushal was known to be politically savvy if not especially skilled as a pilot. He was, in Taj's view, a navigator, in all senses of the word.

And, as the commandant of Yelahanka, a necessary addition to the welcoming committee.

The convoy consisted of two Jeeps, an ambulance and rescue unit, and a cherry picker. They rolled toward the spacecraft without waiting for an order.

As the convoy turned onto the runway, Tea looked stricken, so he said, before she could ask, "Rachel and Pav are fine. There is one serious injury, a man we don't know."

"Oh, God. Taj, it crashed!"

"It could have been worse."

"Tell me how!" This was an argument they had repeated all through their two decades of married life. Taj was a glass-half-full sort, she often said. Whereas Tea's type was *I didn't order your stupid glass*.

"They could have left a smoking crater," he said, unnecessarily.

"Jesus Christ," she snapped. Then she turned on the driver. "Can't we go faster?"

Taj had fought to keep the *Adventure* receiving party small, and he had succeeded—if one neglected to count Tea and the hundreds of Indian Air Force officers and enlisted men and their families and friends crowding the base, lurking, it seemed to Taj, behind every window or outside every fence.

In the official dozen were five from the staff of ISRO Bangalore, including the center's director, Mrs. Melani Remilla; the deputy mayor of the city, Suresh Kateel, representing the Bruhat Bengaluru Mahanagra Palike; also a member of the staff of the governor of Kanatka State and two agents from the Research and Analysis Wing in addition to the commandant of Yelahanka and his director of operations.

Taj was the twelfth.

But no reporters so far. The Signals Intelligence Directorate had frozen or silenced all networks and was transmitting blocking material on broadcast frequencies that originated from or were received at Yelahanka.

Or so they believed. Taj was skeptical.

Nevertheless, as much as it was possible in the mid-twenty-first century, the landing of this alien vessel carrying refugees from Earth was a private affair.

They cleared the buildings lining the runway, passing a plaque commemorating Taj's ill-fated *Brahma* mission to Keanu. He had been stationed at Yelahanka when selected for space training in 2005, so the base had more or less claimed him. He had driven past the plaque half a dozen times in the last week, each time feeling a pang of regret and shame.

This time, however, he barely glanced at it, as if finally leaving it, and the *Brahma* experience, in the rearview mirror.

Looking ahead, their view still blocked by buildings, Taj wondered what he and Tea and the others would find at the landing site. They had heard the disturbing final exchanges . . . with no knowledge of the type of vehicle *Adventure* was, Taj was no judge of its terminal phase, though it did seem to be falling rather fast, not perfectly controlled. In the last few seconds, when *Adventure* more or less hovered over the runway, he could see that one of its four tail fins was clearly damaged. There was a hole in it big enough to see through.

It was early morning; the runway at Yelahanka ran almost directly east–west. Taj and team had instructed *Adventure* to aim for any of three helicopter pads to the north and west of the runway. Thanks to its problems, *Adventure* hit on the grass apron at the extreme eastern edge of the runway.

Which meant that, as they drove toward *Adventure*, Taj and team were looking directly into the morning sun. The big fat shape of *Adventure*—it reminded Taj of the famous London Pickle—was nothing but a two-dimensional shadow until the convoy managed to come up on its southern side.

Then he got a clear view of the patchwork quilt of thermal tiles, much like the old space shuttle, many of them scarred from the heat of reentry. "Oh my God, Taj! Look at that piece of crap," Tea said. "How could they fly that from Keanu?"

Even though it was uttered by his wife, whom he loved, Taj bristled at the comment; any vehicle capable of crossing half a million kilometers was not a piece of crap.

Yet, with its tilt and damaged fin, it did look "hobo," to use a phrase Taj had picked up from space station Americans. Nevertheless, even half-crumpled the fin was still strong enough to keep the vehicle from toppling.

Up close *Adventure* proved to be as tall as a five-story building . . . almost as tall as Taj's long-lost *Brahma*. The medical unit and the cherry picker were at its base. One of the med techs waved and signaled that there were no toxics. All Taj and Tea could do now was wait, and wonder what the crew's medical need was.

Before the basket of the cherry picker reached it, the hatch opened, flopping downward to provide an egress platform. Stepping out onto it was a figure from years of Taj's nightmares . . . a Sentry! Taller than a human, multi-armed, deadly.

"Oh my God, Taj—!" Tea grabbed his arm. She had not seen any Sentries face-to-face, but she had seen their work.

"General," Kaushal said, using a rank Taj had long since relinquished, "is that what we expected?" He sounded as nervous as any military man would, when surprised.

But this Sentry was carrying a wounded man. From where Taj stood, nothing more could be seen, certainly not the extent of the man's injuries or even his identity—Taj prayed that it was not Pav even as he wondered if he would recognize his son.

With two techs aboard, the cherry picker basket reached the hatch level. The techs took the wounded man from the alien, then began to descend.

Taj's Jeep stopped fifty meters from the base of the craft. "Wait here," Taj told Tea. To his surprise, she did as ordered.

He and Kaushal hurried toward *Adventure* now. What they saw was devastating—a young barefoot Hindi in what would have been normal street attire (white shirt and slacks) a generation back, with a severe head wound, as if the left half of his face had been bashed in. "Get him to the infirmary," Kaushal ordered.

Taj shaded his eyes and looked up at the Sentry, a figure from his past, shouting, "Are there other injuries?"

To his surprise, the creature shook its head and waved its upper arms in a very humanlike set of gestures. "No!" Its voice was muffled by its suit, of course, but could easily have been any of the welcoming party.

Then the Sentry was joined on the platform by four others, all in street clothes. (Taj had expected flight suits of some kind.) A heavyset black man—likely the partner named Toutant. A teenaged girl in shorts and a loose yellow blouse—Yahvi.

A tall man who looked much as Taj once had. "Papa!" He waved. Pav! Lord, he was grown up! Handsome in spite of the day's ordeal.

And with him, a dark-haired woman in her thirties. "It's Rachel, hi!" For a moment, Taj felt confused . . . it was as if he were looking at Megan Stewart, Rachel's mother . . . the same woman he had last seen, alive, on Keanu twenty years ago.

Before this thought could bedevil him further, there was a shriek from behind him—Tea. Waving her hand, moving as she had not moved in a decade, she ran toward the base of *Adventure*.

Rachel was hopping up and down like an excited teenager, which was what she had been during her last meeting with Tea. It was clear that she wanted to scream, and just as clear that, given the wounded man's condition, she could not.

And so Taj Radhakrishnan was reunited with his son and introduced to his now-extended family.

There were hugs and tears all around as the *Adventure* crew descended. Tea and Rachel were linked so completely and for so long that an objective observer might have judged them to be a single organism. There was a special bond between the two, of course. Rachel's mother, Megan, had been killed in 2016 in an accident that cost Zack Stewart command of the *Destiny-5* lunar mission . . . which had then gone to Tea!

A year or so later, Zack Stewart began dating Tea . . . who then became a surrogate mother to fourteen-year-old Rachel. They had apparently gotten along well—it was Taj's impression that at the time, Rachel might have had the edge in maturity.

And if so, it appeared that his granddaughter, who had been standing silently and politely for several minutes, shared her mother's prodigal serenity. Of course, Yahvi's silence could also be caused by sullenness—or, to be entirely fair, the stress of her recent experiences.

Rachel finally turned Tea toward Pav. "Hello, Pav," Tea said, "it's so nice to finally meet you." Then she turned to Taj. "Do you tell him or do I?"

Pav looked at his father with his familiar, quizzical expression. "Tea is my wife," Taj said.

Rachel squealed and hugged Tea again. Pav was more dutiful—understandably. "I guess, then," he said, taking Yahvi by the hand and drawing her forward, "this is your granddaughter, of sorts."

Now Yahvi allowed herself a smile—dazzling, shy. She looked directly at Taj. "What do you want me to call you?"

He was startled by the question—especially in the circumstances.

"How about *Grandfather*?" he said, wondering what the other options were.

Pav hugged Yahvi, then pulled Taj into a three-way hug. It was not a gesture he would have learned in his sixteen years on Earth, but welcome nonetheless. "Can you believe we made it back?"

We Aggregates are your friends and allies! There is no reason to be afraid, or even uncomfortable!

But there are obvious differences. For one thing, we come in a greater variety of shapes and sizes, ranging from the near microscopic to Aggregates that are slightly larger and heavier than most humans.

We have families, too, though human biologists call them "formations." And while we have ancient roots in organic life, for the past two hundred million Earth years we have been machine-based. Think of your computers as mobile units, able to combine and break into smaller entities depending on need, and you'll have the idea.

And while individual Aggregates are usually an assembly of dozens, hundreds, or thousands of smaller, often identical units, don't assume that we are all the same. Interaction with other beings—especially humans!—results in revised programming and behavior.

So, while you may see us marching to the same drummer, remember this: Each Aggregate may be hearing a slightly different tune!

OPENING PARAGRAPHS, *MEET THE AGGREGATES ORIENTATION*,
DR. WILLIAM H. "BOB" BAILEY MIDDLE SCHOOL,
LAS VEGAS, NV, 2031,
SAVED BY WHIT MURRAY

AGGREGATE CARBON-143

CONTEXT: In theory, information moved across the greater Aggregate formations at the speed of thought. An image received by a single unit in Barcelona should, in theory, have been recorded and processed by a random single unit in northern Arizona in one-tenth of a second

(Earth-based Aggregates have adopted human measurements for ease of communication).

In practical terms, however, this time frequently stretched not only to one second, but often to five or even ten seconds—a thousandfold lag! Aggregate Carbon-143/A72 had experienced this so many times she could not retrieve the number (low-priority data was usually overwritten) but never failed to respond with surprise and annoyance.

Carbon-143 knew the reasons. The priority of the information, as predetermined by the dominant formation's algorithms. Other traffic in various networks.

Then there was the final filter: Each descending sub-Aggregate within a formation designated one unit to receive, process, and forward certain types of information.

NARRATIVE: For the Aggregate formation designated Carbon A72, geographically based at Site A in northern Arizona, Free Nation U.S., unit 143 was tasked with the initial receipt of military operational data (among eleven specific types of information) and assigning its value.

One of the humans in Carbon-143's immediate web of contacts once remarked, "Data has to climb a tree," which, after suitable follow-up research to determine the various meanings of the term *tree*, Carbon-143 embraced.

At this moment, monitoring and assigning value to a certain cluster of data, Carbon-143 judged herself to be a small branch far from the main "trunk" of Aggregate Carbon.

It should not have been the case. Operational military data had, in Carbon-143's judgment, significant value to the Aggregate.

But, likely as a result of recent determinations that physical manufacturing was failing to meet assigned quotas, her hierarchy had downgraded operational military data.

Its value must be level four of five in order to justify Carbon-143's immediate presentation. Below four, the data would be processed and placed in the queue.

Carbon-143's standard algorithms judged the data of 13 April 2013 1144 UDT to be level three: valuable but not critical.

But Carbon-143, performing her own content analysis, felt a need to override the algorithm and class the data as level five, for immediate relay and response.

Before taking such a dramatic step, however, she performed one additional review:

ACTION: The formation's ability to operate in what its American hosts termed the Indian subcontinent and China had never been established to a level sufficient for operations. As a rule, the Aggregates could only conduct surveillance.

But when the Free Nation U.S.'s space- and surface-based systems detected the approach of what they named Near-Earth Object Keanu, Aggregate cyberwarfare cells concluded that a visit was likely to the ninety-ninth percentile.

And that a visit with military potential was in the seventieth percentile.

Further, the Aggregate's political cells declared that even if a NEO Keanu–origin visit would necessarily target the Indian subcontinent, a direct military strike against the North American continent, specifically Free Nation U.S., was low probability.

ANALYSIS: The visit, no matter how "peaceful," was quickly rated as a potential military strike. So Aggregate defensive cells activated their links to Free Nation U.S. moribund anti-missile systems as a precautionary measure, while offensive units revived surface and subsurface naval systems, a process that took substantially longer, deploying them to the South Atlantic and to the Pacific.

In accordance with decisions by the affected Aggregates, it was determined that a return to Earth by NEO Keanu entities was not in the best interests of the formation, so offensive means were authorized.

ADDITIONAL NARRATIVE: Cyberwarfare cell prediction B was correct: On 13 April 2040 UDT, inhabitants of NEO Keanu attempted a visit to the Indian subcontinent instead of an overt strike (though defensive systems remain on alert for the possibility that the NEO Keanu entities plan both a visit and a hostile strike).

A subsurface naval vessel with a host crew was in position to launch a weapon at the Keanu vehicle, and did so under prior orders from the Aggregate Iron.

The strike was not direct; the vehicle survived. The units involved have voluntarily restructured themselves and the human hosts have been eradicated.

CONCLUSION: This vital operational military data was rated no higher than level three because of lack of success.

Four seconds elapsed from the moment Carbon-143 received the operational military data and reached her conclusion.

AFTERACTION: Carbon-143 removed herself from the fabrication-assembly facility at Site A, deferring her involvement in the monitoring of mobile-vehicle propulsion quality control, to protests from Carbon-144 and Carbon-145.

She physically stepped into what another human counterpart would call a "sunny Arizona afternoon," and approached Carbon-14, her immediate hierarch, to encourage the swift receipt and processing of the Indian strike message.

Carbon-14 responded: "Tentative agreement, pending response to this query: Why?"

And Carbon-143 answered, "Failure of the strike increases the probably of a reaction from the Keanu-origin entities. Chance of success—and likely damage to the Project—is now higher."

Carbon-14 processed, then responded: "Mathematical probability analysis?"

Carbon-143 could only respond: "No. Nonstandard emotion-based judgment."

"On that basis, this request is denied. Similar requests will result in removal from quality control and data hierarchy and total reprogramming. Persistence could even result in recycling."

Carbon-143 returned to her place inside the facility. She was aware of unwanted data—images and sudden surges in her electrosomatic web—that made her momentarily inefficient at her task. It took, in fact, almost twenty seconds for her to return to optimum efficiency.

She reran the context, analysis, narrative, conclusion, and especially action. The same electrosomatic spike occurred again.

Her human counterparts would have called it "frustration."

It isn't the flight that kills or even stresses an astronaut. What really gets you is the bullshit they put you through after landing.

ANONYMOUS ASTRONAUT, 2011

RACHEL

Once the initial greetings and introductions were complete, Rachel stood back and let Taj and the rescue team prepare to take *Adventure*'s crew to Yelahanka's infirmary.

"I would like the Sentry and Mr. Toutant inside the rescue truck," Taj said.

"Okay," Rachel said. She was still a bit dazed by the landing and the sight of Taj and Tea—*Tea!* The pretty, smart, almost socially hopeless woman her father had turned to in his widowerhood . . . to find her here, married to Taj!

It was one too many shocks.

In their limited contacts, Rachel had made it clear to ISRO that she would defer to them on where the returnees would be taken, and how, and in what order. But little else.

"We would rather not advertise the presence of an alien," Taj added, unnecessarily.

Now that the euphoria of arrival had passed, the other *Adventure* travelers seemed to be as numb as Rachel. Only Yahvi seemed to have any life to her, as she kept looking at the sky and at what must have been, for her, magical distances.

"Feeling okay?" Rachel said, taking her daughter's hand.

"Weird, but okay."

Zeds and Toutant climbed into the rescue truck. Even though it had twice the height of the ambulance and Jeep, it seemed to be a bit of a squeeze for the Sentry. Wing Commander Kaushal rode with them.

Rachel, Pav, and Yahvi boarded the Jeep with Tea and found themselves waiting for Taj.

Before the convoy could leave the landing site, there had been a scramble of luggage and equipment. The *Adventure* travelers each had a small bag—toiletries and a change of clothes. (Yahvi had insisted on bringing Sanjay's bag down from the cabin.) "What is the problem?" Pav said.

Rachel knew why. "Soyuz landing," she told her husband. He made a face, but his father nodded. "When I returned from ISS in June 2014, landing in Kazakhstan, many personal items went missing."

It was pleasing to Rachel to know that even with the quasi-emergency nature of the landing, Taj would not allow *Adventure* to be ransacked. Before departing the landing site, he insisted that they seal the hatch. Of course, as with any customs shipment, those seals could be broken by eager parties undaunted by legalities.

So Taj had encouraged Pav and Toutant to actually lock the hatch.

"Do you trust these guards?" Pav asked his father, as the Jeep finally started rolling away.

"They aren't the usual sort," Taj said. "We did a special screening."

Rachel wondered what that might involve, and how any of that would stop someone from being bribed.

No matter; she could do nothing but trust Taj and ISRO.

As they drove through the empty streets of Yelahanka village, she noticed Taj repeatedly glancing over at his son—now a grown man in his thirties.

"Why don't you ask him?" Rachel said.

"Ask what?" Taj said, surprised by the question.

"All of the things you want to ask him."

Taj smiled, a rare event from what Rachel recalled. She knew he must have a thousand things he wanted to know. Surely he wanted to embrace his son, his son's new wife, and his granddaughter.

But the streets were narrow and the task of getting to safety had priority. So Taj had to settle for brief eye contact and nervous smiles. Rachel sympathized, even as she and Pav and especially Yahvi craned and looked around like tourists.

Pav shouted one question to Taj: "What about Mother?"

"She died ten years ago," Taj said, likely horrified that he had to deliver the news in this manner. Rachel recalled that Taj had separated from his wife, Amitra, Pav's mother, shortly before the *Brahma* mission in 2019. It had been big gossipy news in the astronaut community of the Johnson Space Center, where any "off-nominal" personnel matter was scrutinized like a Dead Sea Scroll. "Ovarian cancer," Taj said.

Pav seemed to take the news calmly, even though Rachel knew he had been close to Amitra. Indeed, they had been with each other the fateful day of the Bangalore Scoop. Rachel reached for Pav's hand.

Tea hugged him from behind.

Thinking of Pav's mother made Rachel think about the humans in her life, pre-Keanu. Not just her father, with whom she'd shared at least one week on the NEO. Or her mother.

But, well, her friend Amy Meyer . . . the other of the two fourteen-year-olds running around the Johnson Space Center during the flight of *Destiny-7*, sneaking food and generally making themselves notorious. Did Rachel remember this correctly? Did one of them actually bring pot onto the center grounds?

Was it her? Or Amy? Not that it mattered now. She found it amusing that, among the many habits and practices of Earth life, HBs had done little with alcohol and almost nothing with recreational drugs. A few of the Houstons had experimented with the "fabrication" of beer and whiskey, and there were probably some who tried the same with marijuana . . . come to think of it, Xavier Toutant once confessed that that had been his business prior to the Houston Scoop. So maybe—

How had Amy Meyer weathered twenty years? Still the cute girl? Or had life, especially life under Reiver domination, destroyed her?

And what about Jillianne Dwight, the poor *Destiny* crew secretary who had had to corral Rachel and Amy during the horrors of that mission—?

The Jeep jostled as they went over a bump. Before they had all recovered, the convoy reached the base hospital's emergency entrance. Here all of them, including the giant Sentry, got out, careful to keep clear of the ambulance team removing the injured man.

A small crowd of officials, military and civilian, was gathering, though they kept a respectful distance, except for a small woman in her sixties. "That is Mrs. Remilla," Taj said, "director of ISRO Bangalore. If anyone is in charge here, she is."

Wing Commander Kaushal reached Taj before Mrs. Remilla could. "Tell Remilla and the others that they can meet the crew inside, not out here. They need checkups."

Rachel saw that Sanjay was headed for emergency surgery. The original plans called for Zeds to be taken to a special chamber inside the hospital; it had formerly been used for altitude training for aircraft crews.

"Rachel Stewart!"

Her head snapped to the sound of the voice, which was in a strange accent, certainly not Hindi-tinged English. She spotted a face at the back of the clutch of dignitaries . . . dark complexioned, younger, in military fatigues but with no rank.

"What do you feel being back on Earth?" the shouter said, pushing himself forward and brandishing a phone.

And he wasn't alone. Suddenly, like roaches boiling out from under a rug when a light goes on, people were emerging from the alleys between buildings, not just reporter types, but older men, women of all ages, children. It was as if the residents of Yelahanka had been cordoned off in this spot . . . and were now breaking free.

Responding to Kaushal's orders, the guards retreated, forming a perimeter around Rachel, Pav, Xavier, Yahvi, and Zeds. Taj and Tea were caught in it, too. The EMTs carrying the stretcher with Sanjay had made it inside, but the crowd had pressed close to the entrance and was almost blocking it.

"Okay, everybody," Rachel said. She had anticipated a situation like this. "I guess we can take a few questions, though as you saw, one of our people is injured—"

Someone shouted, "Who is he?"

"Sanjay Bhat," Pav snapped. "Born and raised right here in Bangalore."

"Is that your daughter?" "What's the girl's name?" "Were you born on Keanu?" Suddenly Yahvi was the target of a barrage of questions.

Bravely, with only a moment's glance at her parents, she answered them.

Rachel noticed Taj making eye contact with Kaushal. The wing commander leaned toward him and said, loud enough for Rachel's ears, "More guards are on the way. We'll have this sorted in a few minutes."

"I thought everyone had been ordered to stay indoors."

"They were." Kaushal shrugged, as if that explained any of this.

"What is your mission?" an obvious reporter shouted to Pav.

"We come in peace," he said, triggering some laughter. "Seriously, we're visitors. More than tourists, maybe, but less than . . . space traders."

"We want to see our old homes," Xavier Toutant said, without being asked or noticed. When a follow-up made it clear to the crowd that Xavier's home was Texas, the crowd reacted as if he had just admitted he was carrying the plague.

"No one goes to Texas," one of the reporters said.

Rachel turned to Taj and Tea. Taj stepped forward.

"We will discuss the United States and the world political situation the moment we are inside."

"To this alien being," another voice shouted. "What are your impressions of Earth?"

Zeds wasn't reluctant at all, which was a pleasant surprise to Rachel. The Sentry was fluent in English, but she had wondered how he would react to being surrounded by humans in open space. "The sky is very large," the Sentry said.

"Rachel Stewart, Rachel Stewart!" It was the original questioner again. "What are *your* impressions, being back on Earth?" the original voice shouted.

"Hard to say," Rachel said. "I was never in Bangalore until today. Has it changed?"

"Everything's changed," a middle-aged woman said.

So far everything had been peaceful, if you simply ignored the shouts for news-style comments from the crew. The biggest disturbance occurred when the sight of the Sentry caused at least one elderly woman to faint. (She had pointed to Zeds and screamed, *"Rakshasa!"*—a Hindi word that Rachel did not need translated: "Demon!")

In a way, Rachel couldn't blame them, not even the reporters who had wormed their way into the group, likely tipped off by friends or paid sources. Humans returning to Earth was the story of the year, especially in a year that probably had little in the way of happy news.

And there was the whole Revenant, back-from-the-dead business. Rachel was surprised that hadn't been the first question.

Then she heard a smashing sound—a dropped bottle, perhaps, or a window. Either way, it was a reminder that the situation was not what she had wanted.

"Kaushal, get them inside!" Taj said.

The additional guards had arrived—possibly causing the smash—pushing the crowds back and clearing a path to the entrance.

Inside, Pav officially introduced his father to Mr. Toutant, who insisted on being called Xavier. Rachel noted that Xavier was unusually subdued, offering none of his usual wisecracks. She hoped it was a temporary situation. It wasn't that she cherished Xavier's wit, though it had its moments. It was just that with Sanjay injured, Xavier was the team's all-around engineer.

Taj quickly arranged for Rachel and the others to have water, at least. After a quick poll of her crew, all of whom still seemed a bit subdued, an offer of food was rejected, for the moment. Rachel's stomach was still performing regular somersaults, triggered by readjustment to gravity and the variety and intensity of smells, which ranged from curry to mold to automobile exhaust.

Even Zeds, who needed twice the calories of the most active human, was willing to wait.

One human was unwilling to wait: Tea took Rachel by the arm, walking her a short way down the hall, away from the others. "Don't hate me."

"God, why would I?"

Tea's eyes were filled with tears. "The last time we saw each other, I was dating your father."

Rachel tried to remember: Yes, sometime during Zack Stewart's *Destiny-7* mission, she had talked with Tea . . . then Zack's girlfriend.

Before Megan Stewart returned to life and complicated matters to an extreme degree.

"I loved your father, you know that, don't you?"

Rachel nodded. An appropriate time after Megan's death—her first death, in 2016—Zack and Tea had started seeing each other . . . which was only a little weird for Rachel, given that Tea had taken Zack's place as commander of the *Destiny-5* lunar mission. They had, as Zack admitted one of the few times he discussed the relationship, "an unusual number of things in common."

Tea didn't need to add that the relationship with Zack had been shattered by Megan's return to life . . . the circumstances were so unique and bizarre that they could not truly be verbalized.

Blinking back tears of her own, Rachel hugged the tall blond woman. "It's all okay. I'm just glad you found someone like Taj."

Taj led them all into the staff conference room.

It was Xavier who spoke first, saying, "Well, we made it, barely. What are you going to do with us?"

Taj told them, "As you can see, reporters are dying to speak to you, naturally, and ISRO has made arrangements for a press conference tomorrow—"

Rachel sat forward. "Let's put a pin in that for now." This was her mission, her group. Her agenda, by necessity, needed to be flexible . . . but it needed to remain her agenda.

Taj accepted this. "Fine. But as you've seen, your return is not secret. There will be immense pressure, and a few planned events will save everyone a great deal of stress—"

"Oh, we'll do events," Rachel said. "But not until we've come to some kind of arrangements with these companies."

"What do you mean?"

"Taj," Rachel said, sounding impatient, "what do you think we want to do here?"

Taj glanced at his grown son, which annoyed Rachel. "I'm over here," she snapped. "*I'm* speaking to you . . . Father."

Mrs. Remilla entered the room at that point, bowing and smiling nervously, and sliding to the back like a parishioner making a late arrival at Mass. Rachel hoped she had heard the exchange; she doubted that women had reached equality with men in this society, even after twenty years.

"My apologies," Taj was saying. "I assumed this was . . . the first step in a return to Earth?"

To Rachel's surprise, and pleasure, Yahvi laughed. "You only return to *home*," the girl said. "This isn't *my* home."

"We are *visiting*," Rachel said. "What happens after the next couple of days, maybe a week or two, is entirely dependent on what we learn.

"And in order to survive here for days, maybe a week or two, we'll need money, won't we?" Here she turned directly toward Mrs. Remilla. "Or is ISRO going to be paying hotel and travel bills for us?"

Taj blustered, as if the thought of money had never occurred to him. "We weren't planning to *charge* you."

"For our landing? Thank you," Rachel said. She indicated the hospital. "And for this medical care? Thank you, again, for not billing us.

"But we have no plans to be guests of the Indian government or ISRO, or the Coalition, or NASA—assuming it even exists. We're going to operate freely, and starting as soon as possible.

"And we will want our own funds." She looked at the others. "It's entirely possible that one or more of us already have money on Earth somewhere, from insurance. Tea, maybe you could tell me what happened to my parents' house. Somebody must have bought it from—?"

"Actually, I handled it," Tea said, "and you're right. That money went into—"

Rachel's nod cut her off. The exchange was one she had simulated, in a way, during the long fall from Keanu. So far it reminded her of her early council meetings when she first became mayor of the HBs, where she had been granted status and some license, but only the power and authority she took. It all felt very familiar.

To Taj and Remilla, she said, "Tell the press to bring their bids when they have them as soon as they have them.

"And we'll need someone who can serve as our agent. After we get done with media access fees, we have scientific and technical matters to discuss." She reached for Taj's hand while glancing at Pav, who stood there, smug, arms folded, proud.

"We would all like you to be our agent, Taj. Tea, too. You're family. But if you'd rather not, please find someone who will.

"Now, where are we spending the night?"

The answer was, first night in the base hospital—which triggered grumbling from Xavier Toutant. "Relax," Pav told him. "We need time to regroup, check our luggage, and get some answers."

They had been talking in the conference room—Taj had not left it for two hours by that time. When Xavier left, Pav turned to his father. "When did you and Tea get married?"

"Fourteen years ago," he said. "We grew close in the aftermath of the mission." It was an inadequate way to describe years of mutual isolation and desolation, their desperate couplings and eventual realization of their mutual affection and need.

"I can imagine. Don't worry; I have no objection. I was just . . . surprised."

Pav walked to the window, which showed only a portion of the base under a hot Bangalore afternoon. "We don't know anything, really, about what's going on here." He looked back. "That's what we came to find out. Is Earth still Earth?"

"Some of it," Taj said. To Rachel, it sounded like an honest answer—if not overly helpful.

"That's what we need to know, as soon as possible. And who better to brief us than my own father?"

YAHVI

Before the briefing, there was lunch, served in the same conference room.
"Does anybody want to lie down or rest?" Rachel said. No one wanted to,
though Yahvi would have enjoyed getting out of this building altogether
and seeing some of India and Earth.

Even if it meant she had to deal with lots of other human beings. But
her parents had warned her, the first day was going to be boring meetings
and lots of logistical crap. So far they'd been right.

One of the few times.

Xavier asked, "Where are we staying tonight?"

"Right here," Taj said. "They had a few unoccupied rooms, so they
converted them."

"Which means they took out the IV units and added an extra lamp," Tea said. Pav laughed.

A couple of Indian Air Force enlisted men brought in trays of covered dishes as well as cartons. "We didn't know what you'd be hungry for," Wing Commander Kaushal said, "so we brought a variety of lunch fixings."

Which turned out to be sandwiches—something Yahvi had seen exactly once in her life—as well as bowls of various vegetables and fruits, along with more exotic items she could not place. And some very strange breaded objects inside the cartons.

Xavier went after the material in the cartons as if it would make him immortal. Taj and Tea as well. Even her parents were digging into the other food.

Yahvi hesitated. None of it looked appealing. And she still wasn't feeling hungry. "Is Zeds getting food?"

"Our specialists are with him now," Mrs. Remilla said. "And I have something for you."

Yahvi glanced at Rachel, who, mouth full, nodded in approval.

The gift turned out to be an electronic device, a small rectangle no bigger than the palm of Yahvi's hand, with frail-looking tendrils attached to it. "It's called a Beta," Remilla said. "It holds hundreds of thousands of popular recordings—everything that hit the top twenty for the past one hundred years." She looked at Rachel. "I couldn't live without mine."

"Are people still making music?" Pav said. "Are there still bands?"

"Yes," Taj said, "though not necessarily where they used to be. We'll be talking about that shortly."

Remilla spent several moments showing Yahvi how the Beta worked; the tendrils had tiny weighted units at their ends that fit into one's ears.

There were only three controls: play/stop, up/down for title/artist, right/left for keyword. "The battery is good for two years," she said. "If you're still on Earth at that time, call me and I'll give you a replacement."

Two years on Earth! The thought terrified Yahvi. But she managed to utter, "Thank you." She had that much social sense.

Shunning the food, she took the Beta to a corner of the room and sat down.

Yahvi Radhakrishnan was a proud yavak.

It was a sensible reaction, since many of the original Bangalores made fun of them as a group, these two-hundred-plus who had been born on Keanu since 2020. Yahvi knew there was something about the word itself—*yavaki* and its comically savage sound—which seemed to tickle the older HB generation. It was especially true when some adults said her name, which meant both "heaven" and "Earth," since it sounded so similar. *Let them have their fun,* she and her friends said at times. *They'll be gone soon and we'll be in charge.*

It wasn't as though Yahvi or anyone her age had invented the term. As nearly as she had been able to determine, sixteen or seventeen years ago, one of the Bangalores, while in full pick-on-the-kids mode, had come up with it.

Yahvi the yavak was taller than her mother and even her father. Slim, even (she had overheard Rachel using this term once) "gawky," though that was when she was eleven and grew seven centimeters in a year. She had her father's coloring and her mother's blue eyes and hair that was, most of the time, an unfortunate blend of the Stewart-Doyle coloring (reddish blond) and the Radhakrishnan curls.

She had spent a lot of time hating the way she looked, something her mother assured her was "normal," which was what HBs continued to use instead of "Earth-like." It was especially obvious when Yahvi pressed Rachel on that point once. Why, for example, was it normal for someone to hate the way she looked?

"Because you might just feel bad. Have zits, for example, or blotchy skin. Or other girls might tease you."

"Why would they tease me?"

"Because they're girls. Or just human beings."

"Won't they hate themselves, too?"

"Some, or all of them at one time or another. But for some people, making others feel bad makes them feel better."

Yahvi had seen evidence of that, so she was still listening. "Why do any of us care what we look like?"

"Well, because of boys, I guess."

And this was where Rachel Stewart-Radhakrishnan's idea of "normal" conflicted with her daughter's: Yahvi never gave any thought to what the boys her age thought of her *looks*.

After all . . . there were only a couple dozen her age. (It could have been worse: The oldest yavaki were nineteen, and there were only four of those.) They had been raised together, taught in the same classrooms. They had worked at the same jobs. They had eaten the same food and, more to the point, dressed the same in T-shirts and shorts.

Nevertheless, the boys often acted like boys, all clumsy muscle and embarrassment. The girls ranged from a couple of tee-hee types that Yahvi couldn't stand to tomboys, which was what Yahvi would have called herself most days.

Though that hadn't stopped her from having sex with Nick Barton-Menon, because he seemed to be the first port of call for girl yavaki on their maiden sexual voyage, and with dear sweet Rook, because she liked him and he seemed to need some encouragement.

(Yavaki weren't exactly encouraged to be sexually active, but no one forbade it, either. Babies were a welcome addition to the population . . . so far.)

The trouble was . . . Yahvi hadn't yet told Rachel about this.

But this moment was to be shared, too. It made it something other than the furtive naughtiness that Rachel had told Yahvi about, even as she recounted her own sexual history, which was entirely Keanu-based and Pav-centric.

The fact that Yahvi had kept it a secret—well, that was a problem. The more time that passed between action and revelation, the worse it got.

Yahvi had actually sat down with her mother and planned to tell her on the very night Rachel told her, instead, about the trip to Earth.

And that wasn't even the biggest secret Yahvi had kept from Rachel.

There was one thing even worse.

And she would never ever tell.

At least, not while they were on Earth.

"I'm going to keep this brief and objective," Taj said.

An hour later they were all back in their chairs in the conference room again—Taj at the lectern, the screen behind him lit up. In the corner of the screen, picture-in-picture, was an image of Zeds in his chamber.

In addition to Yahvi's grandfather—it was still strange to think of this older man as a relative—and Mrs. Remilla and Wing Commander Kaushal, there were two new arrivals: two men who said nothing but watched everything.

"Planet Earth has undergone a number of changes in the past twenty years," Taj said, as the screen displayed two hemispheres: Earth west, showing the Americas, and Earth east, showing Europe, Asia, Africa, and Australia. (Yahvi recognized them from lessons.) The images were typical satellite maps, showing brown or green terrain and far, far too much ocean for her comfort. "In ascending order of likely concern to you, there has been continued global climate change, resulting in higher sea levels and diminished Arctic ice—"

"Interesting use of *diminished*," Pav said. "Why not just say *disappeared*?"

Taj acknowledged his son's interruption with a raised eyebrow and nothing else. "The global economy has been stalled and stagnant for the better part of a decade. There are the usual wars and conflicts—none of them nuclear or critical, but all troubling, naturally." The twin hemispheres blossomed with gross domestic produce numbers, rates of growth or decline—Yahvi saw that most of the figures were red, which she took to be bad. (She'd learned that much about Earth symbology.)

A series of small fire images appeared over parts of Africa, Eastern Europe and Eurasia, and the Korean Peninsula. Those must be conflicts.

"Obviously we were unable to communicate much of this to you during your approach. We have the ability to encrypt signals, but we couldn't assume you could decrypt them."

"Smart assumption," Pav said. "We have the capability, of course, but it would still have required you to upload keys and codes—"

"—which would have been intercepted, yes, yes, yes," Rachel said, showing uncharacteristic impatience. (At least with Pav. She was frequently impatient with Yahvi.) "Obviously there is a more important update you're holding back."

All of the indicators on the screens vanished, leaving the satellite images as they were originally. "Bottom line," Taj said, "as my Houston friends used to say . . . fully one third of the Earth's population and habitable surface is under control of—infected by—the beings we call the Aggregates and you call the Reivers."

He clicked on the computer pad and the Western Hemisphere changed color. All of North America and South America were overlaid with a nasty yellow. So were much of Europe and parts of Africa.

Only the far northern or southern regions seemed immune. China, India, and Australia were the only areas clear of this yellow.

"We knew this," Xavier said, "or we could guess it. But what does it mean? What's happening there?

"Well," Taj said, "that's a good question."

Rectangular video images appeared around the border of the giant map. As Taj spoke, he highlighted each one so that it filled half the screen for a moment. (The images had superimposed identification, which was helpful: Yahvi could recognize most major Earth landmarks and a lot of terrain, but only that.)

What she saw:

A field in Kansas . . . the blue bowl of the sky, golden wheat and a giant tractor-combine rolling past, a human farmer visible in the cab . . . with an angular Reiver "mantis" type riding outside the cab behind him.

The canyons of downtown Manhattan, marvelously dressed people crossing sunny streets . . . with a cluster of Reiver "anteaters" in a crosswalk.

A seaside café in San Francisco—Golden Gate Bridge to the left, seascape to the right—and another cluster of anteaters posing like tourists at a café!

"If that's alien domination," Xavier said, "sign me up." No one laughed—no one but Yahvi. She earned a sharp glance from her father; no response at all from her mother.

Then the images changed.

She saw a lake bottom in Minnesota, dying fish flopping in the mud, the only visible water a small puddle . . . and a strange-looking machine chewing up the shore, as if dredging a new course for a river.

A refugee camp in Louisiana. It looked like refugee camps all through history, she imagined: emaciated people, eyes staring out of dirty faces.

What should have been a beautiful mountain in Montana . . . its top sliced off by a machine that appeared to be a giant cousin of the mud dredger. An avalanche of slag was pouring down one side, spilling onto the landscape.

Downtown Cleveland, leveled as if hit by a nuclear weapon.

Then a factory in El Paso, Texas, row on row of some kind of vehicles. Yahvi realized there were hundreds, and they looked a bit like the military tanks she knew from history class, but bulging with nasty-looking weapons, not just a single cannon barrel. Their turrets were transparent on top and showed that each was driven by a Reiver.

The last . . . a desert landscape, likely Arizona or Nevada . . . and a row of squat, newly built (well, they were shiny and a couple looked unfinished) towers stretching far into the distance, where a mound of some kind rested.

"We have thousands of such images, of course," Taj said. "These are merely samples."

"We've seen similar," Rachel said. "But what is it like? This is the middle of the twenty-first century . . . with radio, TV, Internet, nations just can't be . . . isolated."

"Of course they can!" Pav said. "When I was a kid, there was North Korea. Albania before that."

"But this is *North America*!" Rachel said.

"And South America, too." Xavier was indicating several videos they hadn't gotten to yet.

"Here is the situation," Taj said. "On the surface, the Aggregate Nations look and act much as they did before.

"Internet access to the Americas and much of Europe is firewalled. It sort of works—but you never know what's not going through or coming out."

Pav was shaking his head. "How did this happen? Didn't we *fight*?"

Taj shrugged. "Yes. There are still outbreaks, revolts against the Aggregates . . . and places where their control is far from absolute.

"But you probably know their advantages better than I. They aren't susceptible to most weapons—only to vast amounts of heat, electricity, or chemical-biological attack, which is incredibly difficult to field outside a laboratory or a small battlefield.

"And their initial arrival, eighteen years ago, was not immediately detected."

"No one tracked their vesicle?" Rachel said. She knew that NASA had tracked the hell out of the Houston version.

"It landed in the South Atlantic, entering over the Antarctic, just like you. There were almost no detectors looking that way, and those that did judged it to be a big meteoroid."

Since no one knew, the Aggregates had time to establish themselves and launched their own strikes.

"It started with plagues—from serious influenza right up to substantially more deadly things resembling SARS and Ebola.

"Countries wanted to close their borders, and did. Immigration and travel were restricted—and the barriers remain.

"It stretched to cyberwarfare, doing to data networks what they did to human beings. It's simplistic to say, that's all it took . . . but in truth, that's all it took."

Rachel lowered her head for a moment, a gesture Yahvi recognized. It meant she was getting to serious matters. "How difficult would it be for the six of us"—Yahvi was happy she was still including Sanjay—"to travel to the United States?"

"Openly? As voyagers from Keanu?"

"Let's say yes."

"Possible. I'm sure you'd be *officially* welcome everywhere on the planet, even in Free Nation U.S." He smiled, not pleasantly. "And totally restricted in anything you heard or saw or did, or tried to do."

"What if we traveled less openly?"

"That would be quite difficult," he said. He actually glanced left and right, as if being watched, lowering his voice. "And the first trick would be getting out of India."

Now Rachel stood. "Then it's time we took those steps. Did you say our media agent was waiting?"

"Agents. And I'll get them in here as soon as possible. But first it would be helpful to take some questions from the press."

Yahvi wanted to run. But a look from Rachel caused her to freeze where she was.

She was beginning to wish she had never come to Earth.

QUESTION: For General Radhakrishnan—

TAJ: I am not part of this press conference.

RACHEL: Oh, please—if we have to do this, you do, too.

(laughter)

QUESTION: What are your thoughts, seeing your son for the first time in twenty years—and learning that you have a daughter-in-law and a granddaughter!

TAJ: It's been a great pleasure.

QUESTION: Would you like them to remain on Earth?

TAJ: I haven't considered that.

INTERVIEW AT YELAHANKA,
APRIL 14, 2040

TAJ

Bangalore and the Committee had been in careful communication with Keanu for months prior to *Adventure*'s landing. Careful for the obvious reasons—the NEO's return was apparent to anyone with a telescope. Taj had seen rumors online before any official word reached him, and he was close to the top of the list of those who would be informed.

It was mutually decided that ISRO would acknowledge the "apparent return" of the Near-Earth Object Keanu, and the "hope" that its presumed human inhabitants were alive and well . . . but with no disclosure of the fact of direct contact, nor of the content of any messages.

Some information was exchanged, of course, but the continuing conflicts between India and China on the one side, and the so-called Free

Nations of the Americas and Europe on the other, distracted most people from the Keanu story.

There were those in the astronomy community, not to mention various fringe groups around the world, who kept the matter alive. But they had little hard information—at least as far as Taj and the Committee knew. (He had learned early in his military career to never make the mistake of assuming that you had the *only* intelligence!)

Taj concentrated on arranging the mechanics and protocols for arrival and reception. He had firsthand experience of such an event—one of four humans on Earth who did—and it had not been pleasant.

Returning from their disastrous missions to Keanu in August 2019, survivors Tea Nowinski, Lucas Munaretto, Natalia Yorkina, and Taj Radhakrishnan had splashed down in the *Destiny-7* spacecraft four hundred kilometers west and north of Los Angeles, not far from the Channel Islands.

In terrible shape—dehydrated, starved, filthy, and worst of all, incredibly traumatized by the utter, catastrophic failure of their mission—they were taken aboard a NASA recovery ship.

There they were separated and put in separate rooms—not staterooms, but tiny crew cabins that had been slightly modified to serve as temporary quarters for NASA astronauts. Taj had hoped and expected that he would be met by an ISRO doctor. That had been his first question after alighting from the rescue helicopter, drinking a considerable amount of juice (which he immediately vomited) and taking the shortest and best hot shower of his life.

It was aboard the ship that he learned that many of the Brahma control team were gone—some of them killed in the impact of a Keanu-launched object that destroyed the control center but eventually scooped up several dozen humans and took off with them.

The same thing had happened at Houston . . . which explained the absence of Shane Weldon, the *Destiny* flight director. Veteran astronaut Travis Buell came to welcome them instead.

Tea, Natalia, and Lucas crowded into the cabin at that point. They all looked better than they had upon exiting the *Destiny* spacecraft, without in any way looking good.

"Good," Buell said, "now that you're all here. I'm telling you you're in quarantine."

"We were *always* going to be in quarantine, Trav," Tea snapped. She had flown to the Moon with Buell and, Taj knew, had not come away from the experience with a good relationship with the man.

"For two weeks," Buell said. "This, unfortunately, is indefinite."

"I'm a citizen of India," Taj told him. "Natalia is Russian, Lucas Brazilian. You have no legal grounds to detain us."

"Actually, we do," Buell said, smiling. "You three entered the United States illegally. None of you are even carrying passports."

Taj remembered wanting to laugh. The idea that a crew of space travelers might make an emergency landing had been considered for decades, especially after the first Russians to return on a space shuttle turned out to be without passports. His Brahma crew *had* carried appropriate papers—

—which had been vaporized on Brahma.

"But you *brought* us here!" Natalia said.

Buell seemed to be aware of the ridiculousness of the situation. "I suspect that will be a factor in your favor, should this ever get to a hearing."

"What in God's name do you hope to accomplish?" Tea said. "It's not as though we're planning to hide anything. You know the worst of it, anyway. Everybody does." Indeed, four dead, two vehicles lost, human history changed.

"If anything," Lucas said, "we're eager to talk."

"See, that's the problem," Buell said. "It isn't the postflight debrief that worries everyone. We know you're pros. You'll tell us every detail.

"It's these other . . . events." He was talking about the miraculous reincarnation of Megan Stewart and several other humans—including Pogo Downey, killed on Keanu, then revived. "It's bad enough that there are all these rumors around."

"What kind of rumors?" Natalia snapped. As far as Taj knew, the Russian cosmonaut had never met Buell before. It was surprising how quickly she had developed a dislike for him. "We can't possibly know what's being said here."

Buell stared at all of them. "I'm just going to call them zombies, for the moment. *Space zombies* is the term."

"Travis," Tea said, "you know what happened up there."

"Do I?" he said. "I don't know jack, right now." Buell was quite religious, even by American standards. The idea that alien entities had the ability to bring people back from the dead, even briefly, with no more effort than humans would expend in accessing a website . . . surely that had to have shaken his faith. It had caused Taj to begin to develop his own new sense of Greater Powers in the universe. "But one thing I know is this: We aren't going to allow any of you to be out in public discussing this.

"Not until we all agree on what happened—"

"—and what will be said about what happened," Lucas finished. The World's Greatest Astronaut was nothing if not quick to pick up on things.

As a further demonstration—as if being sequestered on a ship were insufficient—Taj and the others found armed U.S. Marines in every corridor and on every deck as they steamed toward California. "What do they think we're going to do?" Tea said. "Swim for shore?"

It was only after they reached Vandenberg, the day after splashdown, that Buell took Taj aside in the crew quarters. "I want you to know," he said, "that I asked them to have someone else do this."

"Do what?" For a moment Taj had the crazy idea Buell was going to do something to him. That was how fatigued and stressed he was . . . and how bizarre the situation.

"This Bangalore Object, when it struck, damaged the center—"

"Yes, you said it caused damage and killed a dozen people."

"It also," Buell said, shaking with tension and momentarily unable to continue. He took a breath. "It also enveloped at least one hundred others on the grounds. It appears to have taken them into space."

"And my son? Pav?"

"He is officially counted among the missing and presumed—"

"Presumed what, Buell? Captured by aliens?"

"I'm afraid that is exactly what we think. We've been able to track both Objects and they are returning to Keanu." He glanced at his watch. "Predictions are that they will land there in less than two hours."

"That's impossible!"

"And yet . . ." Buell was trying to be sympathetic. "Look," he said, "I have children. I can't imagine what it would be like to lose one—or to have one taken from me like this. I can tell you that NASA and the Coalition are doing everything we can to figure out what is happening, and what we might do."

"I take it a rescue mission is off the table."

Now he saw the Travis Buell that NASA and America loved . . . the feisty, get-'er-done Buell. He seemed to grow several centimeters. "Nothing is off the table, Commander."

But, of course, it was. Within days Keanu had propelled itself out of Earth orbit, resuming its journey into deep space, taking with it 187 humans from Bangalore and Houston.

Including, he learned from a frantic Tea Nowinski, Harley Drake, Shane Weldon, and Rachel Stewart.

Mrs. Remilla and ISRO had been as unenthusiastic about a Landing Day press conference as Taj but were overruled by the government types, notably Suresh Kateel. "The *Adventure* crew members must show themselves and be seen answering questions as soon as possible," Kateel said in their final pre-arrival meeting.

It was odd, because Kateel had never spoken on the subject when it came up earlier—indeed, had rarely spoken at all. He was one of those silent "horse-holders," to use a NASA term, so common in large organizations, possessing titles like *secretary* or *deputy*, but who wielded immense power.

Kateel was an older man, heavy, bespectacled, unremarkable by any objective standards. Yet when he finally uttered an opinion, even Melani Remilla closed her notes and considered the matter decided.

Only Taj had been sufficiently brave, or foolish, to ask why the crew's appearance was so important.

"To prove that they have arrived and are safe," Kateel said. His whole manner suggested that he was not used to making explanations. "Most of all, we want them to address the Revenant business."

That, at least, Taj understood. During the *Brahma-Destiny* mission he had been forced to accept the bizarre notion that a dead human being could not only be resurrected—but could have his or her soul somehow located and extracted from the universe at large to be recombined with a new version of the person's body.

The simple notion that human souls persisted beyond death was, to Taj's mind, the most important discovery in human history.

Yet it had been relegated to second place because it occurred the same week in which humans learned that there were indeed other intelligent races in the universe.

And that our encounters with other races were not fated to be benign.

It was only after returning to Earth that Taj had truly begun to appreciate the enormity of the Revenant discovery. He had not decided what he thought of it yet; it was one of those matters that a true philosopher could spend several lifetimes contemplating, and he was not a philosopher.

He had noticed, however, that the discovery led to a sharp rise in religious fervor among both Hindis and Muslims. He had half-expected the proof of life after death to lead to a rise in martyrdom—how many more suicide bombers could be recruited from fanatics who knew for certain that part of them would definitely survive past the moment of detonation? But Taj had not seen this. Of course, given the Big Brother state that India had become, it wasn't likely he would have—

"This Revenant matter has led to rumors that have evolved and darkened for twenty years," Kateel was saying. "We require the appearance of normality."

There had been no discussion of a truly open press conference. Only that a small group of screened and selected reporters, using equipment provided to them by the Signals Intelligence Directorate, would be allowed to quiz *Adventure*'s crew for an hour, if that, using a list of questions approved by Kateel himself.

So it was that, shortly after Taj's exhausting presentation on the Aggregates, four men and two women were admitted to the conference along with a camera crew of two.

Rachel, Pav, Yahvi, and Xavier were seated at the head of the table where formerly Taj and Mrs. Remilla had been. It was Mrs. Remilla who made the brief introduction, explaining in the most general and uninformative way that *Adventure* traveler Sanjay Bhat was "indisposed." This was followed by a silence that was almost comical, as if the anointed reporters had misplaced their script.

The alien Sentry named Zeds? "Zeds will not be available for this event," Mrs. Remilla said. The imagery on the conference room view screen had changed from strategic global data to an image of *Adventure* on the ground at Yelahanka. The window showing Zeds had been closed. Taj wondered if the Sentry could still access the room. He was not a reporter and had no love for the profession, but surely the chance to question a living, breathing, articulate alien was exciting beyond measure—the thing you dreamed about doing!

This group of reporters had clearly been cowed by Kateel or the intelligence services, because they accepted Remilla's bland restrictions with no visible protest.

Finally, these reporters began to ask the expected questions. To Rachel and Pav, about life on Keanu, what they missed, what they didn't miss. How long they planned to stay. "As long as you'll have us," Pav said, smiling in what his father thought was a forced manner.

Interesting questions, from Taj's point of view: *How long will Keanu remain in Earth orbit? Have you returned permanently?*

And here Rachel offered a dazzling smile and said, "That answer is the same," which told no one anything.

Are you in contact with Keanu? "Yes," Rachel said. *Can the rest of us contact them?* "Very soon," Rachel said.

Speaking of travel—the ship you traveled in, how did you manage to build it? "Oh, we found it lying around," Pav said, a lighter moment that seemed to play well with the reporters. He went on to reveal that *Adventure* had indeed been "found," that it had been built by the Sentries "a really long time ago" and then refurbished.

Can it take off again?

"Once it's refueled," Pav said. Taj wasn't so sure about that, unless *Adventure* was powered by a truly exotic motor; no chemical rocket known to human physics could be that small (and carry that little fuel) and still reach escape velocity.

But Taj had no idea what kind of rocket motor *Adventure* possessed. Or, come to think of it, what cargo it carried.

Nor did he expect to learn the answers here. What troubled him was that he was not sure he would learn the answers from his son, not without considerable effort.

The questions to Yahvi troubled Taj with their triviality—it was like listening to paparazzi chasing a pop star back in the early 2000s—but his mild disgust soon gave way to outrage when he heard his granddaughter's answers. Sexually active! At age fourteen!

Now he was eager to know more about life in the human habitat on Keanu. It sounded like some libertine fantasy, free of all standards of decency.

His face no doubt showing his displeasure, Taj caught Pav's eye and saw only passive acceptance.

His posture must have stiffened, because he felt Tea's hands on his shoulders. "Steady, Grandpa," she whispered.

"Did you hear that?"

She slid into the chair next to him. "Yes, terrible stuff," she said. "The questions—"

"The answers."

Tea looked amused. "I realize this is something I should probably have told you on our wedding night, but I was sexually active at the same age. In Nebraska, USA."

"And your point is?"

"Their life"—she nodded to Rachel, Pav, Yahvi, and Xavier at the other end of the room—"has been incredibly difficult. Remember what that place was like when we left. Imagine what it was like when a hundred and eighty-seven very unhappy people got dumped there.

"They had nothing! They were on a different planet! They had to make it up as they went along! It's a miracle they didn't just starve in the first month. They made a home in an alien environment! They kicked out the Reivers—"

"And sent them here."

"I don't think they *sent* them, darling. And now look," she said. "They came back here to help us! Six of them against a hundred million Reivers and quite a few humans who want to do them harm.

"And you're upset that teenagers *fuck*? Come on, Taj."

All he could do at that point was hope that his silence served as an apology, and turned back to the reporters.

There were almost no questions for Xavier. He was asked what he missed most and snapped, "Sunsets, I guess," which discouraged additional queries.

Finally one reporter dared to ask the question Kateel had wanted. "What can you tell us about the Revenants? Do people die on Keanu, then come back to life?"

Pav said, "No—" But Rachel swiftly intervened, placing her hand on Pav's arm. "That is a very complex subject," she said. "And a press conference isn't really the best place to discuss it. Let's save that for another day, when we've had more time to adjust and be helpful with our answers."

There was some grumbling. Clearly Kateel wasn't the only one who wanted to learn the secrets of life beyond death.

But not today. The press conference ended; Mrs. Remilla took charge of getting the reporters out of the hospital.

And Taj, feeling suddenly every year of his age, was left looking at his son, his daughter-in-law, his granddaughter, and Mr. Toutant . . . wondering what they had become.

National technical means are no longer available to us: The last Indian-built imaging surveillance satellite, RISAT-5, was launched in 2021 and ran out of maneuvering fuel a decade later.

Commercial platforms such as OrbImage and GeoEye have been inaccessible to nations outside the Free Nation sphere and are reportedly no longer functional. (There have been no commercial imaging launches since the Aggregates consolidated their control of Free Nation U.S. in 2023.)

To be blunt, we lack overhead capability.

Combined with travel restrictions and information firewalls, our only sources of intelligence are the so-called undernet, and inferences that can be made from economic studies.

Leading to this conclusion: Free Nation U.S. is in the midst of a construction project that dwarfs the Apollo program and, indeed, compares to the buildup of American nuclear forces (missiles, warheads, aircraft, naval vessels) in the period 1946–1992.

And the center of this construction is a facility located in northern Arizona, an area formerly known as the Arizona Strip.

The purpose of this project is still unknown.

INTELLIGENCE REPORT, RESEARCH AND ANALYSIS WING,
DELHI, 25 MARCH 2040

WHIT

"First trip east?"

Whit Murray blinked at the voice, which belonged to a man a few years older than him—possibly twenty-five. He was tall, thin, with reddish blond hair and beard. A ginger, his mother might have said.

Whit had memories of two stops after his middle-of-the-night arrival, when the train had largely been empty. Where had all these people come from? And who was this strange man next to him? "Yeah."

And why did the guy have a deck of cards in his hand?

The man's voice was surprisingly rich and deep. "Any idea what you're in for?"

"No. Just, something related to my work."

"Which was—?" The man opened his hand and began to slide cards from palm to fingers.

Whit made a face. He was blinking, hoping his eyes would begin to water. "You don't look like a member of THE," he said.

The man laughed. "I'm the last fucking person to be in THE." He pronounced it "Thee" with a long E rather than the preferred "T-H-E," which didn't make Whit any more comfortable. "I am notoriously indiscreet." Freezing his cards in his right hand, he held out his left. "Randall Dehm."

Awkwardly, they shook. "So, Randall, how long have you been working on . . . whatever it is you're working on, including that business with cards?"

"The cards? Since I was eight, right after . . . things changed and it wasn't so easy to play games on the Web or watch TV. Something to do."

"How many tricks have you mastered?" Whit realized he was looking past Dehm as he spoke, taking his first look at the others in the car . . . which itself looked and smelled brand-new. Everyone seemed to be Whit's age—under twenty, certainly, and in a couple of cases, much younger.

All equally dazed, too.

"Exactly eight," Dehm said. "The Count, Do as I Do, Cutting to Aces—"

"They've got names."

Whit was unable to hide the sarcasm. Dehm smiled. "I've been on this project since I was twenty, seven years ago. They . . . recruited me midway through college." He smiled. "The cards, even longer. On my own."

"Oh, a college guy." Whit was immediately jealous. He'd had the grades and test scores for college, but no opportunity. The days of Pell grants and scholarships—the things that allowed his dad to go to UNLV, according to Mom—were long gone. The Aggregates preferred to take "promising young minds" and "channel them." "Where were you studying?"

"Caltech."

That made it even worse. Not only was Caltech where all the best technical people went—okay, maybe MIT—but it was in Los Angeles. Whit had always wanted to go to Los Angeles.

He had always wanted to go anywhere besides Las Vegas.

He realized, in fact, that this train trip to wherever might be his third, possibly his second trip across a state line!

Whit's earlier assignment, programming field calculations for a giant generator, had kept him within Las Vegas city limits, at the former Nellis Air Force Base. (There were still some U.S. military craft there, but no airmen or pilots that Whit and his team were ever allowed to meet. Of course, the giant electrified fence between the Installation and the rest of the base might have had something to do with it.)

The new one was far outside the city, outside the state, in fact. Whit had grabbed his gear from the dorm and hoofed it back to the metro stop in order to catch the oh-dark-thirty bus to the Henderson node.

There he found a special train heading east . . . past Hoover Dam (which he could see from the window, since he happened to be sitting on the right-hand side of the car), then into the trackless waste of north-western Arizona.

Well, not trackless . . . this train had tracks, new ones to Whit's untrained eye.

Dehm squinted past him. "Oh, check this out."

No sooner were the words out of Dehm's mouth than the train turned to the left, and Whit was looking out his window at the most fabulous structure he had ever seen in his life.

Far in the distance, sitting on the high desert under a cobalt-blue desert sky, was some kind of termite mound ten stories tall, rising like an ogre's castle on the north rim of a canyon. It was actually a city in one huge structure—an arcology, to use a term Whit remembered from his reading—but not necessarily a human one. There was no obvious activity, no aircraft or trucks going in and out . . . no ads, no personal touches . . . no color.

Just a squat, intimidating dun-colored structure taking up a huge amount of space and looking as though it had stood for a thousand years.

Detracting from the ancient temple image, however, were two visible rows of slablike power towers—no lines, just the towers themselves—stretching across the landscape from Hoover Dam and nuke plants elsewhere in Arizona, Utah, and California like monoliths.

Surrounding those structures . . . a series of giant flat mirrors on pedestals, all pointing at a common center.

The whole thing looked like Disney World conceived by, say, Attila the Hun.

"How far away are we?" Whit asked.

"Half an hour at least," Dehm said, which meant the mound was even larger than Whit had thought. "We have to go through a couple of tunnels first."

"I've never seen anything like this. We're going to live there?"

"And work there. That's not all . . . the whole top of that canyon, the side away from us . . . Well, just wait. And get used to it, too." Then, with no apparent concern that he might be overheard—and Whit could see that two girls and a boy in the next seat were listening—Dehm added, "It'll be the last home you'll ever know."

Whit was so alarmed that he forgot to be cautious. "What are you talking about?" He didn't really believe this Dehm guy, but why would he say something like that?

"This project is entering its final phase," Dehm said. "That's why they gave the senior people—like me—one last vacation. To say good-bye."

"And that's what they told you."

"Of course not. They just gave everybody in my section leave at the same time, which had never happened before. But there is a sense of completion and finality." Dehm smiled and proudly, stupidly displayed four jacks.

"So what? Then it's on to the next project, right?"

"See, that's just it." And here Dehm managed to lower his voice and glance over his shoulder. The eavesdroppers sat back, though to Whit their eyes remained wide and their ears remained tuned. "What I heard a while ago was that this particular project was kind of a terminal one, that when the Aggregates hit the on button, it would leave the facility and maybe North America and possibly even the entire world pretty much dead."

The train entered a tunnel.

Whit found himself feeling frightened—he wasn't sure why. He had never been afraid of the dark. And it wasn't Dehm's story, because he wasn't sure he believed it, especially since it had all the signs of some weird THE loyalty test.

Maybe it was the sudden reality of separation from the life he knew . . . the sense that he was moving into a new world.

They emerged into harsh desert light. Blinking, Whit turned away from the window and focused on his fellow passengers.

He had seen earlier that they were mostly his age, about evenly split between guys and girls. Dehm, in fact, who was in his own world for the moment, fumbling with his cards, was the oldest person in the car.

One thing they all had in common . . . they all seemed to be alone. No pairs or groups.

And every one of them wore the same look that Whit did: wide-eyed, unreasoning fear.

The train plunged into another tunnel.

QUESTION: For Yahvi Stewart-Radhakrishnan, what's it like growing up on a Near-Earth Object?

YAHVI: I don't know how to answer that. I grew up, I guess.

QUESTION: How do you spend your time?

YAHVI: I go to school and work at my jobs, what else?

QUESTION: Would you like to go shopping?

YAHVI: Is that what teenagers do on Earth?

QUESTION: Some of them.

YAHVI: Then sure, I suppose.

QUESTION: Would you say that growing up on Keanu is different from growing up on Earth?

YAHVI: How would I know? I just got here.   YAHVI, FIRST INTERVIEW

YAHVI

"Why can't I see Zeds?"

Yahvi caught up to her mother after the boring conversation in the meeting room.

"He's in a pressure chamber."

"I heard. So why can't I see him?"

The family stretched across the half-lit hallway, Yahvi on the left, Rachel in the middle, Pav on the right. As she frequently did in conversations like this, Rachel turned to Pav, as if to say, *Listen to your silly daughter.*

Which always infuriated Yahvi. "Mom!"

Rachel opened her mouth to tell Yahvi why not, then closed it. "Actually, there is no good reason. Let's see about Sanjay, then make sure Zeds is okay."

Yahvi never wanted to come to Earth at all. Leave Keanu someday? Sure, if she lived until the NEO reached a destination. But she wasn't holding her breath for that; even with all the enhancements her parents and Harley Drake and Sasha Blaine kept talking about—extending the human life span to hundreds of "years"—well, it still wouldn't be good enough.

Yahvi was ready to admit that having Earth as a target was an improvement over the Architect home world. Earth was a few years distant, at Keanu's rate of travel.

The Architect home world? Something like five thousand years.

"Humans just aren't suited for travel between the stars," Sasha would always say.

"What is it we *are* suited for?" That question came from Nick Barton-Menon, who was the most complete smart-ass in Yahvi's year at school . . . and as cute as he was smart.

The trouble was, he knew it. The double trouble was, everyone tolerated it. Even Sasha Blaine, the giant red-haired goddess of a mathematician, would put up with snarky comments from Nick that would have gotten Yahvi or anyone else sent to the fields for "readjustment."

"Humans are great at starting wars," she would say. (This was not a onetime exchange.) "Lying, cheating, quarreling, poisoning our environments."

"Go, humans!" one of the others said.

"So we're essentially like the Reivers," Nick would say. "Only larger and less able to disassemble ourselves and survive."

"Those are just our bad traits, some of which turn out to be useful. As in dealing with the Reivers." Yahvi had never seen a Reiver; none of the yavaki had. They had been exterminated on Keanu before she was born.

Or so everyone said. Obviously, given the terrifying things they heard about these creatures, their varying shapes and sizes, their insane ability to duplicate themselves, their ability to destroy—that is, reshape to their own needs—anything they touched, every human on Keanu hoped they were gone. Every now and then some yavak, or even one of the older HBs, would report a sighting in some tunnel or one of the other habitats (the Skyphoi habitat was notorious for these events), and there would be a lockdown and panic. Even Nick Barton-Menon would pay attention then.

The problem was . . . apparently a whole bunch of Reiver Aggregates had escaped from Keanu. They had made their way to Earth.

Which was surely bad for Earth, but Yahvi had a difficult time imagining the place, even having seen it looming in the *Adventure* view screen for four days . . . and after walking its surface for several hours.

Of course, she had been limited to the sights and sounds of an Indian Air Force base, and one particular building—hardly a representative sample, as Sasha Blaine would say. But even then, she was ready to conclude that while Earth might be a perfectly fine place for those born there and condemned to live their lives there, it seemed too limited, too confined.

For example, Keanu moved. It was *going places.*

Earth moved, too, of course. In a steady rigid orbit around one sun, the same thing it had been doing for four and a half billion years, and, with luck, for another two or three. That was just striking Yahvi as not much fun.

Of course, it probably reflected her anger at having come close to death . . . and her frustration at being cooped up in this awful hospital away from whatever fun Earth had to offer.

She was more frustrated that she and her parents, and for that matter, Xavier and Zeds, weren't allowed to see Sanjay Bhat, or even to know for sure if he still lived.

Yahvi, Rachel, and Pav went upstairs to the entrance to the intensive care unit only to find Indian Air Force guards and this Wing Commander Kaushal blocking their way. "Your companion is in no condition for visitors," the round little counselor told them. There were no nurses or doctors around, no one who might listen to an appeal.

"We'd like to know his condition," Rachel said, in a voice that Yahvi knew well; it meant, *I'm being patient for now, but the explosion will follow shortly.*

Kaushal was deaf and blind to this, however. "You saw the extent of his head injuries," he said. "He was taken directly to surgery after we arrived here, and no one has emerged to tell me what is going on."

Rather than cloud up and rain all over Kaushal, Rachel turned to Pav. "Where did Taj go?"

"He and Xavier had to talk about securing our cargo—"

Rachel turned back to Kaushal and actually said, "Thank you. We'll come back in an hour."

"Maybe we could get something eat," Pav said. Yahvi felt that they had just eaten, and besides . . . she still felt sick from the crazy near-death experience of a landing, and the smells and sights of the intensive care unit.

Yahvi hadn't gotten to know Sanjay Bhat prior to *Adventure*'s launch—for most of her life, he had just been one of those faceless, humorless, grown-up HBs who spent most of their time in the Temple and hurrying back and forth on Important Work.

Nor had they bonded during the four-day mission. Sanjay had spent most of his time in the lower deck with Xavier, again, likely busy with Important Work. Yahvi could not remember them having a single conversation that went beyond two sentences—and one of them went this: "Don't be such a yavak!"

Meaning, *Don't complain, suck it up, be grateful*. It was a Bangalore attitude that Sanjay seemed to glory in. Yahvi had seen her mother rolling her eyes at Sanjay more than once since launch.

Still, Yahvi felt terrible about what had happened to him.

The three of them found two more Indian Air Force guards outside Zeds's chamber, which was in the back of the hospital building near ventilation equipment that ran so loudly it must have cooled or circulated air for the entire hospital.

This time the guards eagerly stepped aside. Yahvi wondered if they were nervous about the giant four-armed alien at their backs.

The door remained closed; it was thick glass and allowed Rachel, Pav, and Yahvi to show their faces and wave to the Sentry. "How are you?" Rachel shouted.

A speaker on the side of the door burped to life, with Zeds's calm voice. "Shouting is not mandatory. I can hear you quite well."

Pav laughed. "Are you being treated well?"

Zeds stepped closer to the door. He had removed the upper torso and helmet of his environment suit, leaving his large head and face pressed against the glass. One of the HBs had long ago compared Sentry heads to "dolphins with no snouts," which, once Yahvi finally saw a dolphin, made no sense, except for the skin color; there were too many angles and gill-like organs in that head to look like friendly terrestrial sea mammals. "I have the sea, I have nourishment, I am momentarily content."

Behind Zeds, Yahvi could see a pool of some kind—Sentries had dozens of words for water or aquatic environments in their own language, but fell back on "sea" for everything from bathtub to ocean when using English—as well as a large mat that was probably intended as a bed, and a table on which several large bowls rested. They seemed to be half-filled with some kind of bubbling stew.

"How are the schemes progressing?" Zeds said, a sentence that caused Rachel to wince and Pav to laugh a little too loudly. "Our planned recovery is going quite well, thanks to my father and his team."

Yahvi wanted to laugh, too. What was the big deal? Zeds was fluent in English! So what if he occasionally used the wrong word!

Sometimes her parents acted crazy.

After that odd exchange, little was said. Rachel and Pav seemed relieved when Xavier arrived. "Sanjay," he said, in his typically abrupt manner.

"What about him?" Pav said. Yahvi knew that Rachel was not a fan of Xavier's and avoided speaking to him whenever possible.

"Still alive, out of surgery, critical condition."

"How did you find out?"

"Kaushal." Xavier smiled with tiny teeth that Yahvi found creepy. "I had to encourage him a little, to share."

As they left Zeds, hoping to see Sanjay, Yahvi turned to Rachel. "What was the big deal with what Zeds was saying? You guys act like he was making trouble!"

Rachel grabbed Yahvi's arm so firmly it hurt. "We discussed this, Yahvi. We have to operate as if we are being watched and listened to everywhere!"

Yahvi jerked her arm away. "I know that! So what? We don't have anything to hide! We just want to get Sanjay well and get out of here, right?"

She glanced at her father—he was usually her supporter in daughter-mother disputes. But not this time; Pav Radhakrishnan was making a supreme effort to discuss something with Xavier.

The argument lasted only a moment; all their best arguments did. Yahvi simply glared, partly out of shame, partly because she had nothing she could say.

Rachel, as always, played the magnanimous victor. "I'm sorry. It's unfair to put this pressure on you. Try to relax." She smiled. "And I'll try, too."

So things were okay, but only for a moment. Yes, Yahvi was on Earth. Big deal. She missed her friends. She missed being around anyone her own age.

She wanted out of this stupid hospital.

ACTION REPORT

INS Mysore, *13 April 2040*

At approximately 0024 hours IST while on station lat 7°7"5' N, long 78°0"2' E, launch of an unidentified anti-aircraft missile observed from location 11 km WSW.

Launcher appeared to be a submarine, likely U.S. in origin, operating outside territorial waters.

Target was Object 2040-A, as designated by ISTRAC, which was descending from infinite altitude (orbital reentry velocity and trajectory) en route toward Bangalore.

The warhead detonated and Object 2040-A appeared to sustain damage, but insufficient to cause loss of control.

No communication was attempted. The submarine evaded surveillance and its current location is unknown.

LT. CDR. ASHOK SINGH, DIRECTOR OF OPERATIONS

RACHEL

Rachel's long-awaited contact with Keanu began with a sharp pain in her head, a throbbing that began above her right eye and spread across her ear and down her neck. It was so sharp and debilitating that it distorted the vision in her right eye and forced her to lean against the nearest wall.

The only good thing about the timing was that she was alone, on her way back from a "tour" of the *Adventure* crew's "living quarters" inside the Yelahanka base hospital. Pav had let her handle this issue—"I can sleep on a floor, you remember"—and so he had gone with his father to see about the growing list of other problems the new arrivals faced.

Yahvi had lingered in the conference room to play with her new Beta toy, to Rachel's relief. Xavier had decided to check on Zeds.

Somewhere within the pain was a voice: "Keanu calling, in the blind. Rachel, can you hear me? Pav, anyone? Keanu calling. . . ."

"I'm Rachel," she said, trying not to speak aloud. The implant system worked best when the user subvocalized, using facial, dental, and throat muscles to do everything but say the words. Tests had shown that Rachel could make words clear even if the pronunciation varied, so she tried to keep her messages brief and therefore clearer.

It was as if she heard a rustle of leaves in her head, which surprised her until she realized it had to be applause or cheers from Keanu "mission control," which she knew to be a makeshift collection of chairs and screens on the third floor of the Temple. She had recognized Harley Drake's voice—that of the confident pilot-astronaut she had known most of her life—but wondered who else was with him. Sasha Blaine, surely. But she could think of no one else, and it bothered her—a sign that she was far away from her home.

"You made it," he said.

"Yes," she said, but felt she had to add quickly, "Sanjay is hurt."

"Say again?"

She groaned. The pain was constant, and worse yet, now she seemed to be smelling burned rubber. Since there was no rubber burning in the empty hospital hallway, she had to conclude it was her brain on fire—or her olfactory nerve.

As succinctly as she could, she told Harley about the missile attack and the crash landing, Sanjay's injuries and current status. "What does this mean for your, ah, mission plan?" Bless him, Harley could not be anything but an astronaut. *Mission over everything, even human relationships.* She imagined Sasha Blaine shooting Harley a look of annoyance.

"We can't go anywhere until we know more," Rachel said, breaking the message into chunks of two and three words. "We're only on day one, so we haven't been delayed."

"I don't need to remind you about the need for urgency," Harley said.

"You do not," she said.

"Apologies," he said. "It's tough being so far from the action. Glad you made it. What's it like being home?"

Rachel understood Harley's reason for asking the question—it was likely the one thing everyone with him wanted to know, beyond the simple fact of the crew's safety. But she didn't want to have this discussion right now. She felt terrible, and she felt exposed . . . as if the wrong word could ruin everything. "We haven't been outside much," she said. "Confined to a hospital since landing."

For a moment, the pain went away. Then it was back, as Harley said, "Losing the link. Glad to know you made it. Looking forward to more updates when you have them. Everyone here says, 'Good work!'"

Then, mercifully, it was over.

Rachel blinked, then ran her hand through her hair, rubbing the right side of her head. It felt as though she had a fever.

She wondered if Pav and Xavier had had a link, and if they had been similarly affected.

God, what if this happened to Sanjay? What if the transmitter in his head had been discovered or removed by the Indian doctors?

The technology wasn't new—one of the space communications specialists among the HBs knew about similar implants from 2019, and Zhao, to the extent that he shared anything, seemed to know a lot about their design and uses. And surely the Indian welcoming committee would expect *Adventure*'s travelers to have some means of staying in touch with Keanu.

This was not a setback—yet. But it reminded Rachel of the risks she and her family had accepted, and the stakes.

It was Melani Remilla who showed Rachel the living quarters. "We set aside four rooms in this wing," the ISRO director said. "All on the same floor, all relatively private."

They were hospital rooms, of course, with medical monitoring equipment removed and an extra chair and rollaway garment rack added.

As if we were packing several changes of clothes, Rachel thought. They each carried half a dozen versions of the same basic outfit; fashion was not a big deal among the HBs. No one had tried to use the proteus to make a sport coat or a little black cocktail dress.

The whole suite looked more appropriate to the prison ward of some white-collar American jail. The feeling was enhanced by the presence of two armed guards at the nurses' station.

"There are bathrooms in two of the rooms," Remilla said. "They have safety railings, of course. We weren't able to remove them without rebuilding the facilities."

"That we can deal with," Rachel said. "Anything will be better than the accommodations aboard *Adventure.*" The onboard "bathroom" had been a curtained-off set of covered buckets on the cargo deck.

She wondered about Melani Remilla—was she married, did she have children? Was she a real engineer or scientist, or a policy wonk or political appointee? She looked like the former—a bit dowdy and distracted—but acted and sounded like the latter.

And did any of that matter? With luck, Rachel and team would be on their way elsewhere within a day or two, even if Sanjay had to remain behind. There would be other political operatives, flacks, and wheeler-dealers to confront—

"There are so many questions I want to ask you."

Remilla had been silent for so long that the sound of her voice, echoing in this empty hallway, startled Rachel. "I feel the same."

"Which is why we scheduled the group briefings and various conferences . . ." Remilla's voice trailed off.

"You want to ask me something in private, and it feels as though you're cheating the rest of the committee." Rachel was aware that she had the bad habit of finishing other people's thoughts. The high degree of accuracy had failed to make it one of her more popular habits.

But Remilla seemed relieved. "What do you really want to do here?" she said. "You aren't equipped to explore—"

"We will be doing some sightseeing."

Remilla made a skeptical face. *All right,* Rachel thought. *Tell her.* "We want to visit Texas, the U.S."

"That's what I feared."

"It can't be a surprise."

"I understand perfectly—if I'd been taken from my home twenty years in the past, I'd want to visit. But you heard your father-in-law. Texas and the U.S., they are not what you remember. You won't be welcome."

They were about to leave the suite and go back to more public areas. Rachel took Remilla's arm. "And now, a private question from me to you," Rachel said.

"That's only fair," Remilla said, visibly bracing herself.

"The entities that control the Free Nations . . . how have you been able to stop their spread?"

"You heard Taj: a combination of embargo, fences, and other barriers, occasional conflicts. But, truly? I'm not at all certain that we have. I think they remain 'contained' because they *choose* to."

"Which leads to, why?"

"That is the single question that obsesses us all, every government, every scientific body. The Aggregates are working on something big, and likely very nasty."

"What does that mean?"

"The best current theory is that they are building a giant energy weapon that they can use to strike anywhere on the globe, essentially destroying cities and defenses from thousands of kilometers distant—"

"Then moving in?"

Remilla shrugged. "That would be the idea. It's what seems to be obsessing and paralyzing our military, because they have no way of counteracting it."

"What about destroying this energy weapon? It's one giant installation, right?"

"Yes, located deep in the heart of Free Nation U.S."

"India had nuclear missiles twenty years ago."

"And still possesses a handful, but they are all twenty years old . . . and likely to be easy pickings for Aggregate countermeasures."

"So taking a few shots at them would do nothing except get them angry."

"'Stirring the hornets' nest' is the phrase that keeps coming up."

"What do you think?"

Remilla thought for a moment. "I'm not sure it *is* an energy weapon. There is also a great deal of other data about huge buildups of conventional weapons . . . especially land vehicles."

Rachel found that image troubling, and also strange. "So they're planning to invade Mexico?"

"Mexico is already a Free Nation, though there are pockets where even the Aggregates don't go," Remilla said. "But they could use ships to transport these vehicles to Asia."

"It sounds as though you really don't know."

"The matter is above my pay grade, as they say."

"Then how about this matter, at our level," Rachel said. "How well do you know Commander Kaushal?"

Rachel's experience with politicians was limited to the HB Council, but even that relatively limited pool had trained her to recognized wariness and hesitation. She could tell that Melani Remilla's eyes narrowed some fraction of a centimeter—about the same distance her eyebrows rose—even as she said, in a voice that betrayed no change of attitude, "Why do you ask?"

"He seems cautious and controlling."

"He's a military man." Now the ISRO official's expression changed from wariness to something like bemusement.

"My father-in-law is a general, too," Rachel said. "This isn't a case of military-versus-civilian. One of our crew is in dire medical condition and we aren't being given timely information, we aren't being allowed to see him. We are being treated like prisoners.

"I understand his concern for the . . . safety of Earth," Rachel said, feeling as though Melani Remilla could do with a reminder. "But we are six people, one of them a teenager. You've already performed medical examinations; we aren't carrying a plague from space. In fact, given where we've lived for the past two decades, we are more likely to catch some terrestrial bug.

"So think of us as free human beings you welcomed to your lovely nation . . . to your planet . . . who have certain tasks they wish to accomplish, and a limited time in which to accomplish them."

"I'm sure Kaushal can be persuaded to accommodate you," Remilla said, "with one exception." Rachel had a good idea what the exception was, but she forced Remilla to state it. "He will never allow you to go to the U.S."

"I didn't realize it was up to him." She smiled, though she wasn't feeling the humor of the moment. "In fact, I thought it was up to you and ISRO, or possibly this Mr. Kateel and the local government."

"ISRO won't stand in your way, but Kateel wishes he and the local government had never heard of you, so he is likely to support the Indian Air Force, which in this case is Kaushal."

"Why does he care?"

"He thinks you might start a war. Given that Aggregate-controlled U.S. warships came close enough to our coast to shoot at you, I must confess that he has a point."

Rachel smiled. Kaushal was actually quite correct. Well, as her father used to say . . . it's better to know who your enemy is as early as possible. "In that case," Rachel said, "please tell Wing Commander Kaushal that we are grateful for his hospitality and that we have no expectation that he will help us travel to the U.S."

"Which means that you will depend on others?"

"At this moment," Rachel said, and she was quite truthful, "I don't know who that would be."

Both women had asked their questions and now seemed lost with each other. "Your daughter," Remilla finally said. "Is she enjoying the Beta unit?"

"Very much," Rachel said. "If she hasn't said thank you, she will."

Yahvi's obvious fascination with the Beta actually surprised Rachel—her daughter had zero experience with recorded music, and damned little with music of any kind beyond unaccompanied singing. The number of instruments among the HBs was three: a guitar, a flute, and a harmonica. There were a few guitar players in the population, and several who had self-taught over twenty years. But overall, musical instruments were as high on the 3-D printer priority list as fashion accessories, which was to say not very.

But music was music, and you didn't need training to be attracted to shiny toys, Rachel realized. *Especially when you were miserable.*

Finally leaving Remilla, she went off to find Yahvi, Pav, and the others.

First met as a creature, too-tall Frankenstein
You died for the third or tenth or a hundredth time
Yet in my wanderings I hear you feel you
Surrounding me

LINES CARVED ON FACTORY HABITAT WALL BY DALE SCOTT,
2015–2018

DALE

As he approached the Temple with Harley and Sasha, Dale said, "Do the lights ever go out?" He gestured toward the "ceiling" a thousand meters up, where snakelike "glowworms" provided daytime illumination for half the day, powering down to half-light at "sunset" and "dawn," and even lower levels for ten hours of human "night." "Ever have any droughts?" Rain inside the human habitat was benign, short, sweet, nocturnal. It reminded Dale of the old song from *Camelot* about rain falling only after sundown. Like that song, Keanu's systems frequently created a morning fog for plants and crops. It always dissipated by "full morning."

"Why do you ask?" Harley said.

"Why do you care?" Sasha snapped.

He chose to answer Sasha. "I've been in the other habitats and seen that there are hiccups in their daily weather."

"Like a system rebooting?" Harley said.

"God, Harley," Sasha said, "you don't have to discuss these things with him!"

The rebuke was enough to stop Harley from answering . . . and just enough to confirm what Dale had suspected, that Sasha Blaine was still his enemy, and that all might not be paradise in Keanu.

The flatness of the terrain made it difficult for Dale to see much more. There were new buildings, of course, all small, no more than two stories, and largely clustered at the opposite end of the habitat, beyond the Temple structure, which still dominated the "skyline." It seemed that a gate of sorts had been built in the entrance at the far side . . . with some kind of tram or train line extending from it and running toward one cluster of buildings. But all of that was still too far away.

Still, he was amazed at the changes just in the Temple. Formerly, and for years after their arrival, it had been a big, barnlike place with upper floors that resembled a college chemistry lab.

Someone with a sense of design had smoothed out the rough exterior, landscaped the approach, and performed a major renovation on the first-floor atrium—even planting flowers. It now reminded Dale of the lobby of a big-city bank, right down to a reception desk. The walls were white and gray, the furnishings black and chrome. The only feature that reminded Dale of the old atrium was the ramp that led to the upper floors.

Even that had been "improved" by the addition of a conference table in one corner, with more chairs, not just for the table but for spectators.

Harley and Sasha led Dale to that corner. The other humans in the Temple "lobby" turned to stare. Well, Dale thought, they didn't see many strangers.

Waiting for Dale in the conference corner was Jaidev Mahabala. The ISRO engineer, master of manufacturing, had not changed in a decade, to Dale's eyes. He was still small, dangerously slim, permanently nervous.

And of all the HBs who were not Dale Scott fans, Sasha Blaine included, Jaidev was number one.

"Let's get this over with," Sasha said.

"Where's Makali?" Dale said. "And Zhao? I would have thought they'd be part of any council."

"Zhao is a valued member of the council," Sasha said.

"But not so valued that he can't show up?" Dale said. "Or is it me? Never mind . . . Makali is a friend. Was a friend." The Australian-born exobiologist, brilliant and dogged, and attractive as well, had been part of the pioneering Keanu trek team. She and Dale had quarreled then but had seemed to be growing closer in the year afterward.

Makali was just the kind of person to do her own exploring, too. Maybe—

"She's busy at the moment," Harley said, as if that explained anything.

It was clear to Dale that Harley and Sasha were both waiting for him to lay his data cards on the table.

A transparent curtain emerged from both walls, enclosing them in a conference space. "What's this for?" Dale said.

"The Temple is our city hall," Harley said. "This room is the city council chamber. Even if we have to have private conversations, anyone who wants can sit out there and see us."

"So generous."

Never known for his patience, Jaidev gestured toward the table. "Sit." Without waiting, he took the chair at the head. "Why are you back?"

Jaidev was several decades younger, yet he made Dale feel like a student reciting for an aged, ill-tempered professor. Just for a moment, Jaidev's attitude made Dale so angry that he almost stormed out. But, no, that was twenty-years-in-the-past Dale. "As I told Harley and Sasha," he said, trying to keep calm, "I have learned that the Reivers are on Earth, as we suspected.

"They control something like forty percent of the planet, including all the best manufacturing and high-tech facilities outside China, primarily in the United States.

"Here's the worst of it: They are hard at work on some large project that will be bad for organic life, which is no surprise, given that everything the little bastards do is bad for organic life . . . but this might also be fatal for Earth as a planet.

"More to the immediate point, they know where Rachel and the others are. They will never allow them to visit the U.S. They tried to kill them once; they'll try to do it again."

Jaidev closed his eyes and drummed his fingers. That wasn't the extent of his twitchiness—he also tapped a foot. "And how do you know these matters?"

With a great deal of pride—no other human had managed to reach such a lofty level of communion with Keanu—he told them.

Beginning almost two decades ago, four habitats had turned out to be off-limits to Dale. Human, Sentry, Skyphoi, and the blasted one.

Reachable, however was a fifth . . . the Factory habitat, a genuine cityscape that filled a volume larger than any two of the others.

It was here that Dale spent ten years wandering, exploring, probing, and in some cases, defacing . . . entirely alone. The Factory was a fascinating place if you craved solitude and the company of exotic ten-thousand-year-old machines doing God knows what for who knows what reason.

But he believed that he had learned some of the Factory's secrets, and one of the most important was accessing its amazing data intercept and retrieval systems.

Dale knew that in their first years on Keanu, Jaidev and Sanjay and that bunch had made several trips to the surface to erect communications dishes that they'd fabricated with Keanu's nanotech goo—Substance K. But, given the other priorities—food, habitation, immense numbers of other needed items—there had been little time for them to pursue what was seen as a hobby.

And Keanu's trajectory away from Earth, and soon the Sun, made signal intercepts difficult; the NEO was literally flying at right angles "south" from the solar ecliptic plane. While many terrestrial signals propagated in an expanding sphere, others—usually the most interesting—had been confined to fiber-optic networks or transmitted in tightly directed beams. There were also signals that were too weak to be detected at any distance.

At least by the equipment humans would possess in 2019, and especially the equipment that could be knocked together by ill-equipped refugees of that era.

Keanu's systems were a hundred times better. "You won't believe what Keanu itself has been able to pick up."

"Oh, try me," Sasha Blaine said. "The Architects were able to pick up morphogenetic signals and human souls. I wouldn't think that episodes of *The Simpsons* would be a real stretch for them."

Dale turned to her. "I don't claim to have mastered the search engine, but I have learned this: *Anything* that was transmitted anywhere near Earth in the past twenty-four years, ever since Keanu entered the solar system, is here somewhere, stored and theoretically retrievable. I'm not just talking television and radio, but ham radio signals and telephone calls. Billions of telephone calls. Internet posts that went wireless. Obviously, I could only access a fraction of a fraction of a fraction of any of it, and I can only read or understand a tiny bit of that.

"Another thing: Terrestrial encryption means nothing to the Architects and their software.

"It just boggled my mind when I realized what it was doing. It still does, because, FYI, Keanu is still recording."

Jaidev spoke. "You still haven't told us how and where you learned about Rachel's landing and these threats."

"Landing news is everywhere outside India, nonofficial but public transmissions. You could see and hear those if your old antenna were working.

"The threats? That's more subterranean, various blogs and other links. But convincing. A source I trust."

Harley looked at Sasha Blaine, who looked away, through the curtain.

Then Harley looked at Jaidev, who stood up. "Deal with this."

And the Bangalore engineer-leader walked out.

"What does that mean?" Dale said. "That's it?"

"Sorry, Dale," Harley said. "You're not going anywhere for a while."

"What the hell are you talking about?"

"You're a . . . security risk."

"Be serious." Dale knew Harley well enough to know that Harley was serious, and felt stupid about it.

"You've stepped in something."

"I'm guessing you're not going to tell me what."

"Nope."

"You're not even interested in what information I have?"

"Oh, we're interested. We want you where you can be questioned."

Dale wanted to laugh. "What are you going to do . . . clap me in irons?"

Harley said nothing but looked past Dale toward Sasha, and the curtain.

Which had parted, revealing three serious-looking young people, one woman and two men, who were there to take Dale Scott into custody.

THE LATEST:

Word from various places in India confirms arrival of the Keanu folks, including a Sentry! (Can't wait to hear the explanation for that.)

One of the crew is badly injured and reportedly not likely to survive.

All are temporarily sequestered at an air base north of Bangalore, near the site of their landing.

Crowds are being kept at bay, but the whole operation leaks like an old boat—good for us, but potentially bad for the Keanu folks. Not only are they fat targets for the Aggs, but anyone on the Indian subcontinent who has a religious gripe with them, and this appears to be a good number.

Well, we warned them to stay away, right? Anyone remember that?

But, since they're here . . .

COLIN EDGELY TO THE KETTERING GROUP,
APRIL 13, 2040

YAHVI

The first night was awful. Partly it was the weight of the hours, the isolation, the creepy interior of the hospital, the presence of guards . . . combined with Rachel's motherly iciness.

Mostly, though, it was the food. Everything Yahvi had eaten in her life had been produced in the Keanu human habitat, either grown from existing stock the HBs had discovered—some of it not remotely terrestrial—or from prototypes engineered by the proteus after considerable trial and error. And while there were spices and curries suited to the tastes of the Bangalore majority, none of it prepared Yahvi for the variety of exotic dishes she was now supposed to consume.

Half of the food on the table appeared to have non-Indian origin, too. There was some kind of rice dish topped with sliced circular items that Yahvi suspected were meat of some kind. They must have been, because Xavier and even Rachel greedily dug into it. "Not bad for Bangalore jambalaya," Xavier said.

There were even boxes of food from places with names like McDonald's and Pizza Hut. "Where on Earth did you get these?" Rachel said.

"Come on, baby," Pav said, "there were franchises in Bangalore when I lived here."

"I just wonder who the franchise money goes to these days," Xavier said. "Those were American companies. Are we supporting the Reivers by eating this?" It was clear he wasn't expecting an answer, as he happily tipped a flat, wedge-shaped object toward his mouth and bit into it. "God, pepperoni," he said, his mouth full. "You know, I could never get this quite right in the habitat."

"Or pastrami or steak or any red meat," Rachel said.

"Not even chicken."

The HBs had few animals, for one thing. For another, the idea of slaughtering any for food was repugnant to most of the imported population—and as far as Yahvi knew, *everyone* in her generation.

She wasn't going near the hut pizza or large mack or whatever the supposed "American" food was. Dealing with the Indian cuisine was bad enough.

So she picked at her food and soon gave up the effort. As any mother would, Rachel noticed. "There's nothing you like?"

"No."

"Not even the naan?"

"It's not like they make it at home."

"It's just got onion in it."

"What's onion?"

Rachel's eyes narrowed. "You know what onion is . . ." She tasted another dish that Yahvi had rejected. "Oh, never mind; that's coconut."

"What is that and why would anyone eat it?"

Xavier laughed. "Try this," he said, holding out a dish that had a whitish tube-shaped object smothered in other items. "It's a plantain. Kind of like a banana."

"I never had a banana, so . . ."

Rachel forced a smile. "Why don't you just eat what looks and tastes good? It's not as though you'll starve." Then she turned back to Pav and Taj.

Yahvi ventured a few more bites, then picked up the Beta unit and walked out. All through the day, the conference room had begun to feel exactly like the flight deck of *Adventure*. Which was a place she found interesting at first but soon began to loathe.

Not that the halls of the Yelahanka Air Base hospital were a great improvement over the conference room. Rachel had told her she could go "anywhere," except for the surgeries and recovery rooms, and the loading dock, and the entrance. Well, she could probably walk up to the entrance—but she couldn't go out.

Not that she wanted to go out. The conference room was only a few meters from the reception desk and the main entrance. Yahvi lingered there behind the door, looking through the window, watching things for a few moments. There was an Indian Air Force guard at the desk, with another pair seated on opposite sides of the small lobby. All three men looked bored; Yahvi suspected that one of the men in the chairs was actually asleep.

Beyond them, a set of glass doors showed very little, except that night had arrived.

What if she did just walk past the guards and out into the night? Then what? She knew that the hospital was located in the heart of a large base, so leaving it would require a long walk . . . possibly the longest walk in a straight line she had ever made.

What lay outside the fences and gates? Stores? A highway? Homes? Empty fields? Her parents might know; her grandfather would certainly know, but what good would the information do her? Any real "exploration" would require mechanized transport, and she had no access to that. (Until riding in the Jeep from the landing site to the hospital, Yahvi's only experience with vehicular travel had been in the Keanu trolley while working on Substance K collection.)

She was stuck here until someone got them out, to another city, another country, another continent.

At this moment Yahvi would have been happy to get back aboard

Adventure and go home. There were many HBs, especially the yavaki, who would have been perfectly happy to keep on living aboard Keanu.

A third door opened behind her, and she was suddenly surrounded by bodies and voices. Four young women, none of them much older than Yahvi, all wearing bland smocklike garb in either light blue or green.

One of them smiled. Another one said, "Hi!"

But the other two, the ones wearing blue, reacted with alarm, grabbing the friendlier pair. "Don't you know who she is?" one of them said.

Yahvi was puzzled. Why would anyone be afraid of her? If anyone should be nervous in social encounters, it should be her. "I'm Yahvi," she said.

"We know." So said the one in blue who had warned the others. "Aren't you supposed to be locked up—?"

"No," Yahvi said.

"Like that thing in the chamber?"

So that was the problem! "Don't be afraid of Zeds," she said.

"It's not just him. We wish all of you would just leave!"

And she tried to tug the others along.

But one of the girls in green wasn't ready to leave and began arguing with the girl in blue. Yahvi could barely follow the exchange, especially since she couldn't help noticing the way the girls had enhanced their looks. They all wore makeup and jewelry—glittery things in their earlobes, bracelets, necklaces.

And their fragrance! There was a bit of a cooking air about them (the girls in green must work in the cafeteria), but what was most prominent was a floral scent. She wanted to ask them—even the one who didn't like her—why they did this and what were the rules, and where did one obtain these substances.

But just like that the argument was over. The two girls in blue marched out. "They're nurse assistants," the girl in green said. "Stuck-up."

"I'm sorry." Yahvi knew what *stuck-up* meant.

"And Surina is very religious."

Yahvi had been hearing that all day, that "religious" humans were among those most troubled by *Adventure*'s mission. It baffled her. There were a few religious people among the HBs, probably evenly split between Christians and Hindus. But, as far as Yahvi knew, none of the yavaki had ever expressed a belief in a supreme being or whatever it was religions were supposed to have. Maybe that was the problem. "We're not here to make trouble."

"I don't think it's you, but where you came from."

"And what you might do," the other girl in green said. "With your magic powers." She made a spooky sound, which made the first girl laugh.

"But you're not afraid of me."

"Well, no. I mean, you seem to be just like us—"

"Well, taller," the second girl said. That was true: Yahvi was a head taller than any of the four girls.

"Where are you going?"

"Out! It's Saturday night!"

Yahvi smiled. "So . . ." She had barely gotten used to "days." Yes, the HBs used the calendar they had grown up with . . . but there was nothing special about Saturday night, or Sunday morning.

"We have dates," the first girl said. "Well, I do." She nudged her friend. "Her boyfriend was deployed last week—"

"Deployed?"

"Sent to the coast on alert," the second girl said. From the expression on her face, this wasn't a good thing.

"In case we're invaded," the first girl said. Her giggles suggested that she didn't really see the danger.

"By the Reivers?" Yahvi said.

The girls looked confused. Yahvi tried to explain. "The Aggregates. The ones who control most of Earth."

"Yes. Everyone's sick of it," the first girl said. Then: "Does your alien friend speak English?"

"Or Hindi?" the second girl said.

"Both," Yahvi said. "Go by and talk to him. Tell him I said hello." As she said it, she realized she could have allayed some of her loneliness and sense of dislocation by visiting Zeds—who was almost certainly feeling the same thing.

Then the hallway door opened again. It was the two nursing assistants, now accompanied by the guards from the lobby. "There she is."

"You shouldn't be out here like this," one of the guards said.

"What, I should be in a different hallway?" She was getting angry. She looked to her two acquaintances in green; they seemed intimidated by the guards and the two nursing assistants.

"Never mind," Yahvi said. "I'm leaving."

She turned away and went through the doors, deeper into the hospital.

She would find Zeds and wish him a good night, even as she pondered the encounter with girls her age—how strange they were, how different their lives were.

All the while realizing that, as far as they were concerned, Yahvi was just as alien as Zeds.

QUESTION: For Rachel . . . Why did you turn Keanu around and bring it back to Earth?

RACHEL: Because I was going to be a bit too old to really enjoy the next closest destination.

QUESTION: Which was—?

RACHEL: At least forty light-years distant, or as we calculated it, based on our highest possible speed . . . really, really far off.

INTERVIEW AT YELAHANKA,
APRIL 14, 2040

RACHEL

Just as the meal was ending, moments after Yahvi had slipped out, Rachel began to feel dizzy and nauseated. It reminded her of morning sickness—and the sudden possibility that she might be pregnant added a whole new layer of stress to the moment. She and Pav were still making love—though, for a variety of good reasons, not since leaving Keanu. They weren't using birth control, either, since everyone wanted the HB population to expand . . . but not right this minute!

Then she realized it was Keanu calling.

She glanced at Pav, who showed no sign that he was being contacted. So she excused herself and went out into the hallway.

Where the connection proved to be almost useless. She managed to learn that Sasha was calling, and heard mention of Dale Scott and a "warning."

She managed to respond with a confirmation and a status update—which was status quo, Sanjay still critical and not seen.

Then it was gone, a most unsatisfying few moments.

Before she could return to the conference room, Taj joined her. "It turns out, the Aggregates did try to kill you," he said.

Rachel smiled bitterly. "You mean, our tail section didn't just fall off?"

Taj looked unhappy, whether with Rachel's flippant response or the fact that his news wasn't really news. "No, you were the target of a submarine-launched missile."

"Well, we assumed we might be shot at. It was one of the reasons we came here rather than the U.S."

"Didn't you consider equipping yourself with defensive missiles?"

Was this the "danger" Sasha had just tried to warn her about? "Taj, we were lucky to get *Adventure* flying, period. We just didn't have the time to invent and install an anti-missile system. Besides, we were just as likely to have been hit by a laser. Or conventional weapons."

"I understand." He got a curious smile on his face. "During the Keanu landings—I don't know if you knew or remember this—your father's team thought we had put a missile on *Brahma*." He shook his head at the memory.

Rachel had indeed heard that: At the time of the *Destiny* and *Brahma* missions there had been tension between the United States and India in particular, so much that some NASA people believed that *Brahma*'s crew would do anything to beat *Destiny* to the Keanu landing—even shoot at them.

"Have you told Pav about the attack?"

"Yes." A simple answer, but it annoyed her. She was the leader of the crew, yet Taj persisted in giving key information to Pav! *Because he was his son? Or because he was male?*

Maybe it was the fact that she hadn't really enjoyed the meal, that Yahvi was worrying her, or that the poor communication session with Keanu reminded her of the burdens of being female, Rachel decided she'd had enough.

"Fine," she snapped. "Since you two are talking, tell him that I'm going to see Sanjay, then Zeds."

"But Kaushal—"

She was walking away before Taj could finish reminding her that

Wing Commander Kaushal didn't want her "bothering" the doctors or patient.

There must have been something in her manner—Rachel knew that in certain situations she had a lean-forward, purposeful stride that tended to enhance her power—but the moment she arrived at the ICU and announced that she was here to see Sanjay Bhat, Wing Commander Kaushal emerged from around a corner. He closed a cell phone and said, "Give me one moment to summon the surgeon."

He walked away, leaving Rachel wondering what had changed his mind about allowing her access to Sanjay. She also wondered whom he had been talking to. And, while she waited, where was Pav?

Kaushal returned with not one but three doctors, all of them in white lab coats. "They will tell you everything they can," Kaushal said. The five of them slipped into the team conference room.

No introductions were offered and, frankly, Rachel didn't care. Her eye immediately went to the X-rays on the light board.

The obvious senior doctor, a tall, stooped Hindi with glasses and wavy gray hair, spoke. "The patient was unconscious upon arrival. Our initial diagnosis showed that his left frontal cranium had been struck by a heavy object.

"Fortunately, the object was largely flat—"

"Except for a few protruding switches," the second doctor said. He was much younger and seemed to Rachel to be impatient.

"The flat surface resulted in a blunt-force injury that was spread over a considerable area. It was as if he had fallen onto a floor or street from a height of perhaps two meters.

"There was some lateralization; his left pupil was blown. The bones were fractured across the entire area."

"Would I be right," Rachel said, "in thinking that the front and left part of his head got mashed in?"

"Crudely." The doctor seemed testy; obviously he was not used to interruptions. "But, yes, the skull was deformed. There was considerable brain swelling, which we alleviated by drilling these holes." His pointer glided across three tiny dark spots.

"After twenty-four hours, the swelling has subsided, though the patient's head still shows a great degree of trauma—"

Just listening to the cold, grim precision of the diagnosis made Rachel want to weep. Given what she had seen in the cockpit, she had suspected that Sanjay's injury would be severe, but here was proof.

The senior surgeon continued, but Rachel could no longer understand his words. She finally blurted, "I want to see him."

They took her around the corner to a hospital room, and there lay poor Sanjay, the left half of his head covered in thick bandages, the usual monitors recording a steady but slow heartbeat.

Rachel reached for his hand. To her dismay, it was cold and limp, like that of a corpse. Sanjay had been part of Jaidev's group, spending his days constantly busy improving life in the habitat. Did he have a lover? He was old enough to have memories of Earth . . . were there family members or friends he wanted to see here? She remembered a brother—then cursed herself for her lack of knowledge. Some leader she was turning out to be! She finally asked, "What is the prognosis?"

"All we can say is that he's stable."

Stable! What a horrible state!

Rachel let go of Sanjay's hand and walked out.

As a leader, as a wife, and especially as a mother, Rachel had developed several operating rules.

Rule number one: Face the bad news because it doesn't get better with time.

She had accomplished that with the visit to Sanjay.

Now it was time to deal with Zeds. Focusing on the challenges of making the Sentry happy, or finding a way to give him useful work, kept her from wondering where Pav had gone and why he was leaving this to her. There was no one she could ask—as she slipped down the stairs from the second-floor ICU to the ground floor and its high-altitude chamber, she passed no one at all.

Once she was on the ground floor, she saw only a couple of medical people, and a single guard outside Zeds's chamber. No Taj, no Tea, no Yahvi or Xavier.

Rachel almost regretted walking away from Kaushal and the surgeons so abruptly.

Of course, she could have diverted to the conference room to retrace her steps and find her missing husband and family members. But that would have forced her to ignore rule number one.

Sure enough, Zeds was chafing at the confinement. "We discussed this, did we not?" she said. She was working through Zeds's mechanical translator, usually a smooth process, aided by the fact that Rachel knew some Sentry Sign, and Zeds had a lifetime of vocalized English and Hindi.

"Mental preparation is no substitute for the experience."

"You hate it." Here she used Sentry Sign.

"I don't use that term," her Sentry friend said, in his typically obtuse way. "I would simply prefer to be allowed out of this chamber."

"You'll have to wear an environment suit."

"We discussed this, did we not?" Zeds was also fond of echoing human statements, usually with the exact tone and a pretty fair imitation of one's voice. This made the Sentry fairly unpopular with most humans.

"And you said you would prefer to minimize those events, due to the discomfort—"

"My current feeling is that I would be more comfortable wrapped in the suit and walking around than unwrapped and confined here." He was sitting, as Sentries do, in a kind of yoga posture, knees up, his arms wrapped around his body and legs, with zero eye contact. Which was understandable, since even sitting down he was as tall as Rachel.

"I will do what I can," she said, "as soon as I can." Then she added, "How are you finding the meals?" Zeds had spent enough time in the human habitat on Keanu to have sampled, and learned to like, certain human foods. His physiology allowed him to receive some nourishment from them, too.

But those foods were largely unique to Keanu; they were now in Bangalore, India, and while Pav had made heroic efforts to identify foods that were similar to those in the Sentry diet, it all seemed to have become seafood chowder. (The Yelahanka and ISRO authorities had insisted on equating "aquatic race" with a diet of shellfish.)

Based on the amount still left in the one bowl Rachel could see, the

Indian shellfish remained untouched. No doubt this contributed to Zeds's testiness.

"I have been subsisting on my emergency rations."

"I will work on that, too. And promptly."

Few Sentries, out of the hundreds in their Keanu population, wanted anything to do with humans. But Zeds not only tolerated humans, he sought them out, integrating himself into Rachel's world to the extent he could. (He had to wear, at minimum, breathing support gear, and often more than that.) Rachel was never sure exactly why.

Zeds was a connate of DSA, herself a connate of Dash, the Sentry who had been part of Rachel's father's final "journey" across Keanu twenty years ago. Perhaps there was some genetic disposition to reaching out to "aliens" . . . maybe he was just curious.

For all that Rachel liked Zeds, she had resisted the idea of bringing him on this trip for exactly these reasons; he complicated everything.

But she knew, instinctively, that he would be useful.

And what the hell . . . *Adventure* belonged to his people. And it was one of Rachel's other rules . . . when in doubt, be fair.

Pav met her before she reached the conference room, and he seemed upset. "I've been looking for you for an hour."

"You couldn't have looked very hard," she said. "This is a big building, but how many places would I be?"

"Good point," he said. One thing she loved about him was his ability—rare in men, in her experience—to accept correction or pushback without feeling wounded.

Or, at least, not showing it.

"Actually, I had contact." That explained it; that throbbing in one's head would make anyone look pale and shaken.

Pav's conversation with Keanu turned out to be longer than Rachel's. He had told them about the missile attack on *Adventure* and learned that there had been major progress on the backup plan led by Zhao.

She asked him if Harley or Sasha had discussed Dale Scott. "Yes!" Pav said. "Why the hell did he return to the living?"

"I don't know," Rachel said. "I can't take that as a good sign."

Pav smiled. "Good things rarely follow Dale."

Then Rachel yawned. She realized that she wanted only to sit down, or better yet, lie down.

Pav saw this and took her into his arms. "We've got a huge day tomorrow—the agent meeting. . . ."

"And figuring out just what the hell our real next step is."

"Let's just go to bed."

Kilroy was here
Kilroy was there
Kilroy was everywhere

GRAFFITO SCRIBBLED BY DALE SCOTT
AT MANY PLACES INSIDE KEANU'S FACTORY

DALE

They hadn't had to drag him; the guards just casually marched Dale to a small hut—one of several occupying a patch of ground behind the Temple, halfway to the "north" wall. "Is this your jail?" he said.

"We don't have a jail," the young man snapped, clearly insulted. But the woman was more forthcoming. "Occasionally people need a time-out. Sometimes they just want to get some mental or physical space."

"Ah, so these are meditation cells."

That effectively ended the conversation.

The hut was exactly that: four walls with a cot. No entertainment devices, not that Dale had seen any such items in twenty years.

But also no sink, faucet, or toilet. As he stood in the dark space—it was probably three meters across in both directions, lit only by two slit windows near the top—he spread his hands and said, "Suppose I need to urinate."

"Yell and you'll be escorted," the man said. Then he closed the door, locking it.

So much for meditation, Dale thought.

Within moments he was alone again . . . as he had been for most of the past two decades.

But now he was confined.

And hungry.

Food was one of the reasons he had had problems with the HBs.

On his earliest walkabouts, before he removed himself entirely from the human habitat, he had been able to take some food with him.

In his first months in the Factory, he had grown quite adept at theft. But that was ultimately unsatisfying; the fields and supplies most accessible to him were limited in their menu.

And he had had an unpleasant encounter with Xavier Toutant, the self-proclaimed King of Food. Seeing Dale heading toward the passageway early one morning (like poachers throughout human history, Dale had found that he was most effective when the "farmers" were asleep), the fat young man had shown surprising speed in intercepting him.

"You know, you could just *ask*, you asshole. Nobody needs to go hungry here."

"Then who cares? You'll just make more, anyway."

"It's just good manners."

"I gave them up for Lent."

He had brushed past Xavier, who had waited until seconds before Dale disappeared into a cleft in the rocks to throw a rock at him!

Dale had continued to poach, but less often. He had turned his attention to finding a proteus station inside the Factory. He believed that he would recognize one, since he had spent hours with the unit in the human habitat Temple.

The search was a bit like locating a particular distillery in a town the size of Dublin, but with no map.

So he had searched, systematically, starting from one of the giant dishlike pools of Substance K that dotted the Factory.

Dale had been lucky; within a few weeks he had located not just one likely proteus printer, but a building filled with them . . . and other buildings next to that one. The section reminded him of server farms in formerly distressed areas of downtown Los Angeles. He dubbed this area the Nanotech Quarter.

He spent at least a year mastering the system to where he could have won a contest with Jaidev. By the end of that time he was able to produce his own food. He even created a "garden" in an open space near his living quarters.

Such things already existed in the Factory, though none of them seemed to have been occupied for an extremely long time. (Even in the carefully controlled and engineered environments within Keanu, especially the Factory, dust accumulated. In a few structures, Dale saw signs of dead Reivers, powdery residue that ranged from film to heaping mounds, likely what was left of the smallest to the larger, anteater-like Aggregates, all killed in the plague the HBs had engineered and launched.)

Not one of the structures was truly optimized for human habitation. The Architect Dale had met was literally twice as tall as he was, and some buildings seemed suited for a being like that. Others had three floors where a human building would have one, suggesting that their inhabitants were really short, or very flat.

Dale's ultimate "home" was an open area under the overhang of a building entrance. Given its nature, the Factory had no regular rain or fog . . . until the day it did, which came as a surprise.

It had happened only once or twice a year, but there was no predictability that Dale could see—no correlation between the sudden rains and occasional failure of the ceiling glowworms. (The first time Dale found himself in absolute total darkness, he had foolishly tried to run—slamming into a wall and breaking his nose.)

Fortified by his own solid if uninspired menu, Dale spent another two years using the Factory systems to learn about Keanu . . . where its power came from, how it propelled itself, how the transit system operated (or in this case, didn't), how Keanu was able to create different gravity fields in the habitats . . . how it turned energy into the nanotech goo known as Substance K.

How it created the "vesicles," the spherical space balloons that managed to launch off Keanu and land on Earth—then return with samples and humans. (Or launch off Keanu carrying a few hundred thousand Reivers . . . and never return.)

He never learned more than a fraction of what he wanted to know. No human could—and certainly no human rummaging through the system without a guide or a key.

One thing did strike Dale, however: Some of Keanu's systems were off-nominal, either failed (the transit system) or failing (the weird reboots in the environmental support). That was certainly troubling . . . not that he could do anything about it.

Yet.

Eventually Dale tired of these explorations and decided to concentrate on experiments. More precisely, on making direct contact with Keanu itself.

The idea of Keanu being an individual wasn't his—Zack Stewart suggested as much during that first week, after his own encounters with the Architect . . . whom Zack considered the voice of Keanu itself.

It was only contemplating the still-murky link between the Architect and the human Revenants that led Dale to agree with Zack's conclusion. An entity the size of a small planet, with God only knew what sense of time passing, with a life span of ten thousand years, would naturally require some kind of avatar in order to communicate with tinier beings whose lives were limited to one hundred years.

One question had lingered for Dale: If Architect = Keanu, why the need for human or Sentry or Skyphoi Revenants? His familiarity with the Factory gave him one vital piece of information: The Architects were the original builders of Keanu, its first crew. So even a Revenant Architect was limited in its ability to communicate; thanks to its size and slower mental processing (compared to humans), it was still out of phase.

Then, considering the whole phasing business encouraged Dale to wonder about the microscopic Reivers. They seemed to have had solved the Keanu-Architect problem by combining into larger creatures. Which then made him wonder if beings the size and scale of Keanu did the same thing: Were there conscious entities the size of solar systems and even galaxies? He spent days pondering the matter, eventually tabling it for future consideration.

Dale tried the various Factory machines, searching for something that might serve as a communicator. He devoted the better part of a year to fabricating his own with the proteus, basing it on what he knew of telephones . . . and wound up with a clever piece of useless junk.

There were whole months when he ignored the systems and returned to his wandering ways.

Finally, after exhausting every other possibility, he had hit on a method worth trying . . . that of putting his body in direct contact with the NEO. He had tried it clothed, then naked. With unmarked skin, and tattoos.

He had lain down wet, then dry. Facedown, faceup.

Eventually it had worked. Eventually he found himself in a trance, experiencing visions, and visions that seemed to leave him informed, somehow. Connected.

The process had yet to work consistently or predictably, but now, here, tonight, in jail, Dale felt he had to try.

After a simple meal delivered by one of his guards, as soon as "night" fell and the HB community went into sleep mode—or whatever they did; they got noticeably quieter—Dale stripped off his ragged jumpsuit, leaving himself naked.

Thin to the point of scrawny, pale to the point of translucent, he looked like *The Illustrated Man* from one of his childhood books . . . except that the illustrations had been drawn by a blind person with no artistic talent at all, but an apparent fascination with various symbols, religious and technical—cross, Star of David, crescent, mixed with sigma and delta—and even a few from the world of magic.

It wasn't just the self-made tattoos that made Dale's body a visual horror, it was the piercings and homemade shunts.

He still had some Keanu-made wires sticking out of his midsection.

There was a floor to his jail hut, but it was made of light brown tiles that he was able to claw open. He peeled half a dozen of them off the floor, exposing the Substance K–derived regolith underneath.

Then Dale scraped out a shallow depression. Someone walking in on him would have thought he was digging a grave, but that someone would have been wrong.

The dugout portion wasn't to commit his body to this alien soil—it was to enhance communication, the same way he had once struck old battery nodes together, knocking off corrosion to improve contact.

Arms at his side, Dale Scott lay on his back in the dirt of Keanu and commanded his breathing to grow shallower, freeing his mind, soothing his spirit.

Within minutes—or possibly an hour, he was never able to tell—he experienced the feeling that he was lying on his back on the surface of some object in space, hurtling toward the stars . . . it was a familiar sensation, one he had experienced many times as a child in his backyard in California, staring for a long time at the night sky.

But with full sensation. Cold and heat. Electronic pulses blasting through him just below the threshold of real pain.

And the sound inside his head, like the voices of all humanity and possibly beings beyond humanity.

At some point—he had never been able to determine how long this process took—he was in a receptive state, feeling as though his eyes were open and trying to watch a multitude of objects, some of them television or computer screens, others pages from documents, still others images, both still and moving, all accompanied by a cacophony of more familiar sounds . . . voices in a dozen languages, music, static.

But mostly screens.

It wasn't all serene. Some images frightened him. Some sickened him. A few made him feel as though he were being assaulted.

It was as if some mechanism inside Keanu's vast system were reading his thoughts—even sensing unconscious needs, which might explain the torrent of what a younger Dale Scott would call porn—and displaying data that matched it.

He saw snippets and samples of news reports broadcast from Earth. Even though the Keanu system seemed to bias its selections toward those Dale would understand, very few of these reports were in English, but since all were accompanied by graphics—images of the individuals in *Adventure*'s crew and the same shot, obviously a controlled info dump, of the spacecraft at its landing site—he could pick up some information.

He wondered where the American broadcasts were, but only briefly; he had learned that broadcasts from Free Nation U.S. were fluff and filler, cleansed of anything troubling or informational.

Then, as if the Keanu system moved up a level of difficulty, he was given a sample of blog posts and e-mails that mentioned "Rachel Stewart" or "Sentry" or *"Adventure"* . . . much as the National Security Agency's I-Trap system had been able to collect similar items with keywords like "terrorism" or "C-4" or "suicide bomber" when Dale was a teenager. This was an endless stream, ninety percent of it consisting of people's questions or observations to each other—eighty percent of that in languages other than English.

But there were nuggets. And just noticing those caused Keanu's great engine to pin them somewhere in Dale's internal dream vision, where he could concentrate on them. He was especially taken with blog posts from several groups in Australia—the word *Kettering* kept coming up. The word had historical connotations for Dale, though he could not remember them (and Keanu's system had not shown an ability to rummage through his personal memories . . . so far).

Kettering posts seemed to have lots of information on Rachel and her crew . . . especially when Dale tracked them back to the source, and ran into encryption firewalls.

He had performed this exercise the night before, in the Factory, which was where he had learned that Rachel's team was near Bangalore and the object of several different threats.

He formed a thought: *Are they safe now?*

And he was hit with such an intense flood of imagery and data that it made him cry out. He saw military vehicles—surface and subsurface ships. He saw drones ranging in size from a large airplane down to a hummingbird floating in a night sky. He saw an aerostat.

He saw surveillance images of city streets—Bangalore?

Then, another level up, where Keanu decrypted the feed from these sources and saw what they were seeing and feeding. Selected imagery from the drones, for example. Simple views of control rooms. Empty streets. Highways.

A distant facility—this Bangalore air base.

There were flashes of data from Kettering and its sources, too—the group seemed to have sources deep within at least one military organization.

Dale felt alarm—just as bad now as it was the first time. Poor Rachel.

Then his summoning of Rachel's name created a link, somewhere in his mind, to Makali Pillay . . . all of them had been together on the Great Trek twenty years ago.

And here the imagery in Dale Scott's dream state changed. It was no longer searched and filtered from sources on Earth; it was clear and close and direct.

It was information from inside Keanu.

He saw Makali Pillay—aged a decade, but still recognizably herself—wearing a bizarre costume of some kind as she floated in a habitat with several Skyphoi!

Even in his dreamlike state, he could chortle with smug satisfaction: *You dumb bastards, you told me bullshit about Makali, so she stayed in my mind.*

Makali led, in one of those odd little connections, to Zhao. Where had *he* gone?

He was elsewhere in Keanu, too . . . in a chamber Dale did not immediately recognize, but clearly working on something important and urgent.

Makali and Zhao—what was it?

He wanted to find them, go where they were.

He wanted out of this jail—

He opened his eyes now and saw that he was staring up at the "night" sky of the human habitat. The roof and walls of the hut had vanished as if they'd never existed.

Before he could sit up, a drop of rain hit him in the mouth.

It was followed by more rain.

He actually swallowed some water before feeling strong enough to get up.

When he did, grabbing his shabby clothes, all he thought was that a bit of rain might mean he was leaving tracks as he removed himself from the habitat.

No worry. Harley and the others, once they realized that their jail had disappeared and that they were no longer dealing with plain old Dale Scott, wouldn't dare follow him.

Day Two

SATURDAY, APRIL 14, 2040

QUESTION: What was there about life on Earth that you missed most?

PAV: Very little.

QUESTION: Seriously?

PAV: Look, throughout human history, most people lived their lives within a thirty-kilometer radius. Our habitat was pretty close to that.

QUESTION: That might have been true prior to the nineteenth century, but you were born in 2003. You grew up with travel and cities and commerce—

PAV: True. But on Keanu, we were mostly trying to survive . . . like humans born prior to the nineteenth century.

INTERVIEW AT YELAHANKA,
APRIL 14, 2040

RACHEL

"It's worse than we thought," Pav told her, when they stepped out into their second Bangalore morning. Both of them blinked like prisoners released from a cell, even though the sky was overcast, threatening rain.

Rachel's first night of Earth sleep in twenty years had been restful— she believed she had truly slept at least five hours—but for a series of strange dreams, including the predictable one in which she was still inside the Temple on Keanu, late to the launch of *Adventure*.

In another, she was back in the home in Houston she shared with her father and mother—though her current age. And Yvonne Hall, the astronaut turned Revenant, simply called her on the phone to tell her, "I'm here for you."

Rachel had awakened at that point, feeling foolishly, possibly insanely reassured—the predictable residue of a dream.

Before beating herself up, however, she had to consider this vital point: All three of those people, Father, Mother, and Yvonne, had died . . . and two had become Revenants. They were proof that the Architects of Keanu had a handle on the existence of consciousness or personality beyond physical death.

Would it be crazy to assume that their technology extended to communication from beyond the grave? To invading your dreams with actual messages?

Rachel said to Pav, "Did you ever smoke?"

"Cigarettes? Of course I smoked! I spent part of my childhood in Russia! Why?"

"I never did," Rachel said. "But right now . . . it's supposed to help you think, isn't it?"

"That's what they say." He put his arm around her. "You don't need nicotine to help you think."

"I feel as though I need something. A boost."

"We're sticking to our plan. Land, make contact, learn as much as we can, then—"

"Then move, yes. But so far we're doing exactly what we expected, and that bothers me."

"Because you're a pessimist."

"A realist."

"Well, then, realist, keep this in mind: Our plan didn't include having Sanjay get critically injured."

Rachel sighed. "And what do we do about Sanjay? Leave him? And Zeds . . . trying to move him is just going to be difficult—"

"Zeds can move himself, and we both know it."

"But not quietly or discreetly, darling. Wherever he goes, people are going to know."

Pav frowned as he looked at her. "We're going clandestine, are we? Maybe you do need to catch me up—"

"I don't *know*. That's the problem. We need Xavier to do what he and Sanjay were going to do, and quickly. We need money, support, transportation."

She sighed. "It's been so strange to find . . . what we've found."

"Come on," Pav said, "we didn't really expect them to be better. We knew the Reivers had reached Earth. I'm just surprised the entire planet isn't buried neck deep in the things."

"Are we sure it isn't?"

Pav started to reply, but smiled instead. "You're right; we only know what we've been told by our hosts. Of course, this is my father we're talking about—"

"And that's why we wanted him to be part of the reception, yes, but—"

"What do we really know? I mean, it's possible he could be a Reiver Aggregate. All of them could be—Remilla, Kaushal."

"Now who's the pessimist?" she said.

"You have rubbed off on me." A horn blared nearby, startling both of them. All around them, the business of Yelahanka Air Base continued as it always had. Buses and Jeeps passed—some distance away, prevented from approaching the hospital—but audible, visible, and smellable.

On the flight line not far away, a jet engine had been revved up . . . likely for maintenance, not preflight. In the relative quiet between revs, they had been able to put their heads close together and be heard. Now, however, the jet was running at military power, it seemed—without break.

"That's a good thing, right?" Rachel said.

"Yes, it means no one can overhear us as we plot." When she shot him a look, he said, "Come on, Rachel, if we are being so closely observed, it's because they *are* suspicious and *assume* we are plotting."

"It just . . . I wish I had more experience." She knew she was displaying more caution than the situation warranted. They had trained themselves to operate "like you are visiting China," Zhao had told them. As a former Guan Bao agent, he knew the means and methods.

Which were constant audio surveillance wherever they went inside a building, tails and shadows whenever they left, and likely directional microphones aimed at them when they spoke outside—as they were now.

"But lipreading is easy to beat," Zhao had told them, "if you're careful, especially if you lean close and block the cameras." And while computer enhancement would easily separate human words from background jet engine noise, it would take time.

"Don't you think they assume we have ways of communicating with . . . Manchester United?" Pav was sensitive on this subject, since he had come up with the code name.

"Why don't you just say 'Keanu' and be done with it?"

It was his turn to shoot her a look. "Fine. They will assume we are in touch, they will assume we are about our own business, and, in fact, they would be far more suspicious if their surveillance showed that we were hiding nothing."

"Which is why," Rachel said, "I wish I had a cigarette."

"I'll ask one of the guards, how about that?"

She took his hand, trying to tell him, in the most secret way possible, that she really wasn't angry with him. She pulled him close, to speak directly into his left ear. "I never expected to be scouting, then attacking an entire continent."

He rocked back and laughed out loud. "Me, neither! And it's time to start, especially . . ."

Rain had started to fall, big fat drops that felt like fingers tapping on Rachel's back and shoulders.

As she and Pav turned, they saw Yahvi in the doorway, looking up, fear on her face.

"Honey," Rachel said, "what's wrong?"

"What is this?"

Rachel realized that her Keanu-born daughter had never experienced rain. The regular habitat mist, yes, but nothing like this tropical pelting.

"It's rain, darling. It won't hurt you."

Then Yahvi sneezed. Rachel and Pav looked at each other. "Come on," Pav said, "inside now!"

Rachel took the lead in putting Yahvi to bed. Thank God for the gift of the Beta!

She and Pav agreed that Rachel would go in search of soup while Pav would locate Xavier and make arrangements for the cargo. "This is suspiciously traditional," Pav said, before departing. "This division of labor."

"These are special circumstances," Rachel said. She hoped, however, that Pav heeded the warning tone: She would rather have been seeing to their cargo than filling this domestic role.

But sometimes a girl needed a mother. As one who had lost hers at exactly this age, Rachel understood.

Leaving Yahvi with her soup, Rachel was met by Taj, who announced, "I just saw Pav. And I am happy to tell you that we have found three potential agents for you!"

That simple phrase infuriated her. *"We"? "For you"?* Rachel knew she was, as Harley Drake would say, spring-loaded. Poor sleep, general tension, Yahvi's condition, Pav's eager escape from domesticity, her father-in-law—in itself an unfamiliar concept—going paternal on her, and talking to Pav first! It all combined to cause Rachel to snap.

"Why don't we roll that back a few pages, and let me see all of the applicants and interested parties so I can pick three. Maybe they'll be the same. But maybe they won't."

She could see Taj's head drop a perceptible quarter of an inch, a gesture clearly indicating a sense of persecution, and one he shared with his son, which was why Rachel recognized it—and grew even more furious.

"There are no applicants," he said, with what Rachel was sure he considered extreme patience, "only three agents that we approached. The landing is still officially classified."

"Perhaps we should move up the announcement."

"It is scheduled for two hours from now. How much earlier can we make it? And still give your agent a head start?"

His answers were logical and correct, which did nothing to make Rachel happier. "You're not empowered to make decisions for us."

Taj stiffened. "I didn't realize I was making decisions. I will resume searching—"

Rachel realized that she had become unpleasant. One of the benefits of reaching her middle thirties was that she eventually recognized that she was losing her temper . . . in time to salvage the moment. "I'm sorry," she said. "The three candidates will be fine. Where was Pav?"

"Enduring a conversation with Mrs. Remilla and her senior staff." The deadpan use of a word like *enduring* was just the thing Pav would have done to soothe Rachel, and it almost worked. "They have him trapped."

"Why?" Aside from general sympathy for her husband and lover, Rachel was concerned for his primary mission, which was the cargo.

"There are questions about your immigration status. A Foreigners Regional Registration Counselor is still not willing to consider issuing temporary visas for your crew." Now Taj smiled, and Rachel saw her husband's face—older, but handsome and engaging. Her anger drained away. "The Sentry's status is a particular challenge, given that he is an extraterrestrial alien."

"Earth is full of such aliens already, you said."

"India is not. The Reivers aren't welcome here. To my knowledge, none have ever tried to enter the country."

"You'd better hope so."

She followed Taj to the conference room, where Pav was indeed sequestered with Remilla and several male bureaucrats. Pav jumped to his feet eagerly, confirming his father's description of a torturous meeting.

He told Rachel what was going on with the visas. "We're cleared to remain in India for thirty days. We're being treated as though we were on a work visa and our cargo as personal possessions not subject to duties."

"Thank you, darling." She put arms around him and kissed him, something she still enjoyed after so many years. (And didn't mind doing in front of others.)

Her gratitude was genuine. She and Pav had spent a great deal of time planning the return to Earth, but concentrated on the technical challenges: trajectories, fuel, targets, communications. They had no real way of knowing what it would be like to be here—and then move forward. Would India be under some kind of martial law?

The meeting was breaking up, thank goodness. Remilla and Taj herded the immigration men out of the room, leaving Rachel and Pav alone. "Tough, huh?"

He smiled. "Among the many things we don't have at home . . . bureaucracies and paperwork."

"Give us time."

"Well, here on Earth, it's only going to get more difficult," Pav said. "We'll be in the news, we'll have this media agent, then . . ."

He yawned.

"Are you as tired as I am?" Rachel said. Pav didn't need to answer; it was on his face. "Let's be old folks at home for the moment," she said, using a phrase her father loved, describing family nights. "Soup for Yahvi, then bed."

"Tomorrow, the world," Pav murmured.

QUESTION: Rachel, you have spoken about the challenges of simply surviving for twenty years in a habitat created by aliens using their technology—

RACHEL: First of all, the habitat was designed and built to accommodate humans.

QUESTION: How?

RACHEL: Ask the Architects.

QUESTION: Then back to my—

RACHEL: The same Architects equipped us with two things . . . one was the proteus, which is a 3-D printer evolved by a few thousand years. It's a device that can replicate or fabricate just about anything, from food to tools to electronic equipment and even chemicals.

QUESTION: Sounds like magic.

RACHEL: Or just technology that's far more advanced than ours. What would Ben Franklin have thought of a computer? We also needed one other thing to make the proteus work, and that was Substance K, which is essentially nanotech goo. Almost everything in Keanu was made of it. After living there for twenty years and eating food derived from it, I'm probably made of Substance K.

INTERVIEW AT YELAHANKA,
APRIL 14, 2040

XAVIER

Xavier Toutant was not part of the big negotiations. It was not his thing, though during the prelaunch preparations he had been quite amused to hear Rachel and Pav and Harley Drake and the others talking about rights deals and money, since not one of the HBs had dealt with the subject since the day they were scooped off Earth in 2019.

Maybe that showed how shortsighted they all were, or possibly they had evolved past such mundane concerns.

At the moment, however, Xavier Toutant was consumed by his job, his mission, which was cargo.

The crew had only taken basic travel gear off *Adventure*—clothes, a little food, toiletries. Everything else that might have been interesting or useful remained aboard the spacecraft, including their own Keanu-built Slates and 3-D printing gear, but most important of all . . . a ton of goo.

Which was what Xavier had been calling it since the day he'd arrived on Keanu as a nineteen-year-old junior fry cook and failed pot dealer. The Bangalores came up with several names for it—NanoTech Slurry, Building Block, and mostly Substance K—but it was still the raw material that, they had discovered, filled whatever part of the interior of Keanu that wasn't good old rock. There were even pipes that allowed Keanu's control system to pump huge gobs of the stuff from one place to another.

The HBs had never learned how to make more of it. Keanu had vats and pools where it was obvious that goo was "grown" from raw materials that you would find in space (water being number one). They had built their own "pipeline" to transfer goo from these pockets back to the human habitat. Maintaining and redirecting that line was one of the most time-consuming jobs in the whole habitat.

Because the things you could do with the goo were . . . anything. Feed it into your proteus, then imprint it with assembly data, and you could make it into a metal machine or a composite structure or a cow or a bowl of gumbo—bowl *and* gumbo, which seriously impressed Xavier the cook.

In the past, goo had been used to make actual human beings. They didn't live long, but that wasn't the fault of the goo.

But it was what made life on Keanu possible. (All the habitats started out as giant empty chambers with a layer of goo that could be "rearranged" into soil, plants, buildings, and then some of the items already mentioned. Built to suit: Humans got an Earth-like habitat, Sentries got an aquatic one, Skyphoi got whatever the fuck they lived in, and so on.)

Adventure had several tanks of goo stored on the lower deck of the vehicle, right below the control module they had lived in for four days. It was Xavier's job to make sure it was still there.

And to figure out how to transfer it, store it, and make it useful.

Because—and this was the real reason Xavier ducked out of the media agent auction—the goo and the "magic" 3-D proteus printing were going to fund the mission, not the crew's "personal stories."

Xavier was happy to spend his time making that a reality. His other goals here on Earth were minimal. All he'd left behind was his momma, and she was close to death the day he was scooped up in 2019. His first mission, once he was able to use a computer, or whatever they called it these days, was to find out when she'd died and where she was buried.

Taj, who in Xavier's mind was turning out to be a good guy, and Wing Commander Kaushal, perhaps a bit less good, offered up a cargo truck, willing hands, and a weapons bunker after Xavier told them, "I'll need secure storage for whatever I take off *Adventure*."

"For how long?" Kaushal said.

"On the order of two weeks." The figure was anywhere between two days and infinity, so two weeks seemed a good compromise.

Did Xavier need refrigeration or temperature control? No. Were there special handling needs? Well, yes—he may have suggested that there was a chance of a dangerous radiation leak.

Which made Wing Commander Kaushal unhappy. "What were you thinking, bringing radioactives to my base?" The look he shot at Taj said, pretty clearly, *I'm not doing this—!*

But Xavier and Pav had war-gamed this argument. "Do you have depleted uranium cannon shells?" he said.

Kaushal stared back. "I can't answer that."

"Fine," Xavier said, "let's just say, for the sake of argument, that you *might* have a case around here somewhere. One case of those shells emits more radioactivity than our entire two tons in a year."

This seemed to mollify Kaushal. It was the absolute truth without being the whole truth: The goo emitted no radiation at all.

But Xavier wanted Kaushal and his team to think it did. It would keep prying hands and eyes away.

He was introduced to Chief Warrant Officer Singh, a man of forty so dark and fat he could have been Xavier's twin. The man's grim, business-like manner gave no hint of brotherly affection, however. It was clear he regarded Xavier with suspicion.

Singh's team included four others in descending seniority and age: a sergeant, a corporal, and two leading aircraftsmen. The latter two were probably twenty years old.

There was another warrant officer, Pandya, who was Singh's opposite in almost every way: ten years younger, fifty kilos lighter, relaxed and often smiling.

He deferred to Singh perfectly, which confirmed Xavier's hunch that he was the representative of the Indian intelligence services.

Xavier had two trucks and the cherry picker at his disposal—quite a fleet for a guy who had never owned a car and hadn't driven in two decades. They headed to the landing site directly after breakfast on the second day, Xavier jammed into the first truck cab with Singh and a driver. Two heavyweights in that small, crammed space, and no air-conditioning. It was the longest half kilometer Xavier had ever ridden.

April in Bangalore was like April in New Orleans, or Houston. Humid and, even before ten in the morning, headed for high heat. Xavier said as much to CWO Singh, who shrugged, as if he were weak. "April is the hottest month here, though not the wettest. That's August."

"That's good," Xavier said. "We only have to risk heatstroke, not drowning." The driver, one of the enlisteds, laughed—to be silenced by a glare from Singh.

They parked, then grabbed masks and gloves, and, once the cherry picker was back in operation, Xavier rode up to the *Adventure* hatch.

All the way up he kept noting the strange tilt to the vehicle and de-bating the need for additional support—a frame, maybe, or even some kind of jacks under the busted fin. The ship rested on hard-packed earth, so Xavier wasn't worried *Adventure* would sink. But it felt wrong to have it looking like the Leaning Tower of Pisa.

One thing he noticed once he reached the hatch level—downtown Bangalore itself, glittering towers that had been lost in the haze, or simply not in his eye line, during his hasty exit yesterday. He started feeling sick and faint, so weak that he had to wrap his gloved hands around the railings of the cherry picker basket. How many millions of people lived here? Nine million? In India altogether, a billion?

He was no stranger to numbers on that scale. Houston had a million people when he lived there, the United States more than a quarter billion.

But for the past two decades he had lived in a habitat ten kilometers long and five or so wide, with fewer than a thousand people. They did rub shoulders from time to time, but he never ever got the sense that he was crowded.

Now, though, even twenty kilometers north of the city center, in what was, by Indian standards, uncrowded suburbia, Xavier felt closed in, suffocated.

The heat didn't help, of course. Nor did Xavier's precarious perch atop a very old piece of Indian equipment.

Not wishing to disgrace himself by vomiting over the side, or even fainting, he opened the hatch and plunged into the cool interior.

Adventure's crew had left batteries running on low, essentially keeping the lights on and the environmental systems running. The sudden, relative cool made Xavier feel better—he wasn't even bothered by the slanting floor.

He opened the hatchway to the storage module . . . all of the containers seemed to have come through the crash landing intact (something he'd worried about just before dozing off last night). There were sixteen identical units, each one about the size of a typical cardboard banker's box from his youth. Fourteen of them held goo; the other two . . . equipment.

He could not off-load all of these things by himself, so he had to allow the enlisted men into *Adventure*. The four of them seemed uninterested in the exotic machine, acting as if they were entering the cargo hold of one of the rotting Antonov transports parked on the apron not far away. They plodded like robots as they set up a chain to pass containers along.

With the weight limits of the cherry picker, it took half a dozen trips down, then up, to get all the containers out of *Adventure* and into the trucks. Xavier realized that by supervising from above—obviously necessary—he had allowed Singh and especially Pandya free rein with the materials on the ground. Either one of them could have been hiding inside a truck, unseen, prying open a container.

Well, nothing he could do about it. He wasn't too worried that they would find anything useful. . . . *Adventure*'s cargo was literally just packages of goo. Even the vital proteus gear was secreted inside goo.

Once everything was loaded up and the crane lowered, Xavier and the team headed for the holding area, a corner of a munitions storage bunker about two hundred meters from the ops area, across the runway. It was more exposed than Xavier liked—his particular bunker and its kin were rounded mounds, wisely separated by several meters of open space, with the whole complex bordered by several dozen yards of mud and grass inside a wicked-looking security fence. There were fences beyond that, marking the boundary of Yelahanka Air Base.

He would have preferred an actual warehouse, a building among other buildings, of course. So that, should the impulse strike him over the next day or two, he could make unscheduled or unescorted visits. True, he would face the usual challenges of evading security—locks, cameras, and whatever new toys had been developed over twenty years.

But he had always found that even layered systems are vulnerable at one point . . . with their human operators.

For example, as the enlisteds were helping him stack and arrange the containers near the entrance to the bunker (which proved to be empty; so much for the alert status of the Indian Air Force at Yelahanka), one of them, the most junior aircraftsman, dropped a container on its corner.

The box ruptured, not only exposing the inner sheathing but tearing it, allowing a puddle of goo to escape.

The young man's eyes—the only expressive part of his face visible over his mask—went wide with fear, either that Xavier would have him arrested or that he might die from exposure.

The sudden silence was apparent to Pandya, who said from outside, "Everything all right in there, Mr. Toutant?" He gave Xavier's name a beautiful French pronunciation.

"Just some final rearranging!"

Then he pulled down his mask and put on his most engaging face. "It's not really dangerous. What's your name?"

He slowly lowered his mask. "Aircraftsman Roi," he said. "I'm so sorry. I'll get a shovel or a—"

Xavier was already bending to the box, righting it and prying off the lid. "Take a look," he said. "You're the first on Earth."

He did, slowly bending toward the container with its wrapped greenish material, like foaming gelatin. "What is it?"

"It's just raw material," Xavier said, an honest if incomplete answer. "It's what we found on Keanu when we arrived twenty years ago. It's very . . . adaptable. You can make almost anything out of it."

Now Roi's eyes went wide in an entirely different manner. This was curiosity, possibly cunning. (It occurred to Xavier that he had been wrong in identifying Pandya as the likely intelligence agent on Singh's squad, that it might well be Aircraftsman Roi. It was also possible that *everyone* on Singh's squad was a spy—that was how he would have done it. But he was now committed to this gambit.)

"You can touch it," Xavier said, demonstrating. It was harmless; had to be, since on Keanu the HBs made food out of it.

Roi dabbed a finger in it, smiled. "How does it work?"

"You need to have the right machine—a 3-D printer, what we call a proteus. You tell the proteus what you need, and, basically, it turns this goo into it. Food, equipment—"

"Money?"

Had him. "Anything," Xavier said. "Especially if you're just thinking of selling some of this to, say, a Chinese entrepreneur—" That was risky, because his sense of this world was twenty years out of date: China might not have entrepreneurs anymore, or if they did, they might be considered evil.

"Mr. Toutant?" Pandya was in the entrance, though the stack of containers kept him from seeing what the group inside were up to.

"One moment," Xavier yelled. "Just a final adjustment!"

He turned away, and Xavier leaned close to Roi. "I would be happy to make you a little gift," he said. He took off one of his gloves. "I could scoop the spilled material into this, and no one would ever know.

"But my colleagues might ask—" Xavier let the last word linger just long enough to earn a knowing smile from Aircraftsman Roi, who then said: "I have two hundred new rupees in my pocket."

"You know, that would be a welcome gift. If I'm asked, I can say I exchanged the material for some money. We don't have any!"

And with that, a deal was closed—and a new friend was made.

It was actually reassuring to Xavier, in a way, to know that some things never change.

And that it was possible he could break out of Yelahanka with minimal effort.

Reaction to the presser: not bad as far as it went, but it didn't go very far.

Confirm that crew includes Rachel Stewart and Pav Radhakrishnan as well as their daughter, Yahvi. Another U.S.-born individual, Mr. Toutant.

But sources say six and that leaves two missing. Wounded? Imprisoned?

Same sources suggest one of the missing two is not human. Can anyone help? It's important!

COLIN EDGELY TO THE KETTERING GROUP,
APRIL 14, 2040

CARBON-143

STATUS: Following a general Aggregate Carbon maneuver, in which each formation relocated from its workplace to the greater staging area, then, following precise circumnavigation, Carbon-143 found herself resuming her modeling with greater vigor.

It should have been anomalous. One of the least questioned verities of Aggregate existence was that their superiority to more organic life forms was due to their high and steady levels of production. Somatic disturbances such as fatigue or lassitude or general unhappiness were not attributes of the Aggregates.

Nevertheless, it had become clear to the formations that, especially in a new planetary environment like Earth's, certain affirming measures helped maintain productivity and contributed to the general sense of purpose. Carbon-143 certainly felt more aligned with her immediate partner, 143/A71, as well as the rest of the A formation.

The march past the rows of vehicles being prepared for action served as a reminder of the scale of the work being performed and impressed upon individual units their relative unimportance and disposability.

Carbon-143 noted the day's lesson.

INPUT: Although no actual data reached her, Carbon-143 detected a tremendous amount of signal noise on her military operational channels. Some action was about to take place. It was too soon to be directly related to the work at Site A—the countdown timer available to all formations and units still stood at minus twenty-five days.

But somewhere on Earth the Aggregates were going into action.

ACTION: None at this time.

HUMANS RETURN FROM KEANU

BANGALORE, APRIL 14—The Indian Space Research Organization confirmed what the rest of the world already suspected: Five humans from the Near-Earth Object Keanu returned to Earth yesterday, landing at a still-undisclosed air base in India. The humans—four of them originally born on Earth and transferred to Keanu by the mysterious Objects in August 2019—are in excellent condition and are expected to make a public statement within the next two days. They are currently being debriefed by government officials and ISRO scientists.

The group includes Rachel Stewart, daughter of American *Destiny* astronaut Zachary Stewart, who commanded the first human vehicle to land on Keanu, and is believed to have died there. Also Pav Radhakrishnan, son of General Taj Radhakrishnan, commander of the Coalition's *Brahma* mission to Keanu in 2019. General Radhakrishnan is chair of the official welcoming committee.

One human, daughter of mission commander Stewart and her husband, Pav Radhakrishnan, was born on the NEO.

Also traveling with the humans is a member of the so-called race of Sentries, extraterrestrial aliens who reportedly lived aboard Keanu for centuries prior to the arrival of humans.   *BANGALORE TIMES*, APRIL 14, 2040

See this, typical of all official reports: Note that there is no mention of the Aggregate attack on their ship, or the severe injuries suffered by one of the crew members.

Why is India hiding the truth? This is what we'd expect from the so-called Free Nations.

COLIN EDGELY TO THE KETTERING GROUP,
APRIL 14, 2040

RACHEL

"May I present the candidates for representation of the *Adventure* saga," Taj said.

There were three smiling people to his left at the front of the conference room. "Miss Arunjee Lim from Popular Malaysia Group." She was a woman Rachel's age, slim, confident, dressed for corporate success and wearing a pair of spectacles that were so thin they vanished when she turned to smile.

"Mr. Urvashi Muraly of *Times Independent*." Male, perhaps a year or two younger than Miss Lim, equally stylish, equally confident. He did not appear to be wearing the magic spectacles.

"And Mr. Edgar Chang of NewSky." This was an older gentleman, heavy, rumpled, looking more like a Hong Kong pawnshop owner than a media genius. "Cheers," he said, revealing a strong Australian accent.

In truth, all Rachel heard was *blah-blah, blah-blah, blah-blah-blah*. Her lack of concentration—or interest—was partly due to the nature of the meeting: She saw the search for a representative as a necessary exercise, but little more than that.

It was also due to a series of static-filled bursts in her head. Keanu was trying to get in touch. She kept biting down to activate her transmitter, silently grunting "Rachel" or "here" or some other single syllable that might travel across four hundred thousand kilometers without resulting in an embarrassing moment in the presentation.

And there was the nagging distraction caused by her concerns about Sanjay. If not for him, they would have been packing to go . . . somewhere else.

Don't blame the victim, she reminded herself.

She almost missed the presentations.

Lim and Muraly had swiftly laid out similar plans: a press conference within twenty-four hours to "introduce" the *Adventure* crew to the world, then exclusive "in-depth" profiles to the highest bidder. "I see four major media groups," Lim said.

"I see three," Muraly said. "But my financial targets might be higher."

That was all short-term. Mid-term, there were "as told to" stories, then "insider views" of the *Adventure* vehicle, "tales of Keanu."

Chang sat silent through the verbal tennis match between Lim and Muraly until: "One useful thing we might do is connect Earth-based families with their lost loved ones on Keanu," he said.

That made Rachel sit up and listen. They had talked about this on Keanu. She glanced at Pav, who nodded as Chang talked about a website and links to humanitarian organizations on the subcontinent.

"What about Free Nation U.S.?" Rachel said. Since that would be important to forty percent of the HBs. "Aren't you, here, sort of at war with them?"

Chang didn't seem fazed by the question. "The model isn't World War Two, though the utter domination and subjugation of North America, Europe, and much of Africa answers very well to that.

"It is more like the cold war, where you had a Soviet bloc that forbade access, did almost no trading, and blocked the flow of information to the West.

"Yet no system is perfect, not even that of the Aggregates, and especially not in the post-Internet age. New Sky has wires into Free Nation U.S. We have facilities, in fact, in the gray zones—"

"Which don't exist!" Arunjee Lim said.

"Whether they exist or not," Rachel said, writing off Lim at that moment, "I'd like to hear about them."

"Gray zones," Chang said, bowing toward Lim, "or rather, 'Zonas Grises,' are geographical areas within Aggregate-controlled nations where it is possible to visit . . . as long as one is discreet."

Now it was Muraly's turn to take a shot at Chang. "Even if these Zonas Grises exist, and I'm not convinced that they do, I don't think the Keanu crew is going to be able to be 'discreet.' Your arrival was surely known to the Aggregates long before your actual landing . . . and with the announcement today, they'll be able to track your every move."

Rachel had to admit that Muraly was correct: She and Pav and the others would have a hard time sneaking into a gray area.

And they weren't supposed to be talking about that, anyway. "Stipulating that a gray area might exist, and that we might have some kind of access to it," Rachel said, "how is that helpful to our mission . . . to connecting the Keanu population with their families and vice versa?"

"The grayest of the gray areas is Mexico," Chang said. "Where you will find numerous pirate transmitters. If you want to get information into or out of Free Nation U.S., that's the place to do it."

Rachel turned to Tea. "What do you think about this?"

Her father's-former-girlfriend-turned-mother-in-law just shook her head. "Oh, honey, I got out of the U.S. fifteen years ago, just when things were getting really bad. I haven't been back since."

"Don't you miss it?"

Tea glanced at Taj, as if concerned that her next words would offend him. "All the fucking time." She sighed. "But it's not the country I grew up in. . . ."

There was more back-and-forth, but Rachel had truly ceased to listen. Lim, Muraly, and Chang were sent off, leaving the three *Adventure* travelers, Taj, and Tea to confer, though to Rachel, the choice was clear and the outcome never in doubt.

It didn't happen without argument, but everyone eventually agreed to let Rachel have Edgar Chang.

In the hallway afterward, she grabbed Pav, who had wanted Muraly. "I didn't really," he said. "I just said that to see the look on your face."

"You bastard!"

"And to see you be what you're supposed to be, which is the leader." He kissed her. "Welcome back."

She welcomed the kiss, and his touch . . . but was troubled by his joking comment. She knew she was the "leader" of the *Adventure* mission; she was the one who had been mayor of the Houston-Bangalores for years.

But in that job, she felt secure . . . she knew the issues, the players, the possibilities. Not here, where the issues were complex, the population vast, even the landscape great and unknowable. The circumstances were unpredictable.

Had she let those factors paralyze her? Had she been reluctant to act? Was she, to use another phrase Zack Stewart loved, punching above her weight?

The only way to answer that would be the results. And the problem with getting results was . . . she and the Adventure crew had only one goal, which was to somehow free Earth from Reiver domination.

At the rate they were going, it would be a thousand years from now, or never.

In spite of her doubts, Rachel expected to sleep more soundly the second night. The bed would be more familiar, as would the noises and smells of the Yelahanka infirmary. And she was tired.

She was also wrong. She and Pav closed the door around eleven P.M. local time—as good as any, given their "space lag," as Xavier called it. Rachel snuggled against Pav, who went to sleep as fast as a human being could.

While Rachel lay there for a good long time

She carried no watch—none of the HBs did—but there was a clock on the nightstand, and it said 1:27. She had not slept at all so far, and it didn't appear that she would.

It was frustrating. Having Edgar Chang on board meant that her team had taken its first public step toward accomplishing its mission . . . and having Xavier returning from *Adventure* with an armful of equipment, and a knowing smirk, meant that the less-public plan was now in motion, too.

All they truly needed was for Sanjay to get well. Or to recover enough to be movable. Having seen him, however, she had to be realistic: He wasn't going anywhere soon.

The brief contacts with Harley Drake and Keanu had been sort of reassuring—Rachel hadn't realized how truly disconnected she had been feeling.

So why the restlessness? And how the hell did Pav manage to lie there snoozing like an exhausted infant? Like Yahvi as a baby—

Yahvi, of course, was another contributor to Rachel's lack of sleep, with her chorus of sneezes, sniffles, and moans heard from the next room. Taj had seen the afternoon signs of an oncoming cold and pre-scribed spicy food, but Yahvi had rejected it—not that Rachel blamed her. (The Keanu diet was bland by any standards, especially the Houston side of it. Yahvi was just as likely to eat a bowl of live insects as a dish of hot curry.)

Yahvi seemed to be quiet now, thank goodness. Rachel had never been a victim of insomnia—she had even been able to fall asleep easily on the hard-packed nanodirt of the Keanu habitat during her first months, before the Bangalore teams "created" hammocks and actual mattresses.

Of course, she had been fourteen then . . . and was thirty-four now.

Exhale. Close eyes. Empty the mind . . . these were all meditation exercises Pav and others had taught her, and they had proved useful, for meditation. As for sleep, she would see—

Then she heard—and felt—a *whump!*

It was significant enough that it forced her to open her eyes, and wait. What could it be? It reminded her of her childhood in Houston, a Dump-ster being emptied early on trash day—

If so, that would be the end of it.

Then she heard a second *whump*, and a third, and a series of fast rattling vibrations.

Pav sat up. "Hear that?"

"Yes," she said. "I'm surprised you did."

"You know me—" He went to the door and paused before opening it, listening for activity in the hallway.

"I want to check on Yahvi," Rachel said.

Pav opened the door and their daughter was there, red-eyed and miserable looking. "Mommy," she said.

As Pav slipped past, Rachel drew Yahvi into the room and sat her on the bed. "How are you feeling?"

"Look at me!"

Rachel had to stifle a smile and a laugh. She felt like a terrible mother, but Yahvi's countenance was comical—red runny nose, her normally pretty blue eyes all bloodshot, her hair a tangled mess. She looked like a cartoon version of herself. "You've looked better," she said, "but it's just a cold."

"What does that mean?"

"It means you stay warm, drink fluids, rest for three days, and it will be gone."

"For you, maybe. What if I don't have immunity? What if this makes me really sick?"

That troublesome thought had been simmering in Rachel's mind, likely another cause of her sleeplessness. She placed the back of her hand on Yahvi's forehead, the way her mother had when she was a child. "You don't have a fever."

"Like that's really scientific. God."

"We'll have one of the Indian doctors check you in the morning."

"That fills me with confidence."

Rachel had to work to keep from laughing again. It was so . . . typical of Yahvi, or any girl her age—indeed, of Rachel herself at that age—to inflate every minor discomfort into a case of the plague. Obviously the girl was ill, and, never having experienced anything like a common terrestrial cold, clearly struggling with it. But she was strong, healthy, and likely to be over it in forty-eight hours or less.

Falling into wise mother mode, as Pav called it, also had the benefit of distracting Rachel from her own situation . . . the lack of sleep, the uncertainty about their next step, and what the hell were those sounds that reminded her of explosions and machine guns?

She had just tucked Yahvi back into her bed when Pav returned, meeting her in the empty hallway. "It's over, whatever it was. The guards seemed relaxed."

"Pav, you know what it sounded like."

"Completely. It sounded like three grenades or mortars, followed by machine-gun fire."

"So—"

"Hey, friends, what's up?" Xavier poked his head out of his room, blinking sleepily. He was wearing nothing but baggy shorts, allowing his notable belly to precede him wherever he turned.

"Investigating a disturbance," Pav said.

"A what?"

Pav looked at Rachel. "What sounded like explosions. Apparently they were not."

Xavier shrugged and scratched his hind parts—never, to Rachel's eyes, an attractive gesture. "I didn't hear anything. You guys woke me up."

"Well, then," Rachel said, "go back to sleep."

"As I said," Pav told him. "It's probably nothing."

Okay, late update:

    We have an opening, a good chance.

    Can't tell you more. But watch this space—

    Until it goes dark. That will be a sign.

COLIN EDGELY TO THE KETTERING GROUP,

APRIL 14, 2040

ZEDS

But it *was* something.

Zeds had been told—repeatedly, by Rachel and Pav and Taj, and at least two other Indian officials—that he was not a prisoner, that the chamber was closed for his protection . . . but not locked.

Nevertheless, the first time he was left alone in the chamber, he had tried the latch . . . and found it locked. He had not attempted to force it that first night, preferring to rest and gather strength, and to more closely observe the workings of the mechanism when he was released the next day, and locked up again that evening.

Zeds wasn't convinced that he could be locked into the chamber; he possessed sheer muscular strength far beyond that of any human. His extra arms provided additional leverage, another force multiplier. He could probably have torn the metal and glass door off its hinges.

But Zeds also possessed a weapon common to Sentries—a tool vest, as Zachary Stewart had named it twenty years past. It was more than that, of course . . . it was a garment that Sentries generally wore when anticipating lengthy excursions outside the sea (which was what they called any aquatic environment larger than a human bathtub). Most of the "pockets" held gas and chemicals that, when combined, created a liquid that could be breathed by a Sentry who would otherwise collapse.

(Harley Drake said it reminded him of the spare oxygen tanks firefighters carried, an image it took Zeds months to understand: What were these "fires" and how where they "fought"?)

The vest also contained any number of helpful items, such as several translating devices, weapons, and tools.

It bulked up under the overall environment suit Zeds was wearing for landing and other excursions and was actually rather uncomfortable. But he had agreed to that because he and Rachel anticipated situations where he might be out of the sea for ten hours or more, far beyond the support limits of a vest.

So, on night two, feeling constrained and also a bit annoyed that he had been eliminated from Rachel's press conference—she and Pav had told him repeatedly that humans might react badly to his presence, and that they would have to be cautious—

Zeds believed differently; half of planet Earth was under the domination of a dangerous alien race! One four-armed ally shouldn't frighten anyone, and might even give some hope that the universe wasn't completely hostile!

He would not blatantly contradict Rachel and Pav; they were good friends, though not, perhaps, as close as Xavier, and certainly not as close as Yahvi, who had grown up with Sentries.

But Zeds felt quite comfortable engaging in activities that had not been specifically forbidden.

Besides, he required less rest than humans. He was no longer capable of entertaining himself in isolation, even with various items in his vest.

He was not a prisoner, so if the door to his chamber happened to be somehow stuck, he was within his rights to open it, was he not?

Which he did, using one of his tools to disassemble the closure mechanism, and another one to remove the hinges.

He had a moment of concern about the depletion of his semiaquatic environment . . . the moist atmosphere quickly dissipated, but that could easily be replaced. The pool in which he rested remained full; it did not evaporate or boil off.

And while he did not anticipate hours of freedom, he chose to wear the external suit. It turned what was likely to be a mundane excursion into a bit of an adventure.

Zeds had heard many tales of human space exploration from Harley Drake and even Dale Scott. He especially enjoyed Drake's account of a "space walk" outside the International Space Station, wrapped in an environment suit, floating at the end of a tether, seeing the Earth hundreds of kilometers below you . . . that was what this felt like.

He had barely taken half a dozen steps when he detected the first anomalous sound—possibly an explosion.

He had prepared himself for an unpleasant encounter with one or more Indian Air Force police, but none showed. He was able to leave the hospital building by a side exit and walk freely into the Bangalore night.

He opened his mask and his vest to fully experience the environment. It was warm and humid, he knew, by human standards . . . notably different from the temperature and humidity the Houston-Bangalores preferred in the Keanu habitat. To an amphibian Sentry, however, evolved in an aquatic environment, the air felt cold and thin . . . likely what a human would feel walking on Mars (well, not that bad; Zeds and Harley Drake had spent considerable time educating him about the difference).

But he was not able to truly enjoy the experience; he was troubled by the nature of the anomalous sound.

There was a fence along the rear perimeter of the hospital—a wire mesh of some kind, its sections strung between metal poles. The fence had been damaged—one entire section had been blown open.

Zeds sensed a team beyond the fence—saw shadows, felt footfalls, heard breathing from multiple beings, half a dozen at least. Their guards? Or assailants.

To his left and rear he detected other humans—four of them—in a position that suggested these were his guards.

There was a flash of light followed by a concussion that flattened the guards and rocked Zeds.

Then a third explosion—there was no longer any doubt about what these were—blew open the fence. The figures from beyond rushed toward it, all of them armed. All were humans with fit profiles wearing black clothing, helmets, and goggles of some kind, likely for night vision.

Three quickly slipped around the building, leaving Zeds to confront one of them.

Had Zeds not been traveling in an environment suit . . . had this encounter taken place on Keanu, for example . . . he might have triggered his vest, with the inflatable, expandable fluid sac frightening his opponent.

And he would have simply opened all four arms, swiftly wrapped up the human, then collapsed into transport mode and rolled away with him.

The suit prevented that. And he had no use for a captive. This man was an assailant, and so were his companions.

He removed two tools from his suit. Just as the opponent saw him—and reacted with obvious surprise, firing a wild burst with his weapon—Zeds lashed out with upper and lower right arms, each with its own blade, neatly dividing the opponent into three sections.

My first kill, he thought. So fast and so easy, little more than a second.

Sentries, he had learned, from Houston-Bangalores, from brief encounters with the Skyphoi, and especially from his own kind, had a history of violence—at least on the long-lost home world, where limited resources created a culture where the struggle for dominance and status was the same as that for survival.

A Sentry had killed Patrick Downey, an American astronaut exploring Keanu twenty years back; another had killed Megan Stewart. Zeds's twice-removed connate, Dash, had killed at least one human as well.

Yes, a history that he now shared . . . it was actually difficult to suppress the surge of sheer pride this swift kill triggered—followed almost immediately by shame. (He had grown up with humans, some of them eager to remind him of past Sentry crimes.)

What if he had erred? What did he truly know about this human's motives or actions?

What if he had made matters worse?

Two more explosions, one right after the other, convinced him his actions had been correct . . . that these men were attackers. Pieces of the hospital building filled the air, raining down on Zeds. His e-suit provided a great deal of protection, but he still found himself taking shelter. Reflexes again.

Then, equally reflexive, he was in motion, running toward the site of the explosions and almost colliding with two of the attackers as they attempted to enter the hospital through a door they had blown open.

Both men reacted with surprise, possibly confusion—for them, fatal delays.

Zeds slashed first right to left, then left to right. Both men were down, in three pieces each.

The view inside the hospital was disturbing—two Indian Air Force guards in bloodied pieces, killed by the explosion. Zeds wondered about Rachel and Pav, Yahvi and Xavier—and Sanjay. Were they safe?

What other actions could he take? There had been three other attackers . . . where were they?

He retraced his steps back to the side of the hospital, where he had originally exited and spotted the attackers. Yes, there were the other members of the team, in full retreat.

Another Indian guard lay on the pavement—still alive, as far as Zeds could tell. He considered offering medical assistance but rejected the idea; he knew nothing of human physiology and could do nothing for the man.

And his appearance might worsen the guard's condition. Best to return to the hospital and summon aid.

As quickly as possible, he made his way back through the side door and down the hallway. He could hear noise in the hospital now and saw four Indian guards hurrying past.

"Please!" Zeds shouted.

One of the hurrying men turned toward Zeds and stopped. It was Wing Commander Kaushal, the stout, energetic Indian Air Force leader who, at full height, reached barely to the middle of Zeds's chest. "What are you doing out here? Are you injured?"

"No," Zeds said. "Why do you ask that?" Of all the humans he had met since landing, Kaushal seemed the least ill-at-ease. Perhaps it was due to his age or seniority.

The wing commander gestured to Zeds's midsection. Looking down, the Sentry realized that the front of his e-suit, and his two right arms, were covered in human blood. "I'm not injured. Sentry blood is a different color," he said. "There is a human outside that door who requires assistance."

Kaushal spoke, and two of the guards sprinted off in the direction Zeds indicated, leaving one behind. "Come with me, please," he said to Zeds.

He didn't wait for comment. Zeds saw no grounds for argument; in any case, he had been on his way back to the chamber.

"Are we under attack?"

"I can't say at the moment," Kaushal said. "How did you come to be so bloody?"

"I encountered three attackers," Zeds said. As they walked, Kaushal's deputy used a communication device—a cell phone, Zeds realized, something he had always heard about but never actually seen—to listen to reports from around the facility.

"They were human?"

"What else would they be?"

Kaushal ignored the question. "So it was self-defense."

Zeds didn't understand what Kaushal meant. "I was simply taking a walk."

"How did you get out?" Kaushal asked.

Zeds considered several possible responses. A complete answer would require many words, so he settled on, "I opened the door."

They had just reached the entrance to the isolation chamber. The heavy steel-and-glass door lay tilted against the wall; the hinges and locks were in pieces on the floor.

Kaushal glanced at his deputy, who was wide-eyed. "You had no help from anyone?"

"No."

Kaushal reached for the door; he couldn't move it. "You may have to wait a while for us to get you safely put away—"

"Commander," the deputy said, waving the phone. Zeds chose that moment to march past Kaushal into the chamber. "I don't need to be put away. I will reseal the door myself."

To demonstrate, he picked up the heavy door and started moving it back into place.

Kaushal and his deputy backed away. The last Zeds saw of them was their backs.

ISRO PRESS RELEASE

Bangalore, April 14, 2040—The five humans and one Sentry in the crew of spaceship *Adventure* are continuing their adjustment to Earth at an air base in southern India in spite of a power system failure. "A transformer providing power to the hospital where the crew resides overloaded and exploded," says Mrs. Melani Remilla, ISRO official supervising *Adventure*'s welcome. "It resulted in quite a fireworks display, but fortunately no one was injured."

The crew will make its first public appearance Saturday at ISRO Headquarters in Bangalore.

Can you believe this bullshit? The Web is filled with reports and images of an attack on Yelahanka Air Base (yes, we know where the crew is being held) in which at least four people were killed. The identity of the attackers isn't known, but ought to be obvious.

Pray for this crew, that somehow they can get free of ISRO.

COLIN EDGELY TO THE KETTERING GROUP,
APRIL 14, 2040

RACHEL

"They're calling it green on green," Taj Radhakrishnan said.

"What does that mean?" Pav said. Rachel noted that her husband was no longer hiding his impatience, not even from his father.

"The attackers were Indian Air Force," Wing Commander Kaushal said. "At least six of them. Three were killed, three got away."

With the exception of Yahvi—Rachel desperately wanted to shelter her daughter from this discussion—they were all in the conference room. Rachel and Pav, Xavier. Zeds on the video link. (Rachel had visited Zeds earlier and been horrified to learn that the Sentry had been part of the firefight.) Taj doing the briefing, Tea sitting next to him.

Next to Tea was Mrs. Remilla, and next to her, Edgar Chang. The gent was now a permanent part of their "team." Also present were Wing Commander Kaushal and his deputy.

"You're certain they were Indian Air Force?" Xavier said.

Kaushal answered: "They were carrying military ID. They were stationed on this base—"

"And you're fine with that?" Xavier snapped.

Kaushal sat up as straight as he could. "What is that supposed to mean?"

"Our attackers wore the same uniform you do! And don't pretend you've been Mr. Helpful so far—"

Now Kaushal stood up. "If you're suggesting that I had any role in this—"

"Commander!" Remilla said. She was literally out of her chair, her hand on the Indian counselor's forearm. "No one is suggesting complicity." She shot a look at Xavier that, to Rachel, clearly meant, *You'd better* not *be suggesting complicity!*

In the calm that descended on the room, Pav said, "Do we have any idea what this was all about? What was the mission?

"Isn't that obvious?" Rachel said. She was pleased that Pav was acting as the voice of reason. That had never been her role. "They were coming to kill us all."

"Or take you prisoner," Kaushal said.

"These soldiers?" Taj said. "Not a chance. They were assassins."

Now Remilla spoke. "Your landing has stirred . . . religious anxieties."

"This goes beyond anxieties," Rachel said.

"Then let's say hatred—the equivalent of a fatwa, if you know what that is."

But here Zeds spoke for the first time. "I would appreciate clarification."

So Remilla explained the meaning of *fatwa*, an Islamic term ordering the faithful to kill an infidel for sins against the faith. "Do you have any evidence that it was Muslims?" Xavier said.

"None," Remilla said, after a nonverbal consultation with Kaushal, who added, "Nor is it Hindi or Christian. But realize that the, ah, religious environment has changed considerably since 2019. There are new movements like Transformational Human Evolution, and new movements like THE tend to be quite sensitive—"

"And aligned with the powers that rule the Free Nations," Edgar Chang said, opening his mouth for the first time. "This has all the signs of an Aggregate operation—using disgruntled or mercenary soldiers as surrogates." He turned to Rachel and Pav. "They are the ones who shot at your spaceship."

"That would have been my first guess," Xavier said. Of all those in *Adventure*'s crew, he was the most obviously terrified of the Reivers and saw their motives behind every action.

Not that, in Rachel's opinion, he was unduly paranoid in this case—

"We have no proof of that, Mr. Chang," Remilla said.

"We'll never have *proof*, Mrs. Remilla."

"Whoever did it," Rachel said, "it's done, and it's shown us that we aren't safe here."

"What could be safer than a military base?" Kaushal said.

"We'd like to find out," Pav said.

"Look," Rachel said, "our original plan was to move off-base within forty-eight hours. We extended that because of Sanjay's condition. It seems that we should go back to that plan."

Now Tea spoke. "And go where?"

"Downtown Bangalore," Xavier said. "Some ritzy hotel where, if nothing else, it costs more to bribe the help than it does here."

"That's ridiculous," Pav snapped.

And Kaushal was about to explode again. "They may have worn the uniform, but those were not my men!"

"Everyone!" Rachel said. "We understand, and shut up," she said, looking at Kaushal, then at Xavier—who was fortunately the kind of person who could be so addressed. "We need to move to a more isolated base, or a ranch of some kind, preferably in another city. Or even another country."

"You can't still be thinking about the U.S.!" Kaushal said. "Even if you could sneak in, that entire country will be hostile."

"What about China?" Tea said. The mention of that name caused Remilla to flinch, too. "I know they're your big enemy these days, but they have strict control over their populace—"

"Or so they like to claim," Remilla said.

"I have contacts in China," Chang said, smiling and spreading his hands in acknowledgment of his surname and ethnic background. "My companies can't operate without that market." He turned to Remilla and Kaushal. "And I can tell you that a horror like last night's attack could not occur there, not if Rachel and the others were sequestered at a military base.

"To be honest, though, it would be extremely difficult to place you on such a base. The most likely—"

"Let's be thinking quickest, too," Rachel said.

"—likely and quickest option would be to get you to a city like Shanghai, into some luxury hotel complex where my media work can commence—"

"And the money can begin to flow," Xavier said.

Rachel saw no better option. "Can you get us out of here tonight?"

"By early morning . . ." Chang frowned. "I don't want to promise what I can't deliver."

"Then please arrange for an early-morning departure," Rachel said, looking toward Pav, then Xavier, then Zeds, and finally Tea and Taj. The humans indicated their acceptance of the plan with nods. Zeds clapped all four hands, which meant the same thing.

Chang cleared his throat. "How many of you will be going?"

Rachel turned to Kaushal. "Sanjay still can't be moved?"

"Under no circumstances!" the commander said. "Moving him would jeopardize his recovery."

"In that case," Rachel said, turning back to Chang, "it's the five of us."

"We're just going to *leave* him?" That was Yahvi, speaking for the first time. Yahvi had found the weakest spot in Rachel's argument. She didn't know whether to hug her daughter for displaying empathy and courage, or tell her to shut up and listen.

"Yes. He's better off here than on the road—"

Pav weighed in. "And we have to move. It's clear we are no longer safe here." He looked at Remilla and Kaushal, as if daring them to argue. They remained silent.

Not Yahvi, however. "What if they come after him again?"

"We can put out a story," Chang said, "let people think he's been moved elsewhere."

"We're going to have to put out a whole bunch of stories," Rachel said.

Chang stood up. "Which means I have a lot of work to do."

Before he could exit, Taj caught him by the arm. "One moment." He turned to his granddaughter. "Yahvi, I will take personal responsibility for Sanjay's care—"

"Aren't you coming with us?" Pav said.

"Yeah, Husband," Tea said. "What about it?"

Taj looked at son, then at his wife. "Tea will go with you. She and I will be in constant communication." He glanced at Chang. "Someone needs to coordinate the travel, and I have the most experience."

"More than I do," Chang said, sounding grateful.

"I can help, too," Pav said. "With Zeds."

"It would have been *nice* to be in communication prior to the announcement of your decision," Tea told Taj, with an edge in her voice that Rachel knew well.

She realized she had to play peacemaker for the various factions. "Tea, I know Taj would have talked this over, but this just came up, right?" Taj nodded.

"It's settled then," Rachel said. "We move tomorrow morning." She pointed to Xavier. "We need to deal with the cargo, too."

She was glad to have something practical to do, because if she allowed herself to consider the odds against the *Adventure* crew right now, she would probably curl up in a panicked ball.

Day Three

SUNDAY, APRIL 15, 2040

TIME TO FIRST LIGHT: Minus 7 days
FIRST LIGHT   22 APRIL 2040 0001:00 MDT
TIME TO FIRE LIGHT: Minus 24 days
FIRE LIGHT   09 MAY 2040 0001:00 MDT

COUNTDOWN CLOCK AT SITE A

CARBON-143

STATUS: Humans assigned to the Project had long reverted to their centuries-old practice of working 6.5 days a week. The formations would have required more—the quotas certainly demanded more—but a decade of observation and interaction had proven that humans working seven days a week not only were not more productive, they actually made more errors.

There were also limits on the resources that could be shipped to Site A and processed for manufacture. So Aggregate Carbon programmed a Saturday workday that ended at 1 P.M.

Absence of humans did not mean that work ceased; far from it. Aggregates usually worked 23.5 out of every 24 hours, with the unused 0.5 hour devoted to system updates and checks or needed rotation of functions.

In addition, every week Aggregates in high-stress activities would have a programmed "refurbishment" session of two hours, in which new downloads from the formation were processed, and possible new aggregations were formed. (Carbon-143 "remembered" that she had been "born" as an aggregate of 11,211 "cells" that had first been aggregated into an intermediate stage of 89 "individuals" before becoming a "unit.")

DATA: In her five years as a unit, Carbon-143 had grown convinced that Aggregates needed additional "downtime" for maintenance, energy reboost, and additional programming in order to function at optimum efficiency. But she had not shaped this observation into an action statement, much less sent it up the information tree. That, as her human counterpart observed in other circumstances, would have been "pointless to the point of idiocy."

ACTION: So it was that Carbon-143 was at her assembly station with the other eleven members of her formation on Saturday afternoon when her human counterpart entered the facility.

"You need to check this out," he was saying to another human: younger, clearly new, and nervous. Both were males—a distinction that did not apply to Aggregates. (Carbon-143 assumed a feminine aspect for linguistic reasons, and because her human counterpart insisted on addressing her in that mode.) But their gender did put the entire formation on alert; they had been programmed to expect a higher probably of mischief from off-duty males than females, especially deep into the leisure hours.

"Won't we get in trouble?" the younger one said.

"Only if we get caught."

"But there are Aggregates all over the place!"

"They don't care, unless we try to break something. It's fucking THE we have to watch out for."

"Okay, then, what if *they* catch us?"

"They won't," the human counterpart said, moving behind other members of Carbon-143's formation and making odd and very likely derogatory hand gestures behind their cranial structures. "They're too busy singing and praying at this hour." The human counterpart actually jumped up on the assembly-line structure.

"Aren't you the least bit curious? Isn't it worth a bit of risk to see what you're working on?"

"I'm working on magnetic fields," the younger one said. "They showed me the generator and I already sketched the power inputs. What else do I need to know?"

"How about what's going through your big old portal?"

"Don't call it a portal. I'm not sure—"

The human counterpart jumped down and took the younger man by the shoulder, turning him. "All those machines you saw lined up out there when we rode in?"

"I'm not sure, everything was so far away—"

"Thousands of them, maybe hundreds of thousands of them. Some of them are trucked in, but the most interesting ones are assembled right here."

"Fine. Noted. Can we go now?"

"First, meet your team. It's only common courtesy."

"Meet an *Aggregate*?"

"Meet one. My girl here," the counterpart said. "The one on the end."

"They all look alike."

"She's always the one on the end, aren't you, baby?"

Carbon-143 was unsure if this direct address required a response. Certainly the cold static of her cross-links with the other eleven members of her formation did not suggest so. But she interrupted her assembly sequence ever so slightly, to allow for a quick nod and turn.

The human counterpart clapped. "Thank you, darling!"

"Randall—"

"Carbon-143, meet Whit Murray."

This statement did require a response; even the formation cross-links approved. Carbon-143 made a more obvious turn and bow.

"Aren't you going to say hello, Whitless?"

"I wish you wouldn't call me that—"

"Mr. Murray, then. Please say hello to Aggregate Carbon-143, like all of us, just a tiny cog in the big machine."

The younger man blinked and held out his hand. "Hi there, Whit Murray."

"She's not going to shake it, sorry."

He lowered his hand. "Does she talk?"

"They do not vocalize as such," Randall Dehm said. "But if you are wearing the proper comm device when you encounter an Aggregate, you will get some kind of response. It all depends on what you ask."

Whit smiled at Carbon-143. "How did you get to know this particular one, then? Without being able to talk."

"Six months ago, I had to do some repairs and reprogramming. No matter how much money and time we spend, sometimes shit breaks. The Aggregates can't stand it, but that's what they get for invading our planet and making us slaves, right?"

Whit appeared to be shocked by this bald, undeniably factual statement. So he said, "I always wondered . . . how come we always see the same types?"

"What do you mean?"

"Aggregates are made up of thousands of individual cells, right? They could form into anything."

Carbon-143 could have explained this, meaning that, had Whit been wearing the "appropriate comm device," she could have uploaded a human-friendly file about nine templates and why they had been chosen—and persisted.

"Don't you like the anteater look?"

"I don't really have an opinion. I was just—"

Randall was standing so close to Carbon-143's left side that the formation's proximity alarm system went on first-level alert. "I like it. I think it's sexy."

Then he laughed and slapped Whit on the arm. "Come on, man. I've got other stuff to show you."

As they left, Carbon-143 had the clear impression that Whit stopped in the exit and looked back.

Meanwhile she tried to control the somatic discharge Randall's remark had caused. It was likely a transient overload triggered by the unusual and prolonged Aggregate-human contact.

CONCLUSION: She could not let it distract it from her work.

The return of humans from Keanu continues to be a major story, topping the looming conflict between the New Coalition and Free Nations over trade and travel.

Four of the five humans and the sole E.T. in the crew have been briefly seen in public; one of the humans was reportedly injured in the crash landing at Yelahanka Air Base on Friday. Beyond that momentary exposure, they have been sequestered. Neither ISRO nor Bangalore government will answer any but the most general questions that interested and responsible citizens are asking:

What do they want? To sightsee? To open up regular trips between Earth and Keanu?

Why are they here and not in the Free Nations, where many of the crew originated?

What do they know of Earth?

What is life like on Keanu? How have they survived?

Have there been further returns of the so-called Revenants? For that matter, did the Revenants ever exist?

More to the point, does Keanu, now looming in the night sky like a death star, pose a threat to Earth—or perhaps only to certain entities on Earth?

It is now rumored that the Keanu travelers will soon emerge from seclusion within the next twenty-four hours, though it is a sad but inevitable sign that they have engaged a publicist and media agent. . . .

Will we have to pay to get answers?

"CAPITAL VIEW" COLUMN BY M. J. MUHAMMAD,
NEW INDIAN EXPRESS, 15 APRIL 2040

XAVIER

Pav's plan, modified by his father and with suggestions from Edgar Chang, rolled into motion just before five A.M. the next morning, when a pair of twenty-five-year-old limousines, an ambulance, and two medium-sized trucks pulled up to the rear hospital entrance—where blood still stained the pavement and the walls still showed bullet marks.

It was raining . . . not the torrential tropical rain expected in Bangalore, just a morning shower.

For that reason, a tent was swiftly erected by enlisteds. This action also effectively kept observers—if there were any—from seeing who got aboard the vehicles in what order. Wing Commander Kaushal was everywhere, guiding the airmen with such vigor that in one case he actually shoved one aside and completed attaching the canvas to the frame himself.

Taj Radhakrishnan watched from farther inside the loading dock. He was pacing like a user waiting for his dealer.

Of course, this was just what Xavier Toutant saw as he and Rachel, Pav and Tea, Yahvi and Zeds slipped through the interior of the loading dock on their way to the ambulance garage.

Edgar Chang was waiting for them as they approached a van and a larger truck emblazoned with the logo of Prasad Stores, apparently a food supplier to Yelahanka. He was not wearing his customary suit and tie, but the more common khakis and white shirt of a clerical worker. He did not look Hindi, of course, but he looked less Chinese.

Xavier realized that Pav was also wearing the same clothing and had also had his hair trimmed. "Pav and I will ride in the van," the agent said. "I'm driving. Pav and I, in fact, are the only ones who know our route."

"Who's driving this thing?" Tea said.

Chang pointed to a grim-faced Chief Warrant Officer Singh— Xavier's associate during the transfer of *Adventure*'s cargo. Not that

Xavier had any doubts that the man was a special agent, but here was proof.

He only hoped that he was one of the agents who could not be bought by their enemies.

"Are we fooling anyone, do you suppose?" Rachel said.

"Well, *I'm* confused," Xavier said. Pav and Tea laughed, but Xavier was only half-kidding. There was the official plan, which involved a somewhat stealthy convoy of five vehicles heading up the Velur Bypass to National Highway 7 and Bengaluru International for a two-and-a-half-hour flight to Delhi. The carefully leaked story was that the Indian capital was a more appropriate temporary home for *Adventure*'s crew—and that superior medical facilities would be better for Sanjay Bhat.

Then there was the real, vastly more stealthy convoy that would leave Yelahanka by the main gate and head east to catch the Thanisandra Main Road, where it would turn south and eventually reach Hindustan Airport, the older facility now, according to Taj, largely devoted to flight test work.

From that point, the plans were vague and kept changing. Rachel and Pav, working with Taj and Tea and this Chang person, had made tentative plans for a flight to Shanghai, or possibly Buenos Aires—the destination kept changing, though the goal always remained the same: get as close to the Free Nation U.S. as possible, as soon as possible.

The giant flaw in any plan was Sanjay's state: miraculously, he had not only survived but been stabilized. While he faced a long recovery and remained technically critical, he was expected to survive.

Chang had released a statement that exaggerated Sanjay's condition, to justify the move to New Delhi. In fact, Sanjay would be staying right there at the Yelahanka Air Base hospital for several more days.

When it was safe, he would be flown to wherever the rest of the crew had come to rest.

Xavier didn't much like the idea of leaving the engineer behind, but he liked the idea of all of them in New Delhi a lot less. He wanted to be in the U.S., "Free Nation" or not, to see for himself what it was like living under Reiver domination . . . and determine what, if anything, could be done about it.

And, more to the point, what was this big double-secret crazy Reiver project—what would it do? How could it be stopped?

The *Adventure* crew needed some kind of base of operations . . . some set of rooms with sufficient power and secrecy and nearby transportation where Xavier (lacking Sanjay's skills) would get the 3-D printers up and running.

The garage was barely large enough to park two ambulances, though tall enough to allow the Prasad Stores truck access. Xavier had been inside the truck two hours ago, when *Adventure*'s cargo had been transferred aboard.

Now, the lift still lowered, the vehicle's rear stood open, revealing that five chairs—each with a seat belt and chest restraint—had been added. "Are we going over rough road?" Rachel said.

"Probably," Tea said. "We're supposed to stay on highways, but even those might be potholed. And we won't have visual cues, so sudden moves will surprise us."

In addition to seats, there was a chest for food and drink.

"Where do we go to the bathroom?" Rachel said.

"We won't be inside long enough to worry about it," Pav said.

"Easy for you to say." But she gave him a hug and was the first to climb aboard.

Xavier extended a hand to Yahvi, which was silly, since the girl was taller and far more lithe than he would ever be. But she accepted it.

And sneezed. Xavier's sympathy for the girl, who had never experienced a cold and was obviously deep in the worst of it, was counterbalanced by his worry that she had infected him. He hadn't had a cold during his time on Keanu; his immune system was surely as compromised as Yahvi's.

And it wasn't as though he was going to be able to wash his hands right this minute. He had to settle for wiping them vigorously on his trousers.

Tea Nowinski climbed up next, though the maneuver was obviously a bit of a strain. She made a face and rubbed her thighs. "I suppose I could have simply waited for the lift."

Then Xavier followed. Standing up inside the truck, he felt cramped already. Four of the chairs were standard human size, but the fifth was a kind of lounger for Zeds. It took up three times as much room.

"I hope Pav was telling the truth about not being in here for long."

Two airmen helped steady Zeds on the lift. It groaned for a moment and brought the Sentry, in his full suit, which still showed bloodstains from the attack, level with the rest of them. The alien ducked and clambered his way to the big chair.

"It feels as though we ought to take a moment," Tea said.

"Like when you flew to ISS?" Rachel said. She turned to Yahvi, who was about to ask what her mother was talking about. "My father told me, and I know Tea lived through it. When they left Star City for the launch site, astronauts and cosmonauts were supposed to stop and sit for a moment, just to reflect and hope for a successful voyage."

"It's an old Russian tradition," Tea said.

"But we're in India," Xavier said. He couldn't help it. He wanted to be rolling.

"How do we perform this ritual?" By speaking up, Zeds effectively made the decision for everyone.

Following Tea and Rachel's directions, Yahvi and Xavier sat on the floor, backs of their thighs touching their feet, hands on top of their thighs. Even Zeds, with a grace and speed that shocked Xavier, made it to the floor in a similar posture.

"Do we say anything?" Yahvi asked, reasonably.

"Just sit for a moment, eyes closed," Tea said.

Xavier counted to five, all the while encouraging the universe and his mother's Jesus to look fondly on their mission.

At that moment Rachel's cell phone beeped and a text from Pav appeared: IGNITION.

They could hear the garage door open. Before they were settled in their chairs, the truck pulled out.

The ride was even less fun than Xavier imagined it, and far longer than the promised hour and a half.

It took all of them several minutes to get safely into chairs and braced after their Russian travel blessing. Tea, in fact, bumped her head. "Okay, this truck is not for me."

They weren't all secured until the truck stopped for several minutes. MAIN GATE, Pav texted.

Then they felt the truck picking up speed, turning first one way, then the other.

They seemed to be on open road. Xavier tried to imagine Chang and Pav in the lead van, guiding them through the predawn darkness, but the only image that came to mind was of a grim Singh hunched over the wheel.

Within moments, the ride smoothed out . . . they were going somewhere, and no bullets were stitching the side of the vehicle. If Xavier listened, he could hear rain on the roof, but that was rather soothing.

Rachel was intent on the phone, occasionally typing messages and presumably reading news of waypoints passed.

Between sniffling and rubbing her red eyes, Yahvi was playing with the music player Remilla had given her. Zeds was inscrutable. Tea had closed her eyes.

Which seemed like a great idea to Xavier.

Then Rachel set the phone aside and nudged him. "Which one is it?"

It took him a moment to realize that she was talking about the transmitter. "Far left, halfway up." The parcel wasn't specially marked, but Xavier had memorized its number and made sure to place it where it could be reached swiftly. "I understand that's a priority."

"I'd hoped you and Sanjay would have it assembled by now. I really hate leaving *Adventure* without a working proteus."

"Give me a secure location and two hours."

"Soon, I hope." She turned away, glancing at Yahvi and Tea. Her profile made her seem quite young—Rachel wasn't any taller than when Xavier had first met her and had broadened only slightly, thanks to motherhood. When not bone-tired, she moved swiftly.

Xavier had to admit that, at various times, he was attracted to her . . . but that was true of many women he knew among the HBs. He had not acted on many of these impulses. Not that there were many or even any opportunities. The human habitat on Keanu was not where you went searching for privacy. You could probably find a place for a tryst, but you had to work at it.

Xavier knew that his inherent laziness was far stronger than his sexual drive. And that his looks and reputation probably did him no good, either.

Strange, though, to be sitting in the back of a truck in a secret convoy on Earth—Earth!—and remembering a momentary crush on Rachel.

Must be the kind of crazy shit that makes us human.

After two-plus hours and God knew how many texts—which Rachel faithfully reported—the truck lurched through a final set of contortions. "Pav says we're almost there."

"No problems?" Tea said, stretching. She had fallen completely asleep; so had Yahvi. Xavier had dozed. His only activity during waking moments had been to explore the supply chest for water and what turned out to be a sad collection of energy bars and fruit.

"None they're telling me," Rachel said.

"What is our next destination?" Zeds said. He had been silent for the entire trip, but Xavier could have kissed the big Sentry now for saying what Xavier could not.

Because these last three days had been nowhere near what Xavier expected when he imagined *Adventure*'s return to Earth—even after the harsh realities of the mission crystallized in his mind. His mission tasks aside—the work he planned to do with Sanjay—he had expected . . . well, maybe a parade. Meetings with scientists, perhaps. Or the head of the United Nations, if that organization still existed.

How about walks in the sunshine? Encounters with other people? Decent meals! Shopping!

And sightseeing! Even *before* being scooped up and hauled away to Keanu, he had never imagined he would be in India. Through a wildly unlikely set of circumstances, he was here, now! So couldn't he see this Taj Mahal?

He had talked to Harley Drake about what happened after spaceflights, and while the ex-astronaut had talked a lot about debriefs and physical adjustments (apparently six months in microgravity took a toll on your muscles, balance, and ability to judge movements) as well as emotional letdowns . . . he had emphasized one welcome, inescapable fact: You went back to your old life.

Xavier wanted to go back to his old life, what was left of it, even for a few days. Being locked up was not to his liking.

It wasn't even smart. Setting aside his own personal desires, he had a mission to perform . . . and it wasn't even started.

"I really wish I knew," Rachel said. "I'm sorry I'm not more of a leader on this. You all knew there was going to be a great deal of . . . improv once we landed."

"Sanjay's injury has cost us time—"

"And flexibility," Tea said.

"Yes, I think we can all agree on that." It was interesting to watch the two of them together. Rachel was twenty-five years younger, yet never deferred to Tea, treating her more like a daughter. And Tea, for that matter, seemed happy to fill that role . . . her facial expressions and tone were closer to Yahvi's than to Rachel's. "Pav and Mr. Chang have been working with Taj and the government—decisions were being made while we drove here."

"Then why don't we know what they were?" Yahvi said. It was as if she and Tea were now double-teaming Rachel. Hell, given what Zeds asked, all Xavier had to do was speak his mind and Rachel would be surrounded.

She was clearly feeling it. "Why don't we just let them open the doors and tell us?"

Which happened in the next ten minutes. Pav was waiting as the door rolled up, revealing that the truck had pulled into a vacant hangar whose door was wide open. The reason they were inside the hangar was obvious: It was still raining outside, with the sky gray, heavy, and low. The top of the nearest building was obscured by fog. The air was the coolest Xavier had felt yet on Earth.

He shivered and thought, *Great: I'm going to be sick for certain.*

The van was parked a few meters away, half-blocking the view from outside. "Everyone okay?"

"Peachy," Rachel said, not waiting for the lift, but jumping down for a hurried embrace. Xavier thought that Pav looked tired and jumpy; maybe Chang was a terrible driver.

"God, this smells better," Tea said. Xavier had to agree; it wasn't just having four humans and a Sentry in an environment suit crammed into close quarters with limited air circulation . . . the interior of the truck had its own collection of stale food smells. (Which, given that this company supplied Yelahanka, made Xavier wonder about some of the food he had eaten since arrival.)

Rachel, Tea, and Yahvi headed for the nearest ladies' room. Xavier was okay for the moment, which allowed him to take in their new and hopefully temporary surroundings as Pav and Singh extracted Zeds from the truck.

Xavier's first impression of Bengaluru was that it looked like Yelahanka, though slightly newer. The runways ran the same direction—due east/west.

But where the buildings and hangars at Yelahanka were almost uniform faded brown, Bengaluru's were brighter—white and bright green—at least in intent. Everything looked faded and worn on a morning like this.

And the base didn't seem to be particularly active. Of course, it was early. Maybe there were noise restrictions.

But, also, maybe there just weren't that many planes flying. If the Reivers could get close enough to the Indian coast to fire a missile at *Adventure*, what other weapons might they be fielding?

He already knew the answer: If they could pay a team of assassins to attack them at Yelahanka, there was really nowhere the crew was safe, not for long.

Even as this thought formed in Xavier's mind, he heard the distant sound of an approaching jet somewhere above the clouds. He had no idea if a plane could land in the rain, or in cloud cover this low.

For a moment he wondered if it was a bomber intending to strike them. But Edgar Chang only looked away from Zeds and Pav long enough to register the same sound. He didn't look particularly alarmed and, in fact, said something to Pav that Xavier couldn't hear.

Zeds began walking freely, performing his own unique Sentry-style stretches (Xavier could only imagine how cramped the giant alien must have felt!). As Rachel, Yahvi, and Tea returned, Xavier caught up with his Sentry friend.

"How are you feeling?"

"Impatient."

Xavier loved the way Zeds always said exactly what he felt. He had none of the social governors that even the least-inhibited human beings possessed.

"What were Chang and Pav talking about?"

"The aircraft is one they hoped to see."

Now, that was interesting—and welcome news. But from where? And more importantly, to where?

Xavier returned to the truck, where Edgar Chang and Chief Warrant Officer Singh were both pacing, phones to their ears. To Xavier's alarm, he noted that as Singh talked, his other hand was removing a revolver from a holster in the small of his back . . . as if checking on its presence and heft.

Meanwhile, Rachel Stewart-Radhakrishnan seemed to be having an argument with her husband as their daughter and Tea looked on, distressed.

"You've never hidden things from me before—at least I don't think you have—"

"I have not," Pav said.

"So why are you starting now?"

"Because I don't know what happened for certain!"

Now Tea spoke: "What about Taj?"

"No word."

Xavier glanced at Yahvi; her eyes and nose were red from her cold, but now it looked as though she'd been crying, too. "Can we catch a brother up?" he said. "And maybe Zeds would like to know." The Sentry had followed him to the gathering.

Rachel gestured for Pav to speak. "The other convoy," he said, clearly struggling for the words. He sighed. "There was an incident."

"Oh, for God's sake, Pav!" Rachel said, as snappish as Xavier had ever heard her. "They're dead, isn't that what you and Chang said? All killed on the road to the other airport?"

Xavier felt sick, though not, when he thought about it a second time, terribly surprised. He waited for Pav to add detail. "The report—Chang got it, and so did your driver—is that a highway bridge failed. Both limos went into the road below and turned over. One of the trucks was damaged, too. No word on the ambulance. The entire party is reported to be dead." Pav quickly pivoted to face Tea. "And so far we don't have definitive information on who was in the convoy at the time. I know my father said he was going along—"

"To help with the ruse, yes," Tea said bitterly.

"Taj is not among the dead," Chang said. He had just gotten off the phone. "There are four fatalities, including Warrant Officer Pandya—" Here Chang nodded toward Warrant Officer Singh. Xavier was surprised at how that news struck him; he'd assumed Pandya was the spy, not a supportive member of the team.

Not someone who would risk his life for them—and lose it.

"Two others were injured and evacuated. Taj is not among them, that's confirmed."

"Do we know where he is?" Pav said.

Chang shook his phone. "Still working on that."

"We should never have left Sanjay," Rachel said. "He's unprotected at Yelahanka."

"I believe the reason Taj stayed behind was to find a moment to remove Sanjay," Chang said. "That was the plan."

"Which one?" Yahvi spoke for the first time. "I can't keep these plans straight."

"Plan 3C," Xavier said. "Not that I want to forget about Sanjay, but here's a stumper: What about us? We got in the truck this morning with this as our destination. Well, folks, here we are . . . standing in a cold empty hangar in the rain.

"Are we flying to China? Are we catching a boat to Japan? What's the deal?"

"Just wait," Pav said.

Out on the runway, a small jet broke through the low clouds, swiftly touching down and rolling out. Xavier would not have been able to identify aircraft types in 2019 beyond big and not-so-big, so he was useless with this one.

But it was not big . . . a corporate or executive jet.

"Is this our ride?" Yahvi said.

Pav put his arm around her. Xavier noticed that he exchanged a look with Chang before answering: "Yes."

"Who are they?" Rachel said.

"Friends," Edgar Chang said.

"I asked my *husband*," Rachel said, more gently than Xavier expected.

Pav smiled, trying desperately—Xavier thought—to return a bit of humor to this tense situation. "It might be better to call them 'old friends never met,'" he said.

The jet was taxiing right up to the front of the hangar; the noise of its twin engines effectively eliminated further exchanges.

Zeds looked intrigued. Tea was grim, her arms across her chest. Yahvi blinked and seemed miserable. Pav had his arm around Rachel.

Now Xavier got a good look at the plane . . . sleek, white, clearly twenty meters from tip to tail. Two pilots were visible in the cockpit. Rows of windows confirmed that it was some kind of passenger craft.

On the tail . . . a baby kangaroo? The word surfaced from his deep memory: a wallaby.

"Is this from Australia?" Xavier shouted. The engines wound down just as he opened his mouth, making him sound so much louder than necessary that the others—even Chang and Singh—laughed.

Singh's lighter moment didn't last long. As the engines fell silent, Xavier and the others could hear latches on the cabin door being opened. As the door swung down, becoming a ladder, Singh raised his pistol, covering the hatchway.

A thin, middle-aged white male with a crest of blond hair stuck his head out. "Don't shoot!" he said, hands up. "We come in peace!"

Xavier saw Singh glance at Chang, who nodded. The weapon was lowered.

Pav stepped forward, hand extended. "Mr. Radhakrishnan, I presume," the man said. His Aussie accent was so strong that *Radhakrishnan* sounded like "Redda kishen."

"My wife, Rachel," Pav said. He quickly introduced all of them, ending with Zeds . . . which caused the Aussie fellow to step back and look up.

When this happened, Yahvi grabbed her mother and said, "Who is this man?"

The man heard her and turned. "Oh, sorry, got your names, forgot to offer mine." He smiled. "Colin Edgely, young lady. Among my other notable accomplishments, I am the man who discovered Keanu."

Rachel said, "I thought that name was familiar. Lovely to meet you, and why are you here?"

Edgely looked at Pav, who cleared his throat and said, "He's come to rescue us."

Mr. Kalyan Bhat of Hebbal, Bengaluru, Karnatka, admits he was shocked by the news that humans had returned from the Near-Earth Object Keanu. "I lived near the control center," he said. "I saw the object rising into the sky." He had a special interest in the event, though Kalyan—who was only thirteen—didn't know it at the time.

"My older brother, Sanjay, was in that thing. I didn't find out for a week."

That shocking news contributed to the death of the boys' mother, Sima. "She was fighting cancer and doing well, but losing Sanjay like that . . . she gave up." Sima Bhat died two years later.

Kalyan and Sanjay's father, Mahavir, a clerk with the State Bank of India in Hebbal, lived until 2037. "I know that losing Sanjay affected him, too. Every year, on the anniversary of the object's takeoff, he would lock himself in his room.

"But when I tried to get him to talk about Sanjay, he wouldn't. There was only one picture of my brother in our house, in my father's bedroom."

As for Kalyan himself, he served in the Indian army during the conflicts of 2029–2031, and became an engineer with DMC Electronics.

"I was thirteen when Sanjay was taken," he said. "I can't wait to see him." He added, "It's like something from an old story—a castaway returning, or someone coming back from the dead."

As for the rumors that Sanjay was injured in *Adventure*'s crash landing, he said, "I hope they're wrong. And if he was injured, I hope he's recovering." Has ISRO or another agency been in touch with him?

"No."

TIMES OF INDIA FEATURE,
APRIL 15, 2040

TAJ

"You said they were going to China!"

Taj was heading for his car when Melani Remilla caught up with him.

They were in the same garage where the *Adventure* convoy had departed earlier that day; Taj had spent the hours since then essentially locked in the conference room, working his phone and calling up news reports on the screens.

The accident on the road to Bengaluru International had shocked him—which in turn surprised him. He had not only agreed to the idea of a second, clandestine convoy . . . it had been his idea! He was the one who always feared that the *Adventure* crew would be targets of violence, and not just from the Aggregates.

Tea often teased him that no matter how cynical he sounded, he was still a romantic. "Poor Taj! Loves flowers and pretty girls and the Moon . . . has to pretend about guns and treachery."

No matter. Knowing Rachel and Pav and the others had lifted off from Bengaluru meant he could go home for a few hours, before returning to the Sanjay vigil—and trying to decide his next move.

Once he got rid of Remilla. "Didn't we all believe they were going to China?"

"That doesn't answer my question, sir!" If Taj had any doubts that Remilla was upset, they vanished.

"Until an hour ago," he told her, and he wasn't lying, "the only information I had was that the crew *would* be going to China. Edgar Chang was arranging it."

"Then who took them to Australia?"

Here Taj was on trickier ground, since he had suspicions, though no data. "That I cannot tell you." Strictly true, if not especially illuminating.

He had known Remilla for more than twenty years, since the *Brahma* days, first as a young female spacecraft engineer specializing in environmental systems, which could not have been an easy job, given the male-dominated ISRO world.

Then, after the arrival of the Aggregates and the subsequent wars and plagues, when India had no money for space exploration aside from spy satellites, Remilla had moved into program management, becoming the last woman standing.

Their interactions over the past year, all of them involving the Keanu return, had been completely professional. He knew nothing of her personal life, though he had some memory of a husband somewhere, and a grown son. During those contacts, Taj had found Remilla to be smart and open—possibly too open when it came to dealing with sharks like Kaushal—but too prey to emotion when things didn't go her way.

Like now. "But you have had more information than the rest of us!"

"Why are you surprised? My son is one of them!"

"So he was telling you secrets!"

"I was spending more time with him than anyone else," Taj said, losing patience with this woman. "So, yes, I undoubtedly heard more than you or Kaushal did."

"You should have told us!"

"I told you everything that was important."

Remilla frowned. Clearly she had no goal other than to express frustration at losing control of a situation that was never in control. "What are they going to do now?"

"I honestly don't know," he said, though he was convinced that, ultimately, the Aggregates were their target. Pav had told him a bit about the Houston-Bangalores and their successful eradication of the Reivers on Keanu twenty years ago. Of course, sanitizing a Near-Earth Object was one thing . . . cleansing half a planet, quite another.

"Will you promise to tell me when they are back in contact?"

"Of course," he said, not at all sure that he would. Remilla's only role now was to make sure that *Adventure* remained unmolested, and that Sanjay Bhat was safe until he could be transferred.

Those happened to be Taj's jobs, too. And he was going to fail at both if he did not get some sleep.

Remilla offered a conciliatory hug, and finally left him.

Taj climbed into his car and started it up, hoping that the drive to his apartment would be trouble-free. He and Tea had spent most of their married life living on Raisina Hill in New Delhi, close to the Ministry of Defence. But with news of Keanu's looming return, they had moved to Bangalore.

It had not been an easy year and a half for Tea. In fact, the entire last decade had been a challenge for his wife. When the Aggregates erected their financial and other walls around the United States, she had faced a choice: Return and submit to the new order, or stay away . . . and lose her pension.

She chose to stay away, and found herself having to make a living as a former astronaut, first woman to walk on the Moon, in a world that had no time for space exploration.

(It wasn't about survival: Taj could support both of them on his general's pension and other investments. But naturally Tea resisted that.)

She had finally found a way to keep busy, making speeches to female students in secondary schools and college classes about opportunities in science and technology—ISRO supported it; more to the point, so did the Ministry of Defence. (The more engineers it could enroll in the coming war with the Aggregates, the better!)

But it was not a happy existence. Tea had grown unhappy, with her work, her future, with India . . . with Taj.

And now she was off with Rachel. Taj was grateful that she finally had something worthwhile to keep her busy. He was quite unhappy, though, that neither of them had been able to work together—he with the "secrets" he had learned from Pav, she with . . . whatever she was gleaning from Rachel—

He had barely pulled out of the garage when he saw movement in his peripheral vision; it was Kaushal with two of his guards literally running out of the hospital. He spotted Taj's car and clearly ordered the guards to pursue him.

Taj chose to hit the pedal and keep driving.

It was ultimately a foolish maneuver. His car was an underpowered electric Tata Sanand III, good for cheap, comfortable commutes, useless for flight.

He was also restricted to Yelahanka Air Base, with its many speed bumps, stop signs, and competing vehicles.

All of which meant that he didn't get far . . . Kaushal's Jeep caught him at the exit gate.

"Why are you running away?" the wing commander said. He was wide-eyed and angrier than Taj had ever seen him.

"I wanted to go home."

Kaushal just stared. It was likely that he was as exhausted as Taj, and almost as likely that he realized it. "You should answer your phone," he muttered. Taj was carrying two of them, but only the one that would connect him to Kaushal was on his person. His official unit was in his briefcase. "And you need to come with me, now."

"What is this all about, Kaushal?"

"It's the *Adventure* man Sanjay."

It was already over by the time Taj and Kaushal reached the ICU.

"He expired without ever regaining consciousness," the senior surgeon said. "Time of death was one forty-five."

Taj rubbed his face. He was torn between relief—he had judged Sanjay Bhat's injuries to be fatal the moment he first saw him—and a growing sense of panic. "Let me see him."

The surgeon stood aside and allowed Taj and Kaushal into the room where Sanjay lay. The IV and other lines had been removed and the sheets rearranged after what, to judge from the pile of bloody cotton and bandages on the floor, must have been a frantic struggle to save the *Adventure* engineer.

The secrets this man held! The things he had seen! The places he had traveled . . . outside the heart of the solar system! Yet he had died as a result of a stupid missile strike!

Then there were the various plans Pav and Rachel had discussed with him—assuming Sanjay recovered, they wanted him flown to their destination. "Wherever we have our cargo," Pav had said.

So much for plans.

Remilla entered, looking shocked. "Oh my God."

"He's gone," Kaushal said, unnecessarily.

"What do we do?"

"I'll call Rachel and tell her," Taj said. He indicated that he wanted to get out of the room, and the others followed.

"Then what?"

"He has a brother," Kaushal said, looking to Remilla for confirmation.

"I'll get in touch with him," Remilla said. "But then what?"

"What?" Taj said.

"The body!" Remilla said. "What do we do? Have a funeral? Ship him to his brother?"

"Let me talk to Rachel," Taj said.

So much for rest.

Day Four

MONDAY, APRIL 16, 2040

Where did they go?

For two generations prior to the arrival of the Aggregates, tabloids and mass-market television shows feasted on stories of "alien abductions," in which lonely humans would be plucked from deserted highways—never from downtown urban streets—and taken off for bizarre sexual or medical examinations in spacecraft.

What about alien disappearances? The crew of the Keanu-based *Adventure* spacecraft has vanished from the base near Bangalore where they were sequestered.

One report had them moving to Delhi, but that turned out to be false—fortunately, since an accident involving what was believed to be the Keanite convoy killed two and injured two others, according to incomplete information released so far.

We are sure of this: No one is speaking about the "aliens" present, not even the Keanites' representative, Edgar Chang, who also seems to have gone dark.

SYDNEY MORNING HERALD,
MONDAY, APRIL 16, 2040

RACHEL

"How long have you been in touch with this Edgely character?"

"Not long," Pav said. "And not often."

The plane bumped, one of many since taking off from Bengaluru.

It was an executive jet, a thirty-year-old Gulfstream 605, according to Edgely. They were flying low over the Indian Ocean and, in Rachel's opinion, coming far too close to nasty-looking storm clouds. The occasional bumps only convinced her that she was in the hands of crazy people.

And Pav had made this happen without telling her!

It wasn't all bad. The turbulence probably added up to twenty minutes out of seven hours of flying. As for the rest of the time, well, the cabin was really luxurious: wide leather seats, soft lighting, carpet. There had been food and beverages shortly after takeoff, served out by Edgely and the two pilots—both Chinese, one male, one female, both younger than Rachel would have believed.

The takeoff had been swift and steep, with Edgely jokingly talking about "avoiding SAMs," which Pav later identified as "surface-to-air missiles."

"Like the thing that shot *Adventure*."

"Correct."

Which made her even more nervous than she had been. All during the escape from Yelahanka she had been focusing on China—what she knew, what they could do there, how long it would take them to move on. The shift to this aircraft and Mr. Colin Edgely and a destination in Australia had forced her to change her mind, never a happy or easy adjustment.

Especially when it was Pav pushing her. "It's all right," he had told her, as they shoved the last of their boxes into the cabin. (Only two thirds of their precious cargo would fit in the aircraft's hold.) "I arranged this."

"Without telling me."

He had made one of his teenaged-boy faces, which infuriated and charmed her, in equal parts.

Then they had said good-bye to Singh and taken off.

Now, Zeds sat on the floor toward the rear of the cabin. Yahvi was next to him. Both were gazing out the windows, apparently rapt. Tea was with them, curled up in a seat asleep.

Xavier sat in the midcabin flipping through a datapad Edgely had brought while also examining several Australian newspapers. He had been quizzing Edgely and Chang about their destination—which would be Darwin in northern Australia—and flying time, which would be eleven hours. "Why Darwin?" he had said, saving Rachel the question.

"Within our range," Edgely said. "And fairly out of the way. Too many prying eyes and ears in Sydney or Melbourne."

Rachel had tuned them out, however, in order to have a private moment with her husband in the forward cabin, who assured her again that his contacts with Edgely had been recent and limited.

"Well, color me relieved," Rachel said. She had never been good at disguising sarcasm. In fact, as Pav once told her during an argument, it was her default setting. "I can't believe you just surprised me like that."

"I didn't want to get your hopes up."

"Since when are you responsible for my hopes? I need facts! I had a right to know!"

"Look," he said, "this is your mission. You're the leader. You always have been. You know I don't question that. But I first heard from Edgely twenty years ago, remember!"

Rachel had not remembered that fact, until Pav reminded her that the Australian astronomer—who had been one of the first discoverers of Keanu as a teenaged amateur in the outback—had sent several messages to the NEO as it departed Earth orbit and the inner solar system back in 2019.

The message had contained warnings about the arrival of the Reivers, later known to most humans on Earth as the Aggregates.

"That was all it was," Pav said. "He posted, I don't know, four or five warnings. I responded with a few messages of my own—where did they land? What are they doing? But never got a response. It was as if we were just leaving messages on a bulletin board somewhere.

"Then, once we started moving back into range of Earth communication, I thought it would be fun to check my old address . . . and found that Colin had continued to post updates on the Reiver invasion for years!

"So I transmitted a hello to him . . . he'd kept the old address just in case, and we exchanged literally three new messages, just me telling him a team would be landing, likely in Bangalore, and that we might need help. Everything else"—he gestured at the plane—"was up to him and his friends."

Rachel glanced back at Edgely. He wasn't much older than she was. "So, what has he been doing all these years?"

"He teaches high school science somewhere in the Northern Territory, he said."

"So a high school science teacher was able to pull off this big rescue, with a very expensive private plane?"

"He's had this group of, hell, I don't know what you'd call it . . . fanboys or enthusiasts, who kept tracking Keanu and passing stories back and forth for the past twenty years."

"This Kettering Group?"

"Yes," Pav said. "They even have a website."

Rachel looked at Edgely. He was thin, even gawky. He was still so happy and excited to be talking with travelers from Keanu that he was bouncing up and down in his chair. Even though he was forty, give or take a year, it was easy for Rachel to see him as a lonely sixteen-year-old astronomy geek, more comfortable with telescopes than girls. "Pav, darling, did it ever occur to you that some or all of those messages could have been Reiver plants? That he has a lot of powerful friends and inside information . . . for a high school science teacher?"

"Quite a lot, actually."

"What convinced you that he was for real?"

He exhaled, then made another goofy face. "Tenure?"

"Meaning?"

"It was just clear to me that the messages I saw now, in the past year, were from the same geeky guy.

"And, maybe I just went on instinct. He was promising nothing, just offering an escape route. Even that never came up until I'd texted him that we'd been attacked and were hoping to get out of Yelahanka.

"And, well, he told me that one of the Kettering guys had made a ton of money—" He smiled and took her hand. "If it makes any difference, I hated not telling you."

"Then we've got that in common." Rachel knew her words were harsh, but her tone was conciliatory. Pav slapped his hand over his heart, as if he'd been shot. Then, wisely, he got up and moved down the cabin.

She was prepared to forgive him, though it might have to wait until they reached Darwin.

Or North America.

There was no room in their relationship for secrets. That was something they had both discussed and agreed on almost twenty years ago, when they first drifted together.

They had not liked each other originally, not during their first real meetings on Keanu, as Scoop refugees from Bangalore (him) and Houston (her). (Both thought they had a passing introduction in the past, on Earth, a logical assumption, since their fathers were both space travelers who had shared a space station mission. But they had been too young then to remember much.)

Then they had shared a wild, intense adventure exploring the innards of Keanu in the company of a dog—and later a Revenant, and still later an actual Architect.

Some relationships are forged in "foxhole" moments, as Harley Drake described them.

Not Rachel and Pav's. After the Keanu core reboot, they had returned to the human habitat exhausted by each other's company and were thrown into the chaos of the post-Reiver struggle for survival.

Of course, the fact that Rachel had seen her father, Zack, going to his death at the climax of that adventure may have contributed to a desire to distance herself from anything or anyone that reminded her of it.

But that hadn't lasted. The blunt reality: There weren't many suitable mates their age. Only eleven other teens had been scooped up in Bangalore and Houston. There were five infants.

The mean age of the rest of the HB population was just over thirty.

Which meant that if Rachel was going to have a boyfriend or a husband close to her age . . . it was going to be Pav or one of four other boys.

She avoided the question for some time. Between ages seventeen and nineteen she had engaged in an intense erotic relationship with Zhao, then in his thirties, the former technical spy from the People's Republic of China—the man who had gunned down Brent Bynum on the first HB arrival day.

Zhao had later proven his stability and value to the entire community . . .

and perhaps it was the fact that he was neither a Houston nor a Bangalore that eventually attracted Rachel.

That had ended eventually. She was just too young for Zhao. His concerns were never hers.

And she had drifted back into Pav's orbit. Looking back, she wasn't sure how it happened, or why, except that one day she realized that she rather liked him. And he was acting very nervous and uncertain around her—

They went off alone one night, and were rarely apart after that.

They had arguments, of course. Disagreements about political matters, practical issues, though not about the things Rachel remembered couples fighting about: money, rivals, whatever.

They had no secrets. Until now.

As far as Rachel knew.

"We'll be at Darwin in an hour."

Rachel looked up. The plane had flown into darkness; the cabin lights seemed brighter. She must have dozed off in her incredibly comfy chair. The lack of recent thumps and bumps allowed her to sleep.

Now Edgar Chang loomed above her.

"Then what?"

He sat next to her, looking even older than he had in their first meetings. Rachel judged him to be in his midsixties . . . she wondered what he had done wrong in his career to be the point man for an operation like this.

Or look at it another way, she thought; maybe Chang was the senior editor of some publication and took this assignment because he wanted it done properly . . . and because it was unique.

She wondered if he would tell her, if she asked. But first things first—

"You wanted to reach Free Nation U.S."

"As soon as possible, yes."

"That's what I'm working on."

"What does that mean, 'working on'?"

Chang smiled and held up his notepad. "It means sending a lot of e-mails to a lot of people in very different locations, including some in Free Nation U.S."

"I thought all that was firewalled."

"As close to a hundred percent as you can get. But, you know, the U.S. is a big place with a lot of open space. Somewhere on some border or out on a prairie—or in the middle of Chicago, maybe—someone has a secret tower and is beaming a signal off some satellite the Aggregates think is dead."

"And what are you learning?"

Chang rubbed his face. Rachel suspected that he had not slept in a day, likely longer. "There are three ways you sneak into Free Nation U.S."

"Walk, fly, or swim?" Pav said, behind her. Rachel patted the chair next to her. She still felt the need to punish her husband a bit, but it was silly to isolate him from important information.

"That's what they were doing when I was living in Houston," Rachel said. Illegal immigration was one of the issues that rose and fell in importance, like the price of gasoline or summer temperatures.

"Some of that still happens," Chang said. "And a good thing, because that's what we're going to be doing. Our choices are to fly across the Canadian border, hike from northern Mexico into Texas, or swim into California."

"Which do you recommend?" Pav said.

"Which method is *safest*?" Rachel added.

Chang looked harried. "*None* of this is safe! If you're thinking of this as some kind of tourist excursion, put that right out of your heads. You are, or will be, once word is out that you're not in Delhi or China, the world's most wanted fugitives. The Aggregates will do everything they can to track you and capture you."

"We know that," Rachel said. "Let's go back to how, or where?"

"Or what you would do if you were in our situation?" Pav said, pointing at Chang.

"Word is that crossing from Mexico, either to California or Arizona, is still the easiest.

"But that raises the larger question: Where do you want to go in Free Nation U.S.? And what do you hope to do there?"

Rachel wasn't sure how to answer Chang—or even if she should. When you stripped away the nonsense about trade or sightseeing, the core of *Adventure*'s mission was reconnaissance. They needed to know the extent of Reiver Aggregate domination of Earth, since clearly it didn't extend to Southeast Asia.

Only then would they be able to consider doing something about it. Assuming they could do anything at all.

But before she could offer Chang some vague nonanswer, Pav spoke again: "Let's just say this, Mr. Chang: We want to get into the western U.S., and as soon as possible. It would be helpful if we also had a nearby base of operations."

Chang closed his notepad. "Then that is what we will try to do. I'll know more when we reach Darwin."

"When will that be?" Rachel said.

"Less than an hour." He considered the situation. "We ought to be in cell phone range already. . . ." He reached for his jacket, which was slung across the next seat.

"Is that secure?" Rachel said. God, now she was sounding like Pav!

"As secure as any broadcast signal can be," he said. "But if you'd rather I waited until we landed—"

At that instant a cell phone rang somewhere in the cabin. Rachel and Chang looked around.

More than a little embarrassed, Pav grinned as he raised his cell phone. "Yes?" he said. Then, as if it would help, he put his free hand over his other ear. "You're breaking up—"

Pav nodded, then clicked off. To Rachel he said, "It's my father. He's going to change locations."

"I'm still amazed that you have these things," Rachel said to Chang.

"Cell phones? The networks were built a generation before the Aggregates arrived. They've infected them, of course—waged cyberwar. But it's one area where we've fought them to a draw—"

The phone rang again and Pav answered it. "I wonder what news he has?" Rachel said.

"Speaking of news," Chang said, "our first task, once we're settled in Darwin, is to release some information about your 'escape' and other activities."

"For God's sake, why?"

"To satisfy the organizations that fronted you the equivalent of ten million dollars." Chang gestured at the plane. "Edgely's friends provided the plane—not the fuel, not the pilots. That all costs money."

"Got it."

"And you'll need every penny where you're—"

"Oh fuck no." That was Pav, suddenly looking stricken.

Rachel gasped. She knew without hearing—

"Sanjay's dead."

SITUATION REPORT

Five of the six members of the Keanu mission *Adventure* departed Yelahanka AB Monday morning, ostensibly headed for Delhi. Sources at Yelahanka suggest that they are actually planning to leave India and make
their way to Free Nation U.S.

The sixth member of *Adventure*'s crew remains at Yelahanka.

This clandestine maneuver seems to have been necessitated by two
separate attacks on the crew, both attributable to forces funded by, or, in
the first case of the submarine-launched missile attack, overtly answer-
able to the Aggregates.

All Aggregate-controlled military forces have elevated their alert status from yellow to orange and seem to be actively pursuing the *Adventure*
crew, treating them as a hostile force allied with, though not controlled by,
India or China.

This alert seems related to the recent consolidation of Aggregate formations in northern Arizona. (See bulletins of 1–7 April 2040.) The motive
behind their apparent withdrawal from larger cities is still unknown and
under investigation.

INTELLIGENCE REPORT, RESEARCH AND ANALYSIS WING,
DELHI, 18 APRIL 2040

DALE

Running through the habitat, naked, with his raggedy clothing in his
arms, Dale was surprised at the ease of his escape.

And the fact that nothing and no one seemed to be moving. The silent stillness reminded him of deadly Sunday nights he had spent in various tank towns during his military career, episodes he had found to be unsettling and nerve-racking, though he could not have said why. After all, he had now spent a good deal of his life as a hermit, living in a place far more isolated than Ten Sleep, Wyoming, on a Sunday night in November. Yet the Factory habitat seemed abuzz with activity compared to the human one.

Maybe it was because of the landscape. The interior of the Factory was like a city, filled from one side to the other with structures of various sizes, some of them seeming, at times, to hum with unknown and likely unknowable activity.

The human habitat in this late hour, by contrast, was dominated by the Temple structure with a scattering of small cabinlike buildings leading from it. But even these were hard to see among the trees in the half-light.

There were no sounds at all. And strangest of all, no apparent movement . . . as if the HBs were toys that had had their batteries removed.

Even close to the "southern" or coreward end of the habitat, where the HBs had constructed a track and mining car system to transport Substance K, things were quiet, as if the equipment had not been used in days.

Dale was still reeling a bit from his communion with Keanu, however, and as he approached the core-side exit, he had one frightening thought:

He had *died*. The reason he saw no one, no movement, no life, was that he no longer existed in that universe. Given what happened with humans who died on Keanu, this wasn't as purely terrifying a notion as it might have been—it was possible to come back.

Though not likely.

This dark fantasy persisted until Dale stubbed a bare toe on a small rock. The pain convinced him that he still lived . . . and encouraged him to put his clothes and sandals on.

Then, feeling as if he were once again completely back in the land of the living, he considered his options. He could return to the Factory and resume his explorations. He would survive; he might even prosper. Let Harley and Sasha and Jaidev and the others go to hell.

But Dale could not forget the original reason he had returned to the HBs . . . his knowledge of trouble for Rachel and the others on Earth, and his larger sense that something truly momentous and game-changing was about to happen . . . something that would affect Keanu.

There was nothing to be gained by returning to the Factory. His mission was onward, ever onward—to find Zhao and Makali.

His close contacts with Keanu left Dale with a three-dimensional real-time model of the NEO in his mind.

It proved to be a terrific guide when he slipped out of the human habitat and began prowling the tunnels that would lead him toward the Skyphoi habitat. (There was only one other choice: the route that led back to the Factory.)

He noted with amusement that the HBs had extended their mining-car operation toward the Skyphoi. The structure of rails, supports, and buckets occupied a third of the space of the tunnel. Like Dale, the HBs must have concluded that the Keanu railcars would never run again.

Or they were simply so desperate to sustain the flow of Substance K that they took the chance. (There were still big pools of Substance K inside the Factory. Dale half-suspected that the random noises he heard there were signs that the manufacturing system was still operating. If the HBs had bothered to find him, they might have saved themselves a lot of work.)

He moved swiftly across the floor of the tunnel, which was hard-packed smooth rock. Someone had strung a row of glowworms across the ceiling, giving some light. (One of the things that kept Dale from exploring every centimeter of Keanu's passageways was the utter lack of illumination.)

As he approached the junction where entry to the Skyphoi habitat was located, Dale wondered if those gasbag creatures had given the HBs help in their operation. It seemed unlikely—and the schematic in Dale's head was no help here, like a Google map that had not been updated.

The Skyphoi *were* involved; some kind of multicolored and asymmetrical piping took up half the entryway, which meant it was large. (The Skyphoi averaged five meters in diameter.)

It didn't connect but ran parallel to the human mining car network that continued on past the Skyphoi nexus.

Dale wondered how long this had been going on, and who among the HBs had the ability to get the Skyphoi involved in anything human. Absent some kind of motivation—like the crisis in 2019 about Keanu's dying power core—the gasbag creatures seemed to emerge only once every decade.

Dale was compelled to search farther. And now, for all his years of wandering within the NEO, he found himself entering Keanu Incognito.

When he accessed the map inside his head, he grew convinced that he was working his way deeper into Keanu's interior . . . as if this particular branch of passageway were a coil winding tighter and tighter around some central shaft. He was amused to realize that, setting aside his eventual need for food and water—which he hoped to find farther on; it would be troublesome as well as humiliating to be forced to return to the human habitat—he could probably accomplish an internal orbit of the NEO . . . the three-dimensional squiggles in his mental map suggested that this passage might eventually lead him back to the Factory, the long way around.

It would still take days, but what a journey! Unfortunately, this voyage was not one of exploration. It was to deal with a crisis.

And, based on what he was seeing now, a mystery.

To Dale's surprise, the mining track and Skyphoi tube continued on. He wondered where they would lead—his Keanu map was fuzzy regarding the space directly in front of him. He assumed there would be another habitat, possibly two . . . but how big?

And who or what would be living in them? If anyone or anything?

Wait! Whether it was the Keanu map inside his head or his own heightened senses, Dale realized that he was being followed!

He slowed long enough to glance behind him, but saw nothing, no one. Heard nothing.

Yet . . . he knew. But what choice did he have? It wasn't as though he could turn and ambush his pursuer. Keep walking—

There, in his peripheral vision—a shadow, meaning there was light behind it.

He began to walk faster, a desire complicated by his instinct to look back. Yes, something bright was behind him in the passageway, and getting closer.

The passageway curved, which allowed him to feel as though he was putting space between himself and the pursuer.

Not far ahead he could see a second branch, too. Which presented him with a decision . . . go right or go left. Or follow the twin rails and pipes straight ahead, to their terminus.

He assumed he would learn nothing by merely escaping. There was also this: Of all the humans living on Keanu, Dale Scott was the closest thing to a master of the NEO that could be found.

Why the hell should he be running away? What was there on Keanu that was a real threat? Even the Skyphoi, while indifferent and uncooperative, were never hostile. He'd never felt unsafe in his few encounters with them.

Suddenly he was at the end of the line . . . the rail and tube structures structure made a curving turn to the left into a large entrance.

And now Dale could hear his pursuer. He could smell something unusual but also somehow familiar. It was the acid tang of the Skyphoi atmosphere.

Which mean that he was about to be caught or at least met by one of the gasbag aliens.

But first—

The entries to habitats were deep, wide at times, and always complicated, usually involving several membranes and, once you penetrated past the initial opening, branching side passages. The membranes played the role that hatches did in spacecraft airlocks, since the atmospheres inside habitats were rarely the same as that in the tunnel system.

Dale slipped through the larger opening and saw immediately that the whole unit had been further rearranged to accommodate the human and Skyphoi pipes. Rather than press on through the obvious central entry, he chose to climb on top of the railcar track and squeeze through a series of membranes that way.

He emerged into a habitat, and immediately had to stop.

First reason . . . there was almost no floor. He was standing on a platform of sorts that jutted into a spherical chamber perhaps a fifth the size of the human or Factory habitats. The platform extended around the perimeter, broken only by the railcar and pipe system. From where Dale stood, he saw that the Skyphoi pipe brought material into the chamber, and the railcars took it away. In the center was a giant filmy balloonlike thing at least thirty meters across that Dale recognized from twenty years past.

A vesicle, the same type of object that had carried the HBs from Houston and Bangalore . . . and had delivered the Reivers to Earth, apparently.

Dale had no idea that anyone knew how to make another one.

This one didn't seem complete . . . the top seemed to be open. Nor was it solid; the entire shell quivered as if made of gelatin—

Shit, he'd let himself get distracted. The Skyphoi had managed to invade this habitat! This one was less than half the size of those he'd known . . . but here it was.

Dale was torn between sudden, unreasoning, but definite fear for his safety and amazement that the large alien gasbags had learned to change their size.

His sense of wonder and curiosity had gotten him into trouble before. Now it had led him into a trap. Well, he had had no choice.

He turned to face his pursuer. Too bad the map in his head and his linkage, however tenuous, with Keanu had failed him.

Seen closer now, this particular Skyphoi seemed odd . . . it wasn't just smaller than those Dale remembered meeting, it was the wrong color and filled with what appeared to be a human shape.

As if, Jonah's whale–style, a Skyphoi had swallowed a man whole.

Which boded ill for Dale's immediate future. Having nowhere to run, he decided to stand his ground. "What do you want?" he said.

To his amazement, the Skyphoi answered! "Fuck you, Scott!"

Then the Skyphoi collapsed, the filmy yellowish bag falling to the surface of the platform and turning to powder . . . leaving an actual human wearing a Sentry-style environment suit.

The human removed the mask. It was Zhao, the Chinese agent who had become one of the HB leaders, the one Dale had asked Harley Drake about.

"So that's where you were?" Dale said. "In the Skyphoi habitat?"

"What are you doing here?"

Dale gestured at the piping. "Following the not-so-yellow-brick road."

"Are you happy you did?"

"I don't know yet. What's it for?"

"Why do you care? You opted out of our activities a long time ago."

"Maybe I'm opting back in." Zhao continued to stare at him. "What?"

"I was merely wondering how long it has been since I've seen you."

"Ten years at least. Why?"

Zhao's face was impassive, unreadable, as always. "I had hoped that your isolation would lead to some kind of personal evolution. Apparently not. You are the same clueless fool I remember."

Zhao was wrong, however. The old Dale would have taken a swing at Zhao for a statement like that. But new Dale, Keanu-attuned Dale, just laughed. "And you are the same arrogant asshole. Depressing, isn't it?

"Now . . . forget trying to prove how superior you are, and tell me what the hell this thing is."

THEY'RE GONE!

Sources in ISRO report that the crew of the Keanu-based spaceship *Adventure*, supposedly on their way to Delhi two days ago, were, in fact, diverted to an undisclosed location and may have left the country.

HEADLINE AND LEAD IN *NEW DELHI TIMES*,
WEDNESDAY, APRIL 18, 2040

RACHEL

Rachel barely noticed the landing, which was smoother than she expected, given the bumpy nature of the last half hour.

It was still night in Darwin, and apparently overcast, so her one glance out the window failed to give her any sense of the size of the city, which seemed to extend to the south of whatever airport they flew into. And their path was east off the ocean.

Besides, she was too busy comforting Yahvi, who had gotten hysterical at the news of Sanjay's death. Even Zeds seemed shocked, retreating into his suit.

Rachel knew that Yahvi had never warmed to Sanjay—that she barely knew him. But deaths were a big deal for the HBs, and death here, now, when the girl was feeling so vulnerable—it had to be shocking.

So she curled up in the seat next to Rachel and sobbed all through the touchdown and the brief taxiing to a stop at what appeared to be a small executive terminal.

Pav sat still and, to unfamiliar eyes, unmoved. But Rachel knew her husband; he was stunned, too.

Xavier and Tea were behind them, not easily seen. Rachel would describe Tea's response as stoic, though with some tears in her eyes.

Xavier looked as though he'd been hit with a hammer. And, in many ways, he had, because without Sanjay, *Adventure*'s success now depended on him.

The plane rolled to a stop. Edgely was first out of his seat as Steve, the male pilot, emerged from the cockpit with the manner of a man in a hurry. "Welcome to Darwin, everyone. And please accept my condolences. Very sad news."

The hatchway opened and Edgely and Steve exited. Chang, Tea, and Xavier started to follow. Tea gestured for Yahvi to join them. The girl sniffed, whether from her lingering cold or sadness it was impossible to tell, and got out.

Rachel lingered, not out of love for the aircraft, but just to give herself some emotional space.

Pav waited, too. Then he took her arm and led her down the stairs.

It was only once they were on the ground that he said, "We have a long list of practical matters to discuss—so long I don't even know where to start."

"Sanjay," she said. "There's a body . . . what do we do?"

"Well, several possibilities: have it frozen and stored; have it shipped to us; have it buried in Bangalore, or cremated there. I think that covers it."

Rachel pondered this unhappy decision as she took in her surroundings. The plane had pulled up to a hangar, one of several in what was obviously the cargo terminal of a large airport.

The sky was moonless, dark—cloudy, night, the smell of rain in the air. She knew it was late, middle of the night, likely three or four A.M.

Yet there were armed guards within sight.

"Are they for us?"

Edgar Chang happened to pass close enough to hear. "Sadly, no. This is the world we live in."

"So, machine guns against the Aggregates?" Pav said.

Chang shrugged. "Useless, of course. It just makes nervous people feel safer."

He smiled and shuffled off. Rachel was amazed at how tired and elderly the man seemed.

"What will it be?" Pav said. "Sanjay?"

"I suppose I have to decide now."

Pav gestured with his phone. "I can reach my father now. Don't know that I'll be able to do that for another ten hours."

"What would you do?"

Pav closed his eyes. Even thinking about this was obviously painful for him, too. "He's Hindu . . ."

"Then have him cremated," Rachel said, surprised that her voice even functioned.

Pav nodded and was about to step away, but she caught his arm. "The rest of it," she said. "What is the plan? Or what was it?"

"Refuel, reload."

"Then?"

"Onward."

"Where? Can this thing fly as far as North America?"

"No."

"Then . . ."

"We stop at Guam, then Hawaii."

Rachel felt sick at the thought, though she wasn't sure if it was the number of stops or just the sheer danger and complexity of the job facing her.

"And this is all arranged and paid for?"

"So far." Pav could see the fear and fatigue. He wrapped his arms around her. "We've got to trust these people. And look, they got us this far."

"How do we know there aren't Reiver soldiers waiting right outside?" She nodded toward the guards at the perimeter. "They seem to think so. . . ."

Pav smiled. "Well, there's only one way to find out."

Darwin was a full-sized city, which meant that its airport was fairly large, with a glittering tower and main terminal . . . and a distant, bustling cargo terminal where the *Adventure* crew's plane had pulled in. Fortunately, it was the middle of the night. Nevertheless, there were still aircraft pulling into the terminal and crews preparing to load or unload them.

Seeing the activity, Rachel said to Pav, "We can't let Zeds out."

"He knows."

"Does he need anything—?"

Pav was smiling. "You forget who you're dealing with, lady. I assigned Yahvi to get water and whatever else he needs for the moment. Right now he's operating on his suit, and we got it tanked up before we left Yelahanka."

"Poor thing. It's like he's a prisoner."

"Are we that much better off?"

Rachel laughed. They weren't. Edgely had asked them to remain within one hangar in Darwin's cargo terminal. "There are bathrooms," he said, "and a bit of a buffet upstairs."

Sanitary facilities and food—that was what Rachel's life was reduced to. It reminded her of the things her father had told her about the realities of spaceflight. "Boredom and repetitious tasks," he said. "And an hour of exercise every day, whether you think you need it or not. What you wind up thinking about is what's next on your meal schedule, and how long is it going to take you to operate the zero-g toilet."

Well, in a way, this trip to Earth was a form of space exploration.

"Speaking of which," Rachel said. She didn't need a bathroom as much as she needed a moment of privacy.

"Go," Pav said.

"What about you?"

He tapped the side of his head. "Going to try to raise Keanu. They need to know about Sanjay."

"From here?" One of the reasons Rachel had resisted leaving *Adventure* was the likely loss of communications with Keanu. Not that they'd been great or even good.

"You never know. It's worth a try."

She emerged from the bathroom to find Edgar Chang and Tea waiting for her. "Edgely has something important to show us."

The high-school-teacher-slash-astronomer had commandeered an office on the second floor of the hangar building. From the pictures on the walls—cargo aircraft going back to the last century—and models of same on the desk, the place belonged to a veteran pilot. Edgely gently removed the models to clear the desk for his datapad.

Pav, Tea, and Xavier joined them. "Where's Yahvi?" Rachel said.

"Ferrying some interesting food-type thing to Zeds," Tea said.

"Here we go then." Edgely had an image on the notepad. "You will recall," he said, sounding and acting every centimeter the secondary school lecturer, "Mr. Chang told you that there were satellites that the Aggregates mistakenly thought to be dead.

"Actually, there were quite a few of them. When your Reivers began showing themselves twenty years back, some operators turned their birds off—or, rather, pretended to. So the human race does have a few overhead assets, if you know whom to ask.

"The trick is, no one has built or launched any new ones in almost twenty years. Maneuvering fuel runs out and solar panels degrade. Satellites don't last forever. And the low-altitude birds, which are the most useful for taking pictures, are subject to atmospheric drag."

"How do you know all this?" Rachel said. Her suspicions, never totally put to rest, were now up and demanding attention.

"Oh, Kettering tracks them," Edgely said. "That's really how the group started . . . English schoolboys were tracking secret Soviet rocket launches back in the 1960s. Some of them grew up and kept up with their hobby.

"The teacher I mentioned, Mr. Hall? He was a junior member, and he later emigrated to Australia and became a teacher in Alice Springs, which is where I grew up." He laughed a little too loudly. "It was so perfectly appropriate!"

"Why?" Pav said.

"Alice Springs was home to a big American satellite downlink station. Just outside town there was a big base, all fenced off, with these giant golf-ball-shaped domes. I mean, even if you had no interest in space and astronomy, you would still be curious!

"I think, in fact, that Mr. Hall had originally come to Alice Springs to work at the facility—lost his job, I guess, and wound up teaching me and a few others at Centralian about satellites and telescopes and . . ." He suddenly stopped. "This is boring and off the subject."

"A little," Rachel said. But she had enjoyed hearing it, because it went a long way to making her feel better about trusting Edgely.

"Er, let's just say I wouldn't have found Keanu without Mr. Hall's help. And I sure wouldn't have been able to get hold of this recon imagery."

He showed his datapad, which displayed a satellite image of a desert landscape.

"Where is this?" Pav said.

"And more to the point," Rachel said. "What?"

"You're looking at southern Utah and northern Arizona, Free Nation U.S. That facility is what the Aggregates and their human allies call Site A, though most everyone calls it the Ring."

It was easy to see why: A giant ring-shaped structure was obvious in the image, a blot on the desert landscape. It had been carved through several mountains and one plateau, too.

"How big is that thing?" Xavier said.

"The Ring itself is over ten kilometers in diameter," Edgely said.

"It appears to be some kind of high-speed particle accelerator," Chang said.

"A bit like the Large Hadron Collider?" Edgely offered.

"Larger—"

"And probably nastier," Tea said. "I've actually been to the LHC, and one big difference is that the real one's underground. So why is this aboveground?"

"I wasn't suggesting that it actually was a particle accelerator," Edgely said, a bit defensively. "The Aggregates or whatever you call them seem to know a lot more about physics than we do."

Chang tapped on a strange-looking structure in the middle of the Ring. "Is that a communications dish or telescope?"

Rachel peered closely at the fuzzy image. "If it were a dish, wouldn't it be inside a dome?" she said, remembering her father's work after Megan's death, how they had visited tracking sites and telescopes.

"They've also got some pretty standard buildings to go with this,"

Pav said. He indicated a collection of rooftops at the center of a couple of roads and rail lines. It was off to one side of the Ring structure. "And a weird-looking mound—"

"Aggregate habitation," Edgely said.

Pav grunted with disgust. "And serious power lines, coming from the south and the west."

"Las Vegas and Phoenix," Edgely said. "We knew there were nuke plants in both places, before the Aggregates. No reason to think they've shut them down since."

"And what is all that?" Rachel said. She indicated what appeared to be fields of rectangular lumps arrayed to the north and east of the Ring, on flat ground.

"Let me," Chang said. He zoomed the picture in. The lumps resolved into vehicles that looked as though they were armored, with rounded turrets and protruding cannon barrels. Some displayed coils, others screens. All of them looked intimidating.

"Any idea what those are?" Rachel said.

"Those look like tanks," Pav said, surprising his wife. "Armored personnel carriers."

"That's what my people think, too," Chang said.

"Why the hell," Tea said, speaking for Rachel and everyone in the office, "would the Aggregates be assembling this . . . invasion force out in the middle of nowhere?"

"Clearly it is associated with the Ring," Chang said.

"Obviously," Tea snapped. Rachel could see that the former astronaut was in her element, dealing with technology and military matters with men who were slow to accept her expertise. *Go, girl.* "I mean, I look at this Ring and think particle beam weapon, some kind of big fricking ray gun."

The fine hairs on Rachel's back tingled. What would be the likely target for a giant Reiver ray gun? It had to be Keanu. The thought was so terrifying and appalling that she couldn't say it out loud.

"But what's not obvious is how that Ring becomes some kind of force multiplier."

No one could offer an explanation.

"I don't think we're going to figure this thing out here," she said. She was hoping they hadn't.

She followed Pav out onto the tarmac. The air was thick, muggy, cool. In other circumstances, she would have enjoyed touring Darwin. For that matter, she would have enjoyed seeing some of Bangalore. Anything beyond the confines of Yelahanka Air Base.

"Were you able to connect with Keanu?"

Pav shook his head. "I think I got a link. You know that weird feeling you get behind your ear? So I transmitted the information—Sanjay, where we are now."

That alarmed Rachel, and Pav noticed. "Nothing more, I promise. I got no response, but there's some chance the message got through."

"Only a small one." She felt agitated and unsure. "We need to tell them about this Ring thing as soon as we can. And before we can do that with any confidence—" She turned, spotted her quarry heading for the aircraft. "Xavier!"

The rotund one detoured toward her. He still looked ashen and dazed, which made Rachel feel a bit worse about what she had to tell him. "We need the transmitter."

"I know. If we would come to rest for more than an hour I might be able to do something—"

"Why can't you work on the plane?"

That stumped him. He turned to look at the vehicle. "Well, it's not stable . . ."

"Come on, even with the bumps we took going around storms, most of the flight was like glass," Rachel said. "Are you telling me you can't get anything done in three or four hours?"

Xavier blinked. "I'm not telling you anything like that. I just didn't know how . . . dire this was."

"It's totally fucking dire. Please, please, please build that transmitter as soon as possible. Even if you only get some of it done on the plane, we'll hold at our next stop to get it running."

"Wait," Xavier said. "The real problem is . . . well, power."

"Where did we get it when all this started on Keanu?"

"From Keanu itself, the whole system. They were tapping into it inside the Temple."

"I have an idea," Pav said. He gestured to Xavier. "Let's talk to Edgely and the pilots."

To Rachel he said, "You should probably find Yahvi and get aboard."

Has anyone heard from Colin?

    As near as I can tell, he's been dark for seventy hours—this from a guy who can't take a breath without posting somewhere, and now that Keanu folks are back? Is something up? Is he all right? Someone tell us!

POSTER ZIRCONX, KETTERING GROUP,
TUESDAY, APRIL 17, 2040

WHIT

If not for the changed landscape outside his window—or just the fact that he *had* a window—Whit Murray could have believed he was still working in Las Vegas. There were the same cubicles, the same lighting, the same workstations.

Even the people looked the same. Most were in their early twenties, with a few outliers who might be Dehm's age, or Whit's. There were probably twenty in the place.

That number didn't include the half dozen THE supervisors, two trios this time—including Counselors Kate, Margot, and Hans, who, along with their fellow monitors, patrolled the lab like herding dogs, silent and still until some worker stretched or showed physical stress of some kind.

Then one of them would swoop . . . gently, it must be said. Even supportively. "Is there a problem? Are you in discomfort? Is a command unclear? Is the task too challenging?"

Whit knew because he had been the subject of THE "support" several times in his previous posting, though there THE counselors had tended to be more gruff and impatient.

Here, though, they were all about helping you do the work, it seemed.

Maybe it was because they were *all*—field modelers and THE action teamsters—new here.

Or maybe it was due to the critical nature of the work.

What made the current level of THE monitoring slightly creepier and more intrusive was that they had three workstations dedicated to them, meaning that any THE agent could sit down and call up a record of every keystroke a modeler made. Whit had had experienced teachers and others checking his work; this was far worse.

"Hello, Whit."

He looked up to see Counselor Kate, the slim redhead from the trio that had "recruited" him in Las Vegas. Still wearing her standard THE uniform, minus the jacket, she looked relaxed, indecently healthy and happy. She lowered herself to a stand that Whit, a longtime baseball player, always called "on-deck circle": one knee up, one on the floor.

Arm on the back of Whit's chair. "How do you like the work so far? The facility?"

"The place is fine." He was able to be truthful; his living quarters were bigger and nicer than where he had lived at Nellis. He wasn't in a bunk bed, for one thing, and he shared his room with only three young men, down from seven.

"But . . ." Kate was offering him an opening.

The only thing lacking so far was free communication, and Whit's experience with THE encouraged him to raise it: "I wish I could talk to my mother."

Kate was all sympathy. "We told her Friday night that you had been called away on a special assignment, and that you would be in touch . . . Tuesday! Right after your shift today." Her whole chirpy manner suggested that this was a wonderful coincidence. Whit also knew that if he hadn't said anything, it wouldn't be happening.

Here came the hand on his shoulder. "Anything else?"

Whit pushed back. Maybe it was exposure to Dehm, maybe it was a sense that time was short and that people with his skills were rare. He might have a tiny bit of leverage.

"I would be more productive if I knew what I was working on."

"You're working on modeling electromagnetic fields. Very, very large and powerful ones. Me, too, by the way." She nodded toward her cubicle.

"I knew that," he said. "But I don't know *why*. Or what for."

Counselor Kate seemed to process this. Whit expected to see her glance toward Counselor Hans or Margot or one of the other three for permission, but she kept her eyes focused on him as she said, "Well, then, ask me."

"We're creating what appears to be a giant cone—or ring—of energy, out here in the middle of nowhere."

"Correct. We can't be messing around with that kind of energy too close to population centers."

"I understand that. I just don't see the use of this energy cone." He decided to press his luck. "Is it a weapon?"

Counselor Kate didn't hesitate. "No, you have my word on that. And, since you have no special reason to trust me, look at this." This time she did glance at Counselor Margot. Apparently having received permission, she called up a new schematic on her screen. It showed a dozen beams of some kind emanating from a projector at the center of the ring. The beams hit the ring, which then projected a gauzy cone into the sky.

Counselor Kate tapped on her mouse pad, pointing the cone in different directions. Apparently it could even be aimed parallel to the Earth's surface. Having some idea of the energies involved, Whit hoped he would never find the cone aimed at him.

"Cool," he said, trying not to be sarcastic. "What does the cone do besides make a pretty shape?"

"It literally bends space."

"Okay," he said, not entirely sure that he understood that—or accepted it.

"The ring accelerates subatomic particles to hypervelocities. When they collide with certain other particles, a . . . distortion is created. A wave of particles."

"Sounds very quantum."

Kate nodded so slightly that it was impossible to know whether she agreed or thought he was teasing her. "This . . . wavicle"—she smiled, pleased with her coinage—"somehow compresses or distorts the structure of space. Think of it as taking two ends of a flat tablecloth and bringing them together. You still have all the fabric, but you've connected the ends." She smiled broadly now, pleased that she remembered an important lesson.

"And once we've made this connection?"

"Oh, objects can move from one end to the other without taking the long way around."

Whit smiled. "We're back to why."

"One possibility is to send material from one world to another without using spaceships."

"What, it just opens a door in the universe?"

"That would be a simplistic and, uh, incomplete way of describing it."

"I bet. Considering how power drops off the farther you get from the generator . . . "

"If you're picturing some cone of empty space stretching across the galaxy, don't. The cone is only effective to a distance of several thousand kilometers. It creates . . . and here I'm using English-language terms for concepts that are not only mathematical, but Aggregate math. It creates a . . . well, a transition."

"That isn't remotely helpful," Whit said.

"It's the best I can do. I can tell you that more than a thousand Aggregate cells are currently mapping the transition."

"How can you speak about mapping something when it's all theory?"

Now Counselor Kate's smile, formerly warm and helpful, became faintly indulgent, as if she had exhausted her patience. "It's a theory that the Aggregates have been . . . pondering for five thousand years."

"Let me get this straight," he said. As he tried to shape his feelings into words, he couldn't help seeing the wide eyes of his fellow field-modelers. Their thoughts were clear: *Better him than us.* "This ring or cone causes some kind of transition or disruption in space so large that you could send something solid through it?" He had read about experiments, pre-Aggregate days, that postulated the superluminal—faster than light speed—transfer of information.

But *objects? Living things?* Not according to the physics he'd studied.

Counselor Kate killed the image. She was suddenly more serious, less like someone trying to sell soap or jewelry. "I'm not saying that is the purpose. It's one of several theoretical possibilities."

Whit stared at her. He suspected that any further questions might elevate him to a suspect category, but what the hell: "What is that countdown clock?"

"It's pointing us all toward what we call 'First Light,' which is an all-up test, and 'Fire Light,' which is the time when the whole cone is ready to go online."

"'First Light' is only five days from now!"

"Yes. The whole project was accelerated in the past few months." She smiled brightly. "It's why you and the others were transferred from your other jobs."

"So there's no time to waste."

"Very perceptive, Mr. Murray."

When he was allowed to step out for lunch, Whit found Randall Dehm already sitting on top of a lunch table in the sun, dark glasses on his face, the remains of a sandwich on the table next to him. "Join me."

"You've already eaten."

He slid off the tabletop. "I can eat more."

And, as Whit ordered a wrap and a drink, Dehm did the same. "Walk with me."

"I only have fifteen minutes."

"Then eat as you walk."

Dehm led him to the edge of the platform, where a railing separated them from a drop of ten stories. "What do you see out there?"

Whit squinted. In the foreground were other buildings, including his residence. The usual electrical and environmental support required for a desert facility. One thing immediately struck Whit as odd: Site A wasn't more than five years old, yet everything looked as though it was falling apart. There were bricks missing from walls, various bits of weatherstripping and UV protection already peeling from windows, walls that had never been painted and looked as though they never would be.

Had the Aggregates gone cheap on Site A? "I see a big bunch of rundown buildings."

"Well, that's because no one expects this place to be permanent," Dehm said. "But beyond that."

Whit blinked. What he could see was a vast open space that seemed to be filled with dun-colored vehicles in a variety of shapes and sizes. It reminded him of the one remaining automobile lot in Vegas, Auto Land, where he used to see row upon row of nearly identical silvery vehicles.

"This project has created a lot of work for some people. Plants down in Oklahoma and Texas, I hear. Can you imagine building all these things with Aggregates looking over their shoulders? No wonder there's been no money to build a fucking bridge in this country for the past few years."

"How do *you* know all this stuff?"

"Everybody who's been here a few months knows the same thing."

"But why are you telling me? Charity?"

Dehm rubbed his face. "Maybe I just like to talk. Show off."

"Maybe you're setting me up as a security risk."

Dehm laughed. "I'm not that powerful." He jerked his head toward the interior of the building. "If you were a risk, the lovely Counselor Kate wouldn't have been talking to you."

"Then I just don't understand—"

"They're trying to keep you *motivated*, man. You realize you were the top of your field."

"I realize no such thing."

"Well, get used to it, while you can. When they moved the clock forward and we had to add staff, they searched outside the college pool for smart folks who were your age or younger. Your test scores and work evals showed that you were ninety-ninth percentile. I'm not saying there's no one else in Free Nation U.S. who isn't as good or as fast . . . I'm just saying you were a number one draft choice."

"And everyone thinks I'll work better if I know what I'm working on?"

"Well, I do. And so, apparently, does THE."

"But you're not them."

"No."

"Which takes me back to—"

Dehm extended his arms as if he planned to launch himself off this high building like an eagle. Then he turned. "I don't trust this project," he said. "I don't think it's good for Americans, and I'm pretty damn sure it's going to be bad for whoever is on the receiving end of it.

"But I can't shut it down! And thanks to my own personality traits—I happen to be one of those people who will follow orders pretty blindly without question—I am happiest when things get done.

"So I want this done, over with, complete. So I can go back to California."

He plucked a coin out of Whit's ear. "So you know what I know. Can you please just push this project to the finish line?"

"As soon as I finish my lunch."

Dehm laughed, then walked away.

Whit had actually lost interest in his lunch. Because the sight of all those war machines made him think not about the assembly plants, but about the mines and pits where this raw material had been found. Or the forges or toxic fabrication plants where it had been transformed into suitable material.

His father had been sentenced to one of those places for daring to speak his mind.

However important that was, it was history now, a side issue. Because Whit Murray had put two and two and two-squared together. (After all, he had just received two indications that his calculating skills were superior.) Take this quantum ring and cone opening a "portal" in space, and add this army of badass machines, and you could only come up with one purpose:

The Aggregates were going to invade someone.

The only remaining question was . . . who?

Day Five

TUESDAY, APRIL 17, 2040

Ever since the arrival of the Aggregates, we have assumed that their presence was an invasion, a hostile takeover of an independent nation, a blot
on the Constitution, a betrayal of our Founding Fathers—fill in the blank
with your standard phrase.

Thousands have died in the service of this belief, or call it a myth. Here
we are twenty years later, with unemployment at record lows, student test
scores at record highs, no reported racial or ethnic conflicts, and the
Cubs finally winning a World Series.

Can anyone say "Utopia"?

Yes, there are still problems: The Free Nation coalition faces threats
from without (though it appears we are on the verge of some kind of reso-
lution) . . . and Keanu rises in our night sky, its purpose unknown.

But it seems to me that we all need to step back from our previous
positions and ask ourselves if the Aggregates haven't been a good thing
rather than evil? BLOGGER MINNESOTA SLIM, NEWSNIGHT&DAY.COM

Who wrote this? Some Aggregate? You are a traitor to the human race.

EXCHANGE POSTED 0811 EDT 17 APRIL 2040
EXCHANGE DELETED 0812 EDT 17 APRIL 2040

XAVIER

Fortunately, the small proteus printer did not require a large amount of
energy. Working with the pilots, Pav and Chang had managed to
scrounge up four batteries for electric vehicles.

It was up to Xavier to get the power from the batteries to the printer, which involved a bit of old-fashioned baring and bending of wires.

But before the plane was two hours out of Darwin, Xavier had managed to get the printer powered up. At which point the real work would begin.

Rachel and Pav had dedicated the entire aft half of the cabin to him.

Zeds helped, though not in a way Xavier would have predicted. The Sentry possessed above-average skill with the proteus and could, in an emergency, have taken over from Xavier in the fabrication of the transmitter.

For the first hours of the flight to Guam, however, the Sentry provided pure muscle, stabilizing the small, light basic printer on its work "bench," which was actually a pair of hastily sawed boards stretched across a row of seats.

It turned out to be very helpful, because the climb out of Darwin and over the Arafura Sea, and especially crossing Papua New Guinea, was moderately bumpy . . . not enough to have bothered Xavier much had he been strapped in his seat, but vastly annoying when it came to creating connections for wires in order to power up the printer.

The bumpiness was even more destructive once Xavier and Zeds completed the wiring and fired up the printer, because then their job was to feed wads of Substance K into it, removing components for assembly after several minutes of fabrication.

"Fucking goo," Xavier muttered more than once, each time earning a bizarre titter of some kind from Zeds. (Apparently the Sentry was amused by human profanity, or at least Xavier's use of same.)

"How's it going back here?" Xavier looked up, four hours into the flight, to find Rachel holding out a beverage in a bottle and a sandwich. Behind her Yahvi had refreshments for Zeds. As Xavier stood up and stretched—a painful maneuver that made him wonder just how long he had been frozen in that awkward praying position—Yahvi slid past him to sit next to the Sentry. Xavier envied her ease with the giant alien. Although Xavier was friendly with Zeds, he was still surprised and occasionally shocked by the Sentry's actions.

Maybe you have to grow up with them, he thought. *Like a dog raised with a cat.* But animals didn't always get along, no matter how you raised them. People were even worse; true, the HBs seemed to be a relatively peaceful bunch . . . mainly because they shared everything. "Everyone is equally poor," as Harley Drake liked to say. Not so the citizens of New Orleans; Houston, Texas; and the formerly Free Nation U.S., in Xavier's experience.

And since humans were always ripping on each other, trying to steal from or kill each other . . . how did anyone expect humans and *aliens* to get along?

"So," Xavier said to Rachel, "Guam."

"I know no more about it than you do."

"The air force had a base there, as I recall," Xavier said. "I wonder if the Free Nations still own it."

"Good question," Rachel said. Her voice betrayed her worry. "Mr. Chang?" The ancient agent worked his way back from the front of the cabin. "I know you and Mr. Edgely and your team have been very careful in arranging our trip, so just reassure me: We aren't flying into an airport controlled by the Aggregates."

Before Chang could answer, Edgely joined them. "Ah, that's difficult to say."

"Try," Rachel said. Now Tea was turning toward them, listening from her seat. Pav, too.

"Guam is allied with Free Nation U.S.," Chang said. "We are sure we can land, refuel, and take off without encountering their customs—"

"And our next stop is Hawaii, which is *definitely* part of Free Nation U.S."

"Wait a minute, we're being exposed to the Aggregates twice?"

"It's geography," Chang said. "We don't have access to an aircraft that can fly the Pacific nonstop. Even if we did, we would have been tracked and detected. Going small, as we have, with the transponder turned off, there are only a few places you can refuel. All of them have some interaction with Free Nation U.S." He blinked. "It would have been possible to take passage on a containership, but that would have required weeks. You wanted to get to Mexico as fast as possible; this is the optimum route."

"It's so risky!" Rachel said, sounding shrill—which was unusual for her. Which made Xavier even more uneasy . . . If Rachel was freaking out, what should the rest of the team be feeling?

"Yes," Chang said. "We could all be arrested. We could all wind up in some Aggregate prison somewhere—"

"Or worse," Edgely said, with a nervous giggle that made Xavier even more uncomfortable.

Chang stepped close to Rachel and put his hand on her arm. "This is what I always tell myself whenever I'm on a plane and the weather is bad or the flight is rough—"

"You mean, like this one?" Rachel said. There was no humor in her voice.

"Yes," Chang said, persisting. "I tell myself that the pilot wants to live, too."

Chang pointed at Edgely. "He's in this, I'm in this, we're all sharing the risk."

Rachel took a step forward and gave Chang a brief hug. If she said something, Xavier couldn't hear it. But it seemed to defuse things. Rachel went forward with Tea. Yahvi joined them, and even Zeds, his giant form forcing the Sentry to move down the aisle crabwise.

Xavier was alone with Chang. As he kept an eye on the proteus, still slowly sucking in Substance K through a tube, then excreting pieces of the transmitter, Xavier said, "So you guys have made this happen by throwing around a lot of money."

"Every penny the rights earned," Chang said.

"How many pennies are we talking? It can't be a secret, right?"

Chang blinked; he seemed to be performing calculations. "For a package that included an hour exclusive live interview, personal stories both broadcast and print, pictures, a future book . . . twenty million Hong Kong dollars. I don't know how many pennies that is; I'm a producer, not an accountant."

"Is that a lot?" Xavier said. "Remember, I last dealt with U.S. dollars around 2019, when a new car cost, say, twenty thousand dollars. Not that I could ever afford one."

"Currencies were seriously depressed by the Aggregate arrival and the collapse of the world's economies. The fee the big companies paid to your group is the equivalent of fifty million U.S. dollars of your time, possibly more."

Xavier couldn't imagine a figure like that—hell, he had trouble picturing one thousand dollars. How big a wad would fifty million be? "I bet it was tricky to actually collect it—"

"You have no idea."

"And then move it around in secret."

Before Chang could respond, the proteus made a coughing sound, then stopped: No fluid moved in, and the piece of material stopped before it could fully emerge.

A foul smell filled the cabin.

"What the fucking hell—?"

"Back to the drawing board, I see."

Xavier was torn between wanting to punch Chang, just for attitude and possibly distracting him, and wanting to run away. Not that it was possible to leave the plane.

It was just that Xavier had never known a proteus to *fail*.

And he was afraid that when it did, the next event would be spectacular and deadly.

He examined the unit, which was the size of an old-fashioned desktop computer with screen. Nothing appeared to be wrong; it had just stopped working.

But it was emitting wisps of smoke.

Xavier glanced at the pieces of the transmitter. Eleven were required; he had nine.

"How long to Guam?" he said to Chang.

"Four hours. Are we in danger?"

Xavier wasn't sure, and even if he had been, he was not going to let Chang know. "Tell the pilot to *fly faster*."

Of all the severe paradigm shifts attributable to the *Destiny-Brahma* encounters with Keanu—the proof of extraterrestrial life, the glimpse of a large galaxy-spanning conflict between two types of alien races, the demonstration of technologies sufficiently advanced from human experience to be totally magical—the one with the greatest impact and most far-ranging effects has been hard evidence that human personalities survive beyond death.

This single revelation, with the evidence of the four so-called Revenants, easily and unquestionably ranks as the most momentous in human history, displacing the discovery of fire or any other pretender to the throne. Entire religions—including those that have served as the most powerful and sustaining political entities in human history—have been founded on much less.

And yet . . . humanity has not been transformed by this knowledge. The established religions still exist, though some of their power and influence has been diminished.

One new movement—Transformational Human Evolution—has arisen, claiming to incorporate the Revenant concept in a new mode of ethics and actions.

But THE is still limited to Free Nation U.S. and a few allied countries. It is inextricably tied to the Aggregate aliens.

If only the human race had been free to truly explore the implications of the Keanu Revenants. But the arrival of the Aggregates has essentially frozen religious-moral inquiry even as it has brought political and technological evolution to a halt.

GERALD MCDOW, *INTRODUCTION TO STASIS:*
THE HUMAN RACE'S LOST LEGACY POST-2020,
CONTRACTED TO YALE UNIVERSITY PRESS, UNPUBLISHED

YAHVI

For Yahvi, the trip from Bangalore to Darwin had already eclipsed the flight from Keanu as the worst trip in her life.

But now she judged Darwin to Guam to be worse than the first two combined. It was not only bumpier, but when the proteus started spasming, it became terrifying. She decided that she did not like travel and that she would be better off at home in the habitat.

At least there she wouldn't be doing what she'd been doing for the past three hours, which was wondering how she was going to die. Would it be smoke inhalation? Or would the plane catch on fire, burning her and the others to death?

Or would it just dive into the ocean from an altitude of ten thousand meters? Yahvi knew enough about Earth history to know that all these things had happened to people—choking to death, burning in agony, smashing into the ocean at hundreds of kilometers an hour, breathing one second, the next . . . what? Blackness? Yahvi had fallen on her face once, and it was easy, she thought, to take that shock and pain and multiply it by a hundred or a thousand or infinity.

No, she couldn't. The horror was beyond her imagining.

And while she knew her grandmother and a handful of other humans had come back from being dead, they hadn't lived very long—and not very happily, either.

It had been several years since she had confronted this issue. The last time was when she was twelve—

Over the years, the HBs had transformed a small corner of the habitat into a human cemetery. Here, Yahvi knew, was where her grandmother Megan Doyle Stewart was buried, as well as a dozen HBs who had died in accidents or of various ailments since 2019, especially Daksha, the Bangalore engineer everyone loved. Also one of the yavaki, born with a life-limiting condition.

In keeping with Hindu traditions, there were almost no monuments . . . those that existed were small and handmade.

There were monuments to four humans who had perished, but whose remains were not recovered, among them Shane Weldon and Vikram Nayar, lost in space along with the prototype X-38 vehicle. . . . Also the Revenant Camilla and Zack Stewart, both of them vaporized in Keanu's core during the "restart."

Several animals had emerged from the Beehive in the early days. There had been cows (cherished by the Bangalores, ultimately butchered by the Houstons, which almost caused a war inside the habitat), and birds, and even a crocodile.

And also a dog named Cowboy, a Revenant, a long-lost pet belonging to Shane Weldon.

Cowboy had lived almost eighteen years in his second life, dying of old age just after Yahvi and her cohort hit the dangerous age of eleven.

The dog was buried in a glade at the opposite end of the habitat from the human cemetery . . . much closer to the Beehive.

Oh, the Beehive—it was the one place in the habitat children were forbidden to enter.

So, naturally, it was the first place Yahvi and her friends went when they began to roam the habitat freely.

It was Nick Barton-Menon who suggested the wicked task of digging up Cowboy.

"God, why?" Yahvi said.

"He wants to see what he looks like," Rook said.

"Use your imagination!" Yahvi said.

"Don't be a turd," Nick said, shoving Rook. "I know what it looks like. I want to try an experiment!"

"You're not an engineer," Yahvi said.

"No one's an engineer for this," Nick said.

"For what?"

"For doing what the Beehive is for," Nick said, smiling like a very bad young man. "To bring things back to life."

Yahvi wasn't at all sure this was a good idea in practical terms. She knew it wasn't a good idea in moral terms; her grandmother had become a Revenant. But only for a few tragic days.

"It was all the Architect's doing," Rachel had explained, the one time she discussed the matter with Yahvi. "We all think, now, that it was him, or Keanu, or both of them, trying to find a way to communicate with us."

"Seems cruel."

"I don't think they planned for the Revenants to die. I think the whole system was barely functioning."

Which, now that Yahvi thought about it, was a good reason not to go messing around with it.

She said as much to Nick.

Who had an answer, of course. "We aren't trying to revive a human being," he said. "Just a dog."

So, to Yahvi's disgust, the three of them, with the help of Ellen Walker-Shanti and Dulari Smith, used "borrowed" shovels and, after much difficulty, managed to uncover the shriveled, barely recognizable remains of Cowboy.

The sight was just sad, more soft bones than anything else. Some fur.

"Shane Weldon would kill us all if he saw this," Yahvi said.

"Then let's make sure he doesn't," Nick said.

Rook had been ordered to bring a tarp, equipment left over from the original HB recreational vehicle, half of which still occupied a place of honor not far from the Temple. "How the heck did you get this?" Yahvi asked. All of the original HB materials were treated like historical artifacts. Most were kept in a special exhibit inside the Temple.

Not all, apparently. "I swiped it from the RV," Rook said. "I figured we'd need something kind of rubbery." It was true that, given the limits on HB manufacturing, blankets were as rare as anything else. And there had been no reason for anyone to fabricate a rubberized sheet like this.

And when Nick actually moved the remains with his bare hands, Yahvi felt like throwing up.

Then Nick and Rook and Ellen, who was taller and stronger than any of them, raised the sheet bearing the dog's remains and began scuttling toward the Beehive, a couple of hundred meters distant.

"You two cover this over," Nick told Yahvi and Dulari. That didn't take long; the soil was light and loose. Of course, even scraping it all back into the grave left an obvious depression.

"This will fool no one," Yahvi said.

Dulari shrugged. She likely didn't care. Yahvi was sure she only came along because she had a crush on Nick.

Bringing up the rear, Yahvi and Dulari found that they had to act as lookouts, a post that required no orders or encouragement. Yahvi kept glancing back toward the Temple and the living area, wondering if some adult just happened to be checking on the girls' quarters.

Or if one of the other girls just happened to wake up and realize that three were missing.

This wasn't usually a huge problem; girls were frequently sneaking off to meet boys. Dulari, in fact, was one of the most active sneaks. But tonight . . . all it would take was one curious parent who decided to search toward the Beehive. Or, just as dangerously, happened to catch them coming back—

"Yahvi, come on!" It was Nick, furious with her for falling behind.

The others had carried their sad burden into the Beehive entrance, a cave mouth twice as tall as Yahvi and at least twice as wide as it was tall. It looked rocky, dirty, and moist, as if the evening mist-rains clung to it . . . or, more creepily, as if water or some other fluid were oozing out of it.

The whole area smelled, too.

Inside it was dark, except for a kind of yellowish glow from the many different-sized cells that lined the walls as high up as any of them could reach. All of the cells were roughly rectangular—"like coffins," Rachel had told her, which then prompted a discussion about what a coffin was—and all had been laid open, leaving dried-out shards of some kind of casing in their openings.

"Okay," Yahvi said, "we're here with the thing. Now what?"

Brows furrowed, as if considering a problem in math, Nick was surveying the walls of cells. "Find one that looks as though it might work."

"I think you'll be looking a long time," Rook dared to say. He rarely challenged Nick.

"And how will we know?" Ellen said.

"Look for one that seems . . . fresh."

"And I don't think you have any idea how these things worked," Yahvi told Nick.

"How would you know?" he snapped. "I've been talking to Jaidev for a whole year."

"Jaidev doesn't know everything," Yahvi said, though he was considered the smartest of all the HBs. She was a bit offended that Nick had overlooked her mother when making inquiries.

"Jaidev knows more than we do," Nick snapped. "And tells more than anyone else."

"Then why hasn't he tried this experiment?" Ellen said.

Nick ignored that, though Yahvi thought it an excellent question. She had a pretty good idea why no one had done much experimenting with the Beehive since it stopped working almost twenty years ago, after disgorging human Revenants and several dozen terrestrial animal Revenants: It was just too terrifying to imagine what life in the habitat would be like if those who died kept coming back!

Yet, here they were, five teens thinking they were smarter than the adults. Of course, Nick *was* smarter than most of them, possibly even Jaidev.

Which made this even more dangerous.

He had completed his survey. "Let's try this one," he said, indicating a cell toward the back of the Beehive, near the other exit, which had been blocked off by HBs in the past. (On the other side, they said, was vacuum: a tunnel leading to the surface of Keanu.) Its lowest point even with Yahvi's waist, the cell appeared large enough to hold a human being, which troubled Yahvi—what if this was the cell her grandmother had emerged from? It just seemed wrong, even more wrong than digging up Cowboy in the first place.

"You're picking that one because you can reach it," she said to Nick.

Nick shot her a look that, had his eyes been heat weapons, would have burned her to the ground.

But that didn't stop him. With Rook and Ellen's help, Nick raised the tarp containing the dog's remains to the cell, then dumped them inside. The whole process looked crude, as far from scientific as it was possible to get.

Yahvi kept stepping back, her heart pounding. Now was likely to be the time Rachel or Pav or some other adult walked in. What on earth would she say? She had no excuse. She would simply have to stand there and suffer the consequences . . . or possibly run.

Once the remains had been completely placed in the cell, they rolled up the tarp. (Yahvi wondered what Rook was going to do with it . . . she hoped he wouldn't just try to put it back where he found it.) "And now what do we do?" she said.

"Pray?" That was Dulari, with a typically inane suggestion. Yahvi remembered that Dulari's family was one of the few openly religious among the HBs.

"Not necessary," Nick said, regaining his normal confidence. "Jaidev said that the one amazing thing about the Revenant process is how it seemed autonomous, almost like magic. They figured out later that it was all Keanu's control systems starting and stopping it, after they'd retrieved whatever morphogenetic pattern they needed—"

"But how did they know to find whichever morpho-whatever pattern that was?" Rook asked that question, and it made Yahvi want to kiss him, not because she needed the answer; she just wanted to see Nick flounder.

"They never did figure that out," Nick said. "But given that their technology is probably ten thousand years more advanced than ours—"

At that instant, a shudder went through the Beehive. Yahvi and the others found themselves outside before they could complete a thought. Nothing magical about it; they were just so terrified they turned and ran.

Yahvi had never been brave enough to return to the Beehive.

But Nick had. The Cowboy-kidnappers had never been a group, but they surely avoided contact after their creepy adventure.

One day, however, several months before the *Adventure* launch, Yahvi had found Nick lurking around the Temple. She assumed he had just returned from a shift on the Substance K conveyor. "Are they working you too hard?" Yahvi said. She had endured her own first shifts on the conveyor and found the work incredibly tiring. And Nick, pale, even unsteady on his feet, seemed to have had it worse.

But he said, "No."

Yahvi wasn't the type to accept an answer that struck her as ridiculous. "You look like death."

"I guess I can tell you if I can tell anyone." Then he glanced around, as if afraid of being overheard. "I went back to the Beehive."

By that time Yahvi had tried to forget about the Beehive. She was angered by the reminder. "You asshole!"

Nick didn't notice. "It was gone, Yahvi."

"What?"

"The *dog*." Apparently Nick had made his way to the cell where the five of them had left Cowboy's remains. "The cell was empty!"

"So someone came along and dug him out of there, just like we dug him out of the ground."

"Maybe," Nick said. "But that cell looked . . . fresh, like it had worked again."

"What are you saying? When was this?"

"Two days ago. And what the hell do you think it means? There's a Revenant Cowboy running around!"

"And that's what you're doing? Looking for him?"

Nick nodded.

She had not wanted to hear more. She had not wanted to know anything about this.

She had run from Nick and not looked back . . . and did not talk to him again prior to *Adventure*'s launch.

She never heard of anyone seeing a dog in the habitat.

It was after the third—or thirtieth—bump that Yahvi said, "I want to go home."

They had been confined to their seats for more than an hour, ever since the problems in the back of the cabin with Xavier's machine, and the bad weather. Yahvi wasn't sure which had come first, though it seemed as though the sudden turbulence had damaged the proteus.

She was in her seat in the second row, on the left side of the cabin. Chang and Colin Edgely were in the first row, right side, hunched over their stupid datapads.

Pav sat to Yahvi's left, in the window seat. Rachel was across the aisle to her right. She said, "We'll be home soon enough."

"When?"

"A few weeks," her father said, "maybe less." Which only made Yahvi more angry; she was arguing with her *mother*.

"That's bullshit," she said.

"Don't swear at your father," Rachel said.

"Then bullshit to *you*."

Yahvi knew that would ignite her father, but Rachel was fast, holding up her hand and silencing Pav. "I'm going to say that that's fair," she said to Yahvi. "We brought you along on this. We knew it might be dangerous—"

The plane bumped again. The little bell that Yahvi had grown to loathe rang again, and the *Fasten seat belts* sign came on.

Yahvi could feel the plane descending. It went so fast that for a moment she could have believed she was back in *Adventure*! From Yahvi's aisle seat, it was difficult to see much through the windows, but it was all dark clouds. God! What were these people doing to her?

She turned to look at Rachel.

And what Yahvi saw on her mother's face made her anger vanish, to be replaced by total fear.

Rachel was afraid they could die!

And if *her mother* felt that way—

Yahvi did not want to die in this plane, in this stupid seat.

She began to undo her buckle.

Across the aisle, Rachel said, "Pav!"

A seat removed from Yahvi, her father grabbed her arm. "Stay where you are!"

But she was not going to stay here! She jerked her arm away from her father and lurched out of the seat, heading toward the rear of the plane. Surely that would be safer if they hit something . . . and maybe they would crash-land—

There was considerable noise behind her, Rachel speaking forcefully to Pav, Tea offering to help, none of them moving very quickly as Yahvi reached the middle of the cabin, where she had a clear view of Xavier in his seat, still struggling with his stupid proteus. It was no longer making smoke, thank goodness, but it was still in pieces, and with the plane bumping and diving, Xavier was doing very little good.

But he was at the back of the plane—

Yahvi felt herself lifted off her feet and pulled backward. For a frightening moment she thought it was the plane doing something awful.

Then she realized it was Zeds! The Sentry had grabbed her and pulled her into the seatless space where he had been strapped. Yahvi struggled but only long enough to establish that Zeds was going to hold on to her, and there was nothing she could do about it. He was, after all, forty percent taller and a hundred percent heavier.

And had twice as many arms.

None of this kept her from saying, "Let me go!"

"You shouldn't be out of your seat," he said.

"I'll go back."

"It's too dangerous to be moving."

She struggled again; nothing doing. Zeds was still in his e-suit, though he had shed his gloves. She felt as though she had been abducted by a humanoid machine of some kind . . . a child's toy. It hurt being pressed up against the straps and tools on the front of the suit.

Yahvi said as much.

"You won't be damaged," Zeds said. "Just inconvenienced."

"Mom!" she called. "Make him let me go!"

But Rachel didn't answer. It was probably because the plane started shuddering worse than at any previous time. Whether it was because she was not strapped down, or because circumstances were different, she had a sense of real forward motion now, mixed with a stomach-clenching rocking motion and even a bit of side-to-side.

She had heard Pav talk about roller coasters and seen imagery . . . *This must be what it's like,* she thought. *Only you don't die on a roller coaster.*

She must have made a noise—probably a whimper—because Zeds spoke again. "This is difficult, but not impossible. We are probably descending out of the storm."

"You don't know that."

With one of his free upper hands, Zeds pointed toward the window behind Yahvi. "I have been seeing more clear sky and fewer clouds."

But he still wouldn't let her go. So she tried another tack. "Aren't you afraid?" she said. "This is really not your world."

"My world is not my world," he said. Zeds often made joking comments; Yahvi realized, after a moment of confusion, that this was one of them.

It took her so long, in fact, that by the time she realized it, the airplane had stopped bumping and the seat belt sign was off.

And Xavier Toutant was saying, "I think I've got it now."

Day Six

WEDNESDAY, APRIL 18, 2040

NYC REPORTS PROGRESS ON LOWER MANHATTAN LEVEE

PRES GERRY TO VISIT MEXICO CITY RE BORDER ISSUES

SEC DEF: U.S. CONSIDERING MISSION TO KEANU

LILY MEDINA SEPARATED AFTER ONE WEEK! NEW
PERSONAL RECORD

PACIFIC STORMS DO NOT THREATEN CALIFORNIA

HEADLINES, *NATIONAL TIMES*,
7 P.M., WEDNESDAY, APRIL 18, 2040

CARBON-143

SITUATION: Midway through a standard workday, Aggregate Carbon-143 and her units were summarily ordered off the line and instructed to form up on the exit platform. The orders came from the highest branch of the information tree.

As one, each disengaged from her workstation, moved back, then rotated to the right before marching out.

Carbon-143 was curious about the value of the maneuver. According to the countdown to First Light, the program was running behind. Surely no information or somatic improvement session was more important than catching up!

As she and her sisters—to perpetuate the human usage—left the assembly and operations building, Carbon-143 noted that other Aggregates were leaving, too, as if the assembly were being abandoned. She scanned up and down her trees and across their branches for information on a possible mechanical malfunction or possible human attack, these being the only two causes that would seem to require such a drastic, formation-wide movement.

Then they received orders to proceed to the storage and staging area, the collection of newly arrived and outfitted vehicles that seemed to stretch to the far horizon.

NARRATIVE: As other formations joined up as they proceeded out of the assembly area, the number of Aggregates grew from 144 to 1,728. Carbon-143 realized that as a unit she was not authorized or programmed for emotions such as pride, but she found an obscure moment of satisfaction in being part of such an impressive team . . . marching in the bright sun with her sisters, if she were careless enough to use human-centric terms.

She found that having even a few seconds off the assembly line was a pleasant diversion—and there was another use of "emotion." She entertained the idea of informing number eleven in her line, or even the unit above them. But only for a few seconds. She did not believe there was any objective basis to suspect that her productivity had suffered. Indeed, in the daily tag-ups she was never ranked below the middle of her twelve.

She also wondered, even more briefly, how number eleven would react if she shared either of these ideas. So far their information exchanges had been purely factual. Eleven was, in fact, identical with Ten or another of the others in the element.

Carbon-143's third inappropriate thought was to wonder this: Suppose Eleven or Ten or Three had these same thoughts! It made sense. The Aggregates were identical at assembly. And while it was true that being a Twelve in a unit meant a slightly different range of experiences from a One, they were so minute as to be lost in the noise of other data.

Or so Carbon-143 had been taught. Perhaps this was untrue.

She was not prepared to test this theory, however.

ACTION: They arrived at a corner of the storage lot. As directed, Carbon-143 moved toward the twelfth vehicle in the first row and initiated contact. A schematic of the vehicle appeared in her internal screen.

DATA: The vehicle was known as an 11F732, which to Carbon-143 implied that there might be 731 other 11Fs. This particular model massed five thousand, two hundred kilograms. It was largely made of a titanium-based composite shell for durability. Its complement of weapons consisted of a 155-millimeter howitzer (the 732, the data showed, was based on an existing Free Nation U.S. Army model for simplicity and speed of design) as well as a device Carbon-143 only knew by name: a Model 3 Field Disruptor, which appeared to be a narrow rigid coil wrapped around a coppery rail mounted atop the cannon.

The interior of the 732 consisted of a electric engine with a generator for the Field Disruptor weapon as well as ammunition storage for the cannon.

There was room for a single Aggregate, with the appropriate navigational, communications, and weapons control interfaces.

The units were ordered inside the 732s for "fit checks," which Carbon-143 was happy to perform. If nothing else, this procedure was another stimulating diversion from her usual duties.

She wriggled through the topside hatch into the 732. It was not an easy fit, but Aggregates were flexible. Carbon-143 rearranged her left side limbs, flattening herself to asymmetry and improving the interfaces.

There was a delay. Some of the units and formations had to travel farther to reach their assigned vehicles. Carbon-143's data Net showed that some of those vehicles were either massively larger or substantially smaller than the 732, which required appropriate adjustments: several units bonding temporarily to control the larger vehicle, and some Aggregates forced to nearly disassemble themselves so they could make the proper interfaces.

The delay allowed Carbon-143 several minutes in which she could freely access the larger weapon system grid. Most of the information was purely logistical: numbers of vehicles (currently 2,011, with more arriving), plans for their movement to and through the Ring. She was fascinated to see how long it would take to transfer more than two thousand tracked vehicles through the Ring itself: ten hours optimum, twelve to fifteen likely.

There was still no easily accessible information on the ultimate destination for this army. Until this moment, Carbon-143 had not even thought of the vehicles as weapons aimed at targets. These tanks and tracked weapons carriers seemed well suited to attacks on a human armored force.

But looking at the vehicle data, she was no longer certain; some of the vehicles were amphibious or even capable of operating underwater. Others were capable of flight, or at least hopping maneuvers. Still others seemed designed to operate in a vacuum; they carried their own internal atmosphere supplies for weapons and operators. (Even though the Aggregates had machine origins, they still required oxygen and water.)

And the largest vehicles were actually intended to operate in space! They had propulsion and reaction control systems to go with weapons packages that replaced cannon with missiles in addition to the coiled disruptors.

She was forced to one obvious conclusion: This army might not be invading Earth, but some other world.

Carbon-143 wanted to download all of this but had insufficient memory space—or official access. So she continued to flick through different fields.

And somehow wound up down the tree that dealt with the Ring and its operations, specifically the section on First Light. Since that was her immediate mission, she dug into it.

The first thing that struck her was the mention of radiation to be released during First Light and the subsequent Fire Light—the actual launch of the army.

The figures were astonishing: The longer the Ring operated, putting out energy, the steeper the increase in horrific side effects. The units of measurement were Aggregate standards and scaled through a variety of different dimensions, but Carbon-143 performed several quick conversions and came to this conclusion:

If the Ring operated for the optimum twelve hours, it might indeed successfully launch its two-thousand-plus vehicles at its target . . . while subjecting Free Nation U.S. to a level of thermal and ionizing radiation equal to ten thousand standard nuclear weapons.

The rest of the world would not be spared; even on the opposite side of the planet, the radiation would be sufficiently high to end all human life and most animal life.

Ignition of the Ring for Fire Light was the equivalent of crashing an asteroid into planet Earth.

Carbon-143 had noted the lack of rigor and substandard materials used in the construction of the Site A buildings, and now she knew why:

The Ring was not meant to be used repeatedly, it was designed to be used once . . . like a nuclear bomb.

And it would leave nothing but a scorched Earth behind.

This was not only tragic for humans . . . it was unhappy news for the Aggregates, too. Though they were more robust than humans and terrestrial animals, they were still vulnerable to destruction from exposure to high heat or radiation.

Carbon-143 could not replicate the reasoning or motivation for the construction of the Site A Ring. It did suggest that the entire formation of formations considered Earth to be, at best, a temporary jumping-off point . . . that its ultimate destination lay across time and space.

ANALYSIS: Aggregate Carbon-143 did not want to remain at Site A or indeed on planet Earth after First Light.

QUERY: Would she share this information with Dehm?

Yahvi Stewart-Radhakrishnan is a remarkable young woman.

It's not her looks, though they are striking, or her exotic heritage—she is the granddaughter of two pioneering astronauts, including India's first, General Taj Radhakrishnan.

It's that she's the first teenager to visit Earth.

That's right—Yahvi was born in the human habitat of the Near-Earth Object Keanu, arriving in Bangalore last week with her parents aboard the spaceship *Adventure*.

Today she is shopping in Shanghai. What has she learned from her week on Earth? "You've all got so much stuff here! And everything is so far away!"

The biggest difference between her friends on Keanu and the young women she's met so far? "Music and clothes! We really don't have them."

EXCLUSIVE WEB AND 'CAST FROM EDGAR CHANG

I never said any of this!   YAHVI TO EC

RACHEL

The landing on Guam—which took place late morning, local time, under a clear tropical sky—had been a trial. While the storm-related bounces and jounces had ended, the approach seemed to require a dozen different turns, some wrenching, all of them tedious.

Yahvi was still locked in Zeds's embrace; Rachel decided to leave her there, since the Sentry could protect her as well as any seat belt.

It was Tea who lost patience first. "Chang, tell us what the fuck we're doing. I hope this isn't evasive action because someone wants to shoot us down."

Hearing that, Rachel sat up straight. But Chang said, "Guam is safe to approach. Steve is just maneuvering to get us in a traffic pattern so we appear to have flown from China."

During the final minutes, Rachel twisted and looked back at Xavier, who had his head down in his makeshift lab. "What do you suppose he's doing?" she said to Pav.

"I think he's made a fresh start," he said.

"Here? I thought the power was too low or too intermittent or there were too many bumps—"

"Xavier is a resourceful guy. You know . . . he's the kind of guy where you lock all the doors and he still crawls in through the window."

When they had glided in and then finally come to a stop at another dismal cargo terminal, Rachel and Pav, Tea, Chang, Edgely, and especially Yahvi and Zeds were eager to get out of the plane.

Xavier chose to remain behind. "I need another hour," he said.

Pav was going to pursue the argument, but Rachel grabbed his arm. "Let him be," she said. "We need that transmitter."

The layover in Guam was much like the one in Darwin, except for daylight, the predominantly Asian Pacific staff, and the more decrepit nature of the buildings. "How long will we be on the ground?" Rachel asked Chang.

The agent already had his face in his datapad. When he raised it to answer, he was more vague than Rachel liked. "Longer than Darwin," he said. "You can eat, take showers."

"'Longer than Darwin' is fairly imprecise," Rachel said, unwilling to let Chang evade the question. "It doesn't take more than an hour to refuel, right?"

Chang and Edgely exchanged a look, which infuriated Rachel. "Goddammit," she said. "You two better tell me what's going on or we're going to have serious problems."

Her anger was fueled by fatigue, of course, but also frustration at being at the mercy of two people she didn't really know . . . on a world that was as alien to her as Mars or the Architect home world might be.

Fortunately, Edgely was always eager to share. "We're waiting on a second plane."

"To fly us?" Pav said.

"To fly in formation *with* us," Chang said.

"Why?" Rachel said.

Chang sighed. "We have almost no hope of entering Free Nation airspace undetected."

"I thought we were flying into Mexico!"

Edgely slipped into teacher mode, growing almost indecently enthusiastic. "Oh, we are! But we come close to Free Nation airspace. They will track us. As you already know, they have air-, land-, and sea-based military."

"The other plane is actually a decoy," Chang said.

Edgely placed his hands in front of him, palms down, right hand half a dozen centimeters above the left. "When we reach Free Nation's radar range, we will be flying one above the other, at different altitudes.

"The two planes will show as a single blip. As we get close enough to the western coast of North America to be tracked with some fidelity, our plane will descend below tracking altitude and divert into Mexico while the target plane will turn north and fly parallel to the California coast."

"Are you expecting it to be attacked?" Pav said.

"Yes," Chang said. "But the transponder will show that it's a Chinese commercial aircraft—it will be contacted and warned off, and will turn back."

"You must have found some brave people to fly that thing," Tea said.

"Expensive people," Chang said.

"But also brave," Edgely said. "They have a narrow fuel margin. They have to fly toward California long enough to draw all the tracking—"

"And targeting," Chang said.

"—but not so long that they exhaust their fuel. They have to turn around and head back to Hawaii. There's no place else for them to land."

"Meanwhile," Rachel said, "where are we?"

"On the ground in northern Mexico," Chang said.

You hope, Rachel thought. *And I hope so, too.*

Two hours later her spirits had improved. She had showered, eaten, and assured herself that her daughter was also fed and cheered up and that Zeds was as good as he could be.

Tea had managed to clean up, too. "I feel so shallow, but I really enjoyed that," she said. They were alone in a hallway on the second floor of the hangar building, where an executive had a fancy suite that included a private bath. Rachel had used it first, then gone for a bite with Pav while Tea took her turn. Now Tea regarded her. "So, how is all the shit you're dealing with?"

Rachel smiled. "There's no way back and nowhere to turn."

"All you can do is go forward with your eyes open and your head high."

"Even if it kills me."

Tea laughed. "I'm with you, Rachel. Right behind you maybe, so I don't catch the first bullet. But whatever happens, we're all in it, too."

"That's what bothers me," Rachel said. "I don't mind risking my life—"

"But you've got Pav and Yahvi—"

"And all the others." She blinked and just started crying. "I already lost Sanjay!"

"*You* didn't lose him," Tea said. "If the Reivers hadn't shot your ship, you wouldn't have had that rough landing. *They* killed him, not you."

"They injured him. But I left him to die. . . ."

"Oh, honey, I talked to Taj. Your poor Sanjay was dead the moment they took him out of your ship. You did what you had to do . . . you acted, you led. You got us out of there."

"To what? Being flown across the Pacific by people we don't know? Waiting for a decoy plane so we don't get blown out of the sky trying to invade America?"

Tea regarded her. "Take it from one of your team . . . you're doing great. Keep moving forward."

Tea's words did their magic: Rachel felt comforted, though she suspected her improved feeling might also be due to being clean, or possibly just her hearty lunch.

No matter the source, she would need all her strength. She desperately needed to connect with Keanu and Harley Drake, because key information needed to be sent . . . and decisions made.

Her first target was Xavier, who was proudly emerging from the plane as promised, almost two hours after landing. "Here's our transmitter," he said, holding out a misshapen gray box the size of a pillow as if it were the gift of the ages. Rachel wanted to laugh. Raised in the United States for the first fourteen years of her life, she thought machines should be like Apple products, smartly designed, symmetrical, polished . . . not the wacky lumps that passed for them on Keanu.

Xavier, who clearly had a more charitable view of these products, noted Rachel's resistance. "It works," he said. "I just tested it."

Given the size of the unit, they had to find her a table in a relatively private place in which to work. Then she had Xavier tell Pav she wanted to be left alone, a feeling that surprised her, since she was so reliant on him.

She was realizing that she needed to regroup, to run through her internal list of tasks. It was how she had functioned best as mayor, as some version of the "leader" Tea had cited—indeed, how she had functioned best as wife and mother.

Her biggest weakness was that she still relied on Harley Drake and Sasha Blaine, and on Jaidev and Zhao and Makali Pillay and so many others for not just support, but to be the mature ones, the better informed.

To be her parents. Rachel was sufficiently self-aware to know that she had never recovered from losing Megan, then Zack, along with her entire life on Earth, within two years.

She had disagreed with all of them at one time or another, or found them to be in error on one subject or another. Now, here on Guam, on her way to a terrifying Reiver Aggregate facility in the former United States . . . she tried not to feel panic, to wish for one of the adults to confidently guide her.

She reminded herself she was not twelve again, but thirty-four, older than the men who had worked in mission control during the Apollo program . . . older than soldiers, sailors, pilots . . . older than Jesus when he went to the cross.

So why didn't she feel more sure of herself?

Maybe no one did, not even generals or presidents or ship captains in the middle of storms.

None of it mattered, anyway. Unless Rachel surrendered the authority the others had granted her, giving up and telling Pav or Edgar Chang to make the decisions from this moment on . . . Tea's advice was the only one to follow.

Forward.

Xavier's transmitter worked beautifully. The moment Rachel switched it on, she heard Harley Drake's voice as clearly as if they were in adjacent rooms inside the Temple. "About time," Harley said. He was never one for idle chat. As long as Rachel had known Harley, it seemed that conversations rarely began, they just resumed.

They had a tremendous amount of catch-up to do, about the decoy trip out of Yelahanka, the flight to Darwin, the Chang-Edgely involvement . . . the nature of the Reiver Ring in the United States, and their plans for the ultimate assault on it.

Ultimately, their conversation lasted fifty minutes and left Rachel with a headache that affected her vision.

The most maddening aspect was the four-second lag between the time her words left Earth and were received on Keanu, and vice versa. Rachel had experienced it to some degree on the voyage from Keanu to Earth, but not like this. It turned what should have been a conversation into a series of statements.

Finally, she had been compelled to discuss the terrible thing that had happened to Sanjay. "We had gotten the message," Harley said. "We've already told the community and held a service."

Then Rachel had to admit that they had done nothing of the sort for their colleague . . . that she had abandoned him in the hospital at Yelahanka, that she had no idea what had happened with his body—

"Stop yourself," Harley told her. "You left him with Taj, and that's all you could do under the circumstances. I don't want you to beat yourself up about this any longer, is that clear?"

Rachel reluctantly told Harley that she would.

Then Harley said, "By the way, Dale is working in league with Zhao."

"I'm sure you know what you're doing," Rachel said, not feeling that way at all.

"We're watching him very carefully," Harley said. "And Sasha tells me we are about to lose you. . . ."

The signal ended abruptly, as the antenna on Keanu's surface rotated below the horizon as seen from the Pacific Ocean.

The exchange left her feeling better—at least Harley and the others knew Rachel's situation. It was up to them to execute their half of the operation, or rather their two thirds of it.

For the first time on her trip to Earth, Rachel began to feel as though she was the beneficiary of some decent luck.

They would need it. By returning to Earth orbit, she and the other leaders had essentially painted a big red target on the Near-Earth Object, bringing Keanu within range of some kind of Reiver planet-killer beam.

Rachel was turning toward Xavier, to thank him for the use of the communicator, when Edgely arrived.

"The second plane is on approach."

Greetings! Emerging from radio and other silence to say . . . all is well.

I've been traveling, seeing the sights, working on fulfilling a lifetime dream. (For those of you who have been following me for twenty years, you know what I mean.)

Which is all I can say here. "But soft, we are observed!"

Hoping for some news I can talk about soon!

COLIN EDGELY TO THE KETTERING GROUP,
APRIL 18, 2040

DALE

"What exactly do you know?"

Once he had penetrated the vesicle factory and been confronted by Zhao, Dale knew he could no longer escape. Zhao had closed and locked the exit from the habitat, even though Dale was fairly sure he could still find a way out.

But he didn't particularly want to. Something in his head—not the map, but some part of the connection with Keanu's controlling intelligence—told him that *this* was where he needed to be, and possibly that Zhao was the one human to meet.

The former spy had shed his Skyphoi environment suit and was busy checking on the odd-looking, lumpish proteus-created controls that operated a set of spray guns and other devices that were slowly but steadily building the vesicle. He was talking to Dale, but not concentrating on him.

"Shouldn't I be asking you?" Dale said.

Now Zhao turned away from his work to face him. "I realize you can't help being an ass, but please try. Surely you know that Harley told me you had resurfaced with some vague warnings."

"I wouldn't call them vague."

"And you still have the incredibly annoying habit of picking on a modifier and arguing about that instead of the substance of an entire sentence. Fine, to repeat while also expanding: What exactly do you know about the dangers to the *Adventure* crew?"

"That their approach had been detected and tracked, that some hostile force fired on them . . ." Dale trailed off, since Zhao kept nodding as if he already knew that much. Well, if he had talked to Harley, he did.

"Anything specific?"

Dale weighed his answer. During his trek from the human habitat, he had felt a growing certainty that Rachel and her team were in danger again. But in order to fully access the Keanu data banks, Dale needed to engage in his naked interface . . . and there had been no opportunity.

Nevertheless, earlier memories seemed to have grown clearer. "The Reivers have a big project that is about to go live. When they pull the trigger, a lot of humans are going to die."

"Did you tell Harley this?"

"No. It wasn't—"

"I should take you back to the habitat and lock you up so everyone can hear your big secrets. You did escape, correct?"

"Ask Harley. He kept insisting I wasn't a prisoner, or that if I was, it wasn't his decision."

"Oh, you were. And in a sense, are." Zhao smiled, never a happy look. "But then, so are we all."

Zhao nodded beyond Dale. He turned and saw half a dozen HBs approaching, two women among them, and one of them, amazingly, appeared to be Makali Pillay, the Aussie exobiologist who had shared Dale and Zack Stewart's long, weird trek across the surface of Keanu. They did not seem hostile; they didn't even seem to notice Dale, but rather fanned out to work on the vesicle. Zhao said. "To be honest, there's no point in locking you up. Things are moving too fast. We actually need some help."

"Doing what?"

"Getting this ready for launch."

"To Earth?"

"Well, it's not going to the fucking Moon!"

"But you already sent *Adventure* there!"

"And look how that's going! They're in everyone's crosshairs. I know it seems like we sent six people up against an entire planet, but come on, Dale. We're going after the Reivers, but not with *Adventure*."

He pointed to the giant, almost-complete vesicle. "With this."

Like all of the HBs, Dale Scott had arrived at Keanu in one of two vesicles . . . giant sample return craft launched by Keanu toward Earth.

There had been a third Object, which the Reivers had used twenty years ago to make their escape. Dale had never discovered how to fabricate another one; in the many areas of the Keanu library he had accessed, he had never even found a reference to the vesicles.

Which meant nothing more than that there was a vast amount of information about Keanu he had yet to learn.

It did bother him that somehow Zhao or Jaidev had managed the trick. It made him feel a bit less special.

But his momentary pique was tiny compared to the wonder of seeing a vesicle being not just fabricated but, in a way, grown. Simply learning how took hours, time in which Dale found himself tolerated if not actually welcomed.

"I can sort of see how you'd replicate the shell of this thing," Dale said to Zhao, joining the former spy at his workstation. "But how do you equip it for war against the Reivers?"

"The basic systems were already in the library," Zhao said, confirming that he had indeed accessed the system—which was news to Dale. "We've spent the last two years weaponizing it."

"What do you use against a whole planet?" A chilling thought occurred to him. "It's not a bomb, is it?" Dale didn't think Zhao would launch a planet-killing weapon, even making the giant assumption that he possessed such a device, since it would kill millions or billions of humans along with the target Reivers, but power did strange things to men, so . . .

"Nothing like that," Zhao said. "Even before we left Earth, bombs were no longer the weapon of choice, unless you were a terrorist. It's all chemical-biological or cyber."

"Like what we did to the Reivers before." The alien Aggregates had been exterminated in Keanu by a designer virus fabricated by Jaidev in the Temple laboratory.

"Exactly," Zhao said. "We assume the Reivers have evolved their defenses." He smiled. "But we've evolved, too. We have the option of going after not just their populations, but against their networks and ability to communicate." He pointed to the vesicle. "We've got half a dozen ways of attacking them.

"And, of course, we have stealth and surprise."

"While the Reivers are panting after Rachel's crew, you're going to hit them from behind."

"Assuming we ever get this fucking thing launched."

"What can I do?" The words were out of his mouth before he truly thought about them. *So much for your enlightened communion with Keanu,* he thought. Well, before becoming an astronaut, Dale Scott spent years as a military fighter pilot.

Maybe he just wanted to kill something again. Especially Reivers.

Or maybe this was all about working with people once more, even people who despised him.

More hours and another day passed, an intoxicating time for Dale in which he almost forgot to eat. His job was to monitor the extrusion of the shell material from three different hoses. Looking like foaming white goo, the smart-shape material quickly hardened and soon enclosed the entire vesicle.

The others on the team—none of them familiar to Dale from years past—largely dealt with the interior equipment, which they were assembling and collecting on the platform that encircled the vesicle. Which caused Dale to approach Makali and ask, "How do you get this stuff inside? Does the shell eventually develop hatches?"

She stared at him for a long moment, as if she didn't recognize him. She was certainly recognizable—clearly in her late forties now, with lines around her eyes and hair cropped like most of the HB women. But she had retained her athletic figure; in fact, she looked leaner and in better shape than Dale remembered. "You know, when I came in here, I said to myself, 'That looks like Dale Scott, but it can't be. Dale went walkabout a long time ago. . . .'"

"I'm back."

"To stay?"

Dale shrugged. "To help."

Makali had her arms crossed, a clear nonverbal sign that she was uneasy with him. Which was an unexpected posture for her—she had been so confident, in your face. Well, Dale had not only changed physically, he was a different person, too.

"In that case," she said, glancing toward Zhao, who merely nodded his approval of the exchange, "if you're going to help, you ought to have the answers.

"No hatches, no windows. The whole vesicle expands or contracts. The skin becomes so thin and permeable, you can push through it. Then it closes up again."

Dale remembered seeing the Bangalore vesicle rotating slowly after it thumped down . . . then expanding to gather in a hundred human beings along with a considerable amount of soil and even a couple of automobiles.

"I always wondered what propelled it."

"Well, it gets expelled from Keanu—"

"Like a bullet, I know," Dale said. "But both of those things took off from Earth—"

"We think it's the skin itself," Makali said. "As the whole thing spins, some of the material on the bottom begins to boil, using *boil* in a very crude sense. It turns into some kind of propellant." She smiled. "Why? Planning to take a hop to Earth and come back?"

Dale shrugged. It was just the engineering side of his mind.

But Makali's statement made him think: He could go with the invading force. He could return to Earth!

Before he could ponder those possibilities, there was some disturbance in the group surrounding Zhao.

It was Jaidev himself. He barely registered Dale's anomalous presence. "You need to see something," he told Zhao. "We all do, back in the habitat."

"But I'm busy here! I have a lot to do before we can launch."

"This may change everything," Jaidev said. "The Beehive is active again."

Day Seven

NIGHT SKY REPORT

The Moon is waxing, Venus getting closer to the Sun each passing night as is Mars, though in different parts of the sky.

Do I include Keanu in this? Tonight it's as close to the Moon as it's likely to be, and ought to be spectacular. (The shadows will be weird, I tell you that.)

But it all feels so temporary. Anybody have any idea whether Keanu is GOING TO STAY?

POSTER GILLAM, KETTERING GROUP,
APRIL 19, 2040

TAJ

"We've got a serious problem."

Taj was awakened by his phone, which was lying on his bed next to his pillow. This was not its usual overnight resting place, but given the threats facing Tea, Pav, Rachel, Yahvi, and the others, it was an obvious choice. Taj had lain down in an agitated state, fearing that he faced a restless night. But the clock proved that he had slept; being sixty-six and operating on perhaps four hours of rest in the past five days might have been a factor.

But he was asleep no longer. Short of breath, confused, he had forced himself to answer the phone and found Remilla on the line. It was just past five in the morning. Though Taj could sense that there was some light through the windows, it felt like three A.M. "Radhakrishnan," he said, military fashion.

"It's Melani," Remilla said, sounding just as exhausted as Taj felt, though she had enough energy to say, quickly, "This is not about Pav and his crew."

"Thank you." The ring tone alone had almost given him a heart attack. Taj had had no word from his son since their conversation about Sanjay a day and a half earlier. He had remained at the Yelahanka Air Base hospital long enough to oversee the transfer of Sanjay's body to Hebbai Electric Crematorium, which had been located by Melani Remilla—it happened to be the closest civilian facility.

Upon leaving Yelahanka, he was subject to a strange set of emotions—an odd and unearned nostalgia combined with a firm desire to never trod its grounds again.

Sanjay and the crematorium were the subjects of Remilla's call, which continued: "He is about to be taken out of our hands," she said.

"I didn't realize that ISRO managed dead bodies from outer space."

"The military has taken over."

"I'm military and no one has told me."

"That's my job. The army wants this whole matter resolved. With the crew out of the country, Bhat's remains are the only . . ."

"Loose end?" Of course. "What are they planning?"

"I think they plan to take the body."

"That makes no sense."

"Word is that someone, somewhere, wants it."

"The family is having a cremation later this morning."

"Even that isn't three days!"

Taj was not as religious as many of his colleagues—even though the events of twenty years ago had opened his eyes to the unknown mysteries of human existence—and certainly not devout Hindu.

But he knew the rites, and it was too soon for a cremation! "Why are you telling me?" he said. "Do you expect me to stop it?"

"I have no power," Remilla said. "I only discovered it by accident and thought you ought to know."

He thanked her, then painfully rolled out of bed and splashed some water on his face. He was famished, so he made a quick breakfast as he considered his options.

Attending to lifestyle matters in these strained circumstances reminded him of a typical morning aboard the International Space Station, where daily rituals were so important to an astronaut's mental as well as physical health. Today it gave him a moment to plan, even though, compared to a day in space, he was forced to improvise.

He and Tea had been renting an apartment not far from ISRO headquarters for the past six months, and had never truly moved in. Neither of them was a cook, either, so there was little food on hand. Taj would have preferred some idli cake, for example, or tea. Failing that, eggs and beans for an English breakfast.

What he found was coffee and some kind of granola cereal—Tea's usual fare. Given the circumstances, this would suffice.

His operational choices were equally limited. He had no military command, not even any subordinates. No power or might.

He had few allies. So much of his recent life had centered around Tea that he had neglected his contacts in the defense ministry . . . not that he had any role to play in their covert and often overt war against the Aggregates. He considered telephoning Kaushal but rejected that: The Yelahanka commander was either working for the plotters—or likely to be ineffectual anywhere outside the base.

And even if he had possessed a team that could be called upon, what was the takeaway, to use a phrase from his time with NASA? In success, did he end up with Sanjay's body in a hearse . . . with himself behind the wheel?

What he wanted, he concluded, was respect, for Sanjay Bhat, for the *Adventure* crew and his son and daughter-in-law and granddaughter.

He did have one weapon, however: his phone. Melani Remilla did have some information he did not. He glanced at the clock—5:20.

Taj reached the two-story Hebbai Electric Crematorium at 6:40, parking on a street a block behind the facility. He felt a bit foolish slinking past the loading dock at the rear of the building (with its curious smell of smoke and what he could only think of as cooked meat) while wearing his full dress uniform. But the need for precautions overrode his sense of dignity.

He had fallen asleep in his uniform, so his clothing had required a change, too. And there was nothing like a general's rank and medals to encourage cooperation with certain individuals.

He had unpacked his service pistol and was wearing it, though he did not expect to use it. (He hadn't fired it in years.)

The doors were still locked. The parking lot was empty.

He took up a position near the entrance where he could see without being automatically seen.

He had strategies for waiting. Breathing exercises. *Review steps taken, to be taken. Check equipment again.*

It reminded him of guard duty as a cadet, and the bonus this morning was the sight of a crescent Keanu low in the southern sky. The Moon was close to new this time of month and was no competition at the moment. Keanu's orbit was more inclined, and the NEO was not only farther away from Earth than the Moon, it trailed it by a hundred thousand kilometers, a figure that would change, of course, with every passing day. All of this caused Taj to wonder just how long Keanu would remain in orbit? Another week? A year? A century? He wished he had asked his son.

The door of the crematorium opened.

It was a young Hindu man—twenty at most—in T-shirt and jeans, clothing that was far too casual for a memorial worker. "I'm Ishat," he said, and offered little more. It was obvious he was unhappy about being roused out of bed.

"Call me General Radhakrishnan," Taj said, sweeping past him. "Are you prepared to conduct a cremation?"

"But we aren't open yet!" Ishat said.

"This is an emergency. It's why I telephoned the owner."

"He only told me to meet you, not to—"

Taj held up his hand, silencing Ishat. "I'm telling you what needs to be done, and you're going to do exactly as I say: Prepare the body of Sanjay Bhat for immediate cremation."

Ishat frowned but seemed willing to do as told. "It will take a few minutes."

"Don't start until I tell you," Taj said. "We're waiting for someone."

He returned to the front door, checking his watch. Almost seven. The army and its associates would be arriving within the hour—

A car appeared at the driveway entrance, moving slowly. Taj reflexively placed his hand on his holstered pistol as he watched the vehicle, an ancient electric Sierra, roll closer, then stop.

Kalyan Bhat emerged, looking both sad and bewildered. He was in his thirties, medium build, balding, dressed in a gray suit and tie, both donned in a hurry, to judge from the missed button and indifferent knot. "You would be General Radhakrishnan," he said.

"Mr. Bhat. I'm sorry that we have to meet under these circumstances."

"I remember your flights, sir. India's first astronaut. They made us feel proud."

Taj had heard this a number of times in his life and almost always corrected it: While he was the first citizen of India to command an indigenous spacecraft, the *Brahma*, and had made one earlier flight as well, an Indian astronaut had gone into space back in the 1980s with the Soviets.

Mr. Bhat was too young to remember that, of course. Taj merely nodded his thanks and guided the man into the facility, taking care to watch for additional vehicles. "Thank you for agreeing to come this morning on such short notice."

"This is a very strange situation."

"I understand."

"I was already in the city, hoping to see my brother . . . alive," he finished. "It was so hard to lose him like that." Then Kalyan shook his head, as if appalled at his own rudeness. "I'm sorry, you suffered the same way."

And I am in almost the same situation, he thought. "We can only endure," he said. Then he called. "Mr. Ishat? Would you lock this door for us, please?"

The ceremony was mercifully brief. Sanjay Bhat's body was already in its sheet; his brother declined to view it. "I prefer to remember him alive," he said. "As a young man, the smartest I've ever met."

"His death is a great loss," Taj said. "To my son's community and likely the world at large." He and Pav had spoken only briefly about Sanjay, but Taj had gotten the clear impression that the engineer was a rare talent, one that the humans on Keanu would require.

As would the Keanu humans hoping to accomplish their mission.

"Please tell me, General, why this haste? Why the unusual hour? My brother deserves better. I deserve an explanation."

Taj's innate reluctance to share secrets was enhanced by his need to protect Kalyan. He would have preferred to tell him nothing, especially since he could not be sure that Sanjay's body was about to be stolen. Nevertheless: "You know your brother returned to Earth in an alien spacecraft, correct? That his death was the result of hostile action?" Kalyan nodded. "There are parties who wouldn't offer your brother's remains the proper respect. This is the best alternative."

That seemed to satisfy him. The last prayers were said, by Kalyan and Taj, with Ishat the silent, sullen witness.

Then Sanjay's body was consigned to the flames.

Ishat went off to collect the ashes, leaving Taj and Kalyan alone and now uncomfortable. Before either of them could utter an awkward word, however, the door buzzed.

"Wait here," Taj instructed Kalyan.

Then he ran out to the reception area and glanced through the curtains.

There were now four new vehicles parked in front of the crematorium: two automobiles, an ambulance, and a bus. At the front door were Wing Commander Kaushal and a pair of civilians Taj did not recognize.

Waiting behind them were three members of THE in their distinctive uniforms. Taj wondered how they had managed to enter India, but that concern was quickly reduced to meaninglessness by the next sight:

A *dozen Reiver Aggregates* were emerging from the bus, forming up as one might expect.

Taj took one long moment to snap several images with his phone, then e-mailed them to an address he had created that morning, texting

Pav the same information, in the hopes that it would be retrievable when his son resumed contact.

The buzzer sounded again. Ishat appeared from the rear of the building, looking worried. "Stop right there," Taj ordered him.

"I have to answer the door," the young man said. He held up his phone. "I am getting orders!"

"Fine," Taj said, "but be prepared to be pushed aside. And before you do, count to ten."

"But—" The buzzer sounded again. Now there was pounding on the door, too.

"Ten!" Taj said. And not waiting for further debate, he ran back to Kalyan, taking the man by the arm. "Come with me."

Without knowing where he was going, Taj guided the man deeper into the facility, turning away from the actual crematorium itself and passing several offices.

"My car is out front!"

"So are some very bad people," Taj said. "My car is out back."

They passed up one door because it appeared to be alarmed—why alert the new arrivals to their exit? A second door, at the end of a hall, led to the loading dock Taj had passed on his way in.

He could hear noise from inside the crematorium—raised voices followed by the crash of equipment. Or so he hoped; he had no desire to see young Ishat injured.

"I do not have my brother's ashes," Kalyan said.

"I fear you are unlikely to get them."

Taj listened again; there were voices from people outside the crematorium, circling around it from his left.

He did not want to believe that they were hostile, a threat to his life and Kalyan's. But he had to be careful.

He pressed his keys into Kalyan's hand. "My car is the only one on the next street," he said, nodding to the right. "Go there now and drive away. Don't return to your hotel. Go to the nearest police station."

Kalyan had slowly registered the danger of the situation. Now he displayed full panic. "I don't know how to do this—!"

"Take the keys," Taj said, in what he hoped was his command voice.

"Go to the first car you see, get in, start it, drive away as quickly as you can."

It worked. Kalyan merely blinked, took the keys, and, without another word, turned and ran off.

Taj pulled his service revolver and headed around the building to the left.

Hebbai Electric Crematorium was not large, though the press of neighboring buildings made it difficult for large formations to circle it.

Taj was waiting when the Aggregate formation came around the corner, two by two, a THE counselor in their midst.

"Who are you?" the counselor said. He was, like all THE, in his twenties. He actually appeared to be nervous.

"A hero of India," Taj said, training his pistol on the agent. "Stop talking and stop walking." He found himself distracted by the presence of the Aggregates . . . now a dozen anteater-like beings that came up to his shoulder. These were red and yellow, like characters from a superhero movie, and constantly in motion, each pair taking up a position around Taj that was either for observation or containment. They were not silent, either, but buzzing to each other like giant insects.

Taj kept his pistol aimed at the young man from THE. "I'm going to walk away," he said. "Please inform your alien associates that I will shoot you if there's a problem."

The young man had his hands up in the classic posture. Taj slid to his right, hoping to reach the corner of the next building, so he could turn and run. The fact that he had not run more than two steps in a decade was of minor concern.

At some level of consciousness, he could not believe his situation. Threatened by an entire Aggregate formation in Bangalore? Pursued by body-snatching or grave-robbing criminals allied with India's military?

Then he remembered his mission to Keanu, and the mix of the impossible and the insane he had experienced in that week, and he was forced to conclude: This was only the second most ridiculous thing he'd done in his life.

He was about to test his running skills when he heard, "General Rad-hakrishnan! You must stop!"

In truth, he had nowhere to run . . . only an open alley.

He turned and saw Kaushal walking toward him, two Indian Air Force guards at his side . . . two strange men and all three THE agents behind them.

And the Aggregates flanking them all.

"This is no longer your business," Kaushal said. "We're here for San-jay Bhat's body."

"You're too late. It's been cremated."

"That's a disappointment."

"To you?"

Kaushal grunted. "I'm indifferent."

"Kaushal, what's the point of this? The man is dead."

Kaushal turned toward the others; the humans, all quite agitated, were conferring. The Reivers were arranging themselves in pairs, as if preparing to fan out. "He came from Keanu. Now that you allowed the others to escape, he's all they have, or had."

"But for what—?"

"You were there, General! Dead isn't dead to these people, right?"

"*Cremated* is dead as far as I'm concerned."

The civilians and THE types had come to a decision and were already in motion, some heading back to the crematorium, another group heading for Taj, and a third going the opposite way down the alley, toward Taj's car.

He could not let them catch Kalyan. He had only met the man, their connection was only through the dead brother, the smart move would have been to simply hope he had already gotten away—

Even though Kaushal's guards had guns on him, Taj suddenly started back down the alley toward his car, reaching for his pistol and shouting, "Stop!"

Ahead of him, a THE counselor and a civilian operative halted, but two pairs of Aggregates kept right on going. Taj fired twice, hitting one of the Reiver anteaters high on its back.

The sight—shards of "skin" flew off the Reiver, which stopped immediately—and sound—like breaking glass—were incredibly satisfying. Taj realized that he had unfinished business with these creatures.

But before he finished that thought, he felt a blow in his right side, a deep punch that staggered him even as he registered a gunshot.

Then he was on the pavement, lying on his side, gasping, hurting. There was tremendous commotion around him—voices, shadows.

The last thing he saw was Kaushal looming over him. The last thing he heard was Kaushal saying, "You idiot."

FIRST LIGHT	22 APRIL 2040 0001:00 MDT
FIRE LIGHT	09 MAY 2040 0001:00 MDT
TIME TO FIRST LIGHT	23 hours and counting

COUNTDOWN CLOCK AT SITE A

CARBON-143

SITUATION: Carbon-143 returned to her workstation in a state of communal ecstasy. The knowledge that final Fire Light ignition of the Ring transmitter would have negative effects on organic and quasi-organic human life—quite likely resulting in her own destruction—was outweighed by her sense of triumph. She was designed to take satisfaction in working as part of her formation, which had been accomplished by participation in the assault force launch simulation.

She realized she was also experiencing an anomalous jolt of accomplishment combined with guilt due to her independent cybernetic sleuthing. This was a somatic state she was less familiar with. The only element—rather, individual—likely to assist her with an evaluation of this state was Randall Dehm. But encounters with Dehm were unpredictable. It was quite likely this state would pass long before Carbon-143 had an opportunity to disclose it.

Would she remember it? She would have a record of the facts, naturally, but these new somatic episodes were not formally accessible the way data or procedures were.

NARRATIVE: Two hours and nineteen minutes into the next shift, the entire formation received another general message: "Basic systems update. Disengage."

As one, all twelve elements of the Carbon-143 formation disconnected from the assembly-line equipment and backed away.

Another general message followed: "Resumption of activity anticipated in seven minutes."

Carbon-143 and the others found themselves with unanticipated and unprogrammed time. On the four occasions this had happened in the past, Carbon-143 had remained on station. Three times she had been able to interact with Dehm, whose workstation was adjacent, and whose systems were usually offline at the same time.

She did not have to wait long. Dehm emerged from the next station, looking troubled. Carbon-143 had no skill at initiating conversation with humans, though she had learned the utility of proximity: If you are in his path, he will speak.

This time the maneuver failed!

"I can't talk now."

Dehm rapidly disappeared from the line, leaving Carbon-143 in the position she had assumed, some distance from the other elements, all of them still waiting for the signal to resume activity.

ACTION: She knew she should return to the formation immediately, and turned to execute that maneuver when she found her path blocked by Whit Murray.

"Sorry," he said. He stepped to his left just as Carbon-143 moved to her right.

They were left in the same position. "Sorry, again," he said.

Carbon-143's programming indicated that she should remain where she was, allowing the more mobile and independent organic—Whit Murray—to initiate his own maneuver.

But in the long interval—from her perspective—between accessing that set of commands and initiating them, Carbon-143 realized that Whit had as much potential use as recipient of her information as did Dehm. After all, Dehm had connected them.

She stepped to her left just as Whit tried to get past her for the third time.

Now he stood there, saying, "Do you need something from me?"

Since he had initiated conversation, she felt empowered: "I have information to share."

Whit flinched, a reaction Carbon-143 recognized as surprise. "What? And why me?"

"About the nature of the Ring and its possible side effects on the environment when triggered."

Whit's eyebrows rose, a reaction recognizable as curiosity combined with interest. "What are they?"

As precisely as she could, Carbon-143 referenced the radiation levels that would result from both a test pulse—the so-called First Light—and the operational firing known as Fire Light. "Won't that be bad for all that stuff out there?" he said, jerking his thumb in what he obviously thought was the direction of the tank field. He was mistaken, by at least sixty degrees, but Carbon-143 elected not to offer a correction.

"Extremely."

"It doesn't make sense."

"Not unless the goal is to leave nothing of use behind following the transfer."

Whit opened his mouth to speak, then, strangely, closed it without uttering a word. And Carbon-143 received the formation-wide signal to return to her station.

As she turned toward it, Whit scurried around in front of her. "You can't drop a bomb like that and just walk off."

"I've been ordered back to my station." She could see Eleven and Ten already plugging in. In seconds, her absence would be noted and cause for review.

She kept moving; Whit moved with her. "I've got it. I need to get back, too." He lowered his voice. "We need to talk more. When does your shift end?"

"My shift never ends."

"Oh," he said, "right." He followed Carbon-143 right up to her station. "Can you, uh, send me the material?" He obviously realized, belatedly, that their conversation might be unapproved or troublesome. He actually smiled at Eleven and Ten as he said, with a noticeable increase in volume, "I think we can help the Project."

"I will locate you," Carbon-143 said, suddenly and strangely unsure of her actions.

ANALYSIS: She had returned to her station and resumed her work with no detectable loss of performance. (She had received no queries about delays from higher on the information tree.)

Yet she spent the next twenty minutes in a state of agitation pondering two questions: Had she betrayed the Project by obtaining and now revealing certain information?

Had she betrayed Dehm by speaking with Whit?

She was uncomfortable with the realization that she had insufficient data to answer either question.

INDIAN SPACE HERO WOUNDED IN ROBBERY

Retired general Taj Radhakrishnan, 66, was severely wounded in an apparent attempted robbery in North Bangalore yesterday. He has been taken to Sagar Hospital, where his status is critical.

Reporting is still incomplete, but the incident occurred in the business district of Hebbal near 5th Main Road around 9 A.M. A shopkeeper found the astronaut shot and lying in an alley. His wallet had been taken.

An Air Force pilot by training, Radhakrishnan became the second citizen of India to fly in space in 2014, and again in 2019, when he commanded the ill-fated *Brahma* mission to Near-Earth Object Keanu.

More recently he has been involved in the return of inhabitants of Keanu, one of them his son, Pav.

Dr. Melani Remilla of the Indian Space Research Organization disputed the suggestion that the attack on General Radhakrishnan was related to this activity.

BANGALOREMIRROR.COM (CITY SECTION),
THURSDAY, APRIL 19, 2040

DALE

The trip by railcar from the vesicle factory to the human habitat took half an hour and was so noisy and rattling that conversation was impossible. Crammed into a single car with Makali, Dale found that the only thing the two of them could do was stare at each other awkwardly.

In any case, Dale had little to offer. Word that the Beehive had come to life had driven Zhao, Makali, and the others toward the railcars. Having just made the hike from the human habitat, Dale had been happy to be taken along for the ride, his first since the weird trek of 2019. He heard no invitation, but he heard no warning to get lost or stay out of this.

So far he was serene about his decision to reengage with his fellow humans, though he was disappointed that his communion with Keanu had not proved to be more useful—that is, that he was still having to prove himself.

That might change. In a major improvement over the previous seventy of his seventy-one years, Dale's timing seemed to be good. Of course, his decision to visit the habitat had been spurred by the worrisome messages from the Keanu system about troubles for Rachel and crew on Earth. Nevertheless, he had followed up, and thus learned of the existence of the vesicle and the plans for its use . . . and now the Beehive had come back to life.

He was certain these were all related somehow, though cause and effect were still elusive. But if anyone could discover that linkage, it was Keanu-linked Dale Scott. He just needed more input, as they used to say at NASA.

The trip was not only an improvement over a second long walk through the tunnels, it showed Dale that the rail line was old, battered, and from the discolorations and wear had seen heavy use. Which suggested that the HBs were desperate for Substance K.

Desperate people did risky things . . . like put five humans, including a teenaged girl, and an alien aboard a thousand-year-old vehicle and fire them toward a planet that did not want them.

Such as come up with a cockamamie backup plan involving some kind of secret bioweapon they hoped to sneak into Earth's atmosphere. Unless the Reivers had somehow managed to not only dominate Earth, but to make humanity forget whatever it had learned in the past hundred and fifty years, radar and missile defenses would still be in existence. It seemed to Dale that this vesicle gambit had little chance of success.

And what then? His concern for the outcome was not just academic—his fate was tied to Keanu. How would the Reivers respond to an invasion and/or an attack? Would they be content to let Keanu remain in orbit . . . indefinitely, untouched?

Or would they fire their own weapons? Worse yet, would they invade? They might feel that they had a right to retake the NEO, since it had been their home for a few millennia.

Dale had a sudden, unwanted image of Reiver microbes spreading up the walls of this very tunnel . . . and anteater model aliens marching toward him.

He couldn't allow that. If—*be polite and don't think "when"*—Harley Drake and Jaidev and Zhao's big plans went to shit, Dale should be ready with his option.

Move Keanu.

And who better to pilot the NEO to a new destination, a new destiny, than former astronaut and test pilot, Keanu-linked Dale Scott?

The cars arrived at the loading complex outside the human habitat with a screeching bump. Everyone but Dale exited automatically and wordlessly, even though it appeared there was a turn in the rail that would allow the cargo car to move directly into the habitat.

But Dale chose to follow Makali and Zhao, who walked swiftly, their team members forming up behind them, not only creating a security barrier—deliberate? Or just habit?—but keeping Dale from hearing their words. It was obvious they were talking about the Beehive, and that all were agitated, even steady, unexcitable Zhao.

From the entrance, the whole of the habitat spread out like a landscape painting, neat little buildings clustered among fields and forests, the Temple dominating it all. It was a more pleasing view than Dale's last, over his shoulder during the half-light of "night." He was amused to realize that he had spent sixteen years away from the human habitat, and was now making his second entrance in the same day.

"Keep up, everybody. It's at the far end." Dale wondered why Zhao had to remind the others where the Beehive was located, but realized that two of the vesicle makers were in their twenties and had likely been brought to Keanu as small children with no experience of the place.

Or it might just have been a sign that Zhao liked to tell people what to do.

They reached the Temple within fifteen minutes, where Jaidev was waiting on the steps. "Harley and Sasha are already on their way," he told Zhao. Only then did he spot Dale. "Why the hell are you back?"

"You welcomed me earlier, remember?" Dale said. "You wanted to keep me, too."

Jaidev turned away, as if he could no longer bear to think about this.

As they continued their journey, Zhao asked what had happened. "You know little less than we do," Jaidev said. "Jordana Swale was near the mouth of the Beehive and noticed a strange light."

"I don't know her."

"She's one of the senior farmers," Makali said. "I know her. Very well grounded. I bet she didn't investigate by herself."

"She came to the Temple first," Jaidev said. "I wasn't here and Harley was busy . . ." Here Jaidev glanced at Dale. Then he decided the information wasn't worth hiding. ". . . talking with Rachel. So Sasha went off with Jordana.

"Fifteen minutes later Jordana was back again, saying one of the cells was active."

"That's a lot of back and forth for one woman," Dale said, unable to resist. "Haven't you guys reverse-engineered the Segway yet?"

Everyone ignored him, which diminished Dale's glee not one bit.

The distance from the Temple to the Beehive end of the habitat was seven kilometers, a distance that, when added to his other movements for the day, made for a challenging walk. He began to feel tired. His feet hurt.

Nevertheless, he appreciated a phenomenon he had never experienced on Keanu. Every few hundred meters, more HBs joined them, slipping out of the fields one by one, or emerging from buildings in larger groups. The moving throng grew to more than a hundred, a significant percentage of the population of the habitat. Zhao, Makali, and Dale had to push their way through a crowd. It reminded Dale of a scene from some old movie about Moses.

There were so many people jammed into the narrow entrance that Dale found himself being jostled. "Sorry," the person next to him said. It was a young man, blond, long-haired, clearly nervous. "I don't know you," Dale said, extending his hand. "Dale Scott."

"Hey, the hermit!" the young man said. "Nick. So this must be auspicious, if you're here."

"We'll see," Dale said. He was growing more uncomfortable. Too many people . . . too many chances for conversations he didn't want to have.

But Nick hadn't finished with him. "Were you around the last time the Beehive worked?"

"Yes. It was sort of operating for almost a year after arrival." Or so he remembered. But that had been for terrestrial animals . . . no human Revenants had emerged after Yvonne Hall, and she had not come from this place. (There were other Beehive-like structures within Keanu, even a long-unused one adjacent to the Factory. Dale had never seen evidence that they still functioned.)

The idea of humans returning from the dead, originally repellent, had consumed many hours of thought over the years. He was more tolerant of the idea now. He had often wondered if Zack Stewart, going to his death in Keanu's core, had assumed or hoped he would be reborn . . . even for a handful of days.

Now Harley Drake emerged from the Beehive, not only offering the hope of information, but giving Dale a reason to excuse himself from the conversation with Nick.

He got close enough to the front of the crowd to hear Jaidev say, "Harls, what's going on?"

"Sasha's in there with Jordana," Drake said. "One of those cells is definitely active."

"What size is it?" That was Zhao, always practical.

"Human."

"Okay, then," Makali said. "Who's died?"

"What kind of question is that?" Harley said.

"She's probably wondering if that might give you some idea of who is going to become the next Revenant," Dale said. There was no reaction from Jaidev, Zhao, and the others in front of him. True, there was a lot of noise and he might not have been heard. But it was just as likely that he was being ignored.

Oh well. That might be changing—

Makali Pillay was upset by Harley's response. "Don't bite my head off."

"Sorry," Harley said.

"This is a strange situation," Jaidev said. "I frankly don't know what to do."

"This is fucked up," Harley said. "But it's really what I just heard from Rachel." If Harley was worried about Dale's presence, he didn't show it. "Things are just as bad as we thought down there. The team is in the same shape they were yesterday, but they're on a long haul to try to reach this Reiver weapons site, and even when they get there . . . it's five against a few hundred thousand."

"We knew that," Jaidev said.

"We knew we were sending a handful of people on a scouting mission. Now we have the intel, and it's terrifying." Dale was about to try to inch his way closer when Harley said, "Get over here, Dale. You might surprise us and be useful."

Harley quickly hit the high points of his Rachel tag-up, concentrating on the new Reiver facility with what was surely a beam weapon capable of striking Keanu.

Dale suddenly understood Harley Drake's agitation. "We need the vesicle to be launched as soon as possible."

"It's within a day," Zhao said.

"Make it happen," Jaidev said.

"Then I shouldn't be here." Zhao turned to Makali. He was serious about returning to the vesicle habitat.

"We might as well wait a few more minutes," Makali said. "Let's see what the big deal is."

As Harley's debrief continued, Dale stepped back . . . most of the other HBs had formed their own clusters. One, largely younger, had formed around this Nick: They seemed eager, even happy.

Another group was older, largely Bangalores. They looked like mourners at a funeral. . . . Dale suspected that they had lost a friend during the past year or two and were hoping that they might be witnessing a miracle.

They'd obviously forgotten how short-lived these miracles had been—

"There's Sasha!"

Dale didn't recognized the voice, which came from somewhere behind him.

It was Sasha Blaine, in all her statuesque red-haired glory.

And, leaning on her—he was having trouble walking—was a man Dale didn't recognize. He was naked, or nearly so, wearing some skinlike covering.

"Oh my God," Makali Pillay said. "Is that—?"

"Yes," Jaidev said.

"That's Sanjay Bhat."

QUESTION: What have you missed most about life on Earth?

PAV RADHAKRISHNAN: My family, of course. I only recently learned that my mother passed away several years ago. I have been fortunate to reconnect with my father.

QUESTION: Anything else?

PAV: New faces, I guess. There are fewer than a thousand of us. I attended secondary schools that were larger. (laughs) Sometimes life on Keanu feels like high school . . . in a submarine.

INTERVIEW AT YELAHANKA,
APRIL 14, 2040

RACHEL

"We'll be passing the Channel Islands in the next ten minutes," Colin Edgely told Rachel.

Ten minutes earlier, Pav had awakened her with a gentle touch on her shoulder. She had been reclining in an airline seat under a thin blanket, dreaming about the Architect's home world. The giant alien she had encountered that first week on Keanu had been dead for twenty years, yet a day rarely passed without some thought of him . . . where his people had come from, what they wanted, where they had succeeded in their quests.

Where they had failed.

Jaidev and the other HBs had devoted considerable effort to walking back Keanu's trajectory, but with the limited resources available to them—and too many unknowns, such as the actual amount of time that had passed since Keanu's original launch—they had never been able to settle on a particular star, much less a planet.

Which had not stopped them all from speculating about the type of world that would be home to creatures like the Architect, a large, low-density planet on the scale of Jupiter, but with a breathable atmosphere and tolerable temperatures. Rachel had formed a clear vision of the place, naming it "Homestead" and imagining endless pink steppes, blue mountains, black forests, and white cities that literally floated in the thick atmosphere. Her Homestead was familiar enough that she had dreams about it.

But today's had not been happy. She had felt incredible sadness and impotence as she watched a flying city literally fall out of the sky, slamming into a blue mountain range and being torn apart, Architect bodies scattered—

But it was just a dream, the side effect of an otherwise solid night's sleep. And some kind of strange, dreamlike mirror of the sadness she felt about Sanjay, and the frustrations she experienced with *Adventure*'s ongoing mission.

Okay, she thought, *I have to start turning this around. Be active, not passive.* She almost launched herself out of the seat.

Stretched across the entire row behind Rachel, Yahvi was still asleep. Pav was moving to wake her, too, but Rachel stopped him. "How long has she been out?"

Pav smiled. "No idea. I was dead to the world for five hours."

"Let her sleep as long as possible. It's not as though there's anything she can do until we get to Mexico."

"If then."

"Well, we didn't bring her so we could get work out of her."

"I just think she'd be happier all around if she had a job."

Yahvi had talents that might be useful. Sanjay and her other teachers had frequently taken Rachel and Pav aside to praise their daughter's potential, especially in math. So far, however, Yahvi's greatest accomplishment was getting her own way. "We can turn to her when we need someone verbally beaten into submission."

Then Rachel slipped into the lavatory for a moment, peeing and washing up, emerging to find Chang busy with his datapad, creating his fantasies about the adventures of the *Adventure* crew.

Colin Edgely was ready with coffee and his geographical update.

"Two hundred kilometers northwest of Los Angeles," he said. "We're flying parallel to the coast and should be turning east within half an hour. With luck, we're on the ground shortly afterward."

"What happens to you two once we're in Mexico?" Rachel said. "I assume this plane goes back to where it came from."

"Yes, Chang will turn around and fly back to China by various means," the Aussie astronomer said. "As for me—" Here his face grew rosy with embarrassment. "I'd like to come along."

"Don't you have students to go back to? Or your family?"

Edgely grinned. "Family knows I'm on my voyage of personal discovery. I met my wife through Kettering, you know." Until this moment Rachel hadn't known that Edgely *had* a wife.

"As for school, I took a leave. My boss isn't a member of Kettering, but he's sympathetic to the mania. Everyone in Alice Springs knows a bit about space tracking and such, anyway."

"So you want to come along."

"Nothing would give me more pleasure," he said. "To see this through."

To see this through. Rachel wondered what that meant. "I don't think we'd have gotten this far without you," she said, with total sincerity. "So stay as long as you want, as long as you know—"

"That it could be risky? I understand." He gestured toward the left-side windows. "The riskiest maneuver is almost upon us, in fact."

They faced so many unknowns. The first hour after taking off from Guam, she and Pav, Zeds, and Xavier had huddled in the rear of the plane, going over their options.

Pav told them that Chang had arranged for them to land in northern Mexico, near the city of Rosarito. "That country is filled with secret landing strips from the drug days, but few are equipped to handle a jet." He had smiled. "Nevertheless, we have found one."

They would then drive overland to the coast, where they would board a small sub. "This definitely sounds like a smuggling craft," Xavier had said.

"No question. There's barely room for all of us."

"Do we have to smuggle drugs, too?" Zeds said.

For a moment none of them realized that the Sentry was joking. "No," Rachel said, laughing, "only our own cargo."

They would be put ashore somewhere on the California coast between Santa Barbara and San Diego, final destination to be decided en route. "The Free Nation Federales keep changing their countermeasures," Chang said, "so our sub captain will be doing the same."

"So this does still occur," Rachel said. "Drug smuggling."

"Oh my, yes," Chang said. "No government in human history ever stopped it, and even with all their extraterrestrial powers, the Aggregates haven't, either." He smiled. "In many cases, however, the smuggling has gone the other way . . . it used to be people into the U.S. from Mexico. For the past two decades, it's been the other way."

"Speaking of cargo, Chang," Xavier said, standing and indicating several containers. "Your little team of mice will be busy arranging the next leg of our journey. But before we make a move, I need four hours to produce our pharmaceutical package."

"Our what?" Pav said.

"The poison pill," Rachel said.

"Oh." In spite of his claims of having slept well, Pav was still, to Rachel's eyes, a bit slow and unfocused . . . or he would have remembered a key backup portion of their strategy versus the Aggregates, which was to replicate the only strategy that had actually worked against the machinelike aliens: infect them with a fast-evolving, self-replicating poison that destroyed their ability to communicate and reproduce.

It had worked to cleanse Keanu of the Reiver infection twenty years ago, driving the survivors off the NEO and toward Earth.

No one expected success from the same formula, but Jaidev, Sanjay, and other great HB minds had discovered a way to mask a deadly bioweapon as something entirely different—a Substance K–derived battery that stored vast amounts of energy in a very small package. It had been the end product of years of research, since the HBs could use such a device . . . and the subject of an increasingly tedious series of jokes, as the HB researchers pondered the eternal question, "What do Reivers want?"

The cleverest aspect of the backup plan was the presence of an actual poison pill weapon much like the original 2019 version. "It works two

ways," Sanjay had said. "Either the Reivers spot and grab it, missing the
real weapon . . . or they don't see it and it kills them."

All this supposed that Rachel, Pav, and company were captives, or
worse, dead. So it was not an option Rachel had spent much time
pondering.

Nevertheless, Xavier needed time to complete "assembly" of both
packages. "Obviously we won't move until you're ready," Chang told him.

"Just as obviously," Rachel said, "the sooner we are ready to move on
this Reiver ray gun, the better."

"I leave those maneuvers to you," Chang said. "I will remain in Mexico to complete my work, then—"

"Then what?" Pav said, an edge in his voice. "Run back to China in
case we fail? Make sure you're out of the blast radius?"

Chang blinked. When he spoke, he sounded tired. "I'm sorry if you
feel I'm abandoning you, but I'm a journalist and a rather famous one at
that. My absence from China has already been noted. My association
with you is public. If someone sees me here—"

"They'll know we're here, too," Rachel said. "You're right, Edgar.
You've worked wonders getting us this far. From this point on, the
smaller our team, the greater our chance of surprise." Rachel saw that
Colin Edgely was looking away, as if trying to pretend he hadn't increased the size of her team by twenty percent.

Rachel turned to Xavier. "The burden of this falls to you and me."
Both still had friends and even family in Free Nation U.S., most in the
western half of the country. They would use their time in Mexico to
make contact, and hopefully find one who would shelter them as they
prepared for an assault on this Aggregate weapons facility.

Zeds's comment was, "I am troubled that we have the potential to be
detected and detained at almost any point."

"So it's a good thing that's the whole idea, right?" Xavier said.

Jo Zhang, their co-pilot, emerged at that point, a broad smile on her face.
"We're right on track and on schedule." She was, Rachel judged, in her
midthirties—her own age—but seemed to possess a rangy confidence

that Rachel lacked, much like Tea; maybe you had to be that kind of person to operate high-tech flying machines. Or maybe operating them made you confident.

"What about defenses?" Rachel asked. "If we ran into Free Nation forces off India, I would expect a lot more right off California."

"We have access to, ah, certain information about Free Nation vessels. There are bases to the north and especially to the south, at San Diego. We're pretty sure we're tracking them all, and there are no threats at the moment."

"How about aircraft and missiles?"

Jo shrugged, looking, for a moment, quite fatalistic. "They're more difficult to track, especially since there's no international air traffic control data here. And with missiles, well, they can be on the ground one minute, and in your tailpipe the next. But we see no unusual air activity at the moment, and if we do, our decoy makes a run for it and draws them off."

We hope, Rachel thought, as Jo slipped away, into the lav.

Before leaving Guam, Rachel had insisted on thanking the pilots, not just Jo and Steve, who had skillfully flown them from Bangalore to Darwin to Guam, but the two who were to fly that decoy plane.

The decoy pilots turned out to be two grim ex-military jet jockeys, one of them originally from the U.S. His name was Benvides, and he was twenty years older than Rachel. "I remember your father," he said. "I was just out of flight school when the Keanu mission happened. And the Objects hitting. That must have been . . . awesomely weird."

"Let's just say I was unprepared for it."

Benvides laughed. It turned out that he and his family had been stationed in Japan when the Reiver Aggregate invasion occurred. "We wanted to go home, to join the fighting, if nothing else. But we couldn't. There was no real war . . . it was like a total collapse within a few weeks."

"Taj said it was like trying to climb a tree that had rotted from within."

"If you realize that the rot happened overnight due to outside forces, yes. Anyway, I've been waiting twenty years to poke a stick in the Aggregates' eyes, assuming they have eyes."

The other man was a younger Aussie named Quentin. He told Pav he came from a family of bush pilots. "Hoping to get back to that after this," he said.

When Rachel first learned of the two-plane approach requiring the decoy to somehow make it all the way back to Hawaii, she had been terrified for the pilots. But both Benvides and Quentin assured her that they could not only make the trip, they would have a margin. "Your bird's a Gulfstream," Benvides said, "and it's got a lot of range. But we're driving a Dassault Falcon 9 with even more, and we're packing extra fuel instead of passengers and cargo. Don't worry about us." He smiled. "Just make sure you kill all the Reivers."

And now Benvides and Quentin were flying directly above them at the common altitude of ten thousand meters while Rachel's Gulfstream had descended to two thousand and would go even lower.

Jo flashed a smile and a thumbs-up as she emerged from the lav on her way back to the cockpit.

And now Yahvi was up, seemingly cheerful. As she ate breakfast, she looked out the portside windows. "I keep thinking I see land, but I'm not sure."

"It's out there," Rachel assured her. She patted her daughter, then worked her way to the rear of the plane, where Pav had gone to ground.

"Something up?" she said.

Pav wore his secretive face and used his quiet voice. "I didn't want to tell the others, but about an hour ago we got a link to Keanu," Pav said.

"What did you tell them?"

"That we didn't have anything new, except that within three hours we expected to be . . . on station."

Rachel smiled. "Have you heard from your father?"

Pav shook his head.

"Are you worried?"

He shrugged. "We're only linked by cell phone, and that won't work until we're close to land."

Rachel touched her husband's hand. He seemed nervous. "There's something else."

Pav actually glanced over his shoulder, as if he had to worry about being overheard by Zeds and Xavier. "The Beehive is alive again."

Among the many startling bits of news Rachel had heard in this past week, or, indeed, in her life, that was high on the list. "No shit."

"Yes, shit," he said.

"And?"

"They don't know yet. I mean, nothing has come out of it. It's just . . . active again. Glowing." He made an eerie sound and waved his hands.

"Did they do anything to fire it up?" Pav shook his head. "Then what's changed?"

"I've got to believe it has something to do with Dale Scott," Pav said.

At that moment the cockpit door opened. Steve, the male pilot, stuck his head out. "We're descending, making our turn. Everyone buckle in." Unlike Jo, who, based on her accent, seemed to have been raised by Americans, Steve Liu's English was halting and unfamiliar. He was a stocky, serious man in his thirties who reminded Rachel of Zhao, the quiet yet capable former spy who had eventually become one of the Keanu community's leaders. Zhao gave the impression that he knew arts and possessed skills beyond ordinary humans, and Rachel saw a bit of this in Steve. Perhaps she was simply hoping.

As she and Pav took their seats and watched Edgely and Chang buckling in, Rachel felt that sudden, now-familiar rush of adrenaline. It had happened to her so often since leaving Keanu that it was becoming her natural state—and surely a bad sign. You could burn yourself out operating at that level.

She glanced at Pav across the aisle. He nodded an okay as he strapped in. She turned to Yahvi, in the seat next to her, who said, "Is this going to be dangerous?"

"No more dangerous than anything else we've done," Rachel said. "A lot safer than landing *Adventure*."

"That's not saying much." The girl was trying to act brave, but her voice and eyes gave her away. Rachel just squeezed her hand, noting, as she often did, that giving reassurance actually reassured her.

Why it did, she couldn't say. It wasn't as though the universe somehow looked more kindly on humans who offered comfort to others—the universe should, Rachel believed, but there was no evidence that it did.

She was, in fact, appalled at how little she knew of the universe, even though her experience of matters beyond Earth—beyond anything seven billion other humans could ever hope to know—should have given her some insight, some special sense.

Yes, she had proof that alien life existed; hard evidence of that sat within four meters of her. She was convinced that her home world was little more than a speck of sand on some cosmic beach. (And that for the past twenty years she had lived inside an even smaller speck.) She had seen the marvels of amazing alien technology, not just the ability to send an inhabited planetoid from one solar system to another, but to literally demonstrate the power of life and death.

She knew that there was an ancient conflict between at least two types of intelligences in the universe, organic versus machine—and that she and her family had somehow gotten in the middle of it.

To think they and their friends could win . . . could have more effect on the battle than a butterfly could affect a hurricane . . . was probably laughable. Her limited but valuable lessons suggested to her that in big games, the score was always going to be Universe: 1,000,000,000; Individual Human: 0.

Yet here she was . . . here they all were, stuck inside a metal tube, flying over an ocean toward a place they'd never seen, controlled and guarded by some of the most capable and hostile aliens imaginable.

Looked at one way, it was insane. Looked at another, it might have been hilarious.

Looked at as part of the human experience . . . maybe it was just fucking typical.

She could feel the plane diving now . . . quite steeply. If she tried she could almost hear the pilots talking on the other side of the cockpit door. No words, just evidence of communication—squawks, grunts, sounds that had the potential to be words.

Their voices were no longer calm.

That was understandable, right? They were executing a tricky maneuver, diving toward the Pacific, preparing to fly toward land at an altitude of less than five hundred meters. Rachel was not a pilot, but she had grown up with an astronaut for a father, and Zack Stewart had been required to fly in supersonic jets as an "operator." She had heard the grim jokes and sardonic phrases about how "air is easier to fly through than mountain" and "don't turn your plane into a boat."

Looking out the window, she could see nothing but sea and sky—a beautiful sunny afternoon, with a few clouds way off to the north suggesting an approaching storm front. At this height, individual waves were visible . . . long broad rollers heading for the beaches of Mexico.

There were beeps from the cockpit.

Yahvi heard them, too. "Mom . . ."

Rachel had never been one to offer unthinking blanket reassurance. She hated the phrase *It's going to be all right* with a passion, because she had ample evidence that very often things didn't turn out all right.

"It's going to be all right," she said.

She glanced at Pav, who would have said the same thing—and who was incapable of hiding his alarm.

The plane began to maneuver. . . . "We're making S turns," Edgely said, as if he were a newly appointed aeronautical expert.

"Can you see land from your side?" Rachel said. Whatever the type of turns, she was still seeing only sea and sky.

The plane rolled to its right suddenly, making Rachel feel as though she were on a carnival ride. Every occupant of the cabin uttered a "whoa!" or the equivalent.

Then it felt as though they were diving, which could not be good, given that they were only a few hundred meters above the water to begin with.

Yahvi was paralyzed with fear. She clutched Rachel's hand like a potential drowning victim.

The plane began to rise now, its motion pressing Rachel and the others into their seats. *Like a rocket launch,* she thought. As this went on and on, as the plane continued to climb steeply, the rocket-launch analogy seemed even more apt. The whine of the engines grew louder. Rachel thought she heard and felt the airframe shuddering.

"Are we heading back to Keanu?" Pav said, triggering nervous laughter from Chang and, behind them, Xavier.

That two seconds of grim humor quickly gave way to even grimmer fear. This wasn't right—!

As she looked out the window to the north, Rachel saw a fireball.

Yahvi saw it, too. "Mommy, what was that?"

"Our decoy," Xavier said.

Rachel had known that, though it took Xavier's words to supply confirmation. She gasped and uttered, "Oh, no!" Benvides and Quentin!

As their plane leveled out, the light brown coast of Mexico visible on the horizon, Rachel saw two other aircraft in the sky, heading toward them from the left.

From the cockpit came the clear sounds of Steve and Jo in a grim struggle, overlaid with alarming beeps.

They were alone in the sky now, targets for the Aggregates.

THINGS WE DON'T HAVE ON KEANU

Sports teams or most sports, except for cricket and some basketball
Churches
Books on shit like diets, investing, pets, or etiquette. Books, period
Electronics stores
ATMs
Kentucky Fried Chicken or other restaurants

THINGS WE DO HAVE ON KEANU

Music
Markets
Free time

XAVIER TOUTANT, AS QUOTED BY EDGAR CHANG
FOR THE NEWSKY NEWS SERVICE

SANJAY

His memories were completely confused.

Sanjay Bhat remembered the tension of *Adventure*'s final approach to Bangalore and Yelahanka . . . the barely suppressed pride and even glee that a hostile missile had come close to destroying them, but failed.

Then he had watched the last few meters of the descent, his eyes unable to look away from the figures on the control panel, as if rapt, unblinking attention could somehow slow the rates, change them to the numbers he wanted—

Then? The shattering impact, cushioned by couch and belts, the sound of something smashing, the panel flying toward him, blinding, crippling pain—

Followed, seemingly a few moments later, by a cough, a feeling of suffocation, an opening of the eyes to see a brownish-yellow film in front of them.

Clawing, feeling relief that the covering was coming away, terror that he was confined. Had he been buried? Was he in the wreckage of *Adventure*?

Then he was shaken by a series of violent spasms. Fortunately, they passed quickly, leaving him shivering, twitching, but alive . . . and lying on his back inside a golden coffin-sized cell, like a honeycomb.

Along his left side was a wall made of a thin, translucent substance that felt like wax. There were shadows outside! Maybe someone who could get him out!

He turned on his side and reached with his right hand—

And poked a hole through the wall.

The whole thing broke into soft pieces, some falling, some peeled away by the entities outside.

Even though his ears were still covered by the clinging second skin, Sanjay could hear a human female voice calling, "Are you okay? Can you hear me?"

Then arms reached for him, pulling him free.

As he slid out of the cell, he realized that he knew where he was. Like most HBs, he had sneaked into the Beehive at one time—or, in Sanjay's case, several times. And that was where he was, in the Beehive, in the arms of a woman he knew very well . . . Sasha Blaine.

"Thank you," he croaked.

There was the choking sob at the realization that he must have died, followed by the instant elation that he had somehow survived, or rather come back.

"It's okay, Sanj," Sasha Blaine said. "We're here."

Another woman held him, too, this one dark-haired, dark-eyed, not familiar. Sanjay let himself collapse into their arms.

They cleaned him up as well as they could, helping him peel the second skin off his head and face, shoulders, chest and arms, legs. "We ought to leave it around your middle," Sasha said, "until we get you some pants."

Sanjay's response was a spasm of laughter. Yes, his *nudity* was the concern. Not his condition, not the fact that he had been killed on Earth and reborn on Keanu. "What about Rachel?" he said, horrified at the way his throat felt and his voice sounded, like that of a man of a hundred. "Is she still on Earth? What happened? How did I get here?"

"Rachel is still good, as far as we know," Sasha said. She nodded to the woman with her—Sanjay remembered her name now: Jordana, agro sector. "Do you have any memory of what happened?"

It didn't take long to tell her—the approach, the missile, the crash. "That's pretty much what we heard," Sasha said. "And now here you are."

"Having been killed."

"Uh, apparently."

"So I'm a fucking Revenant."

"Well, yes."

"Any idea how?" He looked up at the Beehive. "This hasn't functioned for twenty years." He thought of Jaidev and Zhao, who had devoted hours to the problem, with no success. "Did someone figure out how to turn it back on?"

"No," Sasha said. "I'm kind of hoping you could tell us what happened."

"I told you everything I know." He croaked again. "So far."

"Well, welcome back. Which sounds really stupid, like you've just been away on a trip."

"Well, I have."

Sasha turned to Jordana. "Let's get him out of here. He needs water and God knows what else."

Among the two gigantic mental adjustments Sanjay Bhat was making—realizing he had died, and that he had been reborn as a Revenant back on Keanu—there was a new one, perhaps more important:

No Revenant had lived more than a few days.

He emerged from the Beehive to a crowd larger than any he had seen in his life in the habitat. The HB population of Keanu had no celebrations or events that required such gatherings. "Is this all for me?"

"Everyone heard about the Beehive," Sasha said.

Sanjay found that he could stand . . . that breathing was easier . . . that he seemed to be gaining strength. Aside from the emotional whiplash of going from dead to alive again—not inconsiderable—and the lingering discomfort of wearing strips of second skin and moving with muscles that seemed untested, he felt good. Even great.

He knew that he had been killed by a blow to his face and head. He carefully raised his hand and felt the same set of bones he had always known.

Allowing for the uncertainty of his new, second life span, Sanjay thought, *Keanu brought me back good as new.*

He spotted Jaidev and Harley Drake and Zhao and then, to his amazement, the legendary Dale Scott, looking as old and confused as Sanjay had felt fifteen minutes earlier.

Sanjay raised his hand. "Hi, everyone," he said.

Then he heard a woman scream.

Oh my God, he thought, *Maren.*

Maren Houtman had been Sanjay's lover for the past five years. And had the *Adventure* mission not intervened, likely for years to come, possibly for life. She had become that important to him in that time, though not, he realized with some embarrassment and worry, so important that she had a place in his thoughts until now.

He couldn't possibly tell her that, either. Maren had many virtues, from intelligence and artistry (she had managed the trick of marrying pottery and sculpture to Substance K engineering) to classic Nordic beauty . . . but a sense of humor was not among them. Nor was she truly confident of Sanjay's affections; when they argued, it always seemed to be about the likelihood that he would find someone he preferred to her—

It was probably in her nature. When scooped up by the object at Bangalore back in August 2019, Maren had been a clerical assistant with the European Space Agency supporting her boss during the *Brahma* mission. ESA had no representatives in the *Brahma* crew but was providing tracking and communication data.

She had endured the flight to Keanu and the years of adjustment, loss, and recovery without ever interacting with Sanjay Bhat in a significant way. Maren had just been a thin blond woman who spoke little and busied herself with food preparation and distribution . . . two things Sanjay Bhat avoided.

It was only when she began installing fascinating objects on various HB structures, from representational or abstract pieces to a misguided bust of Zack Stewart, that Sanjay began to notice her. (In fact, their first real conversation had been an argument over what Sanjay thought was the silliness of creating likenesses of deceased humans.)

Now Maren was on him, at him, kissing, holding. She was so distraught that she was hardly able to form words. But he did hear: "They just told me yesterday!"

"What?" he said, his voice sounding better, though still not great.

"That you were . . . were . . ." And then, unable to say *were dead*, she started sobbing.

"Look," Sanjay said, "they were wrong!" He had to admit that he enjoyed the rush of emotion—he was blinking tears himself—as well as the comfort of Maren's strong arms around him.

And her fragrance. Early in their relationship, he had realized that he loved the way Maren smelled.

Now she fastened herself to him with a ferocity he would have loved to reciprocate in a more private setting. She made it difficult for him to walk, not that the pressing crowd of HBs would have allowed much speed. "Let's get you to the Temple," Harley Drake was saying.

Harley's command voice worked its magic. Maren's death grip relaxed and the other HBs moved aside. Sasha and Jordana and Maren formed around him on three sides. All were taller, Sanjay realized, and the variety of coloring—ginger Sasha, blond Maren, and dark Jordana—sent a jolt of smug, unjustified pride through him. *My three graces,* he thought.

Sanjay had taken perhaps a dozen steps and was beginning to feel as good as he had ever felt when the vision in his left eye changed, not so much distorted as overlaid with another image.

What the hell—?

He felt a growing pressure at the back of his skull, and now his right eye was affected, too. The overlay resolved itself into the image of what looked like a giant egg. But that was swiftly replaced by . . . unknown faces, figures, landscapes.

Inside his head he registered . . . static, voices in languages he didn't know, even music.

Then one word: *Ring.* It repeated, *Ring, ring, ring.*

He blinked but kept walking and smiling, telling himself, *This is normal, this is temporary, this is* not *the beginning of my Revenant sell-by moment,* right up to the moment where he fainted and fell on his face.

"Are you awake?" Maren's voice in his ears, low, almost a whisper; her face in his field of view, brows furrowed.

They were in the Temple now, second floor, Sanjay's work home for most of his adult life. Sanjay had been given a pair of trousers and a loose shirt. He was flat on his back on a couch; Maren was sitting on the floor next to him, his hand in hers.

He managed a quiet "Mmmm," but squeezed her hand and pulled her even closer.

His vision cleared. The tableau was utterly familiar and at the same time totally disorienting. Physically and mentally, he had prepared for weeks to leave Keanu—possibly for good. He had had terrific, painful arguments with Maren. "Why do you have to go?"

"I know more about the vehicle than anyone."

"And why did you have to be the expert?"

"I don't know. It's in my nature."

Maren's worst fears had become fact. There was always a risk with any space mission. *Adventure* could have exploded on launch. It could have suffered engine underperformance and drifted into a useless orbit, fatal to its crew.

Its thermal protection system could have failed. Even a small navigation failure would have caused them to miss Earth entirely, dooming them.

Then there was the possibility—certainty, it turned out—that they might be fired upon.

The method and likelihood of a return to Keanu remained uncertain.

When Sanjay considered the nature of the *Adventure* vehicle and mission . . . well, the odds might have actually been weighted in favor of failure and death.

And so far, he had experienced a little of both.

Yet . . . he had made it back. He was in his lover's arms again.

So why did he feel so guilty?

He realized that Sasha, Harley, Zhao, Jaidev, and several others were nearby, either staring at him with obvious concern or pretending not to. "How long was I out?" he said, loudly enough for everyone to hear.

"Fifteen minutes," Harley said. "We had to carry you." A typical Harley comment, which Sanjay appreciated.

"Sorry about that."

Maren was looking at his face. "How do you feel?"

A good question. He felt fine, except for the lingering pressure in his skull. The voices and other sounds were still present. Images kept flickering through his vision . . . they were less intrusive, but still present. It was as if his brain had learned to manage the flow of extraneous data during the fifteen-minute blackout.

And flow of data was what he had to be experiencing. Sanjay knew that one suspected reason for the Revenants' existence had been to communicate, to serve as a bridge between humans and alien intelligences who had not only a different language but unusual biologies and, for that matter, wildly unfamiliar frames of reference. He had heard, for example, that the Architect seemed to possess a sense of time that was far slower than that of humans . . . the same way that an insect's sense of time passing would be far faster.

Sanjay had become a bridge. Fine. His goal was to be a good bridge . . . and to still be standing more than a week hence.

"A little rattled," he told Maren and the others. "Hungry."

So they fed him typical Keanu food, which, given that he was ravenous, was the best thing he had ever tasted. (Another list of regrets for dying when he did . . . no chance to eat a proper Earth meal.) As he ate, he made sure to exchange reassuring looks with Maren while trying to answer questions from Jaidev, Harley, Sasha, and Zhao.

There were the expected ones. His last memory. His first sight and sounds upon revival. "Do you remember anything from in between?" Zhao said.

That question was surprising only because it came from pragmatic Zhao, the last human Sanjay would ever have expected to take interest in life after death.

Sanjay would have been the second least likely, and no matter how he replayed his moments of death and new life, he found no interregnum, no region between, no halfway-between-heaven-and-hell moment. "No. As far as I can tell, there was no gap." He snapped his fingers. "It was that fast."

Maren seemed upset by the whole notion, not that Sanjay could blame her. "How did this *happen*?" she was saying.

"Don't question it," Harley said. "Gift horses and all that—"

Unsurprisingly, this caused Maren to collapse in sobs.

"Oh, for God's sake, Harley," Sasha said.

"I'm a little curious, too," Sanjay said. "I mean, we knew that Keanu had the ability to . . . find an individual human soul and—"

"Please don't call it a soul!" Maren said.

"Fine, a human identity, a personality . . ." As he uttered these terms, he noticed changes in the signals inside his head, as if he were taking part in a kind of guessing game.

"A morphogenetic field," Jaidev offered. Then he smiled. "Whatever the hell that means."

That term resonated inside Sanjay's head. "My particular morphogenetic field was apparently tracked and then retrieved for, uh, reuse?" He smiled at Maren as he said that. She shook her head at the wickedness of it all. But she had stopped sobbing. "I don't think we're ever going to know how," he said. "But maybe we can figure out why."

"Keanu wanted you *back*. That's why," Jaidev said.

"Which is obvious and still tells us nothing," Zhao snapped.

"Keanu also seems to be monitoring us," Sasha said. "It's bad enough if it's watching or listening. It's terrifying to think that somewhere inside Keanu is a . . . a computer system that understands English and Hindi.

But I can accept that. I can imagine it. What I don't know is if Keanu is reading our minds."

"Unlikely," Jaidev said.

"And manipulating morphogenetic fields *is* likely?" Harley said.

"We can't know the answers to those questions," Zhao said. "Not yet. But add this to our list: Assume Keanu has been monitoring us all along, tracking our movements, growth—"

"Births, deaths," Sasha said.

Zhao nodded. "Especially deaths. And ask . . . why did the Beehive stop working? We thought it had been damaged in the rebooting of the core. Right now it seems as though Keanu just turned it off."

"And eventually turned it back on," Sanjay said. "I can't say I'm unhappy it did."

Maren had returned, snuggling up to him and taking his hand.

Now Harley looked at the others, making some nonverbal exchange of information. Then he turned to Sanjay. "Would you be willing to talk to Dale Scott?"

"Why not?"

As Zhao went to retrieve Dale, Sanjay said, "When did he turn up?" Harley and the others briefed him on Dale's sudden return. "Wait, he knew about our troubles?" Sanjay had to laugh. "He actually knew more than I did!"

"You had an excuse," Harley said.

"Yeah, I was pretty dead."

Maren got up. "I don't like this."

"You don't even know Dale Scott," Sanjay said.

"Why are you doing this?" she said. "Why are you putting yourself through it? You should be resting—"

"I've had enough rest," Sanjay snapped, immediately regretting his sharp tone. He did not want to quarrel with Maren. But he faced challenges that were greater and more important, frankly, than their relationship. "Sorry."

She looked at him, then shook her head. "Find me when you feel like it." And walked away.

As Maren left, she passed the arriving scarecrow of Keanu, Dale Scott.

The moment Sanjay saw Dale, the noise inside his head increased. He could feel his heart rate spiking—the imagery was clearer now, the sounds less chaotic.

Something was definitely happening.

Then Dale Scott put his hands to his head.

"Are you feeling that, too?" Sanjay said.

"Probably."

"What do you see or hear?"

"The vesicle, mostly," Dale said.

Which confirmed what Sanjay had thought. "We're on the same wavelength." He knew all about the vesicle and the plan to use it as a secret strike weapon against the Reivers.

"I can speak for all of us, I think," Sasha Blaine said, "when I tell you that you two are freaking us out."

"Sorry," Dale said. "I've spent a lot of time trying to tap into the Keanu system. I don't think I've mastered it." He pointed at Sanjay. "But you've got it."

Yes, he realized, as images and data seemed to come into focus, arranging themselves in accessible columns. He had glimpses of Keanu, both its interior and exterior. He saw Earthscapes, too . . . not just India and the Pacific, but a desert and a giant structure of some kind.

It was all linked, and he could feel the connections without being quite sure how it fit together. Nevertheless, the feeling was electrifying—almost worth dying for.

Almost.

"When do you launch the vesicle?" Sanjay said to Zhao.

"Within hours," Zhao said.

"I need to be on it."

Day Eight

No word now from Colin. It's three hours past the time when he should have reached his destination.

Anyone? Anywhere?

I'm getting a bad feeling. . . .

POSTED ON KETTERING GROUP,
APRIL 20, 2040

XAVIER

The transition from free flight and nervous optimism to airborne captivity and depression took, Xavier Toutant guessed, about five seconds.

That was for him, and he was, as his momma and numerous employers used to say, slow on the uptake. He suspected that for Rachel and Pav, Yahvi, Chang, and Edgely, it was more or less instantaneous.

As for Zeds—

"What is happening?" the Sentry said. He had been in a quiet state akin to hibernation for several hours. It was, Xavier knew, a way of conserving his suit's resources. And no doubt a means of coping with the tedium. He had been able to offer Xavier little assistance beyond holding large items, and the need for that had passed quickly. Xavier's job soon became monitoring the proteus as it prepared the two biological packages.

And with their capture, to finish at least one of them before they landed.

"Okay, you probably saw, we're being escorted," Jo Zhang said. She finally opened the cockpit door ten minutes after the destruction of the decoy plane and the turn toward the coast.

"By whom?" Chang said. He seemed the most shocked of the group.

"Those are U.S. Air Force planes," Jo said.

"Old ones, too," Pav said. "F-22s. They were flying those when I was a kid."

Rachel was slumped in her seat, rubbing her temples. Xavier knew that look; he had seen it frequently in the endless, contentious planning meetings for the *Adventure* flight. "What about Benvides and Quentin?" she said.

Jo hesitated. "I could tell you I don't know, but you don't need bullshit right now. Their plane was destroyed."

"Thank you for your honesty," Edgely said.

Even from the rear of the cabin, dividing his gaze between the proteus next to him and the backs of everyone's heads, Xavier could see that Jo's blunt statement had not made Rachel happy. Her eyes filling with tears, she was shaking her head with great agitation. "Did we have any warning?" she said.

"Nothing," Jo said. "One moment we were doing just fine, preparing to break off, the next . . ."

The only thing keeping Rachel from getting out of her seat and confronting Jo was Yahvi's condition. The girl was sitting next to Rachel, hunched, probably hugging a pillow to keep from screaming. Rachel put her arm around Yahvi and leaned in to her.

Questions were still flying around the cockpit, from Chang and Edgely and Pav to Jo. None of the answers provided any information to Xavier . . . nothing he didn't already know, that is.

They were screwed.

Jo finally said, "I'll let you know the moment we learn anything. Right now, we're just following our escorts."

Leaving his machine to its final assembly, Xavier had started moving forward. "Any idea where?" he said.

"We're flying north over the Los Angeles basin," Jo said. "Steve thinks we're headed for Edwards, since that's the nearest military base."

Xavier sat down next to Rachel. He'd always wanted to see Edwards. Living in Houston on the fringes of the space program and its culture of aviation, Xavier had grown quite familiar with the famous California base and its history of exotic aircraft and space shuttle landings.

But not like this.

"Will you be able to get anything finished?" Rachel was asking him.

"One of the packages. Maybe."

"It should be—"

"The second one."

Rachel nodded, as if to say, *Thank God someone is doing what I need.* "Should you be—?" *Up here with me,* she was going to say.

"It's on auto. I'm going right back. I just wanted to"—he shrugged— "see how you're doing." He inclined his head toward Yahvi, who had herself bent pretzel-like, head bowed, eyes closed, hugging a pillow to her chest.

Rachel didn't bother to fake a smile. "We'll just see, won't we?"

Colin Edgely had been peering out the right-side windows. "Those are F-22s, for sure," he said.

"That's what I said," Pav told him.

"Sorry, mate." The Aussie smiled. "A bit nervous, I guess. Trying to find the silver lining."

"How's that going for you?" Xavier said. He couldn't help it.

"Those planes got close enough to show that the pilots were human. How about that?"

"That's good how?" Pav was taking up the argument.

Edgely was game, however. Xavier was fascinated by the way people responded to stress—including himself. He knew that he tended to wind down, to feel sleepy, like a small animal in the jaws of a larger, hungrier one. This couldn't be true, of course; such a trait would have evolved out of existence due to the early deaths of its holders. So, fine, then, call it calm in the face of danger.

Others, like Rachel and Pav, got tense and couldn't hide it.

Some, like Chang and Yahvi, became tense and quiet.

Then there were those, like Edgely, who just got stupid. "It means we're not dealing with Aggregates." Not until we land, Xavier thought. As did everyone who heard this.

"It's Edwards," Jo told them, popping her head out of the cockpit for a moment. "On the ground in ten minutes."

"Then what?" Pav said. He stood up and stretched. To Xavier, he seemed spring-loaded, ready to fight . . . someone.

"Well," Rachel said, "if they wanted us dead, they would have just blown us out of the sky like the other plane. So I'm guessing it's prison and interrogation."

"Probably some kind of show, too," Edgely said.

"Colin, please stop speaking," Rachel said.

Chang finally spoke. "I'm guessing we should all belt in."

"Thank you for that," Pav said, not hiding the sarcasm.

"Who speaks for us?" Chang said.

"Why would it matter?" Rachel said.

Chang turned toward her. Xavier could see genuine fear on the man's face. "Let me rephrase that: How are we to act? Do you plan to cooperate, or resist?"

"I haven't decided yet," Rachel said. "Are you in a hurry?"

"We might have different agendas," Chang said.

"Meaning you'll, what? Surrender? Rat us out?" Hearing this, Xavier remembered that Chang knew something of their plans. His lassitude vanished, replaced by fear: Even in 2019, it was possible to drug a prisoner and get him to say every secret he knew. He couldn't imagine that the Aggregates were less capable.

He glanced back at the proteus, still laboring away. The second package wasn't going to be done, anyway, but Xavier hated the idea that the Aggregates would know all about it the moment they shot his brain full of truth serum or the Reiver equivalent.

"I can try to bargain," Chang was saying. "My government might have some leverage. The question is . . . do you want to be included? Or is it everyone for himself?"

"Given that we have no weapons," Rachel said, "no idea where we are, and no cavalry to ride to the rescue, I am eager to tell you, sure, do what you can."

Even with Rachel's cold, accurate description of the situation, to Xavier, fighting still sounded like a better idea than simply taking what the Aggregates handed out.

Xavier sat through the by-now-familiar touchdown and used the longer-than-expected taxi to squeeze a few more precious minutes out of his

3-D printer. The package was not complete; he would need another hour, perhaps two. And clearly he wasn't going to get it.

He hoped Rachel and Pav had a Plan C. "We're not going to the main base," Pav said. "They're taking us to the north end."

"Probably more secure," Edgely said. He had recovered from Rachel's rebuke. "And look at that!" He pointed out the window. In spite of his other concerns, Xavier looked, too, seeing a giant cube-shaped structure off to the north and west. It appeared to be featureless, dun-colored, twenty stories for sure, three or four times taller than any of the more normal-looking towers and office buildings that made up the Edwards main base. "Some kind of Aggregate thing, you suppose?"

"Tell you what," Pav said. "Let's just ask when we have time."

The plane stopped in front of a weathered, ancient hangar. Xavier decided to keep the proteus running—what the hell.

Rachel and Pav were out of their seats instantly. Pav went to the door. "Can you see who's out there?" Rachel said. She was headed to the rear of the plane.

"People," Pav said. "No Reivers yet."

Rachel patted Zeds on his massive shoulder, then crouched next to Xavier. "How are we doing?"

Xavier chanced a look and saw the expected armed guards, four helmeted U.S. military types with weapons waiting where the Gulfstream's door and ramp would land. Behind them were half a dozen other humans, three of them in strange black uniforms. "Not finished."

"Shit." Rachel turned to Zeds, then back to Xavier. "Keep it running as long as possible. We don't know if they'll realize what it is."

As she stood up, and Zeds began the process of standing up and moving, the cockpit door opened. Steve and Jo emerged, looking shaken. "Let us go first," Jo said.

Except for Xavier, they were all out of their seats as the door opened, letting in fresh desert air. Such a pretty day, Xavier thought, so much more inviting than Bangalore.

Such a shame.

As Steve and Jo went out, Xavier could hear harsh voices and words from outside. Xavier could make out words. "Down!" "Hands up!"

Two soldiers entered, weapons tracking from person to person. Yahvi whimpered. "For Christ's sake," Pav said. "We're coming out."

At that moment the soldiers registered Zeds's presence. One of them shouted a muffled, "Jesus!" and backed up, bumping into Edgar Chang.

The other soldier misinterpreted that as Chang attacking the soldier, slamming him with the butt of his rifle. "Hey!" Pav shouted, grabbing the first soldier. Suddenly four men were shoving and shouting—the two soldiers, Pav, and Edgely. Chang lay slumped in a seat.

"Leave them alone!" Rachel was shouting. "We aren't resisting!"

Xavier glanced at the proteus. He still needed more time—

Another human entered, a young man in black. "Oh, no," he said, swiftly inserting himself between the combatants and preventing real injury, not that it was possible, in the tight space, for anyone to do much damage with bare hands. The soldiers had not fired their weapons.

"Everyone, I am Counselor Nigel." The young man's voice was confident, relaxed, as if he broke up fights every day. Perhaps the English accent helped. From what Xavier could see he was thin, south of thirty, the kind of person who handles large sums of money with little awareness. "These are my companions, Counselors Cory and Ivetta." Two more young people in black had crowded into the cabin. They were young, too: a thickset man and a petite, dark-haired woman.

Meanwhile, the soldiers backed themselves up against the cockpit bulkhead. "We welcome the crew of *Adventure* to Free Nation U.S."

Rachel slid forward. "Wow, so polite, considering you just shot down one of our planes and killed two of our friends."

"That was regrettable and avoidable," Counselor Nigel said. "We mean you no harm."

"Which is why our pilots are kneeling at gunpoint."

Xavier glanced out the window. Steve and Jo were kneeling on the tarmac, hands behind their heads.

"These are precautions that will end as soon as possible."

Rachel was in Counselor Nigel's face. "Do you want to put the handcuffs on us here and march us out one at a time, or wait until we're outside?"

Counselor Nigel stared at her for a moment, then chose—wisely, Xavier thought—to drop the pretense of normality. "One at a time," he said. He turned to Chang and Edgely. "You two will go first."

Edgely helped Chang to the door. The older man looked badly shaken and unsteady. "Then you, Captain Stewart, followed by your daughter, then Mr. Radhakrishnan," Counselor Nigel said.

Rachel took Yahvi's hand, partly to reassure the girl, partly, Xavier suspected, to show a bit more defiance. "Better leave Zeds for last," Rachel said to Counselor Nigel. "He takes a while."

Then she and Yahvi went through the door.

Xavier glanced at the readouts. He still needed more time, though less than he'd thought earlier. That was one of the problems with the proteus—lack of precision. Ten minutes, possibly.

And the three officers were working their way toward him. "Mr. Toutant," Counselor Nigel said.

"Nice to meet you."

"Would you come with us, please?"

"I'm not actually feeling that good," Xavier said, improvising only slightly. The tense maneuvers had left him momentarily queasy and dizzy. "Can I just rest here for a while?"

"You'd be more comfortable in quarters."

"You mean jail?"

"You're not going to jail."

"Great, then I'd like to rent a car. I've always wanted to see L.A. Maybe you guys could help me with that."

Counselor Nigel's patience expired. He gestured to his companions and the soldiers, who started for Xavier.

Zeds, who had been silent and motionless throughout the whole exchange, stepped forward, blocking the five assailants as easily as an NFL lineman would a group of peewees.

"Mr. Toutant, tell it to step aside!"

"Zeds," Xavier said, trying not to laugh, "try to get out of their way."

"I am," Zeds said, his voice booming in the cabin. Xavier wasn't actually sure that Zeds had deliberately gotten in Nigel's way . . . apparently Nigel and his cronies were confused, too—or they might have shot the Sentry.

Or tried to. Xavier wasn't sure gunfire would be an effective way to stop the big alien.

While the six beings were trying to sort themselves out, Xavier watched the printer and its line to the Plan B container, weighing the moment when he would have to disconnect it.

Minutes. "Hey, Counselor Nigel, everyone. I think I'm feeling better, so let's just all relax—"

Bing! It took Xavier a considerable amount of willpower to keep from looking at the proteus.

Zeds's struggles had ceased. He was now past Counselor Nigel and passing between the two soldiers, who were keeping their weapons trained on him.

"And since we're all being calm about things," Xavier said, hoping to keep everyone's attention on him, not his cargo, "I would love to know how you found us."

"I don't have that information," Counselor Nigel said, "and probably couldn't tell you if I did. Please be aware, however, that entry to Free Nation airspace is tightly controlled. Any unauthorized aircraft was in danger."

"Yeah, I figured," Xavier said. Then he shouted, "Zeds!"

All heads turned toward the Sentry, who, bent over like an old man, paused midway through in the cockpit door. As they looked away, as innocuously as he could, Xavier kicked the connecting tube free of the Plan B container. "Wait for me at the bottom of the stairs!"

The only giveaway was the smell of residual Substance K poison in the tube.

The ruse seemed to have worked: Xavier stepped away from the printer, past Counselor Nigel and his two companions, and was about to be grabbed by the soldiers when he had another thought. "Can we wait just a second?"

He started digging through the Substance K cargo. "Don't do that," Counselor Nigel said. He and his male companion tackled Xavier before he could examine more than four boxes.

But that was sufficient. As he was gently but firmly hauled forward and toward the cabin door, he carried with him the sight of a small unit stuck to the bottom of one of the containers.

It was a bug, almost certainly some kind of tracking device that had told Free Nation U.S. and the Aggregates exactly where Rachel's crew was at all times.

Fucking Kaushal.

The lamestream media has been telling us for years that the Aggregates brought peace and prosperity to North America—that's only the biggest of their lies.

But now they are ignoring the stories of some kind of migration, all the units and formations moving to the southwest, apparently Arizona.

At the same time Keanu is back and sending ships here. Will we be seeing some kind of landing in the desert? If so, will it be Aggregates leaving?

Or more of them arriving?

Or something even worse!?!

POSTER TREYNOLDS, TRUEPOST.COM,
APRIL 20, 2040

WHIT

"L minus eighty-five," a woman's voice said, as Counselor Kate swiped a key and opened the door to Ring mission control.

"You're sure you're not giving me too much time?" Whit said. He joked when nervous. Amazingly, few people ever understood that.

"This is an emergency. We had a dropout."

The twenty hours between his bizarre encounter with Aggregate Carbon-143 and the terminal count to First Light were the strangest and most exhausting in Whit Murray's life.

His THE handler, Counselor Kate, had found him just seconds after the Aggregate creature departed. "Come with me," she said. "You saw the clock."

Fifteen minutes later he was inside Ring mission control, a windowless room whose walls were screens showing the Ring structure and elements, some of them close-ups of pipes and electrical connections, others of nasty-looking military hardware, still others landscapes. Overall, it reminded Whit of old footage he had seen of the moments before rocket launches . . . the giant frosted tubes, the cables, the gantries, the wisps of vapor.

Although every human in the room seemed calm, there was no chatter, no sound except for labored breathing. It was the tensest environment Whit had ever experienced. For a moment he regretted possessing his "talent," or at least letting it be discovered. "Here," Kate said, showing him a new station in the last row, which was empty.

The cubicle looked a lot like his former station—the same chair, the same keyboard and screen. What was different was a cyberlink headset and gloves. "Put these on." Kate picked them up and prepared to help him.

"I've worn them before," he said, though to play games when he was thirteen, not to help control a beam of energy strong enough to microwave a planet.

The headset and gloves were warm, as if someone else had just removed them. Whit wondered what had happened to the previous wearer—on a break, he hoped, as opposed to being taken out and executed for some kind of failure. He wanted to ask Kate what "dropout" meant, but this wasn't the moment.

She wasn't leaving him, however. "I'll be with you." She sat down at the unused station next to Whit's and donned her own headset and gloves.

Then, as his eyes, ears, and brain adjusted to the link, as he felt the familiar meld with the system (he had a mouse pad but would also be able to access new data with the twitch of a facial muscle), Whit forgot about Kate and actually ceased to worry about his role.

He just took in the experience, literally feeling the pulse of power as it built throughout the Ring system, being pulled from grids all over the western Free Nation U.S. One window showed him the grid and the flow of electrons. Another displayed the storage.

Then there was the array of mirrors that would catch the initial burst of energy and shape it. There were hundreds of them—a figure Whit knew as a number, but something quite different as an experience. He felt them all as petals of a gigantic silvery flower, each quivering in a gentle breeze.

In another window was the glory of the portal itself, still a rotating, vibrating wire frame (its shape responded to minute shifts in the aiming of the mirrors) thousands of meters tall . . . like a ghostly sun hovering over the Arizona desert.

He had access to the strike force, too, the rows and rows of vehicles poised to roll through the portal the instant it opened.

And they would be arriving on some other planet, an idea Whit still found unlikely.

Wait, here was a window that showed the target planet!

"Counselor Kate," he said, a bit tentatively. Who else would be listening?

"Yes, Whit."

"Is there some window or program I should be working in?"

"Not today. This is your orientation. We anticipate adjustments after First Light and will be conducting daily sims until launch. Your job is to get to know what's in those windows, because you might wind up working in any one of them."

Much as Whit disliked the sound of daily sims, especially with the end result being the irradiation of Free Nation U.S., he loved being given permission to roam freely.

He had always heard that the Aggregate networks had everything you could possibly want to know. It was the Internet plus the undernet plus whatever the aliens knew. And once you had access, you had total access.

Granted, humans would be unable to understand much of what they would find . . . but that still left a considerable amount of data, such as that dealing with humans and what happened to them.

Like Whit's parents.

Not just yet, though. Better to see what exactly is going on—

"Sixty minutes," the countdown lady said, seemingly whispering right inside his head.

Excellent. As the count progressed, Whit glanced at the operational windows on his screen only long enough to be sure things were still going forward.

The rest of the hour was a glorious dive into a pool of wonder . . . the Aggregate data on the world they planned to invade.

The only drawback was that, unlike other data screens at Site A, which were optimized for human use, specifically human users of English with Arabic numerals, the material on the target world retained Aggregate marking and terminology.

Nevertheless, images needed no captions. And there were no obvious limits to access.

As Whit had come to expect, the material was displayed like a tree, starting with an image of the world itself . . . a sphere with multicolored horizontal bands (red and orange at the poles, becoming bright blue at its equator) and a series of rings around its equator. The planet seemed large even though Whit could not read the scalar notations and saw nothing to compare it to. Maybe it was the resemblance to Jupiter or Saturn.

Interesting: Where Saturn's rings, seen close up, were clearly made of billions of fragments of ice and rock, a quick zoom in showed that the fragments in this world's rings were uniform cubes. *Of what?* Whit wondered. *Or why?*

As the view shifted, Whit saw another startling image of structures beyond the rings . . . at least three moons, all in an orbit that had the same inclination, an obvious sign of artificial placement.

The view swooped close to one of the moons, revealing gridlike structures on a surface that resembled, in many places, a cue ball. It reminded Whit of images of Keanu taken by the departing *Destiny* astronauts back in 2019 as encrusted soil and ice on the NEO's surface boiled off and revealed similar smooth material below. Were these distant moons cousins of Keanu? Was he seeing starships under construction?

It was impressive and even terrifying to think that the inhabitants of this planet had the desire and ability to move and reshape rings and moons.

For that matter, what was this planet's *name*? Every window bore the same notation, but in Aggregate lettering and figures. He would have loved to have just that single term translated, though it was entirely possible, given the Aggregates, that their designation for the target world required a string of sixty-odd figures.

Whit decided to just think of it as "Rainbow," since the progression of its banding seemed to match up with the visible spectrum seen in a rainbow.

Where was Rainbow? Almost certainly very far away. Whit wondered if the planet was a relatively close neighbor of Earth's, possibly circling Alpha Centauri or some star like that. Probably not. A starship like Keanu could make the voyage from Alpha Centauri to Earth. A rational intelligence would choose that mode over the energy portal, if said energy portal left your departure planet a smoking ruin. . . .

But who ever said the Aggregates were rational? By human standards?

And who lived there? Were its inhabitants machinelike bugs similar to the Aggregates? Or something entirely different?

Maybe this was the home of the Sentries or the Skyphoi, some of the other aliens inhabiting Keanu. Either of them could have been Aggregate enemies.

Or humanoids?

So far Whit had to be satisfied with aerial views, satellite imagery showing broad rivers and immense forests, the usual mountains and plains. The undeveloped areas, if that was what they were, looked much like those of planet Earth, allowing for an unusual color tint (everything seemed more purple than green, though that might have been the Aggregate filtering, not true color). Whit guessed that undeveloped landscapes looked pretty much the same everywhere.

(It also seemed that Rainbow was prone to storms. Every relatively close image had a wall of menacing thunderclouds on the horizon. Wider angles had swirling cyclonic structures in their hearts.)

There were cityscapes, too, though, and these were something else . . . one of them covered an entire continent. Whit had seen images of urban sprawl from space, but human cities had winding rivers and freeways and obvious downtowns and parks and twisty streets.

Rainbow's giant cities were like . . . well, they reminded him of circuit boards in their angularity and their utter lack of any apparently organic life.

Of course, he was still seeing everything from a great height. He blinked to see if there were other windows or tools—

Oh, much better. Suddenly Whit was falling very fast, like a passenger on a meteoroid or, more likely, some kind of space probe. Given the way the ground was rushing toward him, not a probe expected to be returned.

The image went black.

Whit clicked: Here was another view, from a more stable platform. Now he was flying above a purple Rainbow forest, thunderclouds ahead of him and likely making the ride a bumpy one (the imagery seemed to vibrate).

It was not just a visual experience: Whit could feel stinging wintry wind on his face, hear air rushing past his ears, smell a mossy fragrance so thick it almost choked him.

He spied a formation in the distant mountains . . . a giant dish embedded in a valley with a tall spike of some kind pointing skyward.

That image died abruptly, too.

A new one . . . now Whit skimmed across a body of water, then low tidal land as he approached a city. Unlike a human habitation, there were no suburbs, no gradual transition from open field to town, just an abrupt *here you are*, flying over blocky golden towers. The wind dropped; he heard a low, rumbling hum; he smelled smoke.

He was swooping low now, barely skirting the tops of the Rainbow buildings. (And unlike human buildings, roofs here seemed to be designed with as much care as the fronts. They probably had some function.)

Suddenly his platform, probably some kind of remotely piloted spycraft, made an abrupt turn and dive . . . now Whit could see creatures in the "streets," and miracle of miracles, they were humanoid, though slow moving—

"Fifteen minutes." Whit heard the countdown voice for the first time in three quarters of an hour. Had he been so absorbed in his "tour" of planet Rainbow that he'd missed the other announcements?

He gave the Ring windows more attention. Most were as they had been earlier: static views, graphic representations of power levels and aiming points, all moving in one direction or another.

One quadrant of Whit's display had an orange overlay, however, and several figures pulsing in red.

Out of the corner of his eye he saw a pair of operators emerging from their cubicles. One seemed quite agitated, gesturing so violently that a trio of THE officers immediately appeared.

Followed by a formation of Aggregates. That was never a good sign.

"Whit!" Counselor Kate's voice hissed in his headset. "Get back to your screen!"

Whit realized he had poked his head up like a prairie dog. He turned away from what was becoming a scuffle and tried to concentrate on his screen, especially his views of planet Rainbow, the city, its slow-moving inhabitants.

He wondered when and how this imagery had been obtained—if Dehm and Carbon-143 were telling the truth, the energy portal was something the Aggregates had never used before. Not only had they never sent themselves or military hardware across the gulf of light-years, they hadn't sent data, either. Both were subject to the same limitations.

If so, it meant that this imagery was old . . . centuries at least. Or, if the rumors about Keanu's age were true, millennia.

It was crazy enough to think about invading a planet—though given the Aggregates' success in taking over a good chunk of Earth, not entirely crazy—but to do so based on information that was current when humans had yet to plant a crop of wheat . . . that was audacious.

The size of Rainbow explained the need for a massive force. (And Whit had seen one tiny window displaying what he believed to be the "order of battle," with the "portal" opening in three different locations on the planet.)

The tour of the Rainbow city ended, and when Whit tried to click to additional images, he found himself back where he started, falling through the atmosphere.

It occurred to Whit that he might not be seeing imagery at all, but rather generated material, like a video game. Hadn't Counselor Kate said there would be simulations? Weren't sims just like games—?

In spite of his misgivings, both about THE enforcement methods and the nasty side effects of the Ring's ignition, Whit couldn't help being excited about being involved with this . . . it sure beat the work he'd been doing in Vegas.

"Five minutes."

Time to pay attention. Everything seemed to be going fine . . . except for the orange displays in the corner of his screen. It didn't seem to be a critical area—the windows were labeled *RANGE* and *I-STRUCTURE* and *ENVIRONMENT.*

Whit wished he could talk to Dehm. It was possible, he supposed, that his older friend was in one of the other cubicle stations. Without Dehm, he was stuck with Counselor Kate. "What's all this orange?"

"Deviations from design."

"Shouldn't they hold until it doesn't deviate?"

"Humans might," Counselor Kate said. "Aggregates won't. They have faith in their designs that we don't."

"Yeah, but some of this material may not be included in their design."

"Do us both a favor and don't tell them."

"I'm only talking to you," he said. He hoped.

"One minute."

At that moment the Aggregate unit passed behind Whit. If reaching the last minute before the First Light hadn't ramped up his heart rate, the presence of a dozen aliens would. It didn't matter that he had grown slightly more comfortable with Carbon-143; Whit still found the Aggregates menacing.

Especially since the formation stopped, leaving at least three of the chunky creatures directly behind Whit and Counselor Kate.

"Thirty seconds."

There were flashes from Whit's screens . . . the mirrors making minute final adjustments. The power levels all reached the top of their various graphs. Whit realized it was silly, but he thought he could *feel* it, as if the entire building were throbbing and ready to explode.

"Twenty," the voice said. "Fifteen. Ten. Systems are enabled."

Whit wondered what it would look like? A big flash? Or would it just be invisible—?

It was a flash, so fast and so bright that it overwhelmed the camera filters and made Whit blink.

A new window opened on Whit's screen showing a ridiculously large cone with rippling edges rising over the desert landscape. Wider and taller and taller and wider, as if it reached to the edge of the Earth's atmosphere.

Still transparent, the edges solidified . . . and then, for an instant, Whit could have sworn he saw dark space inside the cone, and the edge of a planet that could have been Rainbow.

Then there was another flash, less intense but no less startling, this one from the upper left-side screens—the orange ones were now bright red.

The cone collapsed, so quickly and dramatically that Whit hunched, as if he expected a structure as tall as ten mountains to land on his head.

Don't be stupid! he thought. The cone was just an energy field. Though God only knew what particles and rays it threw off as it spun up.

The control center was absolutely quiet, surprising Whit. Where were the alarms, the hooting horns? Because this was clearly very bad news.

No one seemed to be moving, either, not even the Aggregate formation. It was as if everyone were either staring at a screen in numbed shock, or receiving data downloads in a similar state.

Finally he heard: "First Light plus fifteen seconds," from the calm and apparently artificial control center voice. "System shutdown."

Whit loved euphemisms. He would have called the event an "utter failure."

"This is bad," Counselor Kate said, the first truly human thing Whit could recall her saying.

"What happened?"

"What do you think? Something failed and the whole thing crashed!"

"System crash, you mean," Whit said. "It looks as though most of the hardware is still whole." It appeared that way in the windows on the right-hand side of his screen, though it was possible they were screen captures and hadn't been updated, that entire pieces of the massive complex lay in ruins.

"No, I'm seeing a lot of damage to the projectors at segment 270." Whatever that was, likely some portion of the Ring.

"What do you think happened?"

"Really? Somebody ignored a bunch of warnings and went ahead with the test."

"Well, it wasn't me," Whit said, regretting his words the moment he said them. *You get nervous, you make dumb jokes.*

Fortunately, Counselor Kate was too upset to notice. He heard her speaking to others, likely her two THE comrades.

"Operators," the countdown voice said, "please secure all data."

"What does that mean?" Whit said.

Counselor Kate was now standing behind him, reaching over his shoulder to his keyboard. "Freeze your screen so every operation can be analyzed. Like this."

While Whit appreciated the assistance—he had no idea how to "secure all data"—he was concerned that a thorough review would expose his snooping into the invasion of Rainbow world.

Given the complexity of the Ring system, and his peripheral role as a mere observer, it wasn't too likely he would be examined.

Or so he told himself. He could see several silver linings in this dark cloud for the Aggregates.

First, the "invasion" appeared to be off.

Second, North America and most of Earth were spared for a while yet.

The downside, of course, was that a delay still left the Aggregates in charge of Earth.

Now there was general motion in the control center. The nearest Aggregate formation stirred to life, moving in groups of three to block the aisles.

Standing up, Whit could see at least two other formations—two dozen individual units—entering the center.

"All human operators remain on console," the system voice said. "No one is leaving."

Day Nine

SATURDAY, APRIL 21, 2040

SPY PLANE SHOT DOWN OFF CALIFORNIA COAST!

China suspected; no comment from Pentagon

DRAGONSTAR 3 EXPECTED TO WIN WEEKEND

Latest thriller and game opening across Free Nation U.S.

FAITHFUL FLOCK TO ARIZONA

Holy sightings on North Rim

HEADLINES, *NATIONAL TIMES*,
7 P.M., FRIDAY, APRIL 20, 2040

DALE

"There's our hermit now."

Dale almost jumped at the voice behind him: Harley Drake, with Jaidev. Somehow they had sneaked up on him.

Well, there had been chaos in the Temple for the past two hours. People were rushing in and out, many of them immediately heading up the ramps to the upper floors, creating, of all things, an HB traffic jam as they collided with those coming down. There were raised voices, several shoves, and no doubt some bruised feelings.

It would have been a disheartening sight for those, like the recently departed Rachel Stewart-Radhakrishnan, who often said that the HB community was somehow better than any comparable group of Earth-based humans. "Our shared struggle to survive in an incredibly inhospitable environment made us better," she said more than once in Dale's hearing.

To be fair, Rachel had been in her midtwenties then . . . and Dale wasn't perfectly certain that those had been her exact words. But her attitude seemed to be that because they were freed from the whole apparatus of human life in the twenty-first century—no computers, television, fast food, air travel, assault rifles, or runway models—the HBs had been able to create a more perfect world, an idealistic commune of some kind that, unlike most communities, had a clear common goal . . . to free Earth from alien overlords.

There was some truth to that. And at times Dale had allowed himself to wallow in the warm bath of the idea.

But to his mind, over time the HBs turned out to be just as greedy, petty, stupid, and confused as any group of humans.

Witness this day and the circus.

Eating a leftover meal of curry and naan, Dale Scott had been watching calmly, if a bit resentfully, from a corner of the ground floor.

His resentment was partly due to his lack of involvement in the activities, most of which seemed directed at the looming launch of the new Keanu vesicle, the big common goal that struck Dale as only slightly less ludicrous than Rachel's *Adventure* mission. When he was thirteen he had read a lurid paperback with a title like *Seven Against Infinity*. (Had good old Wade Williams written that?) Even then the idea of one small group of humans successfully waging war on a planet filled with hostile aliens struck Dale as unworkable. The reality had not been an improvement.

Compounding the original attempt with a second effort that might involve twice as many humans equipped with exotic weapons—well, it was slightly better but still not in the doable range.

"Shouldn't you two be planning your new invasion of Earth?"

Harley waved a dismissive hand. "Zhao's got that, don't worry."

"When do you launch?"

Harley looked at Jaidev. "Four hours," the engineer from India said. He seemed worn down, far older than his years. Planning invasions must do that to a man.

"You don't seem all that enthusiastic."

Jaidev flopped down on the chair across from Harley. "Too many unknowns."

Jaidev had never had much time for Dale Scott, and vice versa. Dale found the ISRO man arrogant and too certain that he was the smartest individual in the habitat. Jaidev no doubt found Dale too irreverent and untrustworthy.

Nothing had happened to change that . . . yet here he was, apparently open to a conversation. So Dale ventured a question: "Such as whether to send Sanjay Bhat?"

Now Harley Drake sat down, too.

The Sanjay situation was the secondary cause for Dale's pique: His time with the Revenant had been brutally cut short. They had just managed to make a connection, some bizarre link through Keanu, Dale believed. But then Zhao had a question, and while that was being dealt with, Sanjay's girlfriend interrupted the whole affair.

Not that Dale had anything against women. Being too attentive to women had hurt him in the military, at NASA and pretty much everywhere he'd gone. Hell, he could make the argument he wouldn't have wound up on Keanu if not for his involvement with Valya Makarova in Bangalore.

But he preferred women who understood the larger realities. Such as the fact that her boyfriend had actually been killed. Whatever relationship they had had was over, defunct, history. Maren whatever-her-name-was had no further claim on Sanjay's time—or his heart.

Especially since, as Dale and everyone knew . . . his time was limited. Like all Revenants, the man had been reborn for a specific purpose, to communicate a message . . . not to play kissy-face.

Harley smiled. "What do you think, Dale? Knowing what you do, would you send him?"

Dale's impulse was to say, *Absolutely*—this in spite of his eagerness to work with Sanjay. But he wanted to see what cards Jaidev and Harley would play. "What do you two want?"

"I'm for it," Harley said. "Jaidev is a big negative."

Dale turned to Jaidev. "Why?"

The engineer shifted in his chair, as if he resented being questioned by an outcast. "We've spent too much time training the team. The vesicle is smaller than the ones we flew in; resources are strained."

"Oh, come on, you've got the magic printers and Keanu tech!" Dale said. "You're going to send this thing to Earth on a fast burn, right? It's not going to take four days. That's a false argument."

Drake laughed. "He's got you there, Jay."

"All right," Jaidev said. "I'm not sure Sanjay can be trusted."

"He could be a Reiver-powered Revenant?"

"Something like that."

"That's unlikely to the point of non-existence," Dale said. "Even less likely than the chances that your two ships are going to take down the Reivers on Earth."

Jaidev sat up straighter, as if Dale had just poked him. *Good; now he's paying attention.* "We think we have a good chance—"

"Or we wouldn't be risking it," Harley finished.

"Look," Dale said, "I'm arguing against my own interests here—"

"What possible interest could you have in this?" Jaidev spat. "You've been off in the wilderness for sixteen years! A week ago I wanted you in jail, and I'm still not sure that's where you shouldn't be!"

Harley Drake, who had turned into a mature man of reason during the past twenty years, placed a soothing hand on Jaidev's arm. "We talked about this, Jay. We were wrong to lock him up—"

"And no good at it, if you'll recall," Dale said.

"Dale knew things we didn't," Harley said. "And I think he still does." He faced Dale. "Continue, please."

"I know the history of the Revenants as well as anyone," Dale said. "They were always sent as communicators. They always had a purpose. Sanjay's purpose is to help you with your invasion. It can't be anything else."

"Not to talk us out of it?" Jaidev said.

"Has he?"

"No," the engineer said. "But he hasn't offered any particular insights, either." He frowned. "You were the one who said the Reivers might be building some big damn weapon. Shouldn't Sanjay be telling us if it exists, where it is, how we can beat it?"

"Maybe," Dale said. "Or maybe Keanu knows it's nothing to worry about . . . that you already have the ability to evade it or destroy it."

Jaidev closed his eyes briefly. "This is all guesswork."

Now Harley slid forward. "And this is what I've been trying to tell you," he said to Jaidev. "Military operations aren't engineering. There are *never* any certainties; the figures *never* add up."

"'No battle plan survives contact with the enemy,'" Dale said, surprised that he remembered the old quote from Air Command and Staff College.

"All you can do is make the best plans—which we have—then trust your instincts." He turned to Dale again. "And my instinct says, go with Sanjay. One thing we can be sure of is that Keanu or the Architects don't like the Reivers. Why would they bring our man back if not to get rid of them?"

Jaidev stood up. "I'm still not sure."

"You'll never be sure," Harley said. "You want a vote?"

Jaidev snorted. "On the principle that ten average people are smarter than one brilliant one? No, thanks."

"So what are you going to do?" Dale called after him.

Jaidev turned just long enough to say, "You'll find out." Then he pointed to Harley. "And get him out of here."

"Since when did you become Jaidev's errand boy?"

Harley was escorting Dale to the passage that led to the tunnel.

"I can see where you might think that," Harley said, with the smooth, unexcited manner that had served him so well at NASA. "But we voted, and it was unanimous."

"Get me out of the habitat."

"Call it taking you back where you really want to be."

"Even after you picked my brain about Sanjay."

"I can welcome your opinion, especially when I agree with it, even as I dislike your presence."

"You're a complicated man, Drake. Or confused."

"Cautious."

They were almost at the exit. Dale knew he could sneak back in any time he wanted; Harley and Jaidev knew that, too. But it would just make it difficult, and given the pressure of time, impossible to take action in a situation like that. "I really need to talk to Sanjay."

"Not going to happen."

"He's a Revenant, goddammit, Harley. And you know I've got my own connection to Keanu."

"Good for you and so what?"

Dale grabbed Harley's shoulders. "*He* felt it. *I* felt it! It *means* something."

"It means shit. For God's sake, one of you is twenty minutes out of the Beehive and the other is . . . dizzy from hunger and not right in the head."

Rather than slam Harley against the nearest wall, Dale let go of him. "You're so fucking wrong—"

"No," Harley said. "You had your say and I listened. But don't push it. Our whole survival—maybe even the future of the human race—depends on what we do, so it has to be right. You opted out of it a long time ago, and you can't just walk back in now . . . not with some mumbo jumbo about communion with Keanu. It's not happening."

Dale was already walking away. Fuck Harley, fuck Jaidev.

Fuck them all.

It wasn't until he was a hundred meters down the passageway, headed in the general direction of the Factory, that he was able to stop.

He had to—the noise and imagery inside his head had grown worse with every step. It was the Factory he was seeing, several structures he recognized but had never explored in any serious way. They kept leaping out at him, turning upside down and sideways, like children trying to get his attention—

Feeling that he might faint, he leaned against the wall just as a voice called, "Wait!"

Someone was following him. Who, why? Harley had just expelled him from the habitat, so this could hardly be friendly. Dale turned, prepared to fight.

Sanjay Bhat was jogging toward him. "You are making my new life difficult," he said, bending to catch his breath.

The images relaxed and settled. Dale felt a calming warmth—a certainty. "Are you doing that?" he asked Sanjay.

"I'm just the enabler."

"What does it mean?"

"That is still, unfortunately, quite unclear. All I know is, I have been compelled to find you and . . . share this with you."

"A specific location in the Factory."

"Apparently."

"You have no idea why?"

"I hope it will be obvious when you reach it. And you need to reach it soon." Yes, Dale felt that, too.

"What about you?"

Sanjay glanced far down the tunnel the way he had come. "I am headed back to Earth."

"Of your own choice—?"

Sanjay laughed. "Since when have we done anything by our own choice?"

"Do you know why, at least?"

Sanjay waggled a finger at him as he turned to go. "Yes, I do."

Dale couldn't believe the man was leaving. "Tell me! I need to know!"

But Sanjay disappeared into the darkness. Dale took several steps after him but was stricken by a headache so violent that he vomited.

He wiped his mouth and considered his next move. As Sanjay said, there was no choice. In his many failed or partially successful communions with Keanu's systems, Dale had learned that the NEO itself had weapons. It was the biggest, nastiest platform around, too, like an aircraft carrier—

For him it was back to the Factory immediately.

What is it like living under the Aggregates?

Most Americans would probably never know the difference. For example, they still vote for their fellow citizens for city council or mayor or Congress or the Senate. And the president. The Aggregates have "representatives" in Washington and most state capitals that parallel bodies of government, but you never see them. (And there is no Aggregate shadow "president," but rather an entire formation that is in and out of the White House every day.)

Major corporations, and some not so major, also have Aggregate shadows. Again, you don't see them. (Of course, the fact that the Aggregates shadow every media organization means complete censorship of those images.)

Crime and punishment are a whole different deal, because the Aggregate shadows are particularly active in the penal system, scooping up habitual offenders for work camps and disappearing those who don't or won't perform.

What we got: Relatively better national security. Access to new developments in technology. Fewer criminals on the street or in prisons (depending on how loosely you define *criminal*).

What we gave up: Control of our own destiny as a nation. Free speech and press. Due process.

The horrible truth is . . . a lot of Americans accept the Aggregates. For them, life is sweet and trouble-free.

They just don't realize that (a) it isn't theirs any longer, and (b) the Aggregates have a history of using up planets and moving elsewhere, and what's left behind is usually destroyed.

Personal note: I had a good friend who grew up in the Soviet Union when it was still Communist, so a lot like that.

GERALD MCDOW, *INTRODUCTION TO STASIS:*
THE HUMAN RACE'S LOST LEGACY POST-2020,
CONTRACTED TO YALE UNIVERSITY PRESS, UNPUBLISHED

YAHVI

"Mom?"

No answer.

"Dad?"

No.

"Zeds? Xavier?"

Nothing.

If Yahvi Stewart-Radhakrishnan disliked Earth based on her experiences at Yelahanka, her arrival at Edwards made certain she would never think of her parents' home world with anything but loathing. Ever since being hauled up the stairs and shoved into this room by a pair of smiling humans in stupid black suits, she had tried whatever she could: shouting and pounding to start.

Then she had searched for some way to break out of the room. However, with no tools and nothing but a door and a barred window to work on, she had little hope of success. She thought about trying to dig a hole in a wall, but the surface was too hard. Then there were odd little slitted plates at various places—electrical outlets, she realized. (They didn't have such things in the human habitat on Keanu.) But she had nothing to jam into an outlet but a finger, and she knew that wasn't going to do her any good . . . and possibly a great deal of harm.

Forced to leave her Beta unit and bag, Yahvi had been taken off the plane with no immediate violence but still found herself separated from her parents to be held by unfriendly humans in stupid black suits. There were also soldiers with guns, and several other people who all acted very concerned, important, and unhappy.

When Edgar Chang was carried out, followed by Colin Edgely, things had just gotten crazy, with shouting and shoving. The Australian had gotten into a shouting match with one of the officials, a dark-haired man in a suit who had identified himself as Mr. de la Vega, and Edgely had been knocked to the ground.

Rachel and Pav had emerged then, adding to the chaos, which ramped up to a whole new level once everyone got sight of Zeds.

The problem was, the "welcoming committee" seemed divided about its behavior. One group was eager to hit and kick Chang and Edgely, while others kept trying to restrain them.

Neither group seemed to know what to do with Zeds . . . the giant Sentry was goaded to an open area and forced to stand at gunpoint, like a trapped animal.

Soldiers had also carried Xavier Toutant out of the plane, and one of them had shouted something about a possible bomb on board—

That was when everything got worse. Shots were fired and Yahvi was pulled toward the nearest building with such force that she had bruises.

Her last sight of Rachel was her mother reaching for her, shouting for her to "be careful!"

Whatever that meant. She had been careful this whole trip, and look where it had gotten her.

Oh, she was pretty sure they had shot Edgar Chang.

As she was hauled inside the building, she saw something she had had nightmares about . . . an entire wall covered with tiny Reivers, the black units oozing and wriggling like bugs and obviously working with another thing Yahvi never wanted to see:

A whole formation of Reiver anteater types. They were buzzing around like mechanical children, each group of three intent on some action, all of them making Yahvi want to grab a soldier's gun and start shooting.

Now it was night. She had been locked up in a small room with a cot and no furniture or fixtures other than a sink for several hours. She had no idea where her parents were, or Zeds, or Xavier. She was cold and hungry.

And afraid. She had been so afraid for so long she forgot what it was like to be unafraid.

Her room was on the second floor of the building and looked to the east. (With no experience of landscapes and directions, it took Yahvi a few seconds to make the calculation.)

There, in the dark sky, though still lit by the sun setting in the distant west, was a giant cloud rising from the ground. It looked like a fire.

She hoped it was poison gas. She hoped it would kill everyone who took a breath.

"Hello," a voice said.

Yahvi blinked and saw that the door was slightly ajar. She had fallen asleep sitting on the bed with her back to the window. That had been stupid; now she hurt all over.

She stood up as Counselor Nigel and his two companions, Counselors Cory and Ivetta, entered. Counselor Cory was holding a covered tray. "How are you feeling?" Counselor Nigel said.

"Like shit. How do you think?"

"Hostility is unproductive," the female companion, Counselor Ivetta, said.

"You started it."

"You invaded Free Nation U.S.," Counselor Cory said.

Counselor Nigel tried to smile. Yahvi realized that he was quite awkward for his age. He had dark hair, cut close, a rosy complexion and brown eyes. If he'd been closer to her age, she might have found him appealing. "*Argument* is unproductive," he announced, directing it at his companions as well as to Yahvi. "We can offer you food."

"I'd rather see my parents and the others."

"Eventually."

"What did you do to Chang?"

"I have no information about him," Counselor Nigel said.

"Or you just won't share what you know," Yahvi said. "Fine. Give me some food."

Counselor Nigel nodded, and Counselor Cory set the tray on the foot of the bed. He removed the lid, revealing several packaged items unfamiliar to Yahvi. "What do I—?"

"That's right," Counselor Nigel said, "Keanu humans don't have packaging."

He reached out to assist, but Yahvi deftly slid the tray away long enough to tear the first two packages apart. The first one held some kind of sandwich, which smelled pretty good.

The second one held a purple drink that spilled all over the bed.

"Oops," Yahvi said, and drank what was left. Then she devoured the sandwich in four bites.

"Now," she said, offering not a thank-you but rather a belch. "What did you want to talk about?"

Had she not been worried about her parents and other companions, Yahvi might have enjoyed the interrogation by the team from THE. It consisted of each of the black-suited idiots asking her questions about Keanu ("Can't you just read all the stuff that got published? It's sort of true") or the *Adventure* mission ("We came to free you, is that what you want to hear?") or what weapons they carried ("Hands and teeth for me") or would she be willing to submit to THE training ("Do I have to wear those ugly suits?").

Every answer, no matter how snarky or snide it sounded, had this virtue: It happened to be true.

Before the questioning, Counselor Ivetta had produced a small instrument with a pair of wire leads that reminded Yahvi of her lost Beta unit. Yahvi knew without being warned that it was a lie detector. As the woman from THE attached the leads to Yahvi's arm and neck, she asked, "When do I get my things back?"

"The plane and its contents have been legally confiscated by Free Nation U.S." Counselor Cory said.

"But," Counselor Nigel said, "we might be able to retrieve personal items . . ."

If you cooperate. Yahvi was able to finish the sentence for him. Well, she had, in her fashion.

The last exchange led Yahvi to ask a question of her own: "Don't you think I'm going back to Keanu?"

Counselor Nigel assumed his more-in-sorrow-than-anger tone. "Given that your ship was damaged and is thousands of kilometers away, it seems unlikely."

"What would you do if you were me?"

That question seemed to surprise him. "I'd cooperate," he said.

"What happens if I don't?"

Now he just looked at her, blinking. Rachel had told Yahvi once that blinking wasn't a reflexive act, the eyes wetting themselves . . . it was actually the brain's way of reloading information.

Once he'd reloaded, Counselor Nigel said, "I'm going to be honest with you. You may not like us," he said, indicating his companions, "but we represent a growing population that has adjusted to the Aggregates and maybe even made them work for us and not the other way around. We think there is a bright, human-dominated future waiting, if we're smart. It's time for you and your family and your friends to be smart. Consider Transformational Human Evolution."

Counselor Cory took that as a cue to deliver the sales pitch: "No matter what you've heard, THE isn't a religion. It's really just a better way of looking at the way humans and Aggregates can coexist . . . and how we can apply their knowledge to our evolution."

Yahvi registered very little of Counselor Cory's message beyond the explanation for THE. But she had been genuinely interested in Counselor Nigel's answer, right up to the word *adjusted*, which was one of those bullshit words grown-ups were always using to make you to do things their way. So far, in her fourteen years of life, Yahvi had yet to be convinced that grown-up ways were better. Look at this whole trip, which she hadn't wanted to take—hadn't wanted her parents to go on. They'd almost been killed at least two times while failing completely in their mission.

And they had had no fun, none of the seeing-great-sites-of-Earth crap Rachel had promised. The new people they had met? Please.

Yahvi wouldn't have bothered. Going back in time even earlier, she wouldn't have turned Keanu around . . . she and most of the yavaki were agreed on that: Go forward, into the universe. Earth was fucked up to begin with; the Reiver Aggregates only made it slightly worse. A group of a few hundred couldn't change that, no matter how many Keanu-based weapons they cooked up.

But now that she was here—

"What does that mean, 'be smart'?" She pointed to the lie detector. "I've answered all your questions. What else is there?"

"I don't know yet. Offer to help, maybe."

"Oh, come on, you aren't going to tell me you have problems *we* could fix."

"Of course not," Counselor Nigel said. "But right now your strategy and that of your friends seems to be—we're the enemy and you've been taken prisoner. Every interaction is a struggle."

The man from THE was nothing but reasonable, but Yahvi not only didn't trust him or respect him . . . she had no idea what she could do that would make her seem "reasonable."

Yahvi unhooked the lie detector, slid off the bed, and pointed to the window. "By the way, what happened out there?"

"What do you mean?" Counselor Nigel said.

"That big cloud to the east."

Counselor Nigel shrugged. "I must have missed it. Not important."

But Counselor Ivetta was blinking like crazy. Which suggested to Yahvi that this cloud had been caused by something other than a forest fire. Interesting.

"We have to take her now," Counselor Cory said.

"To my parents, I hope."

"Eventually," Counselor Nigel said, opening the door. Yahvi briefly considered resisting, but there were three of them and one of her.

Yahvi didn't like the way that sounded. "What happens first?"

"We're only phase one of the interview process."

He stopped in front of a door farther down a dark hall. Only then did Yahvi see that it was covered with tiny Aggregates.

It opened.

The room was several times larger than the one Yahvi had been held in and looked just like the conference room at Yelahanka, minus the viewing screens and the table.

There was only a single chair . . . and half a dozen anteater Reiver Aggregates, all of them buzzing, chattering, and moving in that disturbing way, some twirling, some vibrating in place, all of them making Yahvi feel as uncomfortable and alone as she'd ever felt.

Counselor Nigel planted Yahvi in the chair, then withdrew from the room. As if responding to a signal, the anteaters closed in, one on each side, one blocking the exit, one facing her.

"You are Yahvi Stewart-Radhakrishnan," the Aggregate thing said in its childlike voice. "You have entered Free Nation U.S. without permission and in a hostile manner."

"Correct," she said. Given her heaving chest and constricted throat, she was lucky she could utter a word.

"What did you hope to accomplish?"

"To reconnect with fellow humans," she said. Then, realizing there was no point in hiding anything, she added, "And to destroy all of you."

A different Aggregate to her left asked the next question. "How would this destruction be accomplished?"

Her parents would freak out if they heard this, but the Aggregates would learn anyway. "By importing a virus that would use your own ability to communicate as a vector."

She had hoped for some kind of response: nothing. Maybe they already knew. Then a third Aggregate, to her right, said, "Are you carrying this virus with you?"

She so wanted to smile and say, "You bet! It's right here in my pocket!" Except that this was no place for jokes . . . and she didn't have a pocket. "It's in our cargo."

From behind her, a different Aggregate said, "Why are you so cooperative?"

"The counselors convinced me it would be to my benefit," she said.

So far the questioning was no more taxing than what Yahvi had experienced with THE—aside from the creepy nature of the questioners. A pause gave her time to remember just what it was she and every human hated about the Reivers.

It wasn't just their resemblance, in one mode, to terrestrial tropical bugs that would swarm and sting. Yahvi thought the anteater model was close to terrifying in its sounds, its inability to be still, its inexplicable behavior.

They reproduced quickly, too, using up resources and quickly imposing their will on everything around them. Creatures that got in the way or failed to get out of the way with sufficient speed were simply . . . eliminated. One fact Rachel had shared with Yahvi before *Adventure*'s launch: The population of the former United States had fallen from 330,000,000 in 2019 to two thirds that. "It might even be less," she had said, "because that isn't a census number, just an ISRO estimate based on acreage for food production and consumption. The Reivers are slowly eliminating human beings."

And that was the problem, Yahvi realized. What she hated about the Reivers was their lack of any detectable emotions or concern for others— or for themselves! Their formations would march into harm's way, being picked off in twos and threes like soldiers in a Civil War charge, never stopping or changing course. What kind of beings gave up their lives so easily? Eagerly?

Maybe you didn't mind dying if you were just one element in a larger machine.

But that was a terrifying thought, too—

They were closing in now. She could actually smell them, a tangy odor that reminded her of the subway passages within Keanu: old, machine-related, nasty.

She wanted to scream.

And then she blacked out.

When she woke up, the Aggregates had backed off . . . and the first sensation she noted was a burning smell. Her? God, the skin on her left leg was blistered! It didn't hurt, really. There was a gel of some kind on it.

Fearing that they had drilled into her skull and detected the transmitter, she touched her head. No, thank God.

But her clothes were in disarray, as if they had stripped and then possibly probed her.

And how long had she been out? It was night; the darkness outside the windows hadn't changed.

She jumped to her feet, towering half a meter over them, shouting, "What did you do to me?"

An Aggregate in the corner said, "You were examined."

She pointed to her leg. "Did you put something in me?" She was afraid that her head wasn't the only possible receptacle.

A different Aggregate spoke. "You were examined."

Was that a yes or a no? God, she hated these things. Her frustration caused her to lose control, weeping and shouting, "I've told you everything I know! I'm a child! And I need to see my parents!"

To her amazement, the Aggregate formation performed a dancelike maneuver, eight of them exiting the room, leaving four to arrange themselves around Yahvi. "Follow the formation," the one to her left said.

That was easy enough, though the damage to her leg made walking tricky. It wasn't the skin that hurt; she experienced sharp pains up and down the leg, as if it had been shot full of electricity.

Which was probably what had happened. Yahvi wondered why the Aggregates had resorted to these harsh techniques—hadn't they been able to tell that she was being truthful?

Maybe they had orders to torture her and it didn't matter what she'd said.

Maybe they were just mean.

The ground floor of the Edwards building was buzzing with so many Aggregate formations that Yahvi thought she would black out again, from the noise, the sight, and, now that she was sensitized to it, the smell. The whole scene suggested chaos.

She saw several THE counselors, too, including Nigel, Cory, and Ivetta, who watched her from across the room with a look that Yahvi found troubling. It was as if they were *surprised* she was still walking, still alive!

Counselor Nigel stepped forward, sliding between whirling Aggregates with a grace Yahvi didn't expect. "We didn't know," he said.

"Didn't know what?" Yahvi said, forced to shout over the buzzing. She waited for an elbow in her ribs from one of her escorts.

"The thing you mentioned." Counselor Nigel looked human and vulnerable for the first time. "It's bad for them."

The thing she had mentioned? Oh, Yahvi thought: the cloud in the east.

Rachel and Pav were sitting outside in a tiny quadrangle filled with metal tables. It was a place for lunch or even a picnic, Yahvi realized, in better times. Or at least in daylight.

They flung themselves at each other. Yahvi heard a groan from her father, and saw, even in the near-darkness, that he had a huge bruise on his face; he had clearly been beaten. "Oh my God, Daddy, did those things do this?"

"Those little shitboxes? Their arms would break if they hit you. No, this was the human guards."

"Your father tried to overcome four-to-one odds," Rachel said, in a tone that Yahvi recognized as teasing. Tonight, though, it was clearly affectionate, possibly even proud.

Looking closely at her mother, she saw signs of distress. "Did they question you?"

"Of course." She held out her arm, displaying the same kind of blistering Yahvi had experienced on her leg. "What about you?"

"It was mostly THE," she said. When Rachel gave a confused look, she added: "Trans-Human Evolutionaries or whatever they call themselves."

"The kids in the black suits," Pav said.

Rachel seemed to accept that. It was too dark for her to see how Yahvi had been damaged, and while Yahvi had no particular desire to spare her mother's feelings . . . this was not the time to offer complaints. "Where is everybody else?"

"Tea was in the room next to us, upstairs," Rachel said.

"They kept you together?" Yahvi said.

"For a while." She made an unhappy face. "I wasn't able to hear everything, but I'm pretty sure she went through what I went through."

"Which was?"

"A billion questions, many threats."

"Was it people or Reivers?"

"People," Rachel said. "There were three Reivers in the room, but they just watched."

"Same with me," Pav said. "The people were bad enough." He seemed to shudder, which made Yahvi want to start crying again. "Xavier is in one of the rooms on this floor," Pav said. "They took him and all our equipment to the same place."

"Probably forcing him to make it work."

Pav smiled. "Good luck getting Xavier to do anything he doesn't want to."

"He doesn't really look like a fighter," Yahvi said.

"You don't have to hit someone to be resistant," Rachel said. "Every daughter knows that, right?"

Yahvi was pleased to hear Rachel joking. It meant that she was bouncing back from the depressing flight and capture.

Pav was less amused. "He can be as passive-aggressive as he wants; the Reivers will turn him inside out to get what they want."

Zeds was captive in another building. "He really slammed a couple of the soldiers around," Pav said.

Rachel turned to him. "Probably giving you ideas, except that he's twice your size."

"I didn't need his encouragement, darling." To Yahvi, he said, "They might have fired on him, but I think they had orders to take him alive."

"You know Zeds," Rachel said. "He only knocked them around enough to show he could. Then he just backed off and said, 'Where do you wish to incarcerate me?'"

Neither of them had seen Edgely. "He was pretty subdued," Rachel said. "I don't think this is turning out to be the adventure he wanted."

"And Mr. Chang?"

"They shot him," Pav said. He did not hesitate, Yahvi noticed.

Rachel added, "That's why your father fought them."

"Why did they kill him?"

"Does it make a difference?" Rachel said.

"They probably saw him as our ringleader. Also, he's Chinese. I think the Reivers really hate and fear them."

Now that the grim and near-grim updates were over, Yahvi realized how tired and sore she was. And still quite uncertain. "So where does that leave us?"

"Prisoners." Rachel smiled. "I have to face the fact that I've totally fucked up this trip. The only thing we've done is stay locked up in rooms or airplanes."

"What did you think you were going to be doing?" Pav said. "Grabbing a gun and shooting Reivers one by one?"

The idea had a certain appeal to Yahvi, even though she'd never held a gun—she'd barely even seen one. "Do either of you know what these things are so upset about?"

Rachel looked at Pav. "You mean, beyond our presence?"

"The cloud in the east. My THE boy said it was bad news for the Reivers. I think it was some kind of accident."

Pav sat up straighter. "You know—"

"Oh, shit," Rachel said. "I overheard one of the humans, not in a black suit, say something about an accident and a facility that was critically damaged." She glanced around and lowered her voice. "The Ring is off that way!"

"It would be nice to think that someone hit our target for us," Pav said.

Rachel was shaking her head. "The word was *accident*, not *attack*. They probably blew some gaskets. And the Reivers never give up; even if the place burned to the ground, they'd build it right back up again."

"Might take a while."

Yahvi saw her opportunity now. "We would still like to get inside it, right?"

"Well, yes," Rachel said. "You know enough to know why."

"Even though our original plan can't possibly work," Pav said. Yahvi knew that her father meant the poison pill strategy.

"What if the Reivers or Aggregates got the idea that the proteus and cargo could help them fix the Ring?" The idea had come to her between two steps as she was marched down the stairs by the Aggregates. She had to assume that their interrogations had told them everything she knew. And even though her parents didn't think they had been subjected to Reiver Aggregate torture, it was likely it had been so intense that they didn't remember.

This idea just seemed right.

"Do we want that?" Pav said.

Rachel was already on her feet. Yahvi knew from experience that her mother thought better when in motion. "No! But we *do* want to get inside the place. I'd rather take the chance we might be bringing them a tool if it puts us in position to wreck the whole thing.

"Now, who wants to be the one to tell them?"

CARBON-143

SITUATION: The critical anomaly aborting the First Light test required immediate action from all Aggregate formations.

All test data was frozen, then transferred to a new unit that initiated failure analysis.

The vehicles of the invading force remained on standby in Staging Areas 1, 2, and 3.

Since assembly functions were on hold, Aggregate Carbon-143's formation was one of those tasked with failure analysis.

NARRATIVE: The order to step back from the assembly station and report immediately to central control caused considerable agitation within the A72 formation, not just with Carbon-143. It was too early in the day for a reboot, and the constant stream of admonitions and encouragements that had been flowing up and down the information trees had a residual effect on every unit: This critical work needed to be accomplished now! Why were they interrupting it?

Carbon-143 noted that her own consternation was shared by eight other members of her formation. This was itself an anomalous condition—a promising one, if one believed, as Carbon-143 did, that the rigid unquestioning conformity of Aggregate existence was not the only or best choice.

As she withdrew from the assembly line, she saw Dehm hurrying past. "Hello?" she said, knowing it was risky. (Suppose the rest of her formation continued on to the control center? How would her late arrival be received or explained?)

"You should stay away from me," he said. Even to Carbon-143's senses, never especially perceptive with human features and emotions, Dehm looked shaken. "We're all under suspicion," he said.

For a moment Carbon-143 lost precise mental function. Any examination of her data use and activities would label her a failed unit, to be followed swiftly by disassembly.

Dehm must have seen some kind of reaction. "Not you," he said. "Humans. Every human in this fucking place."

He hurried off.

Having no destination in mind, Carbon-143 followed her formation to the rest place.

UPDATE: Within an hour, a burst of information informed Aggregate Carbon-143 that four human workers had been suspected of failures in the First Light test. These ranged from late warnings of changing weather conditions to improper coding of mirror convergence algorithms.

No sabotage was suspected. Nevertheless, all four humans had been terminated.

Aggregate Carbon-143 accepted this news calmly. She had been given a warning, after all.

Only then did she see the list of terminated humans and the name *Randall Dehm*.

For several seconds, and the second time in this day, Carbon-143's processing functions failed to operate at optimum utility.

She accessed the name again, and received unwelcome confirmation.

She even accessed imagery from the termination.

Four humans, two men and two women, all thin, all dressed in similar white T-shirts and khaki trousers, all nervous, stood in a dimly lit cell. The image was fixed, from a security camera, and while it appeared that three Aggregates were present, none from formations with recognizable designations—like punitive units.

Dehm's last words were, "Fuck you."

Then he was struck from behind by a bolt of energy, collapsing in a terminal heap.

Carbon-143 broke the link.

Before she could process the experience, she and the entire formation were informed that they were now part of the failure analysis team.

FORECAST: The failure analysis consumed twenty hours, time sufficient for six formations completing separate reviews, with six more repeating each step.

The twelve conclusions agreed on the cause of the First Light failure.

Three primary remediations, as voted by all twelve analysis formations, were (A) greater rigor in adherence to data from the Ring's external environment (weather, especially wind and temperature), (B) repair of the damaged Ring structure, and (C) insertion of a final go/no-go decision maker in the launch commit checklist.

The system code was already being revised to accomplish step A. Revisions would be complete within nine days.

The forecast for step B, repairs, was also nine days, but flagged as unsustainable without additional resources. Carbon-143 knew that additional formations would be deployed, though materials and assembly times were the true forcing factors and would almost certainly dictate a failure to meet that deadline.

Those were mechanical remediations. Step C could be classed as managerial/political.

An entity other than an Aggregate needed to be inserted into the final decision-making process.

(There were other Aggregate modes, though smaller units, the kind that, Carbon-143 realized, she was composed of. These were operating in autonomous mode.)

Her formation was ordered to its overdue thirty-minute downtime.

Carbon-143's eleven colleagues wheeled and departed for their normal recharge stations.

She went in search of Whit Murray.

ACTION: Even though there were 1,724 individual humans within the Ring facility's boundaries (down four in the last two hours), locating an individual was not difficult, not for an Aggregate with access to the locator.

Whit was one of thirty-nine human operators working in Ring control who had been sequestered as part of the investigation. Because he had no operational role or access to go/no-go functions, he had been released early (though with a flag: Examination of his data indicated excessive interest in events and information beyond his assigned function).

He was in the cafeteria with a handful of other humans. Aggregate Carbon-143 did not consider herself an expert on human emotional states, but it was obvious from the shuffling walks and lack of chat that the mood was subdued.

Whit was emerging from a food line with a tray. "Hello," he said. He waited for her to speak; Carbon-143 did not feel this was the appropriate venue for her proposed conversation.

Whit must have realized this. "Let's go over here," he said, leading her to an empty table in the far corner.

As they reached it and Whit set down his tray, Carbon-143 announced, "Randall Dehm is dead."

"What are you talking about?"

She explained. As she did, she noted changes in Whit's physical state. His eyes began to water and his lower lip trembled. He seemed to have lost functional use of his hands.

Finally he sat down. "I can't believe they killed him." He stared at the floor for a moment. "And he didn't do anything wrong!"

"We don't know that." In fact, the failure analysis had indicated some sloppiness on the part of human operators in Dehm's section.

"What's that supposed to mean?"

Carbon-143 regretted her statement. "Please accept my apologies. This is a time of great stress.

"New humans will be inserted into the command system. One will almost certainly be given final go/no-go power for the next light."

"Why?"

"Because Aggregate decision making is flawed." She was stating a simple fact, the result of careful analysis as evident on all decision trees. But further consideration added weight and even horror to that statement.

Aggregate decision making is flawed! Which led to the conclusion that Aggregate actions were incorrect. The destruction of Randall Dehm was wrong.

The inevitable conclusion was that Carbon-143 was now free to make individual decisions. They couldn't possibly be more wrong.

She uttered these words: "Would you be willing to accept this assignment?"

"There's a risk."

"Correct. Failure could result in termination."

Whit smiled coldly. "From what I've learned, around here, success could result in termination. For humans." He stood. "Where and when do I start?"

Day Ten

SUNDAY, APRIL 22, 2040

Fiat justitia, ruat coelum.

("Let justice be done, though the heavens may fall!")

LUCIUS CALPURNIUS PISO CAESONINUS

RACHEL

It was still early morning, perhaps an hour after dawn, when Rachel Stewart-Radhakrishnan emerged, blinking, from the helicopter landing on a pad atop a giant, square building—and gasped.

She had seen many amazing sights in her life, from her father's launch on the *Destiny-7* mission to the terrifying descent of the Houston Object and the looming planetscape of Keanu, but none struck her as perfectly blending impressive, frightening, and awe-inspiring as her first sight of the Ring.

Part of the awe was due to the desert itself, so stark in its early-morning beauty. Then there was her appreciation of the ingenuity required to alter that landscape, not only building a small city where none had existed, but carving out what appeared to be a particle collider more than ten kilometers in diameter.

Then to surround it all with collections of military vehicles so large they probably equaled the entire U.S. Army of Rachel's youth.

Keanu was bigger, but more remote. The Ring was right here in front of her.

"And we thought we were going to take this out all by ourselves," Rachel said, speaking just loudly enough for her husband to hear her. *This* was how you invaded another planet, not with a ragtag band of six in a used spacecraft . . . even if you had a secret backup vehicle.

"We still do, don't we?" Pav said. "Even though they did some of the work for us." He nodded to the north, where a cluster of orange-and-yellow vehicles suggested repairs in progress. Residual smoke or steam supported that conclusion.

Rachel favored Pav with half a smile.

Because one thing had finally gone right, after the horror of the past two days, with the shootdown, the death of Edgar Chang, and the interrogation by the Reivers at Edwards.

Yahvi had come through.

Rachel had accepted her daughter's radical idea of giving the Aggregates what they wanted, and that was proving to be a turning point in their relationship. Sasha Blaine and others had warned her about it over the years, because she'd never experienced it herself—nor had Pav. "It's when the child takes over," Sasha had said. "Where the adult realizes that the kid has a better idea. It's one of the toughest things a parent learns."

"Why?" Rachel had said.

"Because it means you, the parent, are one step closer to obsolescence."

Rachel still wasn't sure she would have truly embraced Yahvi's idea except for what happened a few moments later.

They had been collected from the relatively private lunch area by THE officers and taken to another building, where Xavier and Tea, Zeds, and Edgely were being held. Rachel desperately wanted more privacy, more ability to talk with a bit of freedom (always assuming that someone could be aiming a directional microphone at them). She and Pav and Yahvi had agreed to pitch the idea of the proteus to THE but wanted Xavier and Zeds to hear it from them first.

The building was a kind of lab, which made sense; their human captors and Aggregate allies were surely setting up Xavier's printer and tearing through the Substance K.

Rachel, Pav, and Yahvi were kept in the entryway as most of the gang from THE tried to go through a serious set of security doors. Rachel wondered just what kind of nasty chemicals or devices were normally found here.

The coming and going allowed Rachel and Yahvi a moment of privacy.

Rachel had noted her daughter's pained expression of the last few minutes. "How are you feeling?"

To her surprise, it wasn't the stress of her recent experiences that was causing Yahvi pain. She was actually angry, saying, "I hear voices!"

Rachel had swiftly taken them both into the nearest bathroom. There she told Yahvi that she had a transmitter implanted in her head, and instructed her in its use.

"It sounds like Sasha talking," Yahvi said. "Why is it taking so long? Oh." She remembered the lag.

She was a fast operator. Within moments she had relayed more vital information than Rachel and Pav had gathered in all their prior contacts.

The biggest news . . . the Beehive had come to life and disgorged its first Revenant in twenty years: Sanjay Bhat.

Rachel had had to fight the conflicting urges to scoff in disbelief and shout with excitement. Yes, it was unbelievable. But . . . yes, and double yes, it was wonderful!

"He's fine, though shaky."

And then the next large item. "He's coming here with the vesicle," Yahvi said. "What vesicle is that?"

"Tell you later."

"Well, they're saying 'coming here,' so I can get the idea. You and Dad didn't tell me much, did you?" She listened again, touching the back right of her head and nodding. In spite of the terrible situation they were in, Rachel felt serene and parental. . . . You wanted your child to grow up in safety, of course, but that was never likely to be possible on Keanu. The next best thing was having her grow up and be useful, no matter how dangerous the situation.

Hearing someone entering the bathroom, Rachel pulled Yahvi into a stall. "Why—?" She put her hand on Yahvi's mouth, shushing her.

They both waited, wide-eyed, hearts pounding. A female voice: "You can't stay in here."

"One more minute," Rachel said.

That seemed to satisfy the female THE counselor, since footsteps and a door closing indicated a departure.

Yahvi whispered, "They want to know if we plan to destroy the Ring."

There was the question of the moment. "Hoping to!"

"Is that the thing in northern Arizona?" Yahvi said.

"Yes."

"Someone might have beaten us to it." Yahvi quickly explained about the ominous pillar in the sky, and Counselor Nigel's confirmation of an "event." "Sasha says Sanjay wants us to take control of it instead."

Control? Of the Ring? What the hell—? "What does that mean?"

Yahvi quickly vocalized the question, and Rachel had to wait through the double torture of the lag.

"Don't destroy the Ring until the last possible minute. They want us to find some way to hack into its controls or something. And maybe steer it."

"Oh, is that all?"

The door opened again. Before Rachel could offer another excuse, Yahvi called, "We're done!" Then, in a lower voice to Rachel, "And we are done. Lost the link."

As they washed up, Yahvi said, "When did you put that thing in my head?"

"One night when you were asleep, maybe three weeks ago."

"Why didn't you tell me?"

"You can't tell what you don't know."

"I am so sick of that."

Rachel agreed. She was very sick of trying to accomplish the impossible. Destroy the Ring? Damage it further? Take control of it?

Right now all of those were fantasy.

Next Rachel had had to endure the demonstration of the proteus, a process that surely shortened her life—not that she expected to die of old age as a captive of the Reivers.

Everyone had been gathered in a two-story workspace, where, Pav suggested, aircraft engines might be suspended for repairs. "Look at those rigs hanging from the ceiling."

Half a dozen THE counselors were present, as were several other humans—the ones who had let Chang be killed, notably de la Vega.

And, naturally, a dozen Aggregates, some of them swarming all over *Adventure*'s cargo and the proteus like ants on a spilled Popsicle.

The only good thing about that moment had been seeing Tea and Edgely alive and in good health—neither seemed to have been abused.

Xavier stood with Zeds. Both had obviously been wrung out about the printer and its uses. Xavier looked shaken and subdued. Zeds was stolid and serene, and still in his suit.

"How are you doing?" she asked Xavier, once they had all established that they were largely in one piece.

"Been better."

"And you, Zeds?" she said.

"I share Xavier's state."

That was a surprise; Sentries were usually quite reticent when it came to emotional responses, especially expressions of weakness. Rachel assumed that the de la Vega and THE interrogations produced results from humans . . . what had they gotten from the Sentry?

Then the fun began.

For some reason the Aggregates seemed to think that the Sentry knew more about the Keanu assembler than the humans. Zeds was a capable operator, as was Pav, but neither was at Xavier's level.

Xavier had to talk Zeds through the demo.

Before it really got started, there was a heated discussion about what the proteus could do—and should do. Xavier was clearly trying to be cagey. "It's only as good as its input," he kept saying.

"What kind of input?" de la Vega said. "Electronic? Paper? A model?"

And there Xavier was stuck.

Rachel had to save her friend. "Most of the inputs are preloaded on Keanu," she said. "Without access to its data banks, we are limited to producing only a handful of items."

From behind her came the voice of an Aggregate: "What handful of items did you have preloaded?"

"Weapons," she announced. She didn't bother to address the Reiver that had spoken; she knew that to talk to one was to talk to all of them.

And she didn't have to force herself to smile when she added, "Devices that will kill Aggregates."

Xavier just stared at Rachel. Even Pav looked shocked. "Yay, Mom," Yahvi said.

A murmur passed through all nine humans, too. "Don't worry," Xavier said, picking up on Rachel's lead. "The weapons aren't active."

And then Zeds said, "Yet."

"Then," a different Aggregate said, "we will destroy these devices and the materials they use, for our own safety."

"Let's not be hasty," Rachel said. "Just because the proteus was pre-loaded with weapons doesn't mean that's the *only* thing it can produce."

"But anything that might be useful requires input from Keanu," de la Vega said. He gave off an air of smug superiority mixed with hostility. Even if she didn't blame him for Chang's death, Rachel would have enjoying punching the man in the face.

"Yes," Rachel said. "I believe I said that."

"But . . . we don't have those inputs."

He talked to her as if she were in grade school. Rachel took a breath. When she lived in Houston, her mother had insisted she learn not only to swim, but to dive. There she had been . . . eight years old on the low board at the Clear Lake YWCA pool, trying not to scream at Megan Stewart for making her feel afraid. She had closed her eyes and dived, smacking her belly and filling her nose with water.

That was how she felt at this moment. "We can get a huge variety of downloads when we regain communication with Keanu." She addressed de la Vega. "You removed transmitters from our skulls."

For a moment she thought the man was going to lie or evade. But then: "Yes. Are you telling us to put them back in?" His tone made it clear that wasn't going to happen.

"Unnecessary. You have systems that can easily communicate with Keanu. You could put us on the line and monitor everything we say."

"Conceded. But you haven't convinced me that we should."

Rachel glanced at Pav. She took another breath, hoping she could make this convincing, when her husband said, "Look, you just had a major failure of some kind. You have undoubtedly lost unique equipment and devices that can't easily be reproduced, or certainly not quickly." He pointed at the proteus. "That's what our machine can do."

"Why do you think we've had a failure?"

The trio of THE officers that had dealt with Yahvi displayed their first touches of human vulnerability. They actually got uncomfortable; one of the two men blushed and cleared his throat, a clear sign of nervousness.

"We can see the evidence in the sky," Yahvi said. "And everyone on this base seems to be freaked out. They wouldn't be doing that unless something just went wrong."

De la Vega wasn't giving anything away. But the blushing THE counselor said, in the quietest possible voice, "We confirmed an event."

De la Vega turned to the young man with genuine surprise. "Well, then," he said. "Let's stipulate that we could use some assistance—"

"Take us to the facility," Rachel said. "Let us see the damaged equipment, get its specs and all available data, and feed that to Keanu. They will process it and download instructions to the printer." She nodded toward the towering piles of Substance K. "We can't replicate something the size of a rocket, but we can make several modest-sized electronic components and a whole lot of small ones." She smiled again. "If that would be of use."

"Wait here," de la Vega said, turning and walking out. His two deputies followed, one of them shooting a look at the guilty THE counselor that expressed a remarkable amount of scorn and pity.

Pav, Tea, and Xavier couldn't help jumping up and down like schoolchildren. "Hold on," Rachel said. "I'm not sure we ought to be celebrating." Especially, she thought, with half a dozen THE goons and double that number of Reiver Aggregates watching.

"This is true," Zeds said. "We may only be helping the Reivers complete their weapon while merely postponing our own destruction."

Tea slapped the Sentry on the chest. "Oh, come on, haven't you heard the saying, 'Live to fight another day'?"

"No."

"Well, now you have!"

Rachel glanced at Yahvi. Her daughter had refrained from celebrating but was nodding her approval. Which filled Rachel with good feelings the way praise from her parents used to.

God, our roles are truly reversed—

More quickly than Rachel would have believed, de la Vega and his scornful assistant were back. "We will be leaving within the hour," he said.

This statement kicked the Aggregates into motion. They gathered up the 3-D printer and the boxes of Substance K. "Hey," Xavier said, regaining his sense of humor, "careful with that shit! You need it more than we do!"

As the aliens carried the equipment and cargo away, Xavier said to Rachel, "I sure hope you know what you're doing."

He and Edgely, Pav, and Yahvi headed outside. Tea took Rachel's arm. "That was really, really—"

"Stupid? Fatal?"

Tea smiled. "I was going to say *brave* or possibly even *cunning.*"

"Let's hope you're right and I'm wrong."

Now, hours later, here they all were, at Reiver Central, after a brief, bumpy ride in the cargo section of a large military transport.

Given the way THE people clung to them, she felt that she and the others had been turned into an Aggregate formation. They could only seem to operate as a group of six, plus their minders.

Rachel had asked Yahvi about her THE trio, specifically the blushing male. "That's Counselor Nigel," she said. "He's almost human." She said this loud enough so Nigel could hear. Which was fine, since Rachel and company had no privacy.

Rachel turned to that trio, sitting across from her on metal chairs. "Thank you for being honest."

"Honesty is a tenet of THE," he said.

Pav was next to Rachel. He said, "Even though it can get you in trouble?"

"It's not the honesty," Counselor Nigel said. "It was my prior revelation of secured information that was troublesome."

"What are they going to do to you?" Yahvi said.

"It won't just be me," Counselor Nigel said, glancing at Counselors

Ivetta and Cory. "We operate as a unit. If the actions of one earn a reward, we all share. If the action of one earns punishment—"

"And what does that mean?" Rachel said. "Confinement? Twenty lashes? Loss of your snazzy black uniform?"

Counselor Nigel hesitated before answering. His features softened just enough to make Rachel feel some pity for him. "All of those, along with retraining or, in some circumstances, termination."

Yahvi was shocked. "You mean you could be *executed* for what you told me?"

Now Counselor Ivetta spoke. "All three of us could be terminated." Her humanity was showing, too: fear, and a desire to terminate Counselor Nigel for putting her in this situation.

"It will probably depend on how successful this is," Counselor Nigel said, indicating Rachel and the plane.

"I'm sorry your lives are in my hands," she said, not feeling very sorry at all.

"That's true for all of us," Zeds said out of the darkness.

It was after landing, while all of the passengers were waiting for the cargo ramp at the rear of the plane to drop, that Pav said, "I asked them to contact my father."

"Good idea. Let's make them work for us as much as possible, while we can." Their phones had been confiscated on landing at Edwards.

"It's not like him to go dark, not even leave a message."

"We've hardly had coverage," Rachel said.

"We've had some." He indicated Tea, who seemed lost, distracted by some fascinating detail of the cargo plane's interior. "She's had no word, either."

The aircraft had landed south of St. George, Utah, on a runway that looked raw and new, even in the darkness. (Rachel guessed it was between four and five A.M. local time.)

De la Vega and his assistants had flown with them—in a separate compartment, along with Aggregates and the proteus. Now the human leader divided the party into three groups, each one to be ferried by helicopter to the Ring.

"How much farther?" Colin Edgely asked de la Vega. Rachel felt sorry for the Aussie; he had only been trying to help . . . had been thrilled to play a role in this mission.

Now he was exhausted, a captive in a foreign land, surrounded by strangers, some of them hostile and murderous. By speaking to de la Vega he was essentially saying, *I don't give a shit what you do to me.*

But the human leader simply said, "Forty kilometers. We can't land an aircraft this size at the facility." And turned to other business.

Edgely caught Rachel's eye. He seemed to feel that he had accomplished something valuable, gained some vital information. Well, Rachel thought, whatever made him feel better.

Not that she was in any position to feel superior to Colin Edgely. Her presence here was due to the same random factors. Until August 2019, she had been a typical fourteen-year-old American girl. Yes, her father was an astronaut . . . but that only made her rare, not unique.

She had not dreamed of flying to other worlds, or living on them. Or having to become a leader of a community, and certainly not some kind of space warrior.

Maybe that was how it was for everybody, all those notable figures throughout history.

Time and luck—some of it bad.

Rachel, Tea, and Zeds were separated from the others—though not from Counselor Nigel and his crew—and put aboard a helicopter with Counselor Cory. Rachel didn't like being separated from Pav and Yahvi, but at least they were together.

The Aggregates were all being loaded into a van instead of a helicopter. "Do you suppose they don't like to fly?" Tea said, pointing to them.

"I think they are too numerous," Zeds said.

"Truer words," Rachel said. Tea laughed.

Before they could take off, Counselor Nigel returned and spoke to Rachel. "I'm sorry to say I have very bad news for you. General Radhakrishnan has passed away."

Rachel took the news calmly, while thinking, *Poor Pav!* She had just said, "What happened?" when Tea groaned and reached out.

Oh, God, Rachel thought. Counselor Nigel didn't know that Tea was Taj's wife.

Then the door was locked and the helicopter rattled into the pre-dawn sky.

Rachel had managed to trade places with Zeds—quite a trick in the cramped helicopter cabin—in order to sit next to Tea, who shook with sobs during most of the trip to the Ring. "God, I'm a mess."

"You just got terrible news."

"Poor Taj," she said. She shouted across the cabin at Counselor Nigel. "Did they say anything? What happened to him?"

"Only that he died yesterday in Bangalore."

Hearing this made Tea even sadder. "There's no one to take care of him! I'm not going to be at his funeral!"

"Let's ask de la Vega," Rachel said, including her THE companions in the proposal. "Maybe they'll let you go, compassionate leave?"

"Oh, honey," Tea said. "First you have to have compassion."

Counselors Nigel and Ivetta only exchanged glances, but their silence confirmed Tea's statement. There would be no expression of compassion from the human leader and his Aggregate allies.

The helicopter turned then, giving Rachel a restricted but fascinating view of a reddening eastern sky, desert mesas casting insanely long shadows . . . and a portion of a glittering circular structure: the Ring.

The helicopter landed moments later. As the engines fluttered to a stop, Rachel said to Counselor Nigel, "Does my husband know?"

"No," he said. "My orders were to inform you."

Tea took Rachel's arm again. "I'll tell him," she said, trying to smile through tears. "I'm his stepmother, after all."

Rachel witnessed the dread delivery from several meters away. Tea had forced her way to Pav, but Rachel was held back; the helipad was crowded with two vehicles and disembarking passengers, all being herded toward stairways. Even Zeds, who could easily bulldoze a path, was stuck behind Rachel, and she behind Edgely.

By the time they were inside the building, Pav had already absorbed the blow. He accepted a hug from Rachel. "It's so fucking unfair," he said. "I just got him back!"

He remained stoic. Yahvi, however, wept openly. Xavier and Tea both comforted her. Zeds and Edgely looked on, each ineffectual in his own way.

De la Vega regarded them all with confusion; obviously he didn't know what they were reacting to, and Rachel was damn sure she wouldn't be the one to tell him. "Your equipment will arrive within the hour," he said. "Right now you are going to the operations center to meet the project leaders. They will identify the devices we need and you can communicate that to Keanu."

He turned to other business, leaving Xavier to ask Rachel, "How are we going to do that?"

"With whatever system they have." She had seen several radomes at the perimeter of this facility.

"Fine. What are we looking for? Some specific tool we can use, some information?"

"Really?" Rachel said. "All we're looking for is time."

She glanced out the window at the desert morning, wondering . . . where was the vesicle?

Veteran NewSky TV reporter and on-air personality Edgar Chang died Friday, family and friends have revealed. No details were given, though family members claim he died outside China.

The 65-year-old Chang, well known to NewSky viewers for a generation, had been working with the six returnees from Keanu. They have not been seen in public for a week, since disappearing from an air base near Bangalore, India.

There has been no comment from NewSky.

XINHUA NEWS, APRIL 22, 2040

Does anyone have more information? Chang was with Colin!

KETTERING GROUP, SAME DAY

SANJAY

Sanjay awoke and was angry with himself.

He had so little time remaining! There was no value in wasting it with sleep, even if Keanu used that time to upload information to him. (He had had a series of strange dreams involving falling, being naked or lost in the passages of Keanu, or a mixture of the three.)

Like every member of the HB community, Sanjay knew about the Revenants . . . tortured Pogo Downey, brave Yvonne Hall, tragic Camilla . . . and, of course, the amazing Megan Doyle Stewart.

Their second lives had all been short, with Camilla lasting the longest . . . a little over a week.

Sanjay wanted to become the new Revenant life span record holder.

At the moment—less than a week after being born again in the Beehive—he felt terrific, alert, pain free, manic, and productive in a way that was quite familiar from his work at Bangalore and Keanu.

Not only that, but he was eager to see Earth. He felt he had been cheated by the accident. Now he had cheated death—*How do you like it?*

He wanted to confront the Reivers, too. He had no memory of their earlier presence on Keanu—Zack Stewart and his daughter, Rachel, and Dale Scott were the major players in their expulsion.

But Sanjay had always loathed the whole idea of the creatures, part organic life form, part machine, all-consuming, and totally against everything he valued in life.

He had learned that there was some kind of galactic war between the Reivers and the Architects of Keanu as well as their allies, the Skyphoi and the Sentries. Humans had sided with the Architects; Sanjay had seen no reason to remain neutral. If eradicating the Reivers on Earth would help that effort, he was all for it.

Or so he had believed, right up to the moment of his death. Now, though . . .

"Where are we?"

Sanjay was floating near the rounded nose of the vesicle, a milk-colored egg thirty meters long and twenty wide at its broadest.

Zhao Buoming floated several meters below him, his head inside a silver dispenser that would shortly be spewing deadly material all over Earth. Without turning, a bit of a trick in microgravity, the former spy said, "We are over halfway, and falling fast."

Then Zhao rotated, showing his bare feet to Sanjay, and pushed himself away, toward the base of the vehicle, which was stuffed with life support and guidance equipment. Sanjay knew there had to be some propulsion gear, too, though not much; the vesicle had been blasted out of Keanu like a shell from a cannon. In addition to basic equipment, it also carried several tons of Substance K in a variety of containers. Some of that was being converted into weapons (most had been assembled on Keanu, but certain substances were so dangerous to humans that Jaidev and Drake and Rachel had deferred their final preparation to post-launch).

Sanjay had found the launch punishing, which shouldn't have surprised him; he knew that the vesicle would be fired toward Earth at a high velocity, much like the original Objects that had struck Bangalore and Houston in 2019. A free-fall trip between Earth and Keanu took four days; those had covered the distance in less than one.

But since one of the marvels of Keanu tech was the ability to control gravity, Sanjay had expected the vesicle to be equipped with a field that would mitigate the effects of being blasted off the NEO. No chance; when the countdown (Harley Drake had insisted) reached zero, the vesicle had shot forward with a speed that belied its mass (an egg the size of a small building, weighing as much as a semitruck, should not be capable of such acceleration!), flashing through one of Keanu's passages before emerging into open space.

Like the others in the crew, led by Zhao, Sanjay had been strapped flat on a squishy mat at the base of the vesicle, a sensation that reminded him of the golden fluid packing his reawakening cell in the Beehive. He had instantly experienced pressure, like a giant sitting on his chest, and suffered narrowing of his vision, a sign he was graying out and likely to black out.

Fortunately, the chest-crushing event had lasted less than five minutes. Now, twelve hours later, he was feeling good . . . just angry at having fallen asleep for six of them.

"When do we land?" He pushed off from the nose of the vesicle and slowly descended to its base.

Seeing him, Zhao looked up, a typically sardonic smile on his face. "You mean *hit*, don't you?"

"Stop torturing him," Makali Pillay said. She had been hidden inside the piles of Substance K containers and processing equipment that filled the vesicle interior. "Not very long ago he was dead."

"Whatever term you prefer," Sanjay said to Zhao.

"We land in ten hours," Zhao said. And floated off, leaving Sanjay with Makali.

"He's really consistent in being shitty to people," Makali said. Sanjay had never grown to know her well, since she preferred to spend her time outside the Temple laboratory, working on agro projects (she was the HB's "flower girl," assembling and then planting beautiful nonfood items), or taking her own walkabouts. Makali was the closest thing the community had to a Keanu expert and explorer—Dale Scott without the weirdness.

"A mission like this is not going to soften a man," Sanjay said.

"Still," Makali said, "it would be helpful if he remembered that the enemy is on Earth, not here. Hungry?"

"Always."

Food was prepackaged, to the extent anything on Keanu was packaged: dried fruit, nuts, bars.

Basic though it might have been, Sanjay found the food glorious. And engaging in such a mundane activity allowed him to think back on his life prior to *Adventure* and the frantic moments since.

He was glad he had kept Maren from coming along. She had screamed at him to stay; when that failed, she had turned on Sasha, Harley, and Jaidev, begging them to send her, too.

Sanjay had sided with Jaidev, Harley, and Sasha in refusing. It was bad enough adding a seventh human "passenger" to a vehicle that had been designed to support six. There was some flexibility in the consumables, allowing for a seventh, but not enough to accommodate an eighth human who would be breathing oxygen, drinking water, and requiring food. Maren would just have been baggage.

There was also the Revenant factor. Sanjay hoped that he would live through the completion of the mission.

But what if he didn't? Poor Maren would be experiencing the death of her lover for a *second* time. And even in success, he was still dead, and Maren was Zhao's responsibility.

No.

He asked Makali, "Why did you volunteer for this? Surely you haven't solved all of Keanu's mysteries."

She hooted. "I haven't solved a single one of them, if you want to be factual. But I sort of fancied seeing Earth again—"

"Even though this is essentially a bombing mission."

"Well, no other travel options, right? We didn't build a tourist vesicle. I also figure, this works and Keanu survives. If not . . . I won't be doing much more exoscience because I'll be dead." She seemed embarrassed by the comment. "Sorry."

"It's not a problem," Sanjay said. "Being dead hasn't made me more sensitive." But it had changed him in ways he still didn't understand. Even as he uttered those words to Makali, additional data formed in his head, a process that gave him a brief, quiet, shuddering spasm that was almost sexual.

Momentary pleasure aside, becoming a link between Keanu and humans was proving to be stressful. (Another reason the Revenants didn't last?) There was no *clarity*. Trying to interpret the words, sounds, and images in his head—the implanted memories—was like being an English speaker trying to translate a passage in Chinese to a dolphin.

Last night's data, and this new material . . . it all seemed to deal with the Reiver facility and a vision of a vesicle sitting on a desert landscape not far from it.

"The mission is still dangerous," he heard himself telling Makali. "Unless you were talking in secret after we took off in *Adventure*, no one has really dealt with getting back to Keanu." Even for *Adventure*'s crew, return was always a desirable option, not a concrete plan.

"No matter how dangerous, and whether or not we get back, it's still worth it." Makali snagged the nuts, chomping them in midair. She smiled. "Frankly, I'm tired of the same old faces."

It seemed like a trivial motivation until Sanjay remembered that within the HB community, Makali was famous for tempestuous love affairs and sexual adventurism, at least to the extent that could be practiced in the limited pool of candidates.

So she was risking her life in order to find new partners, which had the virtue of being a basic biological drive.

Which left Sanjay wondering about the other four in the crew, three Bangalores and one Houston. The Bangalores, like Sanjay, were all forty or slightly older—engineers or other Brahma control center functionaries who had been scooped up by the Object.

The Houston team member was a woman slightly older, Bobbi by name. A sales clerk at the Bayport Mall, Bobbi had been the victim of geography (her apartment was near the impact site of the Houston Object) and natural curiosity (she had gone out to see what had happened). Surely her motivation was less primal than Makali's—probably just the urge to go home.

They were all busy monitoring a suite of 3-D printers that were still creating the fast- and self-replicating chemical-biological-cyber weapons that could be (a) dispersed in Earth's atmosphere or (b) dumped in Earth's oceans or (c) quickly spread through soil and groundwater if the vesicle blew up in orbit, crashed in the ocean, or smacked into land.

Thinking about the weapons allowed the new Keanu information to grow clearer in Sanjay's mind—and more urgent. He needed to have this out with Zhao.

He pushed himself toward the vesicle captain. "How much control do we have over our trajectory?"

"Very little," Zhao said.

"As far as you're concerned, we're just a guided meteoroid."

"Meteor at the moment," Zhao said. "A meteoroid when we enter the atmosphere." He smiled, but not happily. "And a meteorite if all that's left is a smoking hole in the ground."

"Becoming a kinetic energy weapon—a giant cannonball—is one of the options, correct?" Sanjay said.

"Yes. Worst-case scenario, we simply crash into this Reiver facility at high speed. That ought to wreck it."

"And us."

"I did call it a worst case."

In the event the vesicle survived its landing—or crash—and if Zhao and team were able to operate undetected, other substances could be delivered via data networks. "That covers everything, I think," Zhao said.

"What's the primary landing site?"

"Aquatic, coast of California. The vesicle will do its thing"—which meant rotate, absorbing terrestrial material while dispersing water- and aerosol-borne weapons—"and we will signal Rachel and the others and hope they can rendezvous.

"Then, *bam!*" Zhao clapped his hands. "Weapons launched, *Adventure* crew rescued, off we go, home to Keanu." Now he regarded Sanjay. "You knew all this."

"We have to change it." So said the voices in his head, quite insistently now.

"To what?" Zhao spoke so loudly that Makali and the others stopped moving.

"To landing as close to the facility as possible, as soon as we can."

"Exposing ourselves to attack? The Reivers flew a vesicle to Earth twenty years ago. We have to assume they know how to breach or destroy one. Hell, we could probably be destroyed by American missiles if we get pounded often enough! And," he said, not waiting for Sanjay to continue his argument, "we lose our waterborne weapons and probably the aerosols, too. Why would we march into this war with a third of our army?"

"The mission is changing."

"I don't see it."

"You don't have my perspective."

Zhao sneered. "This is your Keanu link talking to you."

"You don't believe it? You used to." Sanjay remembered Zhao's tales of his encounter with the Architect, his interactions with Zack Stewart and especially the Revenant Yvonne Hall.

"Seeing Dale Scott as a proponent made me reevaluate Keanu's taste in messengers."

"Dale Scott is not in contact with Keanu—"

"I rather think he is, insane as that sounds—"

"Not the way I am!" Sanjay said.

"For God's sake, Zhao!" Makali joined the argument. "Dale Scott never *died*. Dale Scott never became a *Revenant*!" She pointed at Sanjay. "This is how Keanu and the Architects communicate with us! Listen to him—or call Jaidev and Harley and have them tell you the same thing."

Zhao blinked. "You're right," he said, his voice notably softer and quieter. "I am forced to admit that the pressure is affecting me." He was a brilliant and capable man, the most versatile of all the HBs with his skills in manipulating people as well as machinery. But who could function normally when dealing with the fate of the Earth? "What is the new plan?"

Makali and the other four had not resumed their work but rather drifted closer to Zhao and Sanjay. What was being said might mean whether they lived or died.

"We are no longer a weapons platform; we are now a courier ship. The goal is to get me close enough to the Reiver facility, as soon as possible, to contact Rachel and her team directly."

"We can't get there in much less than ten hours," Zhao said. "Maybe we can accelerate and shave an hour or two."

Sanjay could feel the response that data triggered. Pleasure, but also more urgency. "Do it, then."

"What's so important that you have to tell her?"

"Keanu's systems know what the Reiver facility is—it's called the Ring—and what it's for."

"Which is?"

"To teleport a Reiver army to the Architect home world."

"You just lost me."

Sanjay felt a pressure in his skull so intense that he thought he was having a stroke. His vision blurred for a moment, then returned. "You don't need to understand it. I don't. But you need to accept it."

"The Reivers are opening a portal to another planet . . . in another star system? If they could do that, why did they ever bother with Keanu or the vesicle?"

"It's new technology for them. Untried."

"So maybe it won't work."

"We can't take that chance."

"Doesn't that argue in favor of our original mission?"

Sanjay shook his head. He shared Zhao's position, but he was no longer speaking entirely for himself. "Even if we successfully launch all our weapons, some Reivers will survive . . . and we will have killed thousands or even millions of human beings."

Zhao appeared frustrated. "I just don't see how taking control of the Ring solves the problem of Reivers on Earth. Wouldn't it be better to blow up the damn thing and kill them all?"

"Keanu has a plan for the Ring."

"Oh. And the Reivers?"

"Some will be destroyed. But there is a . . . greater need." Sanjay struggled to articulate the message. The flood of images and data was so intense and so diverse that he couldn't accept it. "I . . . I'm no longer certain that Keanu wants the Reivers destroyed, if that's the price."

Then he vomited, explosively, with all the horrific side effects that meant. "Oh, Jesus," Makali said.

His discomfort was short-lived. As he accepted water and stopped shaking, he said, "Here's how we take control, and why."

As he started speaking, he saw an expression he never thought he would ever see on Zhao Buoming's face:

Surprise.

And then, something that surely passed for excitement. Then Zhao said, "I hope the entire plan doesn't rest on us alone."

Sanjay felt a jolt like a bolt of lightning in his head, and a shiver up his spine, a form of confirmation. "It doesn't," he said, both relieved and disappointed. Relieved because it doubled the chances that this crazy idea might work.

Disappointed because it doubled the chances that Keanu would no longer need him, and he would die as quickly as the earlier Revenants.

QUESTION: For Mr. Toutant, what is your role in the *Adventure* crew?

TOUTANT: Movie star. (laughter)

QUESTION: Seriously.

TOUTANT: Well, I'm not a pilot, I'm not a politician, so (pats his ample stomach) call me ballast.

QUESTION: You're not answering.

TOUTANT: You pick up on things.

INTERVIEW AT YELAHANKA,
APRIL 14, 2040

DALE

Dale Scott had spent years flying Air Force jets on combat missions and routine patrols.

Then, during his decade at NASA, he had access to the sleek T-38 jets, which gave him even more hours of high-performance exhilaration.

He had been also launched into orbit aboard a Russian Soyuz rocket.

None of those experiences approached the thrill and satisfaction he felt in "flying" Keanu, even though his active role lasted less than fifteen minutes.

He had made his way back to the Factory in less than an hour—there was nothing like compulsion, anger, and good directions to shorten a trip.

The control center that Keanu guided him to was a structure he had passed dozens of times over the years. He recalled making plans to check out the place, but that applied to fifty other buildings as well.

When he arrived, he realized that he had stuck his head inside at least once in a dozen years . . . finding nothing but inert, incomprehensible machines and displays.

Today, however, these items were alive and working, as if waiting for him.

By now the messages inside his head had resolved with impressive clarity; he knew exactly what screens to touch, in what order, with what timing.

He executed the intricate series of commands, feeling a glow of satisfaction each time he was successful.

With the final touch, he believed that he felt a shudder in his feet . . . Keanu's propulsion system coming alive.

On one central screen, entire rows and cells of figures began to change.

"Houston, we have ignition," Dale said.

Another screen lit up with the most detailed Keanu schematic he had ever seen—not for the first time in his exile, he wished for an iPhone so he could capture that image. Jaidev Mahabala, Sasha Blaine, and Harley Drake—indeed, any one of the HBs—would have introduced money to the human habitat just to be able to buy the thing.

It showed the spheroid of the NEO, of course; that wasn't surprising. Also visible: a number of habitats that Dale recognized, including the Factory. What fascinated him was seeing at least twice as many habitats as he expected, along with a network of tunnels and passages far more extensive than his explorations had revealed.

There was the core, too, a central cylinder running roughly south to north and containing Keanu's primary power source, the fusion generator Zack Stewart had died restarting.

Near both poles of Keanu were a dozen tubes that were different from the internal tramway or Substance K piping . . . these had a slight conical shape, like trumpets, with their mouths appearing to reach Keanu's surface.

Of course, Dale realized: These were scoops for sucking up interstellar gas and other materials to fuel the power core. (The schematic showed that there were other methods of gathering fuel or energy, including a network of grids on the NEO's surface.)

Spaced equidistantly around Keanu's equator and poles were smaller tubes that Dale recognized as propulsion jets.

And, finally, three other passages . . . vesicle-launching tubes.

Ultimately the schematic was a hodgepodge of different systems added over time. What else would one expect from a ten-thousand-year-old starship? It was likely that none of the equipment was original . . . that it had all been redesigned, upgraded, remade over the millennia.

And, given the variety of habitats, by different races, each with its own technology, and its own relationship to the now-absent or extinct Architects.

Humans were latecomers, Dale realized. And in twenty years had done nothing! *We don't even know what we're living in,* he thought.

But for the moment, one human had been empowered. Dale Scott had activated Keanu's propulsion system for the second time in human history. The first activation, twenty years ago, had stopped Keanu's flight out of the solar system and put the NEO on a long, slow trajectory back toward Earth.

That event had been controlled from the Temple, but only the way that a human space mission could be "controlled" from a backup center . . . basic commands could be given, but little else. The real calculations and decisions took place in the primary centers.

Here in the Factory node, Dale had finer, more precise control than the Temple.

He needed it, because he was not only blasting Keanu out of its circular orbit four hundred thousand kilometers from Earth.

He was sending it on a collision course toward Earth.

He wondered whether Jaidev and the others knew that. In the past month, Keanu had made a burn of its system to slow down enough to be captured by Earth's gravity, so, Dale knew, the backup node in the Temple was still active. But would anybody be watching? Would its rudimentary displays suddenly flash red or sound some kind of alarm?

He would have loved to see the look on Harley Drake's face when he realized that someone else had taken the stick and was flying his NEO.

There was still work to be done, of course. An object the size of Keanu—over one hundred kilometers across—and flying at a velocity that was steadily increasing to ten or twenty thousand kilometers an hour needed to be able to tweak its trajectory.

Because the idea was not to hit *Earth.* The idea was to fly close, within a thousand kilometers, possibly even lower, on a certain path over a certain spot at a certain time.

Dale hoped that someone on Earth would be aiming a camera at Keanu as it approached—and then he realized that every human on the fucking planet would be watching the sky! Having a bright white NEO the size of a major asteroid growing bigger and bigger would send people running for hills and shelters . . . at least, those too stupid to realize that the impact of an object the size of Keanu would be a civilization-ending event.

(The rock that had killed the dinosaurs was a third the diameter of Keanu.)

The smarter ones would hold each other's hands, say their prayers, confront their fate, watching in horrified wonder as the shiny thing grew monstrous in the sky.

What a show that would be!

In spite of his years of solitude and systematic exploration of the Factory and environs, patience had never been prominent in Dale Scott's makeup.

After several hours with no further update of the images and sounds in his head, he began to wonder:

Was Keanu finished with him?

He shouldn't have been surprised. His communion with Keanu had never been consistent; indeed, at times the images and sounds had been absent for days or even months.

But he needed them now.

He returned to the control node and saw that the status screen continued to change. He also found a new panel that showed both "target" Earth, still small and largely in shadow, just a bluish crescent, and the Moon, far closer, half-shadowed, viewed from a completely different perspective; Dale realized he was looking toward its south pole . . . he could make out Shackleton Crater, the landing site for *Destiny-5* more than twenty years ago, a mission he might have commanded instead of Tea Nowinski . . . if not for Zack Stewart.

No, don't look back. Go forward.

But . . . how? Since he had commanded Keanu out of orbit, the NEO had crossed thousands of kilometers. Its speed had increased dramatically.

It was diving toward Earth! Surely Keanu needed his help with that incredibly dangerous operation—

Then he remembered: Keanu's systems didn't always work properly! That had been the problem when the HBs first arrived . . . dead passageways, failed equipment.

And since then . . . the dormant Beehive!

What if the stress of the de-orbit burn had damaged Keanu's ability to communicate with its human links? Obviously the NEO was saying nothing to Dale. Suppose Sanjay on the vesicle was out of comm, too?

Then what? A missing tweak of Keanu's trajectory at this moment could be disastrous!

One option was to run back to the human habitat, to see if the Temple node was online.

But that would take an hour . . . and if Jaidev and the others were in touch with Sanjay, or Keanu itself, then Dale's efforts were not needed.

If not, though, he would have wasted precious time—

He went looking for his communion site.

The scooped-out depression was as Dale had left it. He peeled off his raggedy clothes and lay down, closing his eyes, regulating his breathing . . . all the yogalike techniques he had learned over the years.

Time passed, minutes at most.

Then he felt it—the connection was right there, begging to be made! He opened his mind, reached out, felt it all wash over him, ten or a hundred times more powerful than any link he had previously experienced.

It made him afraid. And it hurt . . . everywhere, chest, brain, legs, arms.

Too much—

Then everything went cold, silent, and dead.

1. (U) MSG NUMBER 51118-47308 (00217) USSTRATCOM/J36

2. (U) FLASH SBSS UPDATE 23APR2040 1811ZULU

3. (S) KEYWORDS "KEANU" "ORBIT" "MANEUVER" "THREAT"

4. (S) Orbital and Earth-based systems recorded propulsive events on NEO Keanu this hour resulting in change-of-orbit maneuver. Delta-V suggests close approach to Earth resulting in threat.

5. (SCI) Impact imminent within forty hours.

INTERNAL COMMUNICATION, U.S. STRATEGIC COMMAND,
FREE NATION U.S., APRIL 22, 2040, 11:12 MST

ZEDS

"Don't do anything I wouldn't do," Xavier Toutant said.

"I don't understand the restriction," Zeds said.

"I meant, try not to kill or injure anyone. At least, not until I tell you."

Zeds and Xavier had been separated from Rachel and the others within moments of their arrival at Site A, hustled into a vehicle, and driven deep inside the long, broad building behind the administration center and its helipad. Their guards were human, not just a THE trio but armed military—and de la Vega.

Zeds barely had time to register the surroundings: the backs of giant mirror towers to the north, part of a ring that extended a long way east and west, then appearing to curve. Also the giant mound that blocked a portion of the view north.

Then they were in a tunnel, and within moments through several doors and into a factory floor filled with Reivers working under dim lights.

Xavier was first to comment, when it became obvious that he and Zeds were going to be working here, too. "We can't see shit."

"We'll fix that in a minute," de la Vega said.

He went off to issue more orders. Only then did Zeds realize that he was surrounded by Reivers of what the humans called the anteater variety, all of them busy at devices that emitted a low, rumbling hum and accomplished nothing Zeds could understand. (His sense of smell told him the walls were crawling with several of the smaller templates, too. His vision was not good enough to confirm this, however.)

He must have reacted in a visible or audible way to prompt Xavier's comment. "It won't be easy," he said.

Xavier slapped him halfway up his back. "Don't worry, this will all be over soon."

"And we may be dead."

"Oh, I know."

Compared to other sentient races, Sentries, Zeds had been told, were fiery by nature, freakishly quick to take action. These traits had recommended them to the Architects as allies in their war against the Reivers.

They had also been their downfall, as their often-blind attacks—so valuable in early battles—eventually allowed the Reivers to develop strategies that defeated them. The colony within the Keanu habitat had ultimately been marginalized, supplanted . . . held as a reserve for that long-off day when the ultimate battle loomed, but used since then as guards or security.

And given the few new races gathered by Keanu, not often then.

The one constant in Sentry existence, however, was hatred of the Reivers—which was reciprocated. It went beyond their encounters with the half-carbon, half-organic beings in the Architect war; it was something in their nature, dry versus wet, aggregate versus individual, small versus large. They had, in fact, nothing in common, and everything in opposition.

DSA, Zeds's direct connate, suggested that the mutual hatred might have roots in an earlier conflict, when some form of the Reivers invaded the watery Sentry world. "We used to live on land as much as water,"

DSA had said, itself a troubling thought. Zeds found it impossible to think of his people living on land by choice; certainly his experiences of the past few days had not caused him to think better of that idea.

This also suggested that the Reiver-Sentry conflict was far older than even the ancient Reiver-Architect war.

All of it made Zeds eager for a fight. Instead, he was locked inside this increasingly uncomfortable environment suit and forced to accomplish tasks better suited to humans.

As Xavier began setting up the proteus, doors kept opening and other vehicles arriving with pieces of equipment, some of them blackened and burned.

Other humans were brought hard copies of documents, something Zeds had only heard about.

Still other humans arrived and began setting up data displays and a communication link.

De la Vega directed all this activity with precision and threats of violence. He was almost Sentry-like in his methods.

And he left Zeds alone, freeing the Sentry to take small steps in each direction, his natural way of judging the size and nature of his environment.

From somewhere nearby he smelled salty water. The mere idea of being freed from the suit and able to submerge for even a short time was maddening. He looked at the many doors—one of them obviously led to that water.

"Hey, I need you," Xavier said. "We've got a lot of work to do and you may have noticed, we have unpleasant supervisors."

Zeds was ordinarily fond of the rotund, smart-mouthed man, but prolonged exposure had reduced his affection, at least for Xavier's dogged methods. Laboring with the proteus printer was not fit work for a Sentry.

Killing Reivers was better.

In the next hour, several good things happened. He and Xavier made direct contact with Keanu, specifically with Jaidev Mahabala. After several moments devoted to pleasantries and catch-up (as well as veiled forebodings), they had uploaded schematics, imagery, and documents to

Keanu. "Even after twenty years, I can't predict what or when something will emerge," Jaidev reported. "But I'll ping you the instant we have it."

For a moment, then, Zeds and Xavier were alone and unmolested. De la Vega had departed some time earlier, no doubt to exercise his particular form of leadership on other humans.

A signal sounded within the factory; the machines stopped, and the ranks of Reiver Aggregates separated from them, formed up, and marched out.

Zeds and Xavier were kept company by a THE trio and as many human guards. "Hey," Xavier shouted, "since we're waiting and you're giving the aliens a coffee break, how about some nourishment?"

The three from THE conferred; two of them exited.

"This is the thing people never seem to realize," Xavier said. "And when I say people, I mean humans, because maybe Sentries are better about this.

"Nothing gets done without logistics. You can't fight wars without bullets, you can't build machines without materials or factories, and you sure as shit can't get any of that done unless you've got people in the right place . . ." And here he smiled and patted his ample middle. "And they've been fed."

"Sentries have no experience with logistics, as you describe it," Zeds told Xavier. "My connate once compared us to humans who live in tropical zones. We would essentially be subsistence fisherpeople willing to spend our days in or near the water, eating and breeding and little else. Perhaps occasional fights."

"Add some music, and you've got New Orleans." Zeds knew little of Earth geography but had learned that his friend Xavier had grown up in this near-tropical American city. "But, come on, you built spacecraft! *Adventure* was so durable we were able to fly it, more or less, after it had been sitting for several hundred years!"

"Vacuum preserves," Zeds said. "And there have always been a fraction of my people who are more ambitious and active. Or we would never have left the sea." Or before that, the land.

"That's true of humans, too. And I am proud to say that I would *happily* be one of those subsistence fisherpeople you mentioned. That's one of my problems with life on Keanu . . . it's just too fucking hard." He smiled again as the two THE officers approached carrying cups and trays of food. "And that was before we decided to turn the NEO into a warship."

It was all human food, of course. Before Zeds could say anything, Xavier snapped to the agents, "Did you happen to notice the fact that he's an alien? With different dietary needs?"

One of them looked chagrined. Again, Xavier spoke: "Show me where you got this stuff and let me pick something I know he can consume. Jesus."

So Xavier went off with the pair that gathered food, leaving Zeds even more alone in the Site A factory, except for a lone THE counselor and the guards, all of them off at a distance.

He decided to investigate the pool. Careful to keep himself within view of the guards—though they must have known there was no possible escape for him—he systematically investigated each door. Naturally, upon reaching the last one, he was finally able to see to a loading dock, and beyond that, a glistening pool of water—not salty in a way he recognized, but still wet and likely restorative. It appeared that the pool existed for equipment of some kind, but that wouldn't bother Zeds . . . as long as there was room enough for his body.

He hoped he would have a chance to test it.

As he turned, he was surprised to see a single Reiver Aggregate, anteater variety, standing in his way.

Anticipating attack, he raised his two upper arms. The Reiver made no motion; it seemed frozen, staring with its blank, faceted eyes. The sight and smell of the creature was so overpowering that Zeds wanted nothing more than to grab the nearest portable object and smash the Reiver into its component units.

Then squash each one.

But he could not attack without some provocation, however slight. And none had been offered. So he said, "What do you want?"

To his amazement, the Reiver spoke. "I am Aggregate Carbon-143 and I have important information for you."

"You *what*?" Xavier said. "With *who*?"

It was ten minutes later. Zeds was back on the factory floor, the

Reiver Aggregate having departed, Xavier having returned with some sort of vegetable stew that might have been Sentry-friendly if cold rather than cooked.

Nevertheless, Zeds ate as he waited for the Reivers to return to their machines. And more importantly, for those machines to rev up and create a sound curtain.

Only then did he recount, in general terms, the bizarre contact with a Reiver Aggregate and her apparent linkage to a human operator in the Site A hierarchy who would be standing by to perform certain actions. "I am to relay this information to Rachel immediately," Zeds said.

"This thing *mentioned* Rachel?"

"No. She said our 'human decision maker,' but the implication was clear."

"What kind of actions?"

"There was considerable detail. In general, it had to do with the activation of the Ring, a change in its size, orientation, and duration of operation. Also that we should make plans to be away from this facility before that activation."

"I hope you remember it all." He looked around. "We need to get Rachel or Pav down here fast."

"I have an idea," Zeds said.

He stood up to his full height . . . and fell over backward.

The suit cushioned the impact, but the floor was still hard.

Xavier seemed genuinely upset. "Jesus, Zeds! Hey!" he called, and bent over him. "What's the idea?" he whispered.

But there was no time to explain. Zeds could hear and feel footsteps as THE officers and guards ran toward him.

He began stripping off his environment suit.

"Whoa, big buddy! What do you think you're doing?"

"I have reached the limits of life support," Zeds announced.

De la Vega had returned, too, joining the throng around Zeds. "What does he mean?" he asked Xavier.

"Ask him, for Christ's sake. He speaks English."

The human leader turned to Zeds. "What's wrong?"

"I have been in this suit for days. Its support has expired and needs renewal." He made a noise that in Sentry language indicated the looming moment of fusion, creating a connate, which to human ears sounded like a horrifying death rattle—or so Rachel had once told him.

Xavier and de la Vega seemed equally alarmed. "I need medical attention," Zeds said.

"What kind of doctor could help him?" de la Vega said.

"Not me," Xavier said.

Then Zeds croaked, "The only human capable of diagnosing me is Yahvi Stewart-Radhakrishnan."

"We'll get her," de la Vega said.

"That's the girl," Xavier said. "Make sure her mother comes, too."

De la Vega was giving orders. Zeds made another horrible noise. "What can we do?"

"I require immersion in water," Zeds said.

Day Eleven

MONDAY, APRIL 23, 2040

KEANU APPROACHES!

No one in government will confirm, but Keanu is maneuvering! Approximately 28 hours ago several eruptions were visible on its surface, consistent with the NEO's original departure from Earth orbit in 2019.

But instead of shrinking in size and luminosity as it did then, Keanu is GROWING.

It is coming CLOSER TO EARTH!

And observers in South America noted a launch of some kind from Keanu shortly after it maneuvered.

Are we being invaded?

Or bombarded?

KETTERING GROUP,
MONDAY, APRIL 23, 2040

WHIT

"How much longer?"

Whit Murray had been speaking into his headset, and thence into the entire Ring control system, for the past two hours, and was getting tired of hearing himself.

He sat in the same mission control as the day of First Light, but now in the center and front. The screens in front of him were different; there were more of them, they showed more data. And in the upper right was a special window all his own . . . a simple purple rectangle with an *OVERRIDE* icon that had not yet been activated but would be at the minus-fifteen-minute point.

It was his job to simply watch and listen; if everything was green and functional and there were no anomalies like weather or a flock of birds, Whit would click the icon and be presented with two additional options: *AUTO* or *MANUAL*. If he selected *AUTO*, things were out of his hands. The Ring's moved-up Fire Light would proceed.

If he selected *MANUAL*, he could *HOLD* the count or *RETURN TO AUTO* or *UPDATE*, then *RETURN TO AUTO*.

It sounded as though he'd been given the keys to a car, but he knew he was not truly in control. There were, he knew, at least eight Aggregate formations in the top level of the Ring Light command structure. Representatives of each formation sat to his right, left, and rear.

But they all had separate functions in the operations of the Ring and its aiming, and especially the planned transportation of all those invasion units through the cone of the Ring. They had to agree on every command decision, and all but one of them had no place for human input.

None but the final one.

"They expect to resume the count within the next twenty minutes." That was Counselor Kate, promoted to voice link at the same time Whit Murray had become the lead "operator." She sounded tired and tense, words that would have described Whit's state, too. Everyone seemed tense; in his hourly breaks from the console, Whit found Aggregates buzzing up and down the hallways outside the center. Those inside—and their human counterparts—seemed jittery, constantly on the move, in contrast to the tomblike stillness of the awful First Light.

Nervous or not, the ultimate go/no-go for the final triggering lay right here with him, Whit Murray, the lucky result of the Aggregates' realization that one human individual might notice something all their other systems would miss.

That, and having a friend on the inside.

Accepting the position was one thing. Enjoying it was something else. He had accepted Carbon-143's offer while in a state of rage and mourning for Dehm; more sober reflection shortly thereafter made him wonder just what he'd gotten himself into.

But it was too late to back out.

Whit had been on the console for seven hours, since late Sunday night. At that time, Fire Light was four hours off.

It still was.

He didn't see the need for the big hurry. What was a few hours, days, months, or even years when you were invading a planet?

And, given that the invasion would leave Earth wrecked, there was even less need for hurry.

But the Aggregates had decided to move everything forward. They would have put Whit at his console Saturday evening, except they were, according to Counselor Kate, waiting for some major replacement parts.

To be delivered or manufactured, Whit wasn't sure. The integration of these parts had consumed the entire night and now most of the morning.

He could only imagine the discomfort human soldiers would be feeling if they were stuck inside the various tanks, weapons carriers, and other vehicles. But who knew with Aggregates? How was that any different from their standard physical location?

The moment he thought terrible things about the Aggregates, he felt bad; there *was* at least one that was different.

How Carbon-143 broke free from her conditioning, or more to the point, why, Whit would have loved to know.

He hoped he would live long enough to ask his Aggregate "friend."

She had not been in contact since offering him this job and giving him a few key instructions:

"When the final command comes, take control of the Ring and disrupt its operations."

"They'll kill me."

"Disrupting the operations will probably kill us all."

"Oh." He thought. "Disrupt how, exactly?"

"Your research will have shown you that the Ring must create a specifically shaped field at just the right moment and with a certain orientation. Change one of those and it will fail. There are also several humans present who will require assistance as they escape this facility. They are visitors from Keanu."

Whit had seen some mention of them on the news. "Why are they here?"

"They are helping with operation of the Ring."

"Then why should I help them?"

For just a moment, Whit thought he detected what, for a human, would have been exasperation. "Because it is necessary."

He had trusted Carbon-143 to this point—there was no reason to stop.

He really wished he could talk to her now, though. He felt isolated, sent out on a mission with instructions that were sure to be difficult or impossible to carry out.

And with little chance of success.

At that moment, Counselor Kate said, "They're resuming!"

And the serene countdown voice noted, "Four hours to Fire Light."

In the control center, all motion ceased. Humans and Aggregates slipped back to their stations so smoothly that Whit hardly registered any motion.

And his heart rate must have doubled. *Oh my God, oh my God,* he thought. *This is really happening!* He was at the heart of the opening of a door to another solar system . . . enabling an alien invasion! Less than two weeks ago he had been a lowly worker bee on a metro stop in Las Vegas!

He thought about his father . . . and Randall Dehm.

He thought about . . . well, everybody in America and the other Free Nations, and how many of them would be alive after today.

He thought about the rest of the planet . . . the same thing for them. Would they be better off with the Aggregates largely gone, or weakened?

Or, their big mission in ruins, assuming that Whit could ruin it— would they be more vulnerable to attack? Or would they be ruthless in taking revenge?

He thought about this target world who-knew-how-many-light-years distant and how his actions might spare them the Aggregate invasion.

As he thought, he followed the progress of the count. He noted imagery from the staging areas as the tanks and tankers and other vehicles lined up in arrow-shaped formations . . . ready for the Ring cone to turn toward them.

He noted the insane amount of traffic on his screen, a constant flow of words, numbers, images . . . as if every component of the Ring facility larger than a cell phone were reporting in. Which was probably what it meant.

Through it all, he kept returning to the purple rectangle on the corner . . . the icon inert, not yet enabled, ready to go live in the last half hour.

The one he would have to click to authorize the final automatic actions of the Ring.

As he stared, a new window appeared next to it, a news camera image of what appeared to be a meteor streaking across the sky.

It was coming from Counselor Kate's station. "What am I seeing?" he asked her, on their private link.

"Apparently Keanu has launched an object toward Earth. The NEO has moved, too, and is coming closer."

"Are we under attack?" He wasn't at all surprised that the humans on Keanu might know about the Ring or be trying to attack it, even if it meant that they would be attacking Whit Murray, too.

"No one seems to know."

"Where is this information coming from?"

"What do you mean?"

"Is this on the Aggregate networks?"

"No," she said. "It's just a Free Nation news feed—"

"Block it," he said.

"But—"

"Goddammit, didn't you just tell me we were entering the terminal phase? We have forty-some minutes to go! Nobody needs any distractions!"

The window vanished from his screen.

"Thank you."

Counselor Kate said nothing.

Whit considered his next steps. The *OVERRIDE* icon would go live in moments, at which point he would click *MANUAL*, and if there was a God, or Aggregate Carbon-143 had done her job, select *UPDATE* and *RETURN TO AUTO*.

Then what? Run? Surrounded by Aggregates, he would be lucky to reach the exit, much less the outdoors, much less someplace safe.

He knew the *Adventure* humans were present and willing to help him . . . but he had no idea how to find them.

All right, then, your plan is hit the right switch, then excuse yourself to go to the bathroom.

Even as he thought it, he knew it was hopeless, lame. He had to accept the fact that his best option was dead hero.

"Murray!" That was Counselor Kate's voice, but not through the link. Whit turned.

Counselor Kate was behind him, and she looked shaken. With her were her two THE companions, Counselors Margot and Hans. They had been present in the control center all during the morning but generally out of Whit's view.

"Step away from the console," Counselor Hans said.

Oh God, Whit thought. He forced himself to say, "Why?"

"Your behavior is suspect," Counselor Margot said.

"You shut down information flow," Counselor Kate said.

"For good reason."

"It's inconsistent with your past behavior," Counselor Hans said. "Step away."

The countdown voice said, "One minute." The *OVERRIDE* icon glowed.

"I think *your* behavior is suspect!" Whit suddenly shouted. He jumped to his feet, pointed at Counselor Hans. "They're trying to wreck the operation!"

The Aggregates to either side buzzed into motion, quickly closing on the trio from THE and giving Whit time to click *MANUAL*, then, as Counselor Hans screamed, "You have to stop him!" *UPDATE* and *AUTO.*

The purple window disappeared.

Other Aggregates joined the struggle. They were no longer needed at their consoles; Fire Light couldn't be stopped now. It was like a rocket with engines igniting just seconds prior to liftoff; shutting it down would only destroy it.

Whit stood back from the console, hands raised. "Fine, I'm suspect? Let's settle this elsewhere." And he allowed himself to be hustled toward the rear of the control room by a trio of Aggregates.

Before they could reach the door, Whit thought he smelled smoke of some kind. Then he saw a cloud of vapor descending from overhead vents.

The door opened, revealing a giant, strange-looking being with four arms.

Then Whit fell down.

RACHEL

"Did you see that?"

Yahvi turned away from the window with such a look of pure joy and wonder that Rachel almost forgot how much trouble they were in. Her child was happy, and that was all that mattered. "It was a glowing ball flying through the sky!"

Rachel joined Yahvi. The window looked south to a corner of one of the staging areas and its collection of vehicles. Beyond that lay a high desert plateau.

And in the sky . . . a bright light moving from the southwest.

"Looks like an aircraft," Pav said.

"It's moving too fast," Rachel said.

So fast, in fact, that it grew to the size of a coin held at arm's length, then vanished somewhere to the east.

"Well," Rachel said, "what do you think?"

Pav's face showed the beginnings of a smile, one of Rachel's favorite looks. "It's what I saw at Bangalore and you saw at Houston."

He was still being a bit too cagey, bless him, but nevertheless confirmed Rachel's hopeful conclusion:

What she had seen flashing across the sky, touching down somewhere nearby, was a vesicle, a Keanu-launched object crewed by Zhao

Buoming and Makali Pillay and, apparently, Sanjay Bhat and several others, and equipped with enough nasty shit to wipe the Reiver Aggregates off the face of the Earth.

And maybe take Rachel and crew back to Keanu.

"I hear you!" Yahvi suddenly said. She walked to the other side of the small room, her hand to her head.

Pav reached for her, ostensibly to keep her from saying anything too revealing, but Rachel stopped him. "Surveillance won't mean anything now. Either it's working or it isn't."

"Is that the vesicle calling?" Tea said.

"Keanu," Yahvi said, her face scrunched up.

"Say that again, please!" Yahvi looked horrified as she and Rachel suffered through the lag. Then Yahvi nodded and told the others: "We have to get to the vesicle *now.*"

"And what then? Fly us back to Keanu?"

"Yes."

"That's going to be difficult," Pav said.

"It can't be more than a few kilometers!" Rachel said.

"And we're surrounded by thousands of Reivers!"

She slapped Pav on the shoulder. "Have a little faith!"

She desperately wanted to take her own advice.

When Rachel and Yahvi reached Zeds, the Sentry was already afloat in his pool, looking more serene than he had since leaving Keanu.

Rachel had no idea what his "malady" was, or what Yahvi was supposed to do about it. But her daughter displayed a surprising flair for improvisation, asking pointed questions about Zeds's physical parameters, then insisting that de la Vega immediately bring her items that someone unfamiliar with Sentry dietary needs would find exotic.

The resulting moments of chaos gave Zeds time to tell Yahvi about the timing of the cyberattack on the Ring and his plans for evasion and escape.

Rachel would have loved to know more, but de la Vega was soon on them. And they were forced to leave Zeds.

While being escorted back to their quarters, they passed Xavier, who was in his glory, giving orders and issuing pointed criticism of those around him like an arrogant chef in a busy kitchen.

He did manage to wink at Rachel.

Returning to their cell with Counselors Cory and Ivetta, they found Pav, Tea, and Colin Edgely being guarded by Counselor Nigel.

"Now what?" Rachel said brightly, once they were all together. "Still restricted to base, I see."

"Actually, to this room," Tea said.

"Could we help Xavier?" Edgely said.

Rachel sympathized; she knew the Aussie astronomer just wanted to get out of the room. But Xavier and Zeds needed no distractions. Everything depended on their success with the Aggregate replacement parts and related actions. "He's doing fine without us," she said.

Counselor Ivetta said, "You'll be here for the next two days."

"Then what? Free to go? That would be great!" Rachel smiled at Tea. "You could be our guide to the Grand Canyon!"

Tea was ready to tweak their captors. "Yeah, I've visited a lot. I bet we could drive there in a couple of hours."

"Why only two days?" Pav said.

Counselor Nigel looked troubled. "Our briefings only cover that time."

At that moment, a boom shook the building. Counselor Cory said, "What was that?"

Counselors Nigel and Ivetta rose. "Let's find out." All three walked out, leaving Rachel to contemplate the meaning of "two days." It could not have been good.

That was when Yahvi squealed.

To Rachel, it felt strange to be locked in one room while important things were going on a few meters away. It was like huddling in your house while a tropical storm raged outside—only silently.

And while grateful for the welcome sight of the vesicle, she longed for a view to the north, toward the Ring itself. Would she be able to see the cone? Would it be like some giant searchlight waving from one direction to another?

Didn't matter.

They could hear shouts through the door, then crashes, as if furniture had been knocked over.

"What's going on out there?" Tea said. She leaned close to the door to hear, then quickly pulled back, fanning the air. "Oh, God, that's nasty—"

"Get to the window," Pav said.

Before Rachel could even speculate about what might be going on, the door opened. It was Xavier, looking sweaty and out of breath. Under his arm he carried two mesh bags filled with gray balls the size of oranges.

"Time to go," he announced. "And you're welcome."

"What's going on?" Edgely said.

"The guards seem to be falling asleep," Xavier said. "But they won't be out for long."

"Where's Zeds?" Rachel said.

"Playing Sandman to a bunch of other guards."

Emerging from their jail cell, they saw a pair of human guards flat out, unconscious. One of them had collapsed on a table, knocking a lamp to the floor. "They look dead," Yahvi said. She didn't sound especially concerned, just curious.

"This stuff really puts you out, I think," Xavier said. "I hope so. It's supposed to work on humans and Reivers."

They all ran for the nearest stairway, passing another guard and an entire THE trio who had been laid out. They stopped at the door to the stairwell.

"I think someone's coming up," Tea said.

Pav turned to Xavier. "Give me one of those bags."

Xavier handed it over. "Just make sure you hit something, so they burst."

Rachel gathered Yahvi, and Tea grabbed Edgely. All four dropped behind a nearby desk as Xavier opened the stairway door and Pav threw one, then two balls through the opening.

There was a shout. Xavier slammed the door.

Everyone waited. Rachel's heart beat so strongly it made her shake.

"We should wait for the gas to clear," Xavier said.

"How long?" Rachel said.

"Only a minute. It mutates when it's exposed to air, supposed to be harmless then."

"What is it?" Edgely asked.

"'Neo-fentanyl,' they say. Sound familiar?"

"Not to me."

Tea said, "And how did you get it?"

"Made it, of course," Xavier said. "At the same time we were turning out new pieces for the Ring. When I uploaded those specs to Keanu, I just wrote on them, *Give me something to knock people out.*" He hefted the bag with a grin. "I wish I'd had this when we landed in India!"

"We should be good now," Xavier said. "Let's roll."

It was a quick trip down two flights of stairs to a loading dock, where several vehicles were parked. There were no guards.

Pav was in his element, running to a green sport-utility vehicle and opening the door. Not finding what he wanted, he moved to the next, then a third. "Keys in this one!"

"No," Xavier said, pointing to a gray van. "This one."

They ran toward it, and Rachel could see that there were items in the back end: a printer and three cartons of Substance K.

"Sorry," Xavier said, "but I stopped here before getting you."

"Smart move, I hope," Rachel said.

The vehicle was big enough to hold them. "Everybody in," she said. She headed for the shotgun seat, then stopped. "All right, a basic question . . . who knows how to drive?"

"Me," Tea said.

"Good," Rachel said. "I never learned—"

"Me neither," Pav said.

"And I'm out of practice," Xavier said.

They had just closed the doors when Yahvi said, "Zeds isn't here!"

Rachel knew that. She also knew that if any of them were to get off Earth, they had to leave this place now. She feared that the Ring was about to ignite, frying everything for kilometers around, and that they were already too late.

"We're going," she said.

Tea started the engine.

"You can't!" Yahvi shrieked, throwing herself at Rachel from the backseat.

"We have to go *now*!" She turned to her daughter. The look on her face must have been savage, because Yahvi retreated as if pulled from behind.

Pav put his arm around her.

The van pulled out.

Emerging from the loading dock into the bright desert sunlight, Rachel wished for sunglasses.

And directions. "Which way?" Tea said, steering them out of a parking lot. A train station lay in front of them. An asphalt road led to the right and one of the giant vehicle staging areas.

A dirt road ran to the left, hugging the base of a hill. "Left!" Rachel said. "The vesicle came down north and east of here, right, Yahvi?"

Yahvi blinked again. "Yes."

"Are you linked?" Xavier said.

"Not really," she said. "I hear bursts, words."

"It would be great if Zhao could vector us in."

The dirt road was bumpy but well traveled, and it took them along the south and east side of the Ring mirrors. Rachel found herself trying to look up at the brilliant squares suspended atop their towers . . . now and then, as the van turned, she saw the huge spire of the central projector.

It appeared to be lit, as if ready to fire.

Then the hill to their right gave way to flatter ground . . . and a clear view of a staging area filled with hundreds, possibly thousands of tanks and other invasion vehicles. Some of them were moving around the edge of the area, kicking up faint geysers of dust.

The others saw it, too. "Oh, shit, what if they start chasing us?" Edgely said.

"I think they're too busy with their invasion," Pav said.

"You hope," Xavier said.

Tea gunned the van, subjecting them to teeth-rattling bounces. "Sorry!" she said.

"Don't worry," Rachel shouted. "Keep going."

She looked out her window, seeing nothing but stark, bare rocky peaks now.

Where was the vesicle?

They drove in silence for another fifteen minutes, passing through rugged canyons and across two different dry washes. Finally Tea said, "I make it a dozen clicks," she said. "Any ideas?"

"Other than keep going?" Rachel said.

"There!" Pav shouted.

Rachel saw it then, too . . . In a high desert meadow was a giant white sphere thirty meters or so across, maybe twice that high, sunk two thirds deep in a field of yellow stalks.

It was rotating slowly.

"End of the road," Tea said. The road continued parallel to the vesicle, then turned back to the north and west.

They stopped and got out. As they did, Rachel saw that a truck had pulled over on the other side of the vesicle. A family of what looked like Native Americans huddled there, fascinated and probably terrified, too. "Get away!" she shouted, waving her arms. But they didn't move.

"I hear them!" Yahvi said. "It's Sanjay!" She bounced up on her toes. "He says to wait, that the whole vesicle is going to expand or something."

Rachel remembered that rainy night in Houston, her need to see the recently landed Object because it was a link to her father, then lost somewhere on Keanu. How, as she and Harley and others had watched, the giant blob grew and grew, its skin becoming just porous enough to absorb them all—

"All right," Rachel said. "We have some decisions to make." She was torn by conflicting emotions but struggled to be the leader. She couldn't believe that her visit to Earth was ending, especially since nothing had gone as planned or expected. There was so much left to do! But no more time. "We're going," she said, pointing to Pav and Yahvi and Xavier. "Tea?"

The tall, striking, blunt, sometimes goofy ex-astronaut had tears in her eyes. "Take me with you. I have nothing here."

Pav hugged her.

"Colin, what about you?" Rachel said.

"Love to take you up on the offer," he said. "But I have a family."

"I understand." She hugged him, realizing that it was their first physical contact of any kind . . . which seemed inadequate, given the man's importance to her and her family. To Tea she said, "We should give him the keys and let him get away."

"Me, too," Xavier said.

Rachel turned to him. "What are you talking about?"

"I'm staying."

"Why?" Yahvi said. She sounded stricken.

Xavier slipped an arm around her and smiled. "Kiddo, there is a shitload of work to do here. Planet's still full of Reivers." He pointed to the van. "But we've got the proteus and Sub K, and me and Edgely here might be able to do something about that."

"Zhao is doing it," Pav said.

"No," Yahvi said. "They couldn't deploy all their weapons. They chose to come for us." She frowned, still listening. "There maybe be new orders."

"Hey," Xavier said, his voice growing more serious. "Once I've got this Reiver thing dealt with, I'm going to figure out how to build a Beehive right here. I think people might really be interested in not being dead forever."

Xavier's ideas always surprised Rachel. She was going to miss him terribly. "You're sure?"

"You know I really hated cooking on Keanu," he said. "This will be better."

Edgely was already in the shotgun seat of the van. Xavier took the keys and ran around to the driver's side. "Which way are you going?" Tea said.

"Always forward," Xavier said, slamming the door and gunning the van.

"Good move," Pav said, pointing back the way they had come.

Dust rose from the road. "How far away are they?" Rachel said.

Pav sighed. "Not far enough."

A tank rolled over the hill into view. It was dark green, tracked, twice the size of their van . . . and sporting a nasty-looking weapon pointed at a forty-five-degree angle. "Now what?" Tea said, jerking a thumb toward the vesicle. "Do they have missiles on that thing?"

"No," Rachel said. "And it won't matter. This could be the first of a hundred of those things." She was out of energy, out of ideas. The vesicle and a return to Keanu was right there! So close . . . even if the vesicle ballooned out now, it would suck up hostile forces, too.

At least Xavier and Edgely might get away.

Without firing, however, the big brutal-looking vehicle slewed to a stop a few meters away.

"Mommy . . ." Yahvi said. They were all rooted where they stood, Rachel realized. Like plants.

The side hatch opened, and Zeds emerged. "What the hell?" Pav said.

Yahvi was running toward the Sentry, throwing herself into both sets of arms.

"I have others," the Sentry announced. And out of the car behind him came Counselor Nigel, looking shaken yet excited. "I want to come with you," he said. "If you'll have me."

"Sure," Yahvi said, surprising Rachel.

One more passenger emerged from the tank . . . a Reiver Aggregate anteater. "Oh, Jesus!" Pav said, and bent to reach for a rock.

Rachel felt like doing the same thing, but Zeds stepped in front of the creature. "This unit has shown independence and initiative. We would not be here without her."

"We can't take a Reiver back to Keanu!" Pav said.

"She will be my responsibility," Zeds said.

He had no right to claim responsibility . . . except that he had risked his life. "Fine," Rachel said, "she comes." Sometimes you had to make quick decisions. And live with them.

"Mom!" Yahvi said. "It's happening!"

Rachel turned, just as the white bulk of the vesicle expanded and enclosed them all.

Keep watching the skies!

LAST LINE OF *THE THING FROM ANOTHER WORLD*
(DALE SCOTT'S FAVORITE MOVIE)

DALE

After what seemed like weeks (twenty minutes had passed since the integration), there was no longer any way of telling where Dale Scott ended and Keanu began. The entity that was formerly Dale Scott had been absorbed and uploaded. There was no longer an *I* or an individual—some residual memories survived, like a drop of cream in a cup of coffee . . . separate, but for how long?

There was no regret, only mutual acceptance. Especially as electronic eyes opened and ears engaged and data flowed. First there was total awareness of Keanu itself, the habitats buzzing with life and energy, then the tunnels and passageways pulsing with fluid—like blood in veins—and, finally, the sense of size. . . . Keanu rotated slowly, feeling to a former human like shoulders being shrugged, like rising from a chair. Then dived forward, in a slow fall—

Beyond a growing awareness of Keanu's self, the universe opened. The crackling storm of solar radiation—it had a smell like woodsmoke and a sound like heavy rain.

Tens of thousands of stars and nebulae colored the sky, some of them feeling so close that there was an urge to reach out and grab a handful—

But close by, there was a world that could be grasped. Or certainly could be known. Images. Data. So many signals and sounds.

Then, more closely, more intelligibly . . . like a three-dimensional image clarifying:

Terrified crowds gathered at religious sites in Asia and Europe.

Radio, television, and Net channels shuddered under the weight of warnings, reassurances, commentaries. . . . What was Keanu doing? Was it out of control? Was it on a suicide dive—impacting Earth would destroy both worlds.

Was it attacking? Missiles in the western region of Free Nation U.S. were armed but not launched, almost certainly because the controlling authorities realized the futility of detonating a bomb on Keanu's surface. Agencies could easily assess the minimal damage caused by the explosion that destroyed *Venture* and *Brahma* in 2019. It would be futile, a pebble bouncing off a containership.

Within the habitats . . . the Skyphoi were indifferent. The Sentries were alarmed. Humans, however, were eager and curious. Voices called out for a view; at least one human was trying to re-create the Keanu protective-suiting system in order to go onto the surface. (He would fail.)

But Keanu itself, Dale himself, saw the sights . . . the blinding snowy landscape of Keanu . . . the huge, shadowed crescent of Earth growing visibly larger with each passing moment.

The former Dale Scott had fragmentary memories of low flights, hazy greenish targets, the grunting release of weapons, the glorious explosion of light.

This was so much better. So, so, so much better.

CARBON-143

CONTEXT: As the countdown to Fire Light entered its final ten minutes, Carbon-143 noted a system-wide surge in data use and access. This information triggered first concern, since additional access might well signal examination of her searches and modifications, then satisfaction, since it also indicated extreme bandwidth consumption and confusion.

NARRATIVE: Assembly ceased at the minus-two-hour point, as the Ring system required every possible unit of energy for Fire Light. The order was hardly necessary; so many units had been withdrawn from assembly and ordered to the staging areas that activity had essentially ceased.

Carbon-143 and her formation were ordered to the staging area and their 732 vehicles, as part of the third wave. She wanted to remain at her station, where she could monitor the data flow from the control center, specifically the actions of Whit Murray.

But that was no longer possible. She could only hope that Whit was able to override the command and take brief control of the process.

And stop the Ring from allowing the invasion and the destruction of most human life.

DATA: As she and her formation emerged from the operations and assembly building and moved toward their staging area, joining up with four other formations, Carbon-143 noticed movement in the shadows to her left. The area was open and used for the delivery of raw materials. There should have been no activity, but there was.

She turned toward it, hoping for additional visual information, and registered an anomalous being known only from historical data: a four-armed entity known by several names, most recently encountered by the Aggregates as a "Sentry" on the Near-Earth Object Keanu.

CONCLUSION: Sentries were hostile to all Aggregates, and Carbon-143 anticipated the commencement of violence. Then she noted a second figure, this one human, staggering next to the Sentry.

"Hey!" the human said, waving to Carbon-143. "It's me, Whit!"

EVEN MORE THINGS WE DON'T HAVE ON KEANU

TV shows and movies, except for the handful on the computers that came
    with us

Automobiles

Cats

Cat videos

Oreo cookies

XAVIER TOUTANT, AS QUOTED BY EDGAR CHANG
FOR THE NEWSKY NEWS SERVICE

XAVIER

"Why are you stopping?"

Xavier had gotten the van out of the meadow and beyond another range of low hills when he suddenly slowed and pulled off the road.

"Don't you want to see?"

"I'm ten thousand kilometers from home," Edgely said. "I want to *flee*."

"Some fucking astronomer you turned out to be."

No matter what Edgely said or did, Xavier wasn't going to miss the show. Especially because—his optimism with Rachel to one side—it might be the last thing he ever experienced.

He had gathered sufficient data from Zeds to know that the ignition of the Reiver Ring was likely to mean bad things for organic life all around the site. There was no way Xavier and Edgely could get far away fast enough.

Now, there was no guarantee it would be bad . . . especially, Zeds said, if something happened to shorten the Ring's operation. Which was apparently the goal.

Xavier could have avoided the risk by going aboard the vesicle, which had just shot itself into the sky behind them. But his time on Earth had convinced him . . . he didn't belong on Keanu. Life there was too limiting for him, professionally and otherwise. Even his romances, such as they were, had grown messy. Had he been living on Earth, he'd have had to leave town or join the Army, as friends had done.

He was willing to risk death to live on Earth again.

And the view was worth it. "Come on, Colin," Xavier said. "Look!"

Edgely was behind him. "Oh, I'm looking."

The Ring above Site A was one of the most spectacular things Xavier ever hoped to see. It was like watching a Ferris wheel the size of a city, glowing and rotating in the sky.

And growing bigger as he watched. "Crazy, isn't it?"

"Not as crazy as this, mate," Edgely said, forcibly turning Xavier to the east.

At first it looked like a full moon, the biggest and brightest he'd ever seen.

But this moon continued to grow brighter, becoming so bright he wanted to squint.

And it was moving, beginning to glow as it created a plasma field with its passage through the incredibly thin but still detectable atmosphere of Earth at a thousand kilometers.

Keanu on approach.

And streaking toward it, another bright light—the vesicle.

Would they make it?

And if they did, where would they be? Even Zeds had been unsure . . . the Sentry thought Keanu was making a close approach, to strike at the Ring and Reivers while allowing Rachel and the others to get home.

But no one knew for sure.

The vesicle seemed to merge with Keanu. Hard to tell . . . Keanu was so big that Xavier felt he was only seeing part of it now.

"The Ring is moving!" Edgely said.

Xavier turned. Good God, the Ring had expanded so much that all he could see now was its lower rim.

And even that was edge-on.

Feeling overwhelmed and about to be crushed, he stepped back, stumbling.

"Don't bother," Edgely said. "There's nowhere to go!"

Here came Keanu, filling the sky, its very passage creating a hot breeze, roaring like an electric waterfall.

He knew he should close his eyes because this collision would be blinding, explosive, deadly . . .

"Oh my God!" Edgely said. "It went through!"

Xavier blinked, and thought he saw the last section of Keanu disappearing through the Ring.

As it vanished, the tower behind them exploded with a zap so loud it hurt their ears. They could see it toppling. Flashes from its destruction were reflected in the mirrors.

Now his eyes hurt, too.

He covered them, looked away, hoped for his vision to return.

And hoped that he wasn't being baked by radiation.

"How are you doing?" Edgely said.

"As well as can be expected. How about you?"

Edgely opened his mouth to speak, then closed it and shrugged.

"Now we move," Xavier said, heading back to the van.

Edgely was still staring at the fractured sky. Finally he turned, shaking his head. "I imagine this is going to be challenging."

"Las Vegas is only a few hours away. It's not Houston or even New Orleans, but amazing things are possible in a place like that."

"Won't police be looking for us?"

Xavier shrugged. "I think everyone is going to be a bit distracted for quite some time."

Epilogue

"Are you up?"

Rachel stirred, opened her eyes. She was in the small residence she shared with Pav. All was quiet, calm, as it should have been.

As if she had never left.

"I think so." Pav lay next to her, spooning her, his voice muffled.

"I suppose it's time," he said.

They both began to stir.

It wouldn't have been difficult to convince Rachel that the past eleven days had been a kind of feverish nightmare . . . that she had never launched to Earth, met other humans, fled across half a planet, escaped from Reiver captivity.

And returned a Reiver to Keanu.

In every morning of their life together, she and Pav had held each other briefly, exchanging kisses, resetting their relationship ahead of the day. Even on Earth.

It was especially necessary today, because they had to go to the Temple now and face Jaidev and Harley and Sasha and the others, all seven hundred of them.

And Yahvi and her new friend, Whit—and her other new friend, Nigel.

And Zeds and Carbon-143/A72.

And Zhao and Makali Pillay, their rescuers—Bobbi and the others aboard the vesicle.

And Sanjay Bhat, still alive, thank God, demonstrating with every breath that Revenants might live longer than a few days. He had relayed a message from Keanu itself, or rather, from Dale Scott, who had vanished while somehow inserting himself into the system. "Keanu wanted to go home," he said, the only real explanation Rachel had received for the NEO's dive through the Ring.

She pondered their new situation, living inside an entity that was now alive and functioning in a new way. Would humans be able to control Keanu? Or were they now just passengers, insects carried by an indifferent, uncaring vessel? She hated that idea, not only because it might lead to her death and the deaths of those she loved.

It was just the wrong way for humans to face the universe.

More immediately, Rachel had yet to consider what might still happen with a working Beehive. Would Pav's father, Taj, reemerge now? Would her own father, Zack? For that matter, what about her mother, Megan?

And what if Keanu chose to create Revenants from people none of them knew, the dead of Earth? Rachel simply didn't know what to expect, if anything.

That much hadn't changed.

They had been back on Keanu a day, by their internal clocks. But Keanu was in a new place, a new space . . . and aimed toward the home world of the Architects. Soon, surely, they would detect signals, perhaps direct communications. They might be welcomed. After all, this was Keanu returning . . . the original Architect warship launched ten thousand years ago.

They might be shot at. They might be destroyed.

They might be ignored. It was impossible to predict. All Rachel knew was that she and the others would deal as best they could.

She wondered, though . . . had their magic leap meant a farewell to Earth? A door had opened to take them here. Might some other door open to take them back one day?

That would be another adventure.

Assuming anything that had happened in the past twenty years was an adventure. Yes, she had had unusual experiences—but so had those she left on Earth. Love was a unique experience. Parenthood. Work. Accomplishment. Failure.

Death.

Adventure was really just life, the days flowing into and out of each other.

And a new day was beginning.

Acknowledgments

Our families have been silent passengers on Keanu's voyage for the past five years, so we thank them: Marina, Sayle, and Milo; Cynthia, Ryan, and Alexandra.

We are also grateful to Simon Lipskar at Writers House, to Ginjer Buchanan at Ace and Bella Pagan at Tor/Macmillan UK, and to Nellie Reed and Lauren Bello at Phantom Four.

Special thanks are also due to those who offered encouragement at various stops along the way: Michael Engelberg, Andre Bormanis, and Emily Mayne, and the gang at HeavensShadowtheTrilogy on Facebook.

D.S.G. & M.C.
Los Angeles, March 2013